THE MARTIAN SENTENCE

THE
MARTIAN
SENTENCE

FROM THE AUTHOR OF **BLACK SILVER** AND
SERGEANT DOOLEY AND THE SUBMARINE RAIDERS

WAYNE ABRAHAMSON

Editors: Jorge David Remy, Jennie Seitz
Cover and Interior Design: Emma Elzinga

Indigo River Publishing
3 West Garden Street, Ste. 718
Pensacola, FL 32502

www.indigoriverpublishing.com

Ordering Information:

Quantity Sales: Special discounts are available for quantity purchases by corporations, associations, and others. For details, contact the publisher at the address above.

Orders by US trade bookstores and wholesalers: Please contact the publisher at the address above.

Printed in the United States of America.

Library of Congress Control Number: 2025906938
ISBN: 978-1-964686-46-2 (paperback)   978-1-964686-47-9 (ebook)

First Edition

With Indigo River Publishing, you can always expect great books, strong voices, and meaningful messages. Most importantly, you'll always find . . . *words worth reading.*

To those who want to write: write.

The Mesoamerican Jungle, AD 650

The towering, blue-faced, yellow-eyed devil was real enough, and the ruptured torsos of their bravest warriors lying in front of the strangely armored heathen proved it so. Behind the demon, the reddish-gray metal bird with one forward-facing, bulging eye, and a rounded beak, standing on three jointed metal legs seemed to approve of the gore. At the demon's feet, a helmet with a face shield made from the clearest of obsidian lay between stubs of maize stalks. The terrifying weapon he used to vanquish his initial attackers hung from a bloodied, and wavering, gloved hand.

Standing in a field of harvested maize, the survivors encircled the blue-faced beast, and the terrifying metal bird he'd climbed out of only minutes ago. They waited. Even though the fire-spitting weapon in his hand remained deadly, the monster began to succumb to the obsidian-tipped spears and arrows piercing his strange suit of clothed armor. Dark-red blood covered the maize stubs at his feet. Realizing they were better off waiting for the flow of blood to ebb, the warriors held their spears, war clubs, and amorphous-bladed daggers at the ready while listening to the creature draw ragged breaths through a gaping mouth. A mouth lined with the most fearsome of teeth.

THE ADVENTURE BEGINS

Copán, Honduras, early June, AD 2020

"Did you find any dinosaurs?" asked the sweating and rotund man.

Geoff Manwaring faced twenty tourists coached in from the cruise-ship terminal in Puerto Cortés but settled his eyes on the man who asked the question. The man was balding, obese, and covered in perspiration from the early June humidity, and his saturated cheap cloth mask sagged from his ears like a full diaper. The sweat also sucked his obnoxiously colorful aloha shirt against his skin.

Bloody Americans, Manwaring thought. *They just keep getting bigger and dumber.*

Thankfully, due to the recent COVID outbreak, this group should be the last for the field school season. Though irritated, he had to remind himself that, indirectly, tourism dollars helped fund his expeditions, including this one. Something the bean counters back at the university never failed to remind him of. "Everybody must serve their sentence," he said under his breath.

The tourists, and Manwaring, stood in the center of the complex's plaza, and his students busied themselves throughout the remnants of the walled-in enclosure. Motioning his hand to the enclosure's salient feature, a rectangular, grass-covered mound behind him, he answered the man's question about the dinosaur. His raised hand clutched his dirt-smeared field book.

"This is an archaeological dig. We are not paleontologists. We are about finding the material remains of past civilizations, not dinosaur bones. Now, getting back to the excavation at hand, we are attempting to determine the extent of the structure under this mound."

Manwaring paused his verbal tour long enough to shake the field book once. Twenty pairs of eyes followed suit.

"This is our third season here. Three years ago, we cleared the site of undergrowth and the smaller trees, leaving us room to map in the extents of the enclosure's walls and the exposed structures within. The second season, we excavated and mapped the cooking area and the well, which you see to my right."

Again, he paused long enough to swing his book-holding hand forward, bringing the pairs of eyes with it. They saw the same thing Manwaring had been looking at for years. The lower two-thirds of two caved-in stone buildings pressing against the damaged stone wall that enclosed them all. A circular hearth, and a knee-high well, both constructed of flat stones, occupied the space in between the constructions.

"We also excavated a midden, or trash deposit located behind the central mound. Through laboratory testing, such as Carbon-14 dating and comparative range dating, we've dated the bones of cooked animals, ceramic shards—or pieces—and the charcoal in the firepit. We determined that a group of Mesoamericans built this complex just before AD 650. However, cultures only occupied this site during two brief periods. Again, right around AD 650 and a bit after AD 1500. Our focus this season, though, is to start exposing the central feature behind me."

Most of the tourists turned their attention to the mound, but six or seven tourists, including three teenagers with white buds inserted into their ears, let their eyes wander about the complex. To them, he knew the view of the tumbled-down limestone blocks enclosing the remains of caved-in stone buildings and tertiary structures was a scene that tourists would see at any Mesoamerican site undergoing archaeological recovery. Well-used paths weaved their way around the bushes, stumps of smaller trees, and the trunks and branches of the larger trees offered shade to most of the stone structures inside the enclosure. One of those trees offering shade to a stela, an ornately carved stone monument honoring I Iuracán, a Mayan god, also put it in danger of falling over. An exposed root grew under the monument's pedestal, tilting it to the point that all it would take would be a minor earthquake tremor to finish the tree root's patient effort.

To him, though, while this site represented years of funded, and satisfying, work, it also presented a mystery. Thinking about that mystery, his mind went back to the work going on behind him.

On top of the mound, now cleared of vegetation, two students walked slowly, one holding a clipboard, while the second unreeled a measuring tape as they paced out the length of the mound's level top. At the base of the sloping mound, other students removed the black earth from two square holes in the ground with square-tipped shovels and dumped the dirt into white five-gallon buckets with strips of orange flagging tape tied to their bails. Three other students, standing to the side of the excavation, sharpened the blades of their shovels with bastard files.

"Once full," Manwaring continued as he reached down to push his field book into the pocket of his cargo pants, they'll carry the buckets to the processing area in the rear corner of the enclosure, where they'll sift the dirt through screens hanging from wooden tripods by rope. After the dirt has gone through the screens, the students will bag any recovered artifacts for later conservation."

Manwaring, still facing the tourists, could see through the back of his head. In the rear corner, beyond the central mound, and next to the rain-worn adobe latrine, were two erect tripods. In front of the tripods, students—either sitting at a picnic table or standing at the tripods—busied themselves with shifting dirt from the hanging, boxed-in screens, bagging artifacts, filling out paperwork, or keeping up with their field book notes. Just like Manwaring, the staff wore clothing, and tools, appropriate for their work: leather boots, baggy pants, loose-fitting, long-sleeve fishing shirts, and holstered Gerber multi-tools and trowels, all now stained with sweat and smeared dirt. Locally made straw cowboy hats completed their dress.

Manwaring did not normally give tours, as the duty of giving tours was rotated through the students; however, he found himself short staffed today. Four students had decided to stop by a local taco stand the previous day, after a day in the field, and they began paying for the decision by sunset. Now, they were at their rented house in the city of Copán, within steps of rental property's two available toilets. The remaining students, and his assistant Bethany Rogers, were already involved in their specific duties, defaulting the duty to him.

"How can you be so specific about the two dates you mentioned earlier?"

Manwaring finished securing the flap over his cargo pant pocket as the balding man asked the question. The same one who asked about the dinosaurs, and who now mopped his scalp with a soggy handkerchief. Manwaring coughed to clear his throat while thinking, *Bloody hell. Didn't I just tell them about the laboratory testing?*

But the irritating man asked another question before Manwaring could answer the first question. "Did you find any sacrificial victims in the well? Any gold objects? You know, to please the gods."

Tired of hearing the often-repeated questions, Manwaring dropped his eyes. He also answered with a lie. One meant to not entice grave robbers to visit the site when he and his staff were not around.

"You're talking about cenotes, not wells. Cenotes are sinkholes, or exposed portions of the limestone strata, filled with freshwater from underground. Also, most cenotes are located on the Yucatan Peninsula, not here in the mountainous jungles." As Manwaring explained the area's geography, the balding man's eye started to wander in disinterest. Other tourists did the same. "And the reason the Mayan paid homage to the cenotes on the Yucatan is that there are no running rivers in the peninsula. And no lakes. All their water is underground, so those cenotes gave them life, community, and purpose. There are available water sources here in the mountains. So, no. There are no sacrificial victims or golden idols in the well behind me."

The three teenagers with the earbuds took an interest in something behind them and pulled back from the line of tourists. Manwaring, on the other hand, forgot about the tourists for a second, and paused to reflect on the lie he'd just told the sweating and obese man.

In reality, they had indeed found the skeletal remains of a man in the well. A man who'd died soon after his thirtieth birthday, and sometime around 1520. And a man of Mesoamerican origin, all of which was normal enough. However, what was not normal was the fact that Manwaring recovered Aztec, not Mayan, weapons along with the human remains. Another oddity they encountered centered around the cremated remains, mostly fragmented dentition, of an individual animal found in the midden behind the central mound. He did not have the means to identify the genus or species of the remains at this site or at their rented fieldhouse-slash-conservation laboratory, so he sent samples to a colleague of his in London. However, even with the advanced laboratory equipment, his friend could not make any sense of the DNA or the fragmented dentition of that animal. Nor could he date the fragments. However, he did detect low levels of radiation contaminating the fragmented remains.

"What was this place? A jail or prison? It looks like a prison."

Manwaring quickly filed away his thoughts about the mystery and looked over at the woman who asked the question, a woman in her mid-thirties, with strawberry-blond hair tied into a ponytail. Her eyes, an inviting bright green, reminded him of people from earlier times. A piece of his life he wanted to forget. Looking at the woman he noticed his hands started to come together. Appreciating a question with a little observation and thought behind it, he pulled himself from the past and pointed them to the walls on either side, he answered her question with a bit more tact than he did answering the man's questions. "Good question, but I feel it was meant to keep people out, not in."

"Okay," the woman accepted, surveying the broken walls around them.

"Is it true that ancient aliens built those pyramids?" asked the blond-haired teenaged girl standing next to the woman. Both held cloth-masks in their hands, and the girl wore peach-colored shorts and a red Carnival cruise-ship T-shirt. The teenager pointed through one of the breaches in the gray limestone wall and at the exposed ruins of Copán off to the west. Backed by a range of forest-covered mountains, the mottled, grayish-brown stone pyramids stood out against the dark verdant backdrop.

The young girl's wide blue eyes exuded innocent anticipation. He answered her anticipation with the same patience that he had answered the woman's question, but for a different reason. The woman's question was based on patient observation. The young girl's question was one heard often, and from men like the fat man in front of him, and one he vehemently disagreed with. However, he knew what it was like to be so young and so full of wonder. And so innocent.

"I am sorry young lady, we must remember that the Mayans, as well as other past cultures, were intelligent and innovative. They created and used technology to build advanced cities, while Europeans were still living in mud huts and hillside dugouts. Europeans would not surpass Mesoamerican accomplishments in architecture, science, mathematics, and astronomy for centuries."

He knew his answer may have been a bit too high brow for the young girl, but he also knew an adult in the crowd would have asked the same question.

"Oh," she said as she turned her head toward the man standing behind her and the woman. "Well, what about the drawings we saw in the brochure?" asked the man, reaching down and tapping the young girl on the shoulder.

The man held a magazine, a paperback, and the folded brochure he'd just mentioned. He had gray hair cut short like a marine, wore a pair of pressed khaki trousers, a red polo shirt, and hiking boots. At about forty years old, and without an ounce of fat, his trim, but muscular, frame created the image of an all-American dad that would have adorned any 1950s automobile or a backyard barbecue advertisement.

Imagining himself in front of a mirror, Manwaring could see what the walking 1950s all-American advertisement was looking at. A nerdy British archaeologist with a slight build, little defined muscle, wearing glasses perched on a hawkish nose, and graying hair pulled into a ponytail. Manwaring's soul ached from jealousy.

"The drawing shows a Mayan reclining in a seat like he's in a spaceship taking off," the man continued. "And there are flames coming out of the bottom of the spaceship. He's also looking through some sort of scope, like he's sighting in celestial measurements. And the spaceship is full of controls, just like on the Apollo capsules. I should know. I was a marine fighter pilot."

Knowing about the image the professed ex-military pilot spoke of, Manwaring saw that the woman with the green eyes tried her best to inspect the underside of her eyebrows. He also saw the other tourists turn to listen to the man and turn to listen to his response.

The mural shown on the wall of a building inside the abandoned city was a rough copy of artwork inscribed into the lid of a stone sarcophagus of a Mayan king. A royal by the name of King Pukal. In short, the exquisitely inscribed stone coffin proved significant for historians and archaeologists in understanding Mayan art, and their culture and history. The coffin also gave rise to the so-called Mayan Astronaut Theory—a premise debunked by academics and researchers.

"That mural is simply a drawing of a Mayan sitting inside an observatory looking through slots in the ceiling," Manwaring answered with a hint of exasperation. "Not a Mayan sitting in a rocket ship. It is all simple coincidence. Again, the Mayans were astute observers of the sky and the world around them. They were also excellent innovators and discoverers of technology. It is ethnocentric for us to believe today that those past civilizations were incapable of creating and using such technology. Historically, whenever modern man encountered such feats of human ingenuity in the New World, they assumed it was ancient aliens, Phoenicians, survivors of Atlantis, or even lost tribes of Israel. I've spent a lifetime studying ancient cultures and civilizations and have yet to encounter evidence of such alien intervention. Additionally, we have yet to discover the physical or forensic remains of any alien species from another planet here on Earth or any type of technology, such as a spacecraft, which proves their presence in our world at any time in the past."

Taking a breath, the man half-closed one eye while using the other one to size up Manwaring.

Manwaring knew what the former marine pilot was appraising. The same person thousands of students have seen over the years. Aside from a man slight in build and with little defined muscle, wearing glasses perched on a hawkish nose and graying hair pulled back into a ponytail, a pocket protector, with pens, tweezers, and a dental pick—that forced one side of his Magellan shirt to sag—only added to his nerdy appearance. Instead of a flight suit and sharp aviator glasses like the man in the red polo may have worn, Manwaring wore a frayed cotton belt with a holstered multi-tool, trowel, and mini Maglite. On his head was a Honduran straw cowboy hat with holes in it.

"Well," the man said, finishing his appraisal, "I read all about ancient aliens in this book, and the author proves that there are spaceports all over South America. Even the Bible talks about angels and demons descending from the skies in fiery chariots. And don't forget the Navy pilots, who've been reporting sightings in the last few years."

The man pulled the paperback book from between the brochure and the magazine. He held the book up for Manwaring's inspection.

It was then that Manwaring recognized the paperback *Chariots of the Gods*. But what really drew Manwaring's attention was the magazine, and the man featured on the cover. A science magazine published just a month ago in May. The cover page showed the image of a rugged-looking man wearing a green flight suit and aviation sunglasses standing in front of a futuristic-looking jet plane poised on a tarmac. A distant desert mountain range backed both the man and the space-age aircraft. Manwaring read the caption printed above the cover's image: *billionaire entrepreneur Angar Einstok's plans for advanced lunar-based industries.*

Manwaring twerked his chin to the left.

Taking a slow, deep breath, and pushing aside the image of Angar Einstok now in his brain, he responded. "The twaddle in your hands, *Chariots of the Gods*, was published decades ago by a semiliterate hotel night clerk, and all the author did was combine a number of tales and legends into a chronology that made for an entertaining tale of groundless supposition."

The man's shoulders squared off under the red polo shirt, while the woman next to him still inspected the underside of her eyebrows. It became obvious to Manwaring now, that this is not the first time the woman, and the girl, had heard the man argue over the issue. While the young girl may have believed her father, the woman was more embarrassed than anything.

Manwaring, trying to think of a way to move the crowd along, noticed the embroidery on the front of the man's shirt. The image on the pocket consisted of the classic alien head with lettering circling the three-inch outline. The letters read *Area 51 Research Association.*

The man was a truther, Manwaring thought. Knowing that any response that did not agree with the man's beliefs would be a waste of breath, he opted not to continue their discussion.

"Well, I know everybody had a long drive here, and there is more to see, so please look around and ask my field crew if you have any questions. You have ten minutes before you need to return to your motor coach, where the driver will take you to the main ruins at Copán."

He turned, removed his glasses, and pulled a bandana from his pants pocket. Starting with his cheeks, he wiped backward to the nape of his neck and under his ponytail, as he stepped toward the mound with the intent of checking in with the crew on top, but the man with the Area 51 shirt left the dispersing crowd and stopped him.

"I know you said the Mayans built all this stuff themselves," the truther continued, "but how do you explain the Nazca Lines? They weren't discovered until the 1950s. When aircraft started flying over the high plains of Peru. There was no way anybody could have laid out those lines unless the ancient Incas had ariel-borne supervisors."

Manwaring stopped and turned to face the man. The crowd behind them split up with half of the group, including the bald fat man, woman, and girl who asked the questions, walking behind the mound to see what artifacts his students were bagging. At the same time, the three teenagers wearing the earbuds walked the opposite way toward the tree shading the nearby limestone stela.

The ornately carved stone monument appeared just as weather-beaten as everything else within the enclosure and was in danger of being tilted over because of the exposed root growing under it. And it was just like the hundreds of other such stelae spread across the region, with most serving as portrait monuments of Mayan leaders and their gods and goddesses. Sculptors worked on at least one side of a stela, sometimes all four sides, and carved animals, figures, and hieroglyphic text; each side formed part of a single composition or honorific motif. In the center of one side would be a depiction of the human, or deity, the monument was meant to honor. This monument honored a being known as Huracán, or One-legged—one of the three gods involved in all three attempts to create humanity—and fashioned during the Mayan post-classic period.

Answering the truther's question, Manwaring kept an eye on the teenagers, Manwaring saw that something on the lower half of the monument caught their attention. They started pointing at the stela and talking excitedly.

"Experimental archaeologists have demonstrated that the people there constructed hot-air balloons out of reeds and animal skins to elevate the supervisors and observers to oversee the construction of those glyphs. The supervisors could even have stood on the slopes of the nearby foothills."

"But how do you explain Teotihuacán? It's known as the Cape Canaveral of Mesoamerica for a reason, and... "

Before the man could finish, Manwaring shouted, "Oy! Hang on!"

The man with the Area 51 polo shirt jumped to the side as Manwaring lurched past him. The British archaeologist quickly made his way toward the teenagers. Two of them remained standing, while the third busied himself, bent over, and picked at the stela with something in his hand. They hadn't heard him because of their earbuds. Manwaring, almost running by now, reached the young man and slapped his hand away from the face of the stone monument.

Startled, the pimply faced young man jerked back while dropping a cruise-ship pass card from his hand. "Hey, man!"

"What in the bloody hell are you doing? What made you think you could bugger up an artifact with a keycard?"

"It's cool, man!" the teenager stated with a dismissive, and angered, tone. He still wore his buds in his ears. "We're just poking around." He looked back at the face of the stela. "I noticed the outline of a secret compartment under that figure on the stomach. We play *Beowulf's Creed,* and in the fourth game, they have hidden compartments in their statues, too."

Manwaring said brusquely through clenched teeth, "This isn't a treasure-hunting video game. This stela is hundreds of years old. And it has nothing to do with video games. Now, get back with the rest of your lot."

The young man snorted while bending over to snatch up his pass card. He muttered *asshole* as he straightened up.

Manwaring ignored the comment while the teenagers stepped past him to join the tourists already queuing up at the motor coach's door.

Taking a cleansing breath, Manwaring returned his attention to the stela.

Just like others, incisions, and intricate carvings of all kinds of animals and Mayan writing covered the surface of this monument. Having spent time last season documenting the monument, he knew it was meant to honor Huracán. The carved relief revealed a man with an elongated skull and a high forehead, a large hooked nose, sleepy eyes, and enormous hooped earrings that hung from his ears. The body was short in length and breadth, and at the waist of the body, the deity's only leg was bent in front of him as if he were sitting. His hands came together in the center of his abdomen, holding a cup against his stomach.

Manwaring squatted to inspect the area the teen had been picking at—the container held in Huracán's hands. He had documented this stela before, and drew sketches of it in his field book, but did they find something he missed? After all, crowded carvings covered the stela's four sides, so missing something could be excused. Adjusting the glasses on the bridge of his nose to get a better look, he reinspected the cup that was used for collecting blood during self-sacrifice. Finding nothing out of the ordinary, he peered under the cup and planted his eyes an outline. One shaped like a slice of sandwich bread. In the center, the carving of an animal, half jaguar half reptile, with a pointy snout protruded from the stone. Though he had documented that section of the stela before he realized today, something different.

Mesoamerican sculptors used a variety of materials such as basalt or obsidian to fashion tools such as chisels. Tools sculptors used to create their carvings in stone blocks but, after today's attention, Manwaring noticed that the incision creating the outline under the blood-collecting cup appeared to be slightly different from other carvings covering the stela's surfaces.

For unknown reasons, Manwaring found himself stuck on that oddity, and after about thirty seconds, it struck him. Someone had used something other than stone chisels to create that outline.

Intrigued about why he hadn't seen it before, he reached down for the trowel holstered to his hip. Pulling it out of the leather holster, he flicked the edge of the tip with his thumb and leaned in to get a better look at the outline. Yes, indeed, somebody had used something other than the tools available to Mayan stone smiths at the time. Using the tip of the trowel, just like the teenager did with his cruise-ship pass card, Manwaring traced the outline and, as grit fell away, his heart started to pound forcibly against the inside of his chest. The sound of metal scraping against the stone added to the mystery before him.

He took a deep breath and blew on the incision. Flecks of stone flew back against his glasses. He removed the glasses from his face and cleaned them with his damp handkerchief. Just as he put his glasses back in place, he heard a voice.

"Geoff, it's half past one, and I told the crew to start wrapping up for the day."

Manwaring jerked his head so hard his ponytail almost slapped his cheek. He saw Bethany Rogers, the project's assistant principal investigator. In her late twenties, with a slight build, freckles, and bobbed blond hair poking out from under the brim of her straw cowboy hat, she wore the same work clothing as everybody else and carried her field notebook in her hand. Straggling tourists were boarding the motor coach behind Bethany. One of his students backed up their white van to another breach in the enclosure's wall. With the engine and AC running, he left the vehicle in park to open the rear doors.

"It's that time already?" he said, glancing at his wristwatch.

While the student made the van ready to receive their equipment, the other students fell into a familiar routine. The students at the picnic table in the rear of the complex started carrying black plastic file boxes and Tupperware totes to the van. Others folded the tripod screening stations and began to carry them, and their shovels, screens, and five-gallon buckets to an aluminum tool shed hidden behind the dirt-covered central building. The mapping crew on top of the mound reeled in the measuring tape, leaving behind pin flags pushed into the dirt, and gingerly stepped down the side of the mound. Lastly, two security guards from the Honduran Tourism Bureau helped a female student with carrying her daypack and empty plastic bucket.

"Right," Manwaring said, standing to reach into his pant pocket for his field book. "Go ahead. I'll be with you in a minute. I am thinking about opening a new unit over here. I'm going to take some notes."

"Right," Bethany said as she turned and walked toward her crew.

Leaving Manwaring to his notetaking, Bethany thought about what had just happened. Manwaring had a reputation for being standoffish or distant, so nobody at this field school paid any attention to his demeanor; however, she noticed something different about him just now. But what that was, she didn't know. When she reached the van, she threw her field book into a tote already half-filled with other field books.

Alone again, Manwaring returned to the incision and pushed against the area with the palm of his hand. It held steady. *Was the incision just the start of another feature that the sculptors hadn't finished?*

He pinched the protruding stub and tweaked it. Still, it didn't move. After taking his hand away, he thought for a moment until it hit him. "Impossible!"

Looking over his shoulder, he saw the last tourist disappear inside the motor coach. He also saw that Bethany and the students were busy closing the site for the day. Returning his attention to The Beast, he stuck his index and middle fingers up under its protruding nostrils. His fingers fit perfectly into two small holes. Like pulling out a dresser drawer, he tugged gingerly at first but then harder when he felt no movement. After two more tugs, he felt the movement. He tugged even harder now, and without warning, the plate gave way. Holding one hand in front of his face, he pulled the two-inch-thick stone cover off his fingers with the other hand and placed it gently on the grass next to him. With an excitement he hadn't felt in years, he reached down to his belt for his mini Maglite. His twitching thumb pushed the rubber-covered button at the end as he pointed it into the chamber. The interior of the chamber was square and slightly smaller than the thick cover plate, and the beam of light gleaned off something shiny and round. With his other hand, he reached into the hole. His hand grabbed a cylinder. He pulled it out and hefted a gold-colored cylinder in his hand. It was the length of his forearm and hand, covered with lines of inscriptions running lengthwise, and sealed at both ends with bulbous caps.

Despite his years of being a Mesoamerican archaeologist with all kinds of finds under his belt, he slowly rose to his feet, awestruck. But as he stood up straight, he quickly recovered his senses. He looked over his shoulder again.

Bethany was still busy supervising the students who were now placing sheets of black plastic over the square units dug into the ground at the base of the mound and securing the plastic in place with sandbags around the edges. The Honduran guards were also busy helping the blond-haired female student with her sandbags.

Seeing everybody's attention was elsewhere, Manwaring dropped the cylinder behind a bush growing out of a tree stump next to him and turned to inspect the ground behind him, pretending to scout out an area to lay out a new excavation unit.

Normally, on Saturdays, he allowed his staff to work until the scheduled cruise-ship tourist groups arrived from Puerto Cortés. Once the tourists left, his staff wrapped up their work and turned in their field books for Manwaring's weekly review so that they could enjoy a short night in the port city. Their Sunday routine included sleeping in at their rented house in Copán. They used the day to rest up and to tend to their dig kits and field gear before Monday. The trip to town also gave Bethany time to pick up her phoned-ahead supply list of items not found in the mountain city. Or to have access to a more reliable FedEx office in case they needed to ship something back to the university. But after seeing what he's just held in his hand, he could not go to the coast this Saturday night. He left the cylinder hidden behind the stump and pushed the cover back in place. Looking around to make sure he did not leave anything out, he walked to the van as his crew finished with the last of the sandbags.

Removing his straw cowboy hat, he wiped his forehead with his bandana while walking to the rear of the van. Replacing his hat and stowing his bandana in his back pocket, he reached into a tote for a scrap of plastic sheeting. Bethany opened the driver's side door and dropped her day pack into the space between the two front seats. "I'll see you back at the fieldhouse," Manwaring said.

"Fine," Bethany answered as she stepped up and sat in the driver's seat.

Manwaring, holding a folded sheet of black plastic, watched his students pile in through the open side doors and slide onto the vinyl-covered bench seats. He closed the rear doors and stepped to the side as Bethany gave the engine some gas. The vehicle's tires crunched the loose gravel as it headed toward the large gap in the enclosure's wall. The Honduran guards, climbing into their own vehicle, a red pickup truck parked off to the side, also fired up their engine. The guards were not supposed to leave until everybody, including Manwaring, were off the site; however, once the young female student they took a liking to was gone, the guards appreciated the food stand down the road and the cold beer sold there.

Now, with everybody gone, he returned to the stela and retrieved the container. After rolling it up in the piece of plastic he retrieved from the van, he cradled it in the crook of his arm and stepped toward the breech in the stone wall. Once outside the wall, he walked the short distance to the gravel parking lot, and his beat-up yellow Geo Tracker. An aged vehicle with a cracked windshield, bald tires, and a missing front bumper. After placing the container in his frayed canvas Alpine backpack on the front passenger seat, he turned the key in the ignition. It took more than one turn of the key, but the worn-out engine finally caught. Letting the engine warm up under the tropical sun, he retrieved a bottle of local whiskey from the pack and uncapped it. Taking a pull, a little whiskey leaked past the corners of his trembling lips.

The afternoon sun flashed through the overhead tree branches as he drove down the long gravel road and toward the suburbs of the modern town of Copán itself. Yet, the Morse-code-like messaging reaching out to him through the trees failed to even make him blink; his mind was elsewhere. Taking sideways glances at the Alpine backpack on the passenger seat, he could not wait to get to their house. The artifact in that pack was none like he had ever seen before. Despite his years as an archaeologist.

Part of his annual funding paid for a sparsely furnished, four-bedroom, two-bath home with a studio apartment, equipped with a half bath, in the backyard. While the house was where they ate and slept, the studio served as their conservation laboratory where they photographed, logged, and started the initial conservation treatment for recovered artifacts. And prepared them for shipment back to the university at the end of the season. Where the artifacts would receive further treatment and study before repatriation back to Honduras. It was also where the tote containing the student's field notebooks remained, waiting for Manwaring's weekly, or weekend, review. At the end of the dig season, he and Bethany would place the filled-out field books into blue curation file boxes for shipment and storage back at the university in England.

While Bethany and most of the students crowded themselves into three of the four bedrooms and the one hallway bathroom in the main house, Manwaring took the master bedroom, and its bathroom, for himself. Because of his position as field director, the privilege defaulted to Manwaring, and one he had no problem with accepting, for more than one reason.

Pulling through the open gate, and past the cinder-block wall enclosing the lot, he parked next to the van already parked in the driveway. He exited his beat-up Geo Tracker, stepped up to the porch, and opened the front door, while carrying his backpack over his shoulder. Bethany, and two young men, the same young men who were part of the group who came down with a case of bad tacos, sat on the living room sofa now freshly showered and wearing clean jeans and Magellan shirts.

So now Stephen and Mark seem well enough to go into town now, Manwaring mused. *Good.*

They drank bottles of Imperial beer while watching a show on the home's only TV, which is one reason four students opted to sleep on the living room floor in sleeping bags every night. Manwaring recognized the show they were watching. A show titled *Expedition Horizon*. One of those treasure-hunting shows with actors past their prime pretending to be archaeologists searching for German U-boats filled with Nazi treasures, or Coronado's lost gold in the American southwest. An open Igloo cooler sat on the floor next to the sofa. As he walked past, he grabbed a beer from the cooler and pulled the magnetized bottle opener from the metal trash can next to the cooler. Ignoring the scene on the TV screen but listening to the rest of the students in their bedrooms and in the hallway bathroom getting ready for a night out on the town, Manwaring popped the cap, letting it drop into the trash can. Raising the bottle to his lips he spoke to them. "Have a good time in Puerto Cortés, lads. And Bethany, while you are in town pick up more bundles of zip ties."

Bethany turned to look up at Manwaring. "You're not coming with us?"

"No," Manwaring said, reaching down to stick the bottle opener back onto the side of the trash can. "The university needs an update before next Friday so they can release the remaining funds from their summer grant.

Don't worry, though, as I have a nice bottle of Tatascan whiskey to keep me company."

"Okay," she said slowly. "But we picked up a dozen bundles last weekend. Remember?"

"Bethany, you'll find out that when it comes to field archaeology, you can never have enough zip ties on hand. Something to remember for the future."

He lifted his beer bottle in salute, turned, and stepped into the hallway to his room. But, as he did, and over the voices of two female students fighting over the mirror in the hallway bathroom, the show's narrator mentioned a name, catching Manwaring's attention.

He turned in time for the show's narrator, a pudgy White man wearing his version of an Indiana Jones fedora, to profile their next guest, Angar Einstok. The screen on the television switched from the narrator standing among ruins of a Roman fortress to a still frame of camouflaged and armed men sliding down ropes hanging from a stationary helicopter hovering above the deck of a ship—a civilian freighter. The caption under the image read: *Angar Einstok and his team of operatives, in conjunction with the Turkish government, seize a pirate ship off the coast of Cyprus.*

"Now that's what I call archaeology," Stephen, one of the young men sitting on the sofa, said. "Repelling out of a helicopter to take down a ship full of pirates and gold from the Ottoman Empire."

Manwaring took an eye off the TV screen and planted it on Stephen. "Just because the pirates looted an ancient site, there is no reason to call that ship boarding archeology. And Einstok is not an archaeologist."

Manwaring stopped his rebuke and turned to face the door to his bedroom. He spoke as he took his first step. "And it's called fast roping: not repelling. There's a difference."

Hearing Manwaring slam the deadbolt into place from inside his bedroom, Bethany again sensed something had happened that day. Though he usually locked himself in his bedroom, coming out only for dinner and to place his crockery in the sink for somebody else to clean before locking himself back in his room, today was different. Was it the way he carried his shoulders? Or was it something extra in his eyes? She could not place it, but she knew something had happened that very afternoon.

"So, if Lord Douchebag isn't coming with us to town," Mark said, pulling Bethany's attention away from Manwaring's bedroom door, "I call shotgun!"

"Thank God," Stephen said. "All he does every Saturday night is ride shotgun, and doodle in a stupid notebook while ignoring us. Then, when we get to town, he disappears. Maybe he's found some sort of weird opium den. Or hangs out in a creepy whorehouse."

Bethany reached into her pants cargo pocket and pulled out her cell phone. "I don't know about any whorehouse or opium den, but he does have a habit of disappearing every time we go into town." Using her thumb to swipe the screen, she looked for a certain phone number while asking the two young men sitting on the sofa with her. "Did you guys finally get rid of whatever you ate last night?"

N ow, alone in his room, Manwaring tossed his straw hat and pack on the bed and took a long pull on the beer bottle—almost emptying it in one swallow. As he caught his breath, he placed the near-empty bottle on the nightstand next to his bed, peeled back the flap of the Alpine backpack, and pulled out the container. He spent the next minute just trying to comprehend what he was holding in his hands. After a long sigh, he stepped over to his desk—a cheap folding table from the local version of Wal-Mart—that was pushed against the wall under the room's only window. Closed gray drapes lorded over a spiral-bound notebook partially filled with doodles, rough sketches, and freethinking, a pen, a laptop in its padded case, a single-bulb lamp, and a twenty-year-old box-like alarm clock. The red digital numbers read 3:04 p.m.

On either side of the table, a six-foot particleboard bookcase filled with reference material, light reading, day-to-day castoffs, and a station where he brewed his own tea or coffee stood sentry. Sitting on the metal folding chair in front of the desk, he set the cylinder on the table and pulled his damp kerchief from his pants pocket. Removing his glasses from his face, he leaned forward while wiping the lenses. Was the cylinder made of gold? White gold? Or even platinum? It was heavy but not too heavy. After cleaning his glasses, he perched them back on his face. Tossing the kerchief on the table, he replaced it with the cylinder, holding it like an ear of corn. As he rolled it slowly, he recognized three of the lines as Aztec or Nahuatl.

Although not literate in Mesoamerican writings, he did have exposure to writings, whether on paper or stone, that the invading Spanish, from centuries before, failed to destroy. As Manwaring viewed those markings on the cylinder, a combination of ideographic proto writing and pictographs augmented by phonetic rebuses started to present themselves. He thought he could also see numbers, represented by dots, and one of them being the number four, expressed by four dots. Like most Mesoamerican writing, the text of the language he had seen on paper, in books, or on stone tended to be large and graphic. He appreciated the clarity of the detail inscribed onto such a small surface area.

Still rolling the cylinder in his hands, he determined the next set of lines as Toltec, and the lines after that as Mayan. Script or logograms complemented by syllabic glyphs, which could appear to some observers as being similar to Japanese writing in structure and format. He also saw a series of numbers including the number four again. The fourth set of lines seemed different in structure and design from the other three, and it took him a second to recognize the form of writing.

Still holding the cylinder like an ear of corn in his shaking hands, he recalled the undergraduate linguistic lectures he had attended. One of those classes, which he enjoyed, was about runology, or the study of Germanic languages.

Now, just like faded ghosts slowly emerging from the walls of an old house, those lectures, and that specific class, returned. Try as he might though, any familiarity between the fourth set of lines and Germanic runes stopped there. He did recognize two symbols, however. One of them looked like a Nazi swastika, and the other appeared to be a pair of lightning bolts parallel to each other. Two jagged lines that adorned the uniform lapels and helmets worn by the German Waffen SS.

As his mind tried to comprehend the significance in front of him, he heard doors closing inside the house and someone calling shotgun outside his window, followed by the van's engine starting. He looked at the old alarm clock. It was now 3:30 p.m. After a not-too-short drive to town, they normally spent six or so hours in town shopping, drinking, sightseeing, and dancing before returning to enjoy a late morning sleep-in.

While he knew he would have hours to himself, he also knew that he would need those hours to comprehend the relic in his hands. He also knew he could not reveal his findings to the world, starting with the others inside the house, at least not yet. He placed the cylinder on the table and lifted his glasses from his nose. Leaving the cylinder and his glasses on the table, he went to get one item that would help him start his journey of discovery. And that started with a statement he repeated often to past students: "Nothing wrong with kitchen-table archeology." On entering the living room, he grabbed two beers from the Igloo cooler and the bottle opener from the side of the metal trash can next to it. Reentering his room, he placed the beer bottle opener against the cylinder. It did not stick.

"Well, it's nonferrous," he said aloud as he lifted the opener from the cylinder and grabbed a beer. "Just like gold."

He drank that beer while studying Aztec writing, and a message began to fall into place in the back of his head. Though he did not consciously translate the Aztec writing verbatim, the message just seemed to fall into place like dice or dominoes cast by God's own hand.

Something about a visitor from the south lofted in the back of his mind.

Setting the empty bottle down, he reached for the second bottle of beer on the table but stopped. Knowing he would be better off having some water, he reached over and grabbed one of the plastic bottles of water standing on the bookshelf, and next to his coffee pot. Grabbing it he straightened up in his chair and twisted the cap off. He sipped some water and set his eyes on the Toltec writing before inspecting the Mayan glyphs again. After a half of a bottle of water, he started to get the idea of a visitor, but from the heavens this time. The number four also appeared again in the text. Suddenly, he realized the potential in front of him. As if to celebrate the epiphany, he brought the bottle of water to his lips and took an exceptionally long swallow. When he brought his eyes level again, they fell on one of the bookshelves standing guard on either side of the desk and draped window.

Among the many books crammed onto its shelves, one particular volume caught his attention. Reaching over, he stuck his finger behind the top of the binder and pulled it down. An image of Napoleon, with his cock hat sitting sidesaddle on his head, riding a camel, filled the book's front cover with the Pyramids of Egypt in the background. He flipped through the pages until he came to the chapter about the scientists and engineers who followed Napoleon's soldiers on their campaign across the Egyptian desert, among them linguists and antiquaries.

As he glanced at those pages, two words popped up. After spending more minutes on that chapter, he looked up and found another book on the shelf. Pulling it down, his eyes focused on the book cover's image, which showed a fragment of a stone tablet with three distinct sets of text inscribed into it. With a growing smile, he read aloud the title above the image: *Secrets of the Rosetta Stone.*

With that thin volume in his hand, Manwaring remembered a statement a journalist made a year ago while drafting an article about him in Mexico. During that interview, she referenced Sherlock Holmes. The reference centered on the idea that Holmes would not exist without Doctor Moriarity, Holmes's archenemy. Manwaring remembered one of the detective's mysteries: *The Adventures of the Dancing Men.* A mystery centered around a written message consisting of a series of stick figures in various positions. The detective, Sherlock Holmes, realized the message was nothing more than a substitution cipher, where each stick figure represented a letter, an English letter. And knowing that the English language had only twenty-six letters in its alphabet, and a limited number of vowels with the letter E used most often, Holmes employed frequency analysis.

Thinking about that mystery novel, Manwaring remembered something a linguistic teacher repeated in his lectures, which focused on the idea that all languages have the same basic components and a singular reason for existing: to communicate.

Manwaring set the book about the Rosetta Stone on the desk and looked at the cylinder. After understanding the mission in front of him, he looked down at the weapons at his disposal. A cheap book about the Rosetta Stone, a pencil, a spiral-bound notebook half full of doodles and free thinking, a bottle of whiskey, a cooler full of beer bottles, hours by himself, and a memory of childhood mystery readings. His eyes landed on the laptop in its padded case. Knowing how easy it had become to hack into computer files, he reached out with his hand and pushed the laptop aside. "Kitchen table archaeology it shall be."

Now, with his arsenal set, he turned his attention back to the cylinder. He picked it up and inspected the bulbous caps at each end, trying to work out how they were attached. He tugged to pull them off. That did not work, so he looked for a secret button or hidden release lever. The caps were devoid of any markings or buttons. He put the cylinder down, and reached for the water bottle, emptying it in one long swallow. He put the bottle back on the table and grabbed the container. Holding it in the crook of his right arm, he reached out with his left and gave the cap of the cylinder a twist. He felt it turn slightly. Excited, he continued to twist it. After ten complete turns, the cap came loose in his hand. He examined the cap and its inside threading and found sheets of paper-like material rolled up and stuffed inside the cylinder.

As a Mesoamerican archaeologist, Manwaring recovered all manner of gold artifacts, most being thousands of years old, buried in the sands of time. Humans placed value on gold because it remained shiny, never corroded, and soft which made it easy to smelt and work. So for the threads and inscriptions to remain undamaged, its makers must have alloyed metals together; however, the magnet from the beer bottle opener did not stick to the cylinder. Another mystery.

Looking at the cylinder, he remembered a piece of equipment in the studio apartment in the backyard, and that being a handheld XRF machine. Shaped like a cashier's scanner, the electronic tool could tell him the exact metal content of the cylinder, including any subsidiary metals or alloys. He also thought about his friend back in Cambridge, who could use laboratory equipment such as a laser ablation machine to trace the source of the metal back to the mountain or river it came from. But he realized that doing so would mean sharing with another person what could be a find of historical dimensions. The question: When, and how should others know about his find? Or should they?

After thinking for a second, he answered his own question, and the answer started with Bethany Rogers, his assistant project leader. Born a British subject, the daughter of a mining engineering consultant, she grew up traveling with her father and his business. The result was a young, multilingual lady with world-travel experience, something she often reminded their students of. Still, she should have been the first person to consult because of her knowledge and experience of minerology and geology; however, she also came off as ambitious. Too ambitious for Manwaring's taste.

Also, like the truther, whose image could have graced any military recruitment poster, Bethany's looks were not a disadvantage to her future. A future set for a person who viewed archaeology as her next cool hobby. Her position here this summer season was merely a steppingstone to her PhD. A career path streamlined by her father's influence at the university, his *Alma mater*. Resentful of the old British class system, Manwaring had earned his doctorate years ago, without the benefit of good looks, connections, or being born into privilege.

He, on the other hand, came from the opposite end of the spectrum. Putting his youth and his disadvantages aside, he had clawed his way to the top of his profession and published a list of achievements and publications a meter long. However, these last few years produced no recent discoveries or publications. But the discovery he held in his hands could change his flight path. His challenge, now, was to be strategic with his discovery. Sighing, he thought about that strategy, and its opponents. One of those opponents graced the cover of the magazine *The Truther* held back at the site. And the same opponent who was featured on the archaeology show, *Expedition Horizon.* Yes, that opponent was one to be wary of.

The red LED numbers of the twenty-year-old alarm clock showed 1:13 a.m. Next to it, the light from the desk lamp's single bulb pulled at his tired eyes. Manwaring rubbed his eyes with one hand while setting his pencil down onto the open spiral-bound notebook. A notebook now almost filled with whatever his mind, and hand, could capture from the cylinder's metal surface, and from the sheets of paper-like material inside it.

As he grabbed for the tumbler of whiskey next to the notebook, he heard the van enter the walled-in driveway next to their fieldhouse. The staccato of metal doors opening and closing replaced the reverberations of the engine as Bethany turned it off. Dismissing the drunken babble of the students, he tilted his head back to think. But his mind devolved into a conflicting, twirling maze of confusing questions. Queries centered on items strewn across his bed.

On the blanket covering the bed were sheets of bark cloth with Mayan text and images. Accompanied by an equal number of plastic paper sheets that contained a sort of alien text, again appearing runic in nature, along with two images, which appeared to be photographs of a human-like creature. One showed a frontal image and the other in profile: the creature had a robust build with bluish skin, almond-shaped yellow eyes, an arrogant-appearing smile revealing sharp teeth, and a bald scalp exposing a long, sloping forehead. The creature's ears and lips were festooned with piercings and jewelry, which looked like gold, inset with brilliant gems. Manwaring remembered how cultures, including the Mayans, often modified their appearances with piercings and filed teeth, and they bound children's heads to reshape their skulls.

As the students clamored for the one available bathroom inside the house, Manwaring reflected on his days as a youth in church and remembered points the priest mentioned in his sermons. Including one passage: *God hath thou made us in his own image?* "Now it makes sense," Manwaring mumbled as he remembered the emails from his laboratory friend in England and the inconclusive results concerning the remains he sent to his friend. It was obvious to Manwaring now that his laboratory friend had no comparison, basis, or datum to go by. Manwaring lifted the tumbler to his lips with a shaking hand and sipped the whiskey. *Or did they make their image into that of their gods?*

Questions raced through his mind including: *Why were there sheets of Mayan bark cloth and what looked like modern photographs on some sort of plastic paper? And why were they hidden in a stela well over seven hundred years old?*

Pulling the tumbler from his lips, he held the glass in front of him as if it were a crystal ball with the liquor inside, being the mystic who could answer those questions through the thick glass. The dim light from the lamp revealed nothing on the thick crystal glass.

Half listening to the students still fighting over the hallway bathroom, he thought about a quote from long ago. He restated it to the glass as if it were his newfound best friend at a London pub. "With wine comes wisdom. Therefore, whiskey must provide the answers?"

Still slowly twisting his hand, he asked the mystic inside the glass. "But what are the questions? Did that alien truther back at the site have something to do with my findings? And what of Bethany? He was able to supervise the dig here during the first two seasons without an assistant field supervisor. It was only this season that the university assigned her. They said she needed to complete another field school in a supervisory position for her doctorate. But why now? Why this season?" He paused to sip the whiskey. "No. I think not, my friend. I think I have found the answers to other questions instead."

Leaning forward to look at the mystic inside his whiskey tumbler in the light of desk lamp, he continued the alcohol-induced conversation. "We have the body of an Aztec warrior, contaminated with radiation, in a Mayan well; therefore, somehow, a group of Aztecs had found out about something special or wanted to hide something special and brought it to this place. A place far from the Aztec Empire. Then, we have the strange ashes and bones found behind the mound. The next, or last questions, then, are, 'what will we find under that mound' and 'what will I be able to decipher from that cylinder, and its contents?'"

Stopping his conversation with the mystic, a pleased smile spread across his face as he brought the glass to his lips and swallowed its remaining contents. Finishing the whiskey, he pulled the glass from his lips while looking at the scrolls. He could not yet read their contents, but he knew that he was looking at an archaeological find of historic importance. He took a second to laugh at the irony of it all. *The world's greatest archaeological discovery was found by an oafish, pimply faced American teenager who couldn't take out the rubbish without using the cell phone to tell him how to do it.*

After understanding the significance of the day, and still hearing movement about the house, he realized he needed to keep his conversation with the whiskey, and the items spread about the desk and the bed to himself. And he needed to secure his findings before the whiskey talked him into a deep sleep. He also knew he would have to summarize that collage of information and the notebook full of disorganized notes for better understanding, until the time was right to announce his find. When that would be he did not know but, as he lowered his glass his hand, he felt the field notebook in the cargo pocket of his trousers. Setting the glass aside, he pulled it out of his pocket and ran his index finger from his other hand slowly along the name and date handwritten on the book's spine in black marker.

He swiveled in his seat to face a corner of the room and the black-lidded tote, which contained basic supplies, including blank field notebooks. He focused his attention on the filled-out field books, from last year's season, in the blue curation boxes in the backyard apartment, and the ones before that season. Thinking about a way to secure the information he would surely pull from that cylinder, he smiled and mumbled, "Shit Sherlock, it has to be the whiskey."

3

Napa Valley, California, early June, AD 2020

"Are you watching that crap again, *Doctor* Elizabeth 'Lizzie' Montgomery-Borden? After all those years of college and medical school?"

Elizabeth was reclining on her bed holding an iced gin and tonic. Wearing faded jeans, an untucked and frayed flannel shirt, and dirt-stained boots, she turned her head toward the voice. A woman dressed like her but wearing a laundry apron stood in the open doorway holding a full laundry basket.

"Grandma, you know that full naming me hasn't worked since I was thirteen."

"Along with ignoring me after, I've told you more than once to make your bed or put away your climbing gear. I almost broke my neck stepping over it."

"Sorry," Elizabeth said. "I'll put the gear away today. Besides, didn't you say Saint Peter always has a wooden nickel waiting for you at the pearly gates?"

"Yes," Grandma answered, "but no need to use it up uselessly."

"Come on in. I'll help you with my underwear."

With that last word, Elizabeth returned her attention to the wall-mounted screen televising a reality show. She sipped on her gin and tonic just as a man in the episode, swinging his metal detector back and forth, started yelling for his friends out of camera view.

Grandma stepped into the room and turned to sit on the bed next to Elizabeth's booted feet and Elizabeth's worn garden gloves. Lowering the basket to the hardwood, she straightened up holding two bottles of pale ale in her hands. "You're smart enough to use that Netflix-thingy to turn on some real classics. Movies with real men. You know, like Lee Marvin. And how often have I told you about wearing boots in bed? Keep that up and you'll end up marrying a pot-bellied handyman who's two mortgage payments behind on his double-wide, and watches reruns of *Jerry Springer*. It's 2020, and you're forty. Time for you to get a life."

Elizabeth, watching an episode of a series titled *The Mysteries of Oak Island*, again took her eyes from the TV mounted against the wall of her childhood bedroom and planted them on the woman who had raised her for most of her life. Both women weighed one and forty pounds each, were solidly built, and displayed a head of voluminous blond hair pulled back and secured into a ponytail.

"It isn't crap, Grandma," Elizabeth replied as she bent her knees slightly and swung her legs off the unmade bed.

Swallowing the last of her drink, she reached for the remote and clicked off the TV. She placed both the glass and the remote on the nightstand on top of a magazine she'd picked up at the airport to read on her way back from the children's hospital in Columbia. She normally did not read *Soldier of Fortune*, but that issue of the magazine, published monthly, featured an interesting man on the front cover, and an article about him inside of it. "Let's get my underwear folded so we can get started on your seedlings."

Grandma pulled a bottle opener from her laundry apron and popped the cap off one of the bottles. She held it out for her granddaughter to grab. "Didn't know you already started."

"I'll take it," Elizabeth said, accepting the pale ale. "By the way, that episode is about Aztec treasure buried in an underground tunnel in Utah. On a spread outside of Kanab. I remember hearing about it during summer vacations from the other kids when we went into town for supplies. They always talked about the Mad Dutchman's Mine hidden somewhere on that property."

"I know that spread," Grandma replied as she placed her bottle on the floor after taking a swallow. Pulling a pair of blue panties from the basket, she folded them in her lap. "We drove by it all the time when Grandpa and I took you fishing. In fact, our campground wasn't too far from there. You always did like to camp out under the stars and collect your treasures. Remember?"

"Yes," Elizabeth replied. "How could I forget the desert's night sky?"

"Anyway, if you listen close enough, you'll always hear tales about the Old West, including stories about the West being home to worm holes and spaceports connecting Kanab to the Egyptian pyramids, Ancient Mesoamerica, and even galaxies. Then, of course, don't forget the odd lost Dutchman's mine, a ranch with strange paranormal activity, or a collapsed cave containing Spanish doubloons. Even as a kid you would always find an old button or casino token and claim it came from Coronado's treasure. Treasures now sitting in those old tin lunch boxes on the shelves in front of us. That said, according to *my* grandmother, the land was bought by a Jacob Schnabel in the early 1880s, and he wasn't Dutch. He came from Germany via Central America, Honduras, I think. But after he got here, he kept to himself on his land, but there were men who snuck onto his land and watched him talking to himself and running around with weird maps and a thick leather-bound book."

"What happened to him?" Elizabeth asked, placing the folded panties on the nightstand next to the magazine with the empty glass on it.

"No one knows," Grandma answered. "People just seemed to notice that he was gone one day. There's always been rumors of a tunnel with three sets of carved stone steps leading down to a subterranean vault of Aztec gold. The start of the tunnel is supposed to be in the back of an arroyo and have a sealed entrance marked with a bull's-eye painted in blue clay paint. While Schnabel was running around the spread, Teddy Roosevelt floated around the same area hunting mule deer and recovering his health. After Schnabel disappeared, the Roosevelt family bought the spread, and eventually, Teddy's younger cousin, Franklin Delano Roosevelt, got interested in the land as well back in the 1920s. It stayed in the family until FDR died right at the end of World War Two. In 1945. After the Second World War, the land passed from owner to owner, but no one has ever found anything concerning Aztec treasure."

Elizabeth accepted a folded T-shirt from her grandmother and placed it with the other pieces of clothing on the nightstand next to the issue of *Soldier of Fortune*.

"It all came back to me while I was watching that show about Oak Island," Elizabeth replied, jerking her thumb toward the TV. "Wasn't there an army airfield or something on the property near Kanab? And didn't Charles Lindbergh fly out of there? And what about FDR? Do you think there's truth to the legend? About the Aztec treasure? There seems to be a connection between Kanab and Oak Island. A Roosevelt connection."

"Oh, you're turning into Nancy Drew again," Grandma answered with a smile. A smile backed by fond memories.

The soft sound of her grandmother's voice took Elizabeth back to her childhood, before she turned thirteen. The room they sat in reflected that loving childhood.

Although larger than the average child's room, the collected and mounted memories of a magical childhood made the room seem so much smaller. Shelves made of pine boards occupied all four walls. Shelving crowded with memories that chronicled both of their lives: brass trophies, blue ribbons, books, and artifacts Elizabeth had collected from the American West, or from her trips to Central America, as a child. Other memories included framed photos of Elizabeth with her parents when they were alive, and the sketches Elizabeth had drawn over the years.

On one of those shelves of those childhood memories was a picture of a young Elizabeth surrounded by other members of the cast from a school Christmas play titled *The Island of Misfit Toys*. A videotape of her acting debut lay flat on the shelf next to the picture. They had watched the videotape together many times since the evening of the play. On another shelf, Elizabeth's old handwritten mysteries were interspersed between the vertical spines of worn paperback novels, mostly Nancy Drew mysteries. Together, they stood at attention between the two old tin lunch boxes Grandma had referred to. One of them was a Roy Rodgers lunch box, and the other, a Disney *Treasure Island* lunch box with a young Jim Hawkins on the front.

"Anyway," Grandma continued, "while Teddy Roosevelt was a governor of New York, vice president, and president, he was also a writer, soldier, historian, hunter, naturalist, conservationist, and explorer, which is probably why he still visited the place after the 1880s. He died in 1919, which is when a younger Franklin Roosevelt started visiting the area. FDR spent time poking around that spread before he became president in 1933. In the 1920s, the family leased out part of that land to the United States Post Office, or whatever they called it back then, who needed to build an emergency airfield for their transcontinental air mail route. That's when Charles Lindbergh flew in and out of there. He was a pilot for the US Army's air mail service. Before his famous solo flight across the Atlantic, of course. Even Henry Ford and Firestone came out to Kanab to test new army trucks and a place to work on airplane development. Some say whatever treasure might've been there was trucked or flown out and ended up in a vault under the Roosevelt family home in New York. But I thought that show you were watching was about a maze-like underground money pit hiding Captain's Kidd's pirate treasure, the Knights Templar golden hoard, or the Hapsburg crown jewels. And on an island off the East Coast of Canada. Wasn't FDR all about that Oak Island business?"

"It does, or is, and he did," Elizabeth responded. "But researchers in that episode said they found Aztec ceramics and other artifacts on Oak Island."

"Whether Oak Island was visited by Vikings, pirates, Templar knights, Aztec warriors, or ancient Germans, I don't know," Grandma continued as she passed over a pair of rolled-up socks and picked up her beer, "but one thing I do know, sure as I sit on this bed here in Napa Valley, is that it's time you get a man in your life. You started on your first college degree at sixteen, won your first beauty contest when you turned eighteen, almost died of a parasitic infection at twenty while in Guatemala with the Peace Corps, and have been an accomplished physician since then. You're forty now, and the last time I checked vibrators do not produce great-grandchildren."

"Grandma!" Elizabeth objected. She pulled the bottle of beer from her lips while accepting her socks. "How many times do you have to remind me of getting married? And having kids. I'm happy the way things are. My position at the hospital is engaging, and the only thing kids and a full-time man would do is screw that up. After having my share of relationships, I realized my vibrator suits me fine."

"Well, la-de-da, Doctor Elizabeth 'Lizzie' Montgomery-Borden. Those relationships you speak of are lucky to last until Labor Day. Then, you discard them like last summer's whites. You bring a man to a family reunion in Utah or a cousin's wedding up to Osseo, Wisconsin. Maybe post a picture on Facebook with you two in Mexico City or hunting deer in Texas. Or bring a man here to Napa Valley for a weekend of wine and cheese. Then poof! The next thing I know is you show up with another victim. Just like that one guy, the one that fell off that cliff when you were biking out there in Kanab. That doctor from New York."

"He was an asshole," Lizzie replied.

"From the photos you put on Facebook, he looked like a royal cheesedick, but at least he was a man. Pretentious asshole or not. That said, what's wrong with a good ol' fashioned Irish bad boy. You know, all Colin Farrell-like."

Grandma paused long enough to sip her beer again and look at the magazine next to the stack of folded clothing.

"How about wrapping your legs around the man on the cover of that magazine. He looks like he can get any woman's ovaries kicked into overdrive. Hell, he can knock the dust off mine. Anyway, I've seen him before on the History Channel. And more than once. The last show I watched was about him deep diving on a Second World War undersea wreck with a specially built submarine. Isn't he an Icelandic archaeologist? That's right up your alley. Also, with both of you being good-looking Scandinavians, think of the children you could produce."

"No wonder Grandpa died. You must've sucked the life out of him, and I mean that in a good way." Elizabeth smiled, ignoring her grandmother's comment about Remington Corbett, the man she drove off a cliff.

Enjoying the image of that man's arm flailing in the sky as he chased his bicycle to the bottom of the canyon, she looked at the magazine. Though she'd never read *Soldier of Fortune* on a regular basis, the image on the front cover and title of the feature article caught her attention at the airport bookstore: "Treasure hunter and aerospace entrepreneur, Angar Einstok, and his team of operatives rescue ancient Peruvian artifacts from international tomb raiders." Above the caption, she saw Einstok and his assault team of seven persons. All of them wore camouflage, battle-dress uniforms, and were laden with their combat gear, including advanced-looking assault rifles slung across their chests.

Behind Einstok and his operatives, a helicopter with a profile that appeared to have come straight from a *Star Wars* movie filled in the background. Both the team and the space-age-appearing craft stood on the rock-strewn ground of Peru's Altiplano, Peru's high desert.

"His name's Einstok," Lizzie explained. "He's a corporate treasure hunter, a camera hog, an aviator, and an aerospace entrepreneur with business assets on every corner of the world. No self-respecting archaeologist would step within ten feet of him. Also, my first degree was in forensic anthropology with a minor in Mesoamerican studies. And I earned that degree well over twenty years ago. I've moved on since then."

"Fair enough," Grandma responded vacantly, holding up one white ankle sock while searching the laundry basket for a match. "But I wouldn't mind strapping that Viking on myself. No sense letting a good man go to waste."

"You old horn dog," Lizzie said slowly as her eyes fell back on the row of Nancy Drew paperbacks and the tin lunch boxes. Her grandmother was right: There's nothing wrong with a good mystery.

The next half hour passed by pleasantly quietly as the women finished folding the laundry and drinking their pale ale.

As Elizabeth took the folded clothing from her grandmother and placed it on the nightstand or bed, her mind revisited the article about Einstok. Though she did not approve of his activities as a corporate treasure hunter, she did approve of the derring-dos written in the article's central story. Writing that would have tickled the fancy of any rabid action-adventure reader: a privately built special operations-capable helicopter capable of flying at extreme altitudes, taking a special operations team to any point on the surface of the planet. In this case, Einstok, flying the helicopter himself, flew his team of operatives to an ancient site on the Altiplano and engaged in a gunbattle with men intent on using explosives to gain access to a suspected underground cache of treasure. In the end, Einstok's team killed all the thieves, and the media credited Einstok with saving another important cultural site from the ravages of greedy treasure hunters.

Again, while she did not approve of his activities, Angar Einstok was still one hell of a man.

Copán, Honduras, AD 2020

A week later, the welcome cooing of a coffee percolator woke Manwaring from a deep, alcohol-induced slumber. Feeling the dryness of his tongue, Manwaring cracked an eye and looked at the old box-like alarm clock on the sparsely topped desk. It read 9:14 a.m. Behind the desk, the closed curtains still lorded over the folding table-cum-desk. He could hear birds chirping from somewhere on the other side of the curtains. He enjoyed their innocent bustle and the smell of the brewing coffee.

Manwaring, like anybody waking up from a good drink, tried to recall the previous night. Turning his head to the right, his open eye looked at the nightstand, where he saw the remnants of the cash he had taken into town with him. Because he only carried cash, he didn't have to worry about a huge, and erroneously signed for, amount on next month's credit-card statement.

Opening the other eye, he recalled the first few hours in Puerto Cortés, before he started seriously drinking. He grinned. A grin that originated the week before. However, that enjoyment disappeared when he started to think about the hours he couldn't remember. Trying to review each blurry slide flashing across the screen in the front of his mind, he pulled his hands from under the covers and held them above his head. Although he enjoyed alcohol daily, it had been years since he got himself blind drunk. Still looking at his hands and keeping them apart, he prayed.

The week before, early Sunday morning, when he heard the staff return from a night in town, Manwaring buried the cylinder, the scrolls from inside it, and the spiral-bound notebook in the tote containing the extra field school supplies. While he understood the significance of his discovery, he knew it would take time to fully develop that understanding before making any public announcements. He could not simply hop on the next plane out of Honduras and wave that cylinder above his head like he was a football team captain hoisting the winning trophy for the cameras. Like a multimillion-dollar lottery ticket, this discovery needed stewardship. He also knew he needed to maintain the discovery's provenance to quell any accusations of creating a hoax.

While he considered himself an ethical archaeologist, there were some who were not as ethical. It was then, that early Sunday morning, when he heard Bethany yelling at a student for peeing on the toilet seat, that he realized his first security threat.

Later that morning, he woke up and started his normal routine, just like everybody else. His usual Sunday was spent alone in the backyard studio apartment catching up on his *work*. When Monday morning arrived, he kept his routine at the site, directing Bethany and the students with their archeology. That night, though, after showering and dropping off his dinner crockery in the kitchen sink like he always did, he returned to his room and locked the door behind him. Those few hours were the most magical hours Manwaring spent recording any single artifact. It was the happiest week of his entire life.

Not trusting his cell phone to take pictures, for fear of hacking, Manwaring used his basic drawing skills and the first half of that week to draw and copy everything he could discern, from the cylinder itself to the scrolls inside it. He hurriedly copied everything into the spiral-bound notepad. The same notepad that Bethany and the others had seen him carry around and doodle in. Being a habitual doodler, no one would ever question its presence out in the open. And if they did happen to get a peek inside the covers, they would consider the scribbling nothing more than a middle-aged archaeologist exercising his mind.

He could have used their laboratory conservation camera, but they kept it in the backyard studio, where the students usually spent a couple of hours after dinner processing artifacts. So sneaking into the building in the middle of the night was out of the question. Bringing the camera into his room was also out of the question, as the sound of a camera shutter going off in the middle of the night would prove disastrous.

After filling the notebook with notes and drawings of the relic, among the notes already there, Manwaring used the last half of the week to summarize the information in a more codified manner. Inside, into a blank, hardback field book using a cheap mechanical pencil.

By Friday night, every bit of information the cylinder, and its contents could offer rested between the covers of a field book. One marked with Bethany Rogers 2020 on the spine, and one smeared with a little dirt from the backyard, sweat from Manwaring's well-used bandana, and a little blood from a cut he'd received out in the field that week. With the goal of making that field book look just like hundreds of other field books, he remembered a cut Bethany received across her palm the previous week. She had smeared some of the blood across the covers while recording notes inside of it.

After including that field book with others inside blue cardboard curation boxes, he wrapped them inside a bigger, single box slated for storage and curation at the university. Since they were over halfway through with the season, and Manwaring sent off his update to the university, they normally sent unnecessary items back early so that they would have less to carry back with them at the end of the dig season. Yesterday, Saturday, Bethany fulfilled one of her duties of visiting the local FedEx store and sending back parcels ahead of them.

The next question was what to do with the cylinder, its contents, and his notebook until he was ready to face the world with his find. For right now, during the remainder of the field school, they were safe while locked inside that bedroom. However, in three weeks' time, the season will be over, along with the lease on the property. Thinking about his schedule after the field school he smiled. While the students would return to their homes, he was scheduled to assist in the restoration of another Mesoamerican site. The same site the truther wearing the Area 51 polo shirt referred to as the "Cape Canaveral of Mesoamerica."

Now, lying in the bed holding his hands in the air above his head, he scrolled through the last blurry slide in the front of his mind. Reassured that those hands had spent an innocent night drinking, he rolled out of bed, wearing only boxer shorts, and poured himself a cup of coffee. A minute later, wearing faded jeans, flip-flops, and a T-shirt, Manwaring unlocked his door and walked down the hallway to the living room, stopping behind the back of the couch. Behind him, he could hear running water coming from the hallway bathroom. He saw nobody in front of him. The students who slept on the living room floor, had rolled up their sleeping bags and were probably in the backyard studio apartment. Sipping his coffee, he smelled freshly baked bread rolls. A Sunday morning responsibility for whoever woke up first was to go to the *panadería* down at the corner for warm rolls and the local newspaper.

While the students preferred to spend their waking minutes catching up on their cellphones, Manwaring enjoyed holding a real newspaper in his hands, even if it was printed in Spanish. Expecting to see a paper sack with its top folded over and full of warm rolls, he looked down at the top of the coffee table and froze in horror.

The photo on the front showed the outline of a body lying on concrete pavement covered with a white sheet. Above the photo, headline read, *Una Prostituta Estrangulada en Puerto Cortés.*

Bahamas, early June, AD 2020

Listening to the overplayed Jimmy Buffet music and bar laughter, both accentuated by the summer night air hanging over Nassau Harbor, Sean Flanagan surveyed the anchored vessel in front of him. Standing on his paddleboard just outside the aurora of the white anchor light mounted to the yacht's masthead, but under the glare of a full moon, he saw a flared bow with a sharp stem, a gleaming white hull with a row of polished brass portholes piercing the hull, and rectangular windows framing the three-story superstructure. Through cracks in the curtains that closed off the windows and portholes, he could see occasional chinks of light escaping from inside. There was also the open fantail, where he'd witnessed parties and meetings the last three days while on his paddleboard, communing with nature.

When not on his paddleboard, Flanagan frequented the bars and beer kiosks scattered along Junkanoo Beach, where he observed the comings and goings from the yacht. While he patronized the bars and restaurants stretched along Nassau's waterfront, he found one that proved most suitable. A beer joint called Junior's. One frequented by locals, including city officials and off-duty police officers. Sitting at the bar, he listened to conversations while pretending to scratch out the world's greatest novel in a notepad and bragging about his nascent literary prowess to any bartender on shift. Unfortunately, his presence at Junior's also attracted the persistent attention of one of the bartenders.

From his eavesdropping, he learned that the Mexican drug czar, along with his security detail and majority of his crew, were coming ashore that night, meaning those left onboard would take advantage of the czar's absence and relax their guard. Sitting at the bar, with his notepad and a bottle of Sands beer in front of him, a plan gathered in his head. *What better way to kill your target when the target, and his security detail, are not around.*

Now, dipping one blade of the double-ended paddle into the water, he put that plan in motion. It was right before sunset when he witnessed his target, and others, step into the yacht's motorboat and go ashore. He also watched as the on-duty deckhand electrically hoisted and folded the gangplank against the deck railing. Coming alongside the hull, he reached up with one end of his double-ended paddle, and used a notch cut into that paddle blade to hook the bottom rail of the main deck railing. Wearing neoprene athletic gloves with finger pads, he pulled himself up using the paddle shaft and grabbed the upper rails, letting the current take the paddleboard from under his feet. He looked forward and aft, along the main deck. Seeing nobody in the shadows, he finished hoisting himself up, rolled over the top rail, and landed on his feet. Stooping to lift the paddle blade from the bottom rail and letting it drop, Flanagan looked at the staircase leading to the aft section of the deck above him. He stepped toward it while listening for any footsteps, and as he did, the light from the moon created a reflection of himself in a drape-backed glass window. Trim and well built, he wore black-gray Barefoot shoes, board shorts, a dark-blue wetsuit vest, a black backpack, and a thick, but trimmed red mustache. All of it topped with a Red Sox baseball cap.

He smiled at his reflection and at his bravado, thinking, *One of these days, your balls will bite you in your stupid Irish ass.*

Returning to the moment, he looked through a crack in the rich blue drapes and saw what should have been the vessel's salon, at least according to the diagram he'd studied over the last three days while drinking beer at Junior's. He saw a room that assumed most of the ship's central section on the main deck. Two men, wearing orange coveralls, sat at a table drinking wine and playing on their cell phones. Another man, wearing a white naval uniform, sat at the bar with a cocktail while watching a soccer match on a wall-mounted large-screen television. Satisfied, Flanagan reached out for the railing of the staircase.

Minutes later, he was standing inside the target's stateroom, with the door closed behind him. Although it was not as large as the salon, Flanagan appreciated the rich furnishings and the glass-enclosed balcony on either side. The furnishings included a beautifully made bed with a nightstand on either side and a wooden desk with bookshelves on either side. Opulent trappings of a once-impoverished, now overly wealthy drug kingpin overwhelmed the stateroom. Satisfied with his research, Flanagan slid the backpack straps off his shoulders and placed the backpack on the carpeted deck. He opened his backpack while thinking about the subject of his contract.

The subject started out a twelve-year-old foot soldier in a drug cartel years ago and ended up a fifty-year-old multimillionaire and the head of one of Mexico's most murderous cartels. While akin to the Mexican drug czar, El Chapo, in stature, the subject matched Pablo Escobar, a Colombian drug czar, in cruelty, action, and vision. Keeping those business practices in mind, the subject had expanded his operations to include dealing in ancient artifacts, international money laundering, human trafficking, and extortion. However, those extracurricular activities also led his target to intrude into territory already established by other gangs in the Boston area.

Peeling back the top flap of the backpack, Flanagan pulled out a crossbow. While he had used a variety of weapons to complete his contracts over the years, he had never used a crossbow before. Relishing the prospect of employing a five-hundred-year-old Iberian weapon for a modern contract, he hefted the weapon in his hands. It had a wooden stock with old steel and brass fittings. He purchased the weapon years ago in Madrid for its antique appearance and novelty, but with the prospect of future use in mind. To date, though, after stripping it down to parade rest, and refurbishing each individual part, he reassembled it and used it only for target practice on a private range. When not shouldering it on the private range, it resided on a fireplace mantle in a cabin outside of Boston.

After retrieving a couple of books from one of the bookshelves in the stateroom, Flanagan stepped up to the headboard and turned to look at the richly stained wooden door. He spent the next minute surveying the room and the angles from the room's furnishings to the door. Finding a suitable firing position, the nightstand next to the bed's headboard, he went to work.

He started by moving a solid brass lamp and a silver chalice full of cocaine apart. During his reconnaissance, Flanagan had seen women brought aboard the vessel, and the state they were in when they left hours later.

Continuing, he positioned the stock of the crossbow between the lamp and chalice and used the two books to elevate the front of the weapon, and to hold the stock down. Stepping back to his pack, he removed a Command picture frame hook, a roll of black wire thread, and his cell phone. Stepping back to the crossbow, he tied the end of the wire thread to the end of the flight groove and stepped backward to the door, unrolling the string as he did. Reaching the door, he held his cell phone in the other hand and used his thumb to find the right app. Like tourists busy flashing their cellphones at whatever caught their interest, he took pictures of the target when he made his few, and brief, visits ashore. Using the app on the cellphone, he recorded the man's exact height along with other tertiary measurements. Holding the wire string tight, he held it against the door and moved both the wire string and cell phone up and down until he found the height of the target's chest, marking the spot on the door with his finger and string. After placing the cellphone in his mouth, he pulled the Command hook from his pocket and set out to complete his remote-firing assembly.

After photographing his work, and retrieving his backpack, he found himself standing next to an open glass door leading out to the balcony facing downtown Nassau. With the empty pack strapped to his back Flanagan took one last look at his work. The crossbow secured to the nightstand with wire and angled exactly right. Another length of that same wire ran from the trigger of the crossbow through more Command hooks, up the wall, across the ceiling, and down to the doorknob. There was no slack in the wire, and just enough tension to pull the trigger when the door opened fully. He looked at the crossbow one more time. While the weapon itself was five hundred years old, the bolt it would fire was not. Made in the workshop behind his cabin, he tipped the twelve-inch hickory wooden bolt with an explosive warhead the size and length of a good cigar. The impact on the target's chest would be fatal, but the addition of a capsule of nerve gas would ensure the completion of his contract.

With a nod of satisfaction, he stepped through the open door and pulled it shut behind him. Stepping up the railing, he reached out with his hands to help himself over it. He looked at the lights of downtown Nassau. *I could have simply wired the door with five pounds of C-4, but then what's the fun in that?*

With that affirmation, he lifted himself over the railing and dropped into Nassau Harbor, holding his Red Sox ball cap in his right hand as he did.

An hour later, and after a shower and change of clothing, Flanagan sat in a chair back at Junior's. With a bottle of Sands beer in his hand, his cell phone in his back pocket, and a paperback book in front of him, he watched as Bahamian police boats surrounded the anchored yacht. The flashing lights dazzled over the black water of Nassau Harbor. He listened to the patrons and bar staff talk about what was going on aboard the yacht. Among the patrons were off-duty police officers monitoring their cell phones. After overhearing a conversation between two officers, Flanagan pulled the cell phone from his pocket and texted a message: *Clean up Aisle Four completed.* Once he hit the send button, he set the phone down and thought about his latest contract. While pleased with the ingenuity of the hit, he started to think about the crossbow he'd left behind. Based on experiences, he realized that it would eventually disappear from the evidence locker and end up in some cop's closet. The sound of a female voice interrupted his thoughts.

"How's your novel going, Flanagan?"

Flanagan turned to look at the well-endowed bartender standing behind the bar.

While Flanagan was not his real name, he responded as if he were born with it. He looked down at the book in front of him before looking up at the bartender. Eastern European-born, she was of medium height with blond hair, a good tan, and store-bought breasts accented by a pink V-necked T-shirt.

"Pretty good, Nikki," he lied, "but I'm just catching up on some light reading for now. And I'll have another Sands when you get a chance."

She nodded as they both heard a patron from the other end of the crowded bar calling her name.

"Be right back," she said as she turned around for a bottle of rye. "And don't forget, we're going out for sandwiches after my shift."

He nodded and returned his attention to the rest of his beer and book. Forgetting about his crossbow, he looked down at the paperback. A fan of military history, Flanagan was halfway through a historical piece about the German general, Erwin Rommel, and his North African campaign. Titled *Rommel's Other Afrika Korps*, the front cover's backdrop was that of the featureless North Africa desert with a burned-out panzer tank in the foreground. Behind the tank, the pyramidion, or capstone, of a pyramid rose in the background. A Nazi swastika bathed in a glow of golden yellow hovered above the pyramid's pyramidion. Under the panzer was a superimposed image of the famous Afrika Corps logo: a slightly bent palm tree with the letters A and K on either side of the trunk.

The book centered around a group of archaeologists and engineers following the tread marks of Rommel's panzers. Just like the academics and the antiquarians who shadowed Napoleon's invasion of Egypt, and the Monuments Men who stayed on the heels of the Allied armies fighting across France and into Germany. Bringing the brown bottle to his lips, Flanagan's thoughts became philosophical, again. An affliction that strikes many men as they enter their forties and wondered how they got to that point in life. Tilting the bottle against his lips, he thought about the year that he started out on this career.

What happened to you, dumb ass? You should be finishing a career as a veteran fighter jet pilot for the Air Force and be neck deep in your NASA application process. "Shit," Flanagan said under his breath.

Over the Atlantic Ocean, early June, AD 2020

"I have the plane, Angar. So, what do you think?"

Letting go of the airplane's controls, Angar Einstok flexed his fingers while rotating his shoulders. As he reached up to adjust his headset, he turned his head to face the left cockpit window inches from his face. "My wing is still there. How about yours, Gojo?"

"Not that you will need it," Gojo stated, "but after the first time I flew with you, I told myself to never let you borrow my lawnmower."

Angar Einstok pulled his attention from outside the cockpit and removed the aviation sunglasses from his face. He reached up to rub the bridge of his nose before scanning the console in front of him. He and Gojo sat in the cockpit of a Brazilian-built C390 twin-engine military transport plane. Blinking his eyes at the sun blaring into the airplane's cockpit windows, he looked over at Einstok Industries chief pilot Captain Albert "Gojo" Majuro, a handsome man of Peruvian and Polynesian descent. His jet-black hair remained neatly combed despite the headset he wore, and the flight maneuvers the plane had just suffered while under Einstok's control.

"Well, despite your efforts at trying to rip it off," Gojo said, "my wing is still intact. And, while I can say the same for Zelda, Munro, and the rest of your team behind us, I won't speak the same for my copilot just yet. He has never flown with you. I know you gave Rand Aviation a security deposit, especially since you're taking an airplane you don't own out over the deep Atlantic for a test flight, and on a real-world mission with real ammunition, but I don't think the deposit will cover cleaning up vomit or shit-filled trousers."

"He is not your copilot just yet," Einstok responded. He replaced his glasses and ran his eyes across the airplane's instruments, including its compass. Their heading: 180 degrees, or due south. "There is no fun in test flying an airplane close to both land and help. Besides, what better way to evaluate an airplane than to take it on a real-world mission? Especially since I'm buying it for that reason."

The Icelandic archaeologist-slash-adventurer-entrepreneur paused to unbuckle his seat belt.

Gojo nodded while adjusting the control yoke in his hand ever so slightly. He also noted the time on his wristwatch, saying as he did so, "You know that I have logged over three hundred hours sitting in the left seat of this exact model, and despite your best efforts, we are still in the air. Therefore, I think it will be a grand replacement for the last aircraft you turned into a pile of scrap in the Urals. So? What do I tell Rand Aviation?"

"You must be working on commission," Einstok said as he leaned forward to push himself from the chief pilot's seat. He paused long enough to look out of the cockpit window, and at the expanse of the Atlantic Ocean thousands of feet beneath them. "Anyway, while we still have an operation to complete, go ahead and tell Rand Aviation I will take it. Zelda will wire the remaining funds to their account momentarily. Also, after my team and I jump, you take Zelda to Dakar to wait for our return there. After you fly us to Italy, return to The Farm. I will send you a list of needed modifications. Tell your maintenance crew they will earn next month's pay."

"Yes, sir," Gojo replied.

"She flies well, Gojo," he said, pushing himself from his seat. "But not that well."

Behind the cockpit, inside the moderately sized cargo hold, illuminated by overhead light fixtures and the square windows lining the fuselage, seven people—wearing sunglasses any army ranger, professional shooter, or fighter jet pilot would be proud to wear—reclined in canvas-webbed seats on either side of the aircraft's cargo hold. Every member of Einstok's team looked like they could have posed for a special operations recruiting poster. Firm, muscular frames pressed against clean, and pressed, civilian clothing. Even the two women in the aircraft's main hold looked capable of holding their own in a good old-fashioned bar fight.

Now that Einstok had completed his test trials, they unbuckled their seat belts and returned to their previous in-flight occupations. While one of them, Zelda sitting closest to the cockpit and separate from the others, concentrated on the laptop poised on her jean-covered thighs, the remaining six each had a closed Manila folder resting in their laps. And one of those persons, Munro Turner stacked two additional items on top of his Manila folder. One, a worn paperback edition of a Jules Verne novel, *From the Earth to the Moon*; the second, a paperback puzzle book with a pen sticking out. However, everybody on Einstok's team delighted in listening to the echoing spasms of Gojo's copilot throwing up in the plane's claustrophobic latrine during Einstok's test trials.

Lining the center of the aircraft's cargo hold and fastened to the metal floor of the plane with straps and cargo netting, were three aluminum pallets loaded waist high with everything they needed for their upcoming mission. The pallet closest to the steps leading up to the waist-high landing just behind the walled-in cockpit was stacked with packed parachutes and dive bags. The middle pallet was topped with Olive Drab Pelican cases containing automatic weapons, ammunition, and night vision goggles. The last pallet, piled with duffels, contained their personal gear.

A man who completed his own appearance with a Viking undercut haircut topped with a top knot leaned forward. He inspected a grayish-brown crab that had come out from under the pallet of duffels.

"Oy, Double Cannon, looks like we've picked up a stowaway," he said to the man sitting next to him. The crab, which could fit into the palm of a human hand, snapped at the air with his claws.

Double Cannon, the biggest member of the team, with ham-sized fists and a fully shaved head and full black beard, responded. "No shit, Nitro. These pallets sat on the tarmac in Tripoli before loading. So who knows what kind of cockroaches crawled into our duffels? Remember that time, in Cairo, when an asp crawled out my bag?"

Nitro continued to inspect the crab while answering. "I remember, because I put that damned snake in your bag. It was a job getting him in there, though. You should've seen your face when that thing popped up out your bag."

"Oh, now you tell me," Double Cannon said, his lips forming a thin line. He raised his fist and popped up his middle finger. "Karma will be a bitch, Bitch."

Nitro did not turn to face Double Cannon's middle finger. Instead, threw out his right booted foot and stomped on the crab. The muted drone of the engines outside the airframe silenced the flattening of the crab's shell.

Double Cannon dropped his fist and turned to look at Nitro. "Did you have to do that?"

Nitro knocked the heel of his boot against the aluminum deck before leaning back into his seat. "No, mate, no I didn't. I just pictured the neck of an IRA piece of shit under the heel of my boot."

Just then, Double Cannon lifted his left leg and let go an enormous fart. The resultant explosion was like a thunderclap inside the hold of the aircraft. Momentarily blocking out the droning of the aircraft's engines outside the plane's fuselage.

The man sitting next to Double Cannon, and on the opposite side of Nitro, Solid Gold, leaned away from the transgressor. "Shit Double Cannon!

Again? We're inside a fucking pressurized aircraft! For Christ's sake!"

Their team leader Munro Turner, a Black Bahamian, looked over the pallet between he and Nitro. He shook his head slightly and turned the corners of his mouth down. He also shot a look of despair at Double Cannon.

Suddenly, two aluminum doors opened, one at each end of the airplane's cargo hold. Nitro and Double Cannon, sitting closest to the bathroom, looked aft at the copilot as he stepped from the tiny space. They smirked at the man wiping the front of his white, button-down shirt and black tie with a paper towel. Both were marked with wet stains. Although a bit pasty-faced to begin with, his short red hair and green eyes made him seem even paler.

"Hey, mate," Nitro said while pointing to his own right shoulder. "You missed a piece of carrot."

The copilot gave both men a sideways look while turning his head to look down at the black epaulet of his uniform shirt. A piece of carrot was stuck to the cloth, and between the epaulet's two yellow stripes.

At the other end of the hold, Angar Einstok exited the cockpit and stood on the landing, closing the cockpit door behind him. Wearing pressed blue jeans, hiking boots, and a white short-sleeved cotton shirt, with three cigars poking out of the shirt pocket, he pulled the aviator sunglasses from his face with one hand and spoke with a voice that overcame the outside drone of the aircraft's engines.

"*Góðan daginn*," Einstok said. He sniffed at the air and directed a stern look at Double Cannon before continuing. "Gojo says we will be landing in the Canary Islands in twenty-eight minutes. We will be on the ground until 1800 hours. While I could have timed our arrival closer to sunset, allowing less time on the ground, I wanted to be close enough to our target in case circumstances changed. Therefore," Einstok paused long enough, again, to look at the copilot, whose name he did not remember, walk past the pallets, and toward him.

The copilot reached the forward pallet and dropped the end of his tie. He tried to hide the wet paper towel in his hand as he looked at Einstok. "Sorry sir, I guess it was something I ate while in Tripoli."

Einstok did not answer, but let the man step up to the landing, pass him, and enter the cockpit before returning his attention to his team.

"You will have a little time to kill, so taking a stroll through town while enjoying coffees won't hurt. Or you could be like Munro and find a park bench to keep up with your reading, or at least complete a sudoku. The bottom line, though, is that you are oil-rig roughnecks heading back to Nigeria, so act like your average, pissed-off oil-rig workers having to return to work after a month's furlough."

Everybody except for Nitro, who had his knee bent and appeared to be inspecting the bottom of his boot, and the woman still concentrating on her laptop, affirmed his order by offering a slight nod or thin smile of acceptance under their tactical sunglasses.

"Good," Einstok said as he looked down the length of pallets and then at Nitro. He shook his head slightly. "Nitro, remember that you are not in an East London pub. Nor are you on the streets of Ulster. Clear?"

Nitro offered a thumbs-up. "Sure, Boss."

Einstok thought about Nitro's history. All he needed was some blue face paint, and he would look like the classic Viking berserker standing at the front of a line of Viking warriors screaming at their enemies. While a modern special operator of the twenty-first century, Nitro's impulsive behavior matched that of the Viking version of a special warrior from a time long past.

Taking his thoughts off Nitro, Einstok gave Double Cannon a second-long look as he raised his wrist and looked at his waterproof, and tactical Rolex. The six people with the folders in their laps looked at their wristwatches before reaching for their folders. The team's leader, Munro Turner, picked up the novel and the puzzle book and set them in the empty seat to his right.

Although Munro wore casual clothing, like the others, the knife-edge creases in his aloha shirt and khaki slacks demarked a professional who paid attention to detail. He even took the time to keep his stout leather hiking boots well-oiled and buffed. He wore a military-style haircut topped with a black baseball cap. A patch with a green hand grenade and golden fire erupting from the top occupied the center of the cap's front. Embroidered across the front of the hat, above the flame-spitting hand grenade, was the French Foreign Legion's motto: *Legio Patria Nostra.*

"We will be over our drop zone, Boa Vista in the Cape Verde Islands, by 2000 hours. We will jump from an altitude of six thousand feet and aim to land one mile seaward of our target. The ship will have its standard lighting for vessels at anchor, and my competitor has hired a security force. Four men. They have two mounted M-60 machine guns on deck, but our contact will stand the security force down from their duties. Zelda has summed up those four individuals in the files in your laps along with their additional weapons outlay. However, as you will see, there should be no issue with those overpaid Walmart detectives. Especially with their team leader. He's ex-US Army and goes by the name of Swanson. He did a short stint with Einstok Industries before I dismissed him, which is why most of you will not recognize the name."

While briefing his team, Einstok pictured the sheets of paper Zelda placed inside those folders, including information on the security personnel and a colored photo of their target: a one-hundred-and-fifty-foot-long salvage vessel with a white hull streaked with running rust. Behind the anchored vessel, a mile distant, he could see an empty, windswept landscape.

"Once in the water, we will use dive weights to sink our parachutes and swim, in formation, to the target. Our contact says that, typically, at that time of night, most people on board are readying equipment for the next day or are packaging whatever they have recovered that day. However, their recovery operation is wrapping up, and they will use tonight to stow their finds and use tomorrow to remove any evidence of their excavations from the seafloor. Our contact has also provided spirits for a post-expedition celebration in the crew's mess, leaving them preoccupied, and all together. Our contact will be on the bow of the vessel smoking a cigarette."

"You said they've been anchored over the site for some time," asked the woman sitting next to Munro Turner. "They haven't been molested at all. By pirates?"

"Yes, Lil' Sumptin,'" Einstok answered with a slight nod. "Zelda reached out to various persons within that sphere of influence and made sure the expedition was left unmolested, which has made our target a bit complacent."

Lil' Sumptin responded with a thumbs-up.

At just five feet, she looked like a kindergartener among NFL linebackers. However, despite her size, she possessed the body of an Olympic gymnast, and an impish presence akin to Tinkerbell having the ability to fieldstrip and reassemble any firearm known to humankind. Einstok thought about their previous operations where she proved her ability to turn the simplest item—a bent lawnmower blade—into devastating handheld, man-killing weapon.

"Good," he said while looking at Zelda, his executive secretary who sat just to his left.

She wore a loose-fitting blouse printed with hibiscus flowers tucked into Levi jeans, which were, in turn, tucked into a pair of hiking shoes topped with thick white socks. Her golden blond hair was pulled into a bun and sunglasses rested on her forehead. Despite her casual dress, no one could miss her strict, businesslike persona, accentuated by the Sig-Sauer holstered at her waist.

"Zelda, I know you would prefer to jump with us, but because of your injury, I can't afford to lose you due to pulled stitches and infection. Also, I need you to stay with the aircraft so that you can take care of the customs officials in Dakar, and those at its airport. Once we jump, Gojo will turn back for the African coast. What we plan to bring into Dakar is important to me, so there is no need to be slight with any monies."

"Yes, Mr. Einstok," Zelda responded as she struck a key on the laptop. She looked down between her thighs at the leather-bound attaché strapped to the aluminum decking under the seat. "I brought enough Euros and US one-hundred-dollar notes in anticipation for that purpose." Leaning back in her seat, she continued, "Also, I am assuming you are purchasing this airplane, so I will deposit the remaining funds with Rand Aviation and sign the paperwork. And I will see the dismissal of the copilot. I am not sure how Gojo vetted him, as he does not make these kinds of errors."

Einstok thought for a second about the man he just mentioned: Swanson.

"You are correct, Zelda. For someone whose resume includes a commission with the Spanish Air Force as a special operations-capable helicopter pilot, that man had a problem with my air trials. Today, no one can be too careful when it comes to industrial espionage. Or sabotage. Please investigate the matter and discharge it as necessary. And make sure you log time sitting in the left seat of my new acquisition after we jump."

Zelda acknowledged with an almost imperceptible nod of her head.

"Excellent. Lastly, once aboard the salvage ship, I will take care of our contact. When you receive word from me, go ahead and withdraw his deposit."

"Yes, sir," Zelda replied, leaving Einstok to return his attention back to his commandos. "Munro, you and Lil' Sumptin' will enter the crew's mess from the aft entryway."

Munro and Lil' Sumptin' gave each other a nod.

"Good." Einstok looked at two other commandos. "Solid Gold and Slingblade, you will enter the mess from the portside entryway."

The two men, sitting next to each other, brought their hands up and fist bumped. Slingblade almost equaled Double Cannon in size, and he wore his hair short, in flat-top fashion. Solid Gold was a trim, muscular, and tanned South African. His Dutch ancestry apparent.

Einstok looked at the remaining two men. "Double Cannon and Nitro. You two will enter from the starboard entryway." Without waiting for a reply, he turned his attention to all of them. "Contain everybody in the mess, get a headcount, and collect all cell phones and other electronic devices immediately. Not including our four *security operatives,* there are twenty-four divers, crewmen, and officers, including my contact. Five of the crew have previous military experience, so discharge any situation as needed."

All of Einstok's operatives nodded slightly as they listened.

"Once we have the ship, and our cargo, I will relay a signal to the pickup boat and research vessel, both of which are already laying off the island to the east, disguised as fishing trawlers. And before anybody asks, we could have used those vessels to board our target, but a seaborne assault could have proved problematic. Besides, I would have no excuse to test fly a new airplane, and this team needs to update their semiannual parachute and swim qualifications. Anyway, the pickup boat will come in so we can transfer select artifacts already aboard the vessel, and then we will be on our merry way to Dakar. Lorries will be waiting at the dock to take us and our recovered items back to this plane. The crew from our salvage ship will dispose of any remaining crew or divers, along with their vessel. There are miles of deep water between the islands and the African coast. Once they settle the matter, they will return to anchor over the site."

As he finished speaking, Munro Turner removed his sunglasses and offered a half wink. Einstok understood the sentiment. Although the members of that team had no compunction with killing, Munro being an ex-French foreign legionnaire understood when and where it might be necessary. Killing simply out of hand was not in Turner's wheelhouse. Einstok understood Turner's stance, but more from a practical point of view. This team was part of Einstok's public image, which could not afford undue public scrutiny.

"What are they doing there?" Solid Gold asked. "You mentioned something about a submerged Greek city?"

"Yes," Einstok answered. "And one which sank thousands of years ago due to underlying volcanic activity. It is a potential location of Atlantis, or at least proof that the Greeks ventured into the Atlantic. The salvage crew has no legal right being there, which proves convenient for me, as they have recovered items that will suit my personal collection nicely."

For the team's benefit, Zelda looked up from her laptop and added, "Our contact has been keeping us up to date, through coded messaging, on what they have recovered, and crated for transport; therefore, allowing for an easier transfer and transit to the coast."

Einstok continued. "The salvagers are secretly looting the site for a competitor of mine and have no permits, so the authorities should take little notice of their disappearance. I also suspect my competitor will not raise any alarms and will write off the derisory dollars he used to fund the operation as a lesson learned. Zelda has already applied for the proper licensing as well as arranged for 'legal' excavation rights. The money that the chief consultants and officials received from my competitor was a pittance compared to my financial intrusion. After our two vessels arrive on scene, divers from my research ship shall redeposit the artifacts I choose not to take back to Dakar. In the morning, my research vessel, legally in place, will announce to the world that, under my direction, I have located evidence that the Greeks did attempt colonize the Atlantic Ocean. I will invite renowned archaeologists to inspect the site and let them monitor my own archaeologists while they document my find."

He paused long enough to look at his wristwatch again.

"If all goes as planned, Gojo should have us at my villa in Tuscany by 1800 hours tomorrow evening. And from there, you all shall be on your way to your furloughs with more-than-adequate bank accounts."

Everybody smiled again.

"That said," Einstok continued, "keep in passive contact with Munro during your leave and avoid any 'embarrassing' or 'notable' entanglements. I have invested substantial funds to have past transgressions forgiven. Be at The Farm by the twentieth of next month."

After the operatives gave their thumbs-up, they opened the Manila folders on their laps.

Stepping down the short staircase from the landing, Einstok reclined in the webbed bucket seat next to Zelda. He pulled two Cohiba cigars from his shirt pocket. Holding one out for Zelda, he looked up at the gray-painted and curved aluminum above his head and slowly inserted the unlit cigar into his mouth. He closed his eyes to savor the rich tobacco.

"Here comes the boring but"—Einstok sighed—"necessary part of business."

"Thank you," Zelda said, pinching the cigar between the fingers of her free hand. "I will enjoy it after your jump, and when I am enroute to Dakar."

Einstok opened his eyes. "An excellent time to enjoy a good cigar, but if you don't mind, I shall enjoy mine before our jump."

"Of course," Zelda said, inserting the cigar into her blouse pocket. "Like you have always said, lighting a cigar at the drop of the hat is simply vulgar."

"Very good, Zelda. Like anything else in life, there must always be a proper pairing as one gives legitimacy to the other. Now, what do you have for me today? How about the Rhinelander Concern. Any news from Max? Let us hope that today is the day. And any more word on that person sniffing about our business? The one you called The Shark?"

Still looking at the airplane's ceiling inches above his head, he enjoyed the unlit cigar.

"I am just as curious about Max's efforts, but nothing yet. And as far as The Shark, I believe he has gone to ground. Let me begin with what we do have. First, I've received a text from our contact within the IRA. The custodian they used for the Bahamian issue has reported a successful cleanup in Aisle Four. Shall I congratulate them?"

Einstok, keeping his face pointed up, turned an eye toward the length of the airplane's cargo hold. His eyes settled on Nitro.

"I did have my reservations with using that custodial technician, especially after having reviewed his résumé, and his lack of discipline, but I appreciated his audaciousness to conduct a cleanup using an explosive- and poisoned-tipped crossbow bolt. Also, I value your intuition with laundering his services through the IRA, just as I am sure they appreciate the sizable bank deposit. Something Nitro does not need to know about, as he would be a bit put out by the fact his employer is trucking with his archenemy. Just deposit the remaining funds to complete the contract. Also, keep track of our janitor. He may prove useful in the future. Next?"

"Yes, sir," Zelda replied as she scrolled down the screen of her tablet. "Our contact within the CIA wants to know if he should continue to push that rumor about Russia paying bounties on American soldiers in Afghanistan?"

As Einstok answered his executive secretary's question, his focus moved from Nitro to Zelda's laptop. "Nothing wrong with an establishment politician looking for a step up in the world by passing on fake news to a gaggle of rabid progressives willing to suck up any tidbit of disinformation. What else?"

"I received the edits for the article that *GQ* will run in next month's edition, and they are asking for a photo to go with the article." Zelda looked up from the screen. "They want to use one of the photos from the Blaylok graduation Commencement."

Einstok slowly rolled the unlit cigar in his mouth one more time before pulling it from his lips. He inspected the dark, wet tobacco while answering. "Since the article is about me paying the student-loan debt for this year's graduating class at Blaylok, using a photo with me shaking hands with a student is fine. While anyone would work, there are two students that have immediate potential."

"I know the two students you are talking about," Zelda answered, returning her eyes to the screen. "One of them has already started his position at the New York City office for the Department of Justice, and the other has just completed his parachute training at Fort Benning and is posted to the 101st Airborne Division. Both assets should become viable by this time next year. Again, like you have stated, nothing defines force projection better than organization and discipline."

"Excellent. Make sure my security division keeps up with the dossiers on the entire graduating class for future reference."

"Yes, sir," Zelda answered with a smile. "Just as you have said before, they may have their thirty pieces of silver, but..."

"I will have my pound of flesh," Einstok finished. "Everybody must mortgage themselves, so it is up to them to account for their choices and serve their sentences."

"I already had the accounting division file those grants with the IRS for tax-deduction purposes." Zelda tapped the screen with her stylus. "Your wife wants to know your schedule. She is in Monte Carlo."

"Very prudent," Einstok said, still inspecting his cigar. "Go ahead tell her I will be in Tuscany by tomorrow evening, and please let her know that I have an addition to the estate garden."

"Very good," Zelda replied.

Taking his attention from the end of his cigar, and placing it on Zelda, Einstok continued, "My wife is still very much interested in meeting you again. It has been a while."

Einstok saw the curious smile on Zelda's face as she looked up from her laptop. He also saw her eyes settle on the wet tip of his cigar pinched between his fingers.

"I remember our weekend in Vienna. She is quite charming, but adventurous at the same time. Let me look at your upcoming schedule to see what I can work in."

"Very well," Einstok said, returning his attention to his cigar. "Next?"

"The board of directors is uneasy about the congressional hearings concerning your planned spaceship facility on the moon. More specifically its location, and the fact that you have already landed, and positioned, exploratory rovers and preparatory modules without any authority or public knowledge. NASA, and their associated interests, had already slated that plat for themselves. They are also concerned about the extension of your new branch of Einstok Industries, TETRA, and its potential monopolization of the lunar surface and space efforts. The board wants to know when you will be back in New York, so they can discuss the issue with you in person. The Senate has already subpoenaed our board members to appear before two committees starting next Monday."

Thinking back to the reason he did, in fact, select that specific location to start his lunar explorations, Einstok answered. "I am not idling myself while waiting for the world bodies to create a treaty, allowing them to divide the moon for themselves and leaving others on the periphery to pick up their scraps. Tell the board members I will be in New York by Friday morning. In the meantime, review your dossiers on every committee member. For details to exploit. If the details are not that unsavory, make them so."

Zelda nodded as she continued to scroll through the screen. "I have already started. Remember Congresswoman Bennington."

Einstok nodded, smiling. "The congresswoman who takes vodka shots off the asses of naked, underage girls."

"Yes. I have also followed up on rumors concerning another committee member. This individual has been indirectly receiving funds, through distant family members, from the Chinese aerospace industry. In return, that person has been voting on tariff legislation in favor of the Chinese, and against the Taiwanese. I see no worries, sir."

"Good," Einstok replied. "Any private citizen who has the wherewithal, and foresight, can do as they wish with the moon, or anything in space for that matter. To hell with any international space treaty. If not for visionaries such as I, no country's space program would have ever gotten off the ground. Even dating back to the 1920s, in Germany, where skilled scientists and private investors combined their efforts to initiate rocket science studies and an interest in space that we all benefit from today. Which means organizations such as NASA would never have gotten off the ground. Anything else?"

"Yes," Zelda replied. "The Secretary of State has a request."

Einstok scoffed. "What the hell does that neutered marsupial want now?"

"He is concerned about the Venezuelan situation and how it will appear in print. He is also concerned about how his role, and those of his 'brothers' and 'sisters' in the creation of the *situation*, might affect future elections in Washington. He is willing to offer any sum so that the president does not find out the truth."

Einstok took a deep breath. "How pedestrian. Offering printed currency. I'm amazed he found his way through the birth canal on his own. Anyway, the president knows what happened in Venezuela, including the use of those foolish ex-Green Berets who paddled ashore in rubber boats in an ill-conceived coup attempt. But the secretary does not know that the president knows. The president plans to keep that information to himself until the time presents itself. You know, such as when a shitstorm of American interference in another country's democratic process spatters all over the president. The president can claim plausible deniability, let out a timely news leak, and throw the secretary in front of a speeding freight train a mile long. It is amazing how Washington politics tends to be so cannibalistic. During times of duress, they shop their own and, with no compunction, consume their victim's guts with relish."

Einstok paused while looking past the cigar and through the skin of the plane's cargo hold. "Zelda, since currency can come in any denominations or specie, who is the richer, a man with twenty million on deposit or a man who holds twenty secrets?"

"Of course, you already know the answer."

"With knowledge, comes leverage, and with leverage, comes control, the truest form of wealth: a king with full coffers has just that, while a pauper with knowledge will never have for want." Einstok paused. "You impressed me with how you personally managed the situation in Venezuela, but I am sorry you had to take a round in the execution of the outcome. Tell the secretary of state that my maintenance crew cleaned up the mess his *siblings* left behind in Venezuela, and that my crew left, for him, and Colonel Rodriguez, a nice, shiny coup that the colonel can proudly display. I've reviewed your version of the story, and I like how you emphasized the colonel's exploits during a key mountain battle, and the capture of those ex-Green Berets. Go ahead and submit it to *Soldier of Fortune* for their next issue. Lastly, make sure one of the dupes at CNN, and at those other news rags, gets a script to run with. Also, remind the secretary that since I had to send you and my maintenance crew to clean up his tipped-over mop bucket, I expect him to not develop amnesia in the future. What is next?"

"First, thank you for your confidence in letting me lead that mission, especially since Turner and his team were more than capable," Zelda said. She looked up from the screen. "Next in line is the president. He would like to meet with you concerning the Space Force. He will be putting his final additions to his plans about its organization and expansion and wants you to advise him on who to nominate for key positions."

"Seems our current political leaders have forgotten a phrase coined by one of America's most intrusive predecessors," Einstok said. "No wonder the American military complex, although they absorb billions of tax dollars yearly, is nothing but a shadow of its former self. Which bodes well for individuals such as I. Especially since the addition of the Space Force will create at least two new four-star generals. Think of it, Zelda, the American army has almost five hundred generals alone. Officers climbing over each other seeking to maintain relevance and vying for a seat at the table set for far less. Officers that I have been able to groom over the years. Tell the president I'll be up for a round of golf this Saturday. The usual course. Anything else?"

"Yes. Our informant in Honduras," Zelda's eyebrows furrowed. "Excuse me."

Letting her view the interruption, Einstok refocused on the cigar in his fingers while listening to the humming drone of the airplane's engines outside.

After a few seconds, Zelda continued. "I just received a communication from Max. Your intuition has paid dividends. His message reads: *The eagle has landed*. Do you have any instructions for Max?"

Einstok turned his eyes to his assault team sitting in the aft section of the aircraft hold. "No. Just tell him to continue his excavations, and to keep me updated. Also, tell him we will meet him at The Farm on the twentieth of next month. Remind him to keep his appetite wetted for Virginia ham and tell him I look forward to having updated reading literature."

Sitting there, listening and feeling the C390 transport plane taking them over the Atlantic Ocean, he thought about what Max might present him with in a month's time. He then started to think about how to best facilitate the information he expected. After thinking a bit, he repeated words he had said only moments before. "Again, everybody who chooses to accept a mortgage must serve their sentence."

"What was that?" Zelda asked.

Einstok opened his eyes and turned them on Zelda. "Just musing aloud. Anyway, you mentioned Honduras. Does Bethany have anything to report?"

"Yes, sir," Zelda replied.

5

Over the Cape Verde Islands, early June, AD 2020

The black air was silent and still as Einstok fell through the clouds. He looked up through his night vision goggles mounted to his black, military-issue, high-cut tactical helmet, lowered in front of his face and at the rectangular black hole his ram-air parachute created in the starlit sky above him. With the canopy properly deployed, he dropped his head to look down at the black sea thousands of feet beneath him. Holding the steering toggles, or brakes, in his hands, he expertly controlled the angle and direction of his descent to an aim point a mile from the lights of their anchored target. Off to his left, he saw the beams of headlights of the occasional vehicles making their way along the few roads crisscrossing the island. Looking up from the black sea, he saw the red pinpricks of infrared chem lights hanging under the other invisible parachutes around him.

Satisfied, Einstok glanced at his wrist-mounted altimeter. One hundred and fifty feet to go. He relaxed his body but tightened his grip on the steering brakes, in readiness to flare the parachute the last few feet of the descent. At twenty-five feet, his shoulders hardened as he pulled down on the toggles. His canopy luffed just before his legs hit the water. Somewhere behind him, the canopy collapsed into the water. Although it was June, the water slipping in between his skin and dark-blue wetsuit chilled him. Grabbing the quick-release buckles of the parachute's harness, Einstok freed himself from the harness, reached down to his combat web gear, and released the brass clip with a six-pound dive weight zip-tied to it. Clipping it to the parachute's harness, he fin-kicked away from the air escaping the material as the weight pulled the parachute under the surface of the black water. The silent whisper of air escaping six other parachutes informed Einstok of the nearness of his team. Einstok waited patiently as the six, infrared, chem lights attached to tactical helmets merged at his position. Spitting saltwater from his mouth, Einstok spoke quietly.

"Let's finish this operation."

Not expecting a verbal response, Einstok turned and fin-kicked toward the ship's lights a mile away. His team fell behind him.

Einstok's fingers grabbed at the plastic rungs of a ladder. One of two ladders hanging over the ship's stern, left by Einstok's contact aboard the vessel. He reached up to his chest and felt the G36 German-made assault weapon secured to his combat webbing. Ready to unclip it as soon as he reached the deck, he lifted the night vision goggles from his face. Reaching down further, he slipped off his swim fins. The others did the same as they gathered behind their leaders.

First to reach the deck, Munro Turner and Einstok saw a light about twenty feet forward of their location mounted to the superstructure above the door leading to the ship's interior. Other lights on either side of the superstructure lining the deck led to the bow. The only other light was the ship's anchor light mounted on top of the ship's radio mast. Aside from the sound of a generator escaping the ship's exhaust stack, they heard the occasional clang from the closing of a steel door or an intermittent, distant laugh.

Einstok unclipped his G36 from his chest and held it in the ready position, letting the short barrel lead the way. Wearing full wetsuits, soled wetsuit booties, and their tactical helmets, the group split into three pairs, leaving Einstok to complete his own purpose.

He reached the two-story superstructure but did not stop there. Continuing forward, with the sound of padded feet following him, he passed the first porthole. An inside cover closed it off. He looked at the next few portholes in line and the weak lights leaking through the curtains covering them. Passing a closed side door, he stopped long enough to peek into an open porthole and through the crack in the curtains. Almost twenty, mostly White, men all wearing work clothes, coveralls, or dungarees, relaxed in the ship's mess. Drinking wine or liquor, and smoking cigarettes under opaque overhead lighting, they played on their cell phones or watched the movie playing on the television screen mounted in a corner of the mess. There were bottles of wine or liquor set up on each of the four tables along with partially full glasses. Opposite Einstok, along the bulkhead were four curtain-covered portholes. The distinctive voice of Harrison Ford came from the television mounted in the corner and rose over the low hub-hub of the men in the mess. *Indiana Jones and the Last Crusade,* specifically a scene where the bad guys searched for the famed diary kept by Indy's father.

Noting three men wearing holstered pistols on their hips, he mumbled the name of the fourth man. The one he did not see.

Ducking under the porthole, Einstok left the men in the mess for his team and moved up to another porthole. He peeked through a crack between the curtains, into the confines of a stateroom, and at two two-tiered bunks squeezed into the small room, seemingly separated only by the door opposite him. One set of bunks was dark and empty. A single bunk lamp illuminated the two men occupying the bottom bunk on the other side of the stateroom. One of the men, a White man, naked except for a leather belt around his waist, and a holstered pistol strapped to his left thigh and hunched over on all fours, grunted as massive Black man, laying over him, forcibly entered him from behind. Watching the men having sex, Einstok remembered when he first met the White man. The man who he knew as Swanson.

Leaving the men to their sex, he continued forward, stopping at the end of the superstructure, under the ship's bridge, or wheelhouse. Sitting on a pair of bitts near the anchor chain, his contact took a long pull off his cigarette. The flaring glow illuminated his narrow, dark-skinned face. The man, with his head tilted backward, exhaled the smoke toward the stars far above him.

Einstok stepped out of the shadow of the superstructure. The man took his eyes from the stars and turned them on Einstok. The perplexed look turned into a smile, but only for a second. Under the starlight, Einstok unsheathed a knife from his combat web gear. At the same time, both heard the burst of gunfire erupt from the open portholes behind them.

"Hello, LeClerc," Einstok said with a grin.

LeClerc dropped his cigarette and stepped backward, but the railing stopped him.

Munro and Lil' Sumptin' approached the steel door leading into the superstructure as the others vanished around its corners. Munro reached out to the knob at the end of the long steel lever that kept the watertight door closed. Lifting the lever, the door cracked open and Lil' Sumptin' stepped forward under Munro's arm. Stepping into the short passageway, they were greeted by a closed door leading into the ship's mess. To their right was another watertight door, one stenciled gear locker. To their left was an open hatchway with a ladder leading into the bowels of ship. The humming drone of a generator welled up from the hatch.

Munro closed the door behind him while Lil' Sumptin' took three steps forward and reached for the doorknob of the interior door. Munro pulled up next to her, waiting for her to make her move. She nodded then turned the knob in her hand. Snapping it open, Munro burst into the room. "Hands up!"

Lil' Sumptin' jumped up next to him as they pointed the short barrels of their assault weapons at the stunned group. Solid Gold and Slingblade shot into the room from their respective doors, and the other two boarders,

Nitro and Double Cannon, burst in through the opposite door. Shocked confusion overtook the faces of those in the messroom. All remained in their chairs, with most shooting their hands into the air, except one man who made a fatal move.

A White man, wearing jeans, a khaki shirt, and a pistol belt reached for the pistol holstered to his hip, but his head exploded before he could lay a hand on it—the thunderclap of gunfire filled the twenty-foot by thirty-foot room.

"You heard the man!" Nitro yelled, peering down the barrel of his assault weapon.

"Damn it, Nitro!" Munro cursed, while finishing the head count. "I got twenty-one! And I don't see Swanson! Lil Sumptin', engine room! Solid Gold and Slingblade, bridge! Double Cannon and Nitro, forward staterooms! Go!"

But before they had a chance to deploy, the muffled crack of an explosion reverberated through the forward bulkhead of the mess and reached their ears.

"I think the Boss just found Swanson," Lil' Sumptin' said.

Back on the bow of the ship, Einstok withdrew his blade from LeClerc's abdomen, letting the dead man slump to the deck. The man's blood ran down the slightly sloping deck toward the superstructure. It glistened under the ship's anchor light, far above both men. Einstok sheathed his knife while turning, avoiding the man's blood as he did. A minute later, he pulled up next to the open porthole and peeked into the stateroom where the two men were having sex. The two men turned out the bunk light, but the ambient light entering through the porthole, and the light leaking through the crack at the bottom of the door silhouetted the most comical sight—the two men were naked facing each other, nose to nose, with ears pressed against the door. The White man, still wearing his belt and holster, held his pistol, a black Glock, in his hand pointing the barrel straight up. Swanson kept his finger inserted into the pistol's trigger guard. Their eyes were as big as the unknown reality threatening them.

As Einstok mentioned, Swanson worked briefly as an operative for Einstok Industries. With the notion of standing up a stand-by special operations team, he had hired six ex-military applicants. Among them was the ex-US Army paratrooper now standing in that stateroom, naked except for his pistol belt and holster. Still in their probationary period, but after completing the initial assessment phase, he gave the newly formed team a mission, one that should have been simple to execute.

Holding his weapon with one hand, Einstok reached up to unclip a hand grenade from his web gear while recalling what had happened with that incident.

Monitoring archaeological digs around the world, Einstok learned to track specific archaeologists, including one Geoff Manwaring, a Mesoamerican archaeologist who had mounted an unannounced expedition into the wilds of Utah. The English university Manwaring worked with had provided basic funding and a security escort, albeit a team of second-rate ex-British Army infantry soldiers. Seeing an opportunity for a simple mission to evaluate the new team, and to add to his coffers, he deployed Swanson and the men. However, after a couple of blunders, Manwaring's team extracted themselves from that gorge with their sought-after relic in hand, leaving Swanson's team bloodied.

Using the fingers of the hand holding the assault rifle to remove the safety wire clip from around the top of the hand grenade, he smiled at the thought of the article chronicling that expedition.

The article, written by an aspiring journalist, had found its way into a mainstream archaeology journal. While Geoff Manwaring had come off as a virtuous man of derring-do, Angar Einstok came off as the evil, and corrupt, man of skullduggery. The writer, a young woman by the name of Penelope, contrasted them as Sherlock Holmes and Doctor Moriarty with the Napoleon of crime being the loser in a game of wits and fortitude.

With the safety clip removed, Einstok held the safety lever, or spoon, down while sticking his finger through the fuse pin ring. *Hell, Swanson wasn't even smart enough to close the porthole cover,* Einstok thought as he raised the hand bomb up to the edge of the open porthole. Einstok pulled out the pin and released his grip on the lever.

Ching!

Letting the spoon pop out, the fuse inside the grenade engaged, creating a distinctive mechanical sound that should have been all too familiar with the ex-paratrooper. A sound he'd heard a hundred times.

Einstok dropped the grenade, and the men shot their eyes toward the porthole. He moved his face from the edge of the porthole just as an explosion on the other side of the half-inch steel cut Swanson's scream of horror short. A cloud of smoke, sparks, and carnage shot from the stateroom's porthole.

"Useless bastard should have stayed in the army," Einstok said to himself.

Shenandoah Valley, Virginia, late July, AD 2020

Angar Einstok relaxed at the antique desk occupying the center of his book-lined study. Shelves armed with some of the finest, and oldest, literature ever printed. A bottle of Springback 1919 whiskey, and a half-empty crystal tumbler assumed their stations on the polished desktop in front of him. A sheet of Einstok Industries stationery occupied the space between the bottle and the glass. Warm sunlight entering through the room's only window, an ornately edged rectangular frame, captured the panoramic view of the historic valley's western, forest-covered hills and fell on the lines of numbers inked on the stationery. The numbers covered two leather-bound volumes. Though Einstok spent his life traveling the world in search of its rarest treasures and becoming wealthy while doing so, he sat in awe of what lay on the desk in front of him.

He reflected on how he and Max Steiner, his man from Antarctica, were able to decipher their find. He and Max had broken the secret code, using a book cipher used by businessmen and politicians over a hundred years ago, to uncover the message hidden in the text of Teddy Roosevelt's autobiography. The handwritten sentiment scripted on the inside cover of the first volume written by Teddy Roosevelt before his death in 1919 revealed that Teddy Roosevelt had gifted this volume to his younger cousin, Franklin Delano Roosevelt. The inked annotation read, *Dear Franklin, please mark my words, and treasure this work, as I know you will find it quite revealing.*

The second volume, written over two hundred years earlier than Teddy Roosevelt's biography, showed its age, as the black-leather front and back covers did their best to protect the vellum pages inside. Under that centuries-old volume rested one other item—a computer-captured photo featuring a metal label plate resting on gray soil. It was the length of a finger and twice as wide, according to the scale under the photo. The plate's manufacturers had stamped the outline of an eagle with its head turned sideways onto the silverish metal along with the letters R and K on either side of the eagle's outline and an angled swastika under the image. While the photo of the metal label was important, what was most significant was the location of the plate.

Thinking about the label's location, Einstok congratulated himself. *So I was right.*

Hearing the distant clopping of horse hooves, he lifted his eyes. The knotty pine windowsill enclosed six horse riders, with two pack horses flanking the riders in front. Pulling up the gravel-paved road, Einstok let out a pleased sigh. He reached into his pants pocket for his cell phone at the same time. "Hello, Zelda. Where are you?"

Her distant voice replied. "We are still in town. Max wanted to get more preserves before flying out for Antarctica tonight. We will be back by noon."

"Good. Don't forget the peach pie."

A minute later, Einstok stood on the historic home's wide front porch holding his whiskey glass. He greeted the riders pulling up to the porch's railing by raising his glass. Munro Turner and Lil' Sumptin' were in the lead, and like the four behind them, wore clean, but wrinkled, camouflage clothing. The eight horses strained their necks to nip at the grass on either side of the gravel-paved driveway.

"The three-day outing in Virginia's back country treated you well." Nodding in approval, Einstok scanned his team, the sidearms holstered on their hips, and the mounts they rode. "Curry your mounts, clean your weapons, and stow your gear. The barbecue is ready, and the bar is open. Munro, join me for lunch. At noon."

"Sir," Munro said as he pulled on his reins. "After we complete a pallet challenge."

"Of course," Einstok responded.

Watching the troop, including the two pack horses loaded with long rifles, compound bows, and modern crossbow encased in soft containers and holstered to canvas panniers, he appreciated the routine of putting his operatives in the field every time they returned to The Farm. Riding horses, refocusing on outdoor skills, and enjoying exercise while going without alcohol provided a restoration of the mind, spirit, and body. He thought about the information behind him and how to pair it with the talent in front of him. Smiling, he turned to wash up for lunch.

Nestled along the western slope Virginia's historic Shenandoah Valley, and under the late July sun, Einstok's training facility, dubbed The Farm, consisted of a one thousand acres of undulating woodland sutured together by running streams, hiking trails, and dirt roads, and scabbed with the occasional open meadows. All infected with deer, bears, mountain lions, and turkeys. Isolated in the center of nature's blessing, like the Swiss Red Cross, were two paved runways, each capable of landing small- to medium-sized jet and propellor-powered aircraft. Adjacent to the crossed runways were support facilities—a maintenance hangar, a parachute loft, an obstacle course, and a shooting range.

South of the airfield, among a spread of oaks, a horse stable, four guest cottages, and a staff residence surrounded an outdoor dining area and an Olympic-sized in-ground pool. Einstok's quarters, a lodge built of local oak, pine, and cedar, and a hundred years old, enjoyed the shade of a dozen oak trees a short distance from the airfield and the guest quarters. A modern, three-car garage, and a helicopter hangar kept the house company.

Even though he expected the information lording over the desk inside, the weeks following the parachute jump onto a competitor's archaeological site in the Atlantic Ocean were momentous. While he kept repeating the words Max messaged from Antarctica in his head, the one image sent from a remote operated vehicle on the moon also never failed to pale in its importance. Both reaffirmed each other's significance and work over the years. While Angar kept multiple operations going at any given time, in various degrees of completion, the one item he placed on the range months ago—when he sent Max and his team to Antarctica and rovers to the moon—simmered nicely.

Though warm, the ceiling fan mounted to the underside of the porch's rafters comforted the four people wearing loose-fitting shirts and jeans as they enjoyed their baked Virginia ham and sides, washed down with iced lemonade fortified with premium vodka.

Serenading their lunch, a pack of coyotes yelped somewhere deep in the forest.

"While I thought nothing could beat Westphalian ham, I find myself at a standstill. That Virginia ham was good," stated Max Steiner, as he lifted the last forkful of peach pie from his plate. "I'm glad I purchased a couple along with the other food stuffs. I know you spent a fortune outfitting our Antarctica expedition, so I hope I am not sounding ungrateful."

Einstok appreciated the middle-aged German's blondish, graying hair and his boyish, Alpine Mountain climber looks.

"Expecting pork raised on peanuts and corn to taste as good as pork raised on acorns and truffles would seem to challenge the quality of the meat, but it appears not to be the case," Einstok replied as he too lifted a fork of peach pie, finishing his dessert. "I will make sure to bring more down with me next week."

"Please do not forget," Max answered, pushing the fork into his mouth and taking a couple of chews. "We will be waiting, along with an envoy from the *Bundestag*. He will thank you in person, on behalf of the German government, for helping to discover and fund the excavation of such a historic site. A find resulting in the repatriation of German 'war dead' and helping to celebrate the achievements of the German people. Even though the site was home to one of Hitler's most insidious ambitions."

Einstok smiled. "While I will take their gratitude, I want to thank you for the find you handed me before representatives of the German government arrived at your excavation."

"Angar, it was your intelligence, knowledge, and intuition that sent me and our Condor Division there, so thanks are not needed," Max said. He picked up his glass of lemonade. "Who knows where that find may have ended up if somebody else had arrived on scene. By the way, how did your meeting go?"

Einstok swallowed his mouthful of pie and picked up his vodka-laced lemonade, listening to the forest surrounding the old lodge. "It started out spotty, but after sharing certain endearing moments with Congresswoman Bennington and the UN Secretary General, both Congress and the UN started to see things my way. Like countries did with Antarctica over a hundred years ago, the current international agreement to divide the moon and Mars into specific areas of influence is marred with skullduggery. The goal of setting aside plats for scientific study while prohibiting any military presence and assigning those plats to the most *responsible* countries with the most aggressive plans to conduct studies is fraught with deceit. I made sure Einstok Industries always had a seat at the grown-ups' table. To get the right portions of the main course, I can start my next phase for TETRA with little interference."

Einstok raised his glass.

Max, Zelda, and Munro followed suit.

Steiner placed his empty glass on the table and pushed his chair back. "I am glad things are coming together and am excited to see the future progressing nicely."

"Trust me," Einstok interjected. "You will see a future that will bless us all."

"I'm sorry, sir." Munro leaned forward while holding his glass in his hands. A drop of condensate fell from the glass of iced lemonade and landed on a thin paperback of a Sherlock Holmes short story—a mystery titled *A Scandal in Bohemia*. Munro paused to pick up a napkin and wipe the drop from the cover. Putting the napkin on his empty plate, Munro continued as his eyes darted between Einstok and Max. "I am sensing something is afoot. I can see the kitchen from my point of view, and the pots on the range, but I am having a time reading the menu. I hope I am not prying."

"Munro, you are not prying," Einstok said, "and I did ask you to join us for a reason. I have seen your reading choices over the years. So I know you will enjoy, and internalize, what you are about to hear."

Munro sat up a bit straighter as his finger ran down the spine of the Victorian-age mystery on the table.

Einstok looked at his lemonade as he nodded slightly. "Please let me see if I can whet your appetite by building a proper bill of fare. But allow me to fill everybody's glasses first."

As Einstok refreshed everybody's lemonade, Munro placed the palm of his hand flat on the Sherlock Holmes's novel. At the same time, Zelda pulled two cigars from her blouse pocket, and Max reached into his shirt pocket for a box of matches.

Having operated with Max before, Munro knew of his Condor Division—a team of researchers who specialized in anything German. It started with the Germanic people who fought invading Roman armies, and ended with Germany's unification in the early 1870s, its involvement in two world wars, the collapse of the Third Reich in the mid-1940s, and the activities of Nazis in a post-war world. Over the years, the Condor Division uncovered more than enough Nazi-stolen treasures—namely, gold, gems, and art—to put the Monuments Men to shame. The division's leader, Max Stiener, was a man well chosen for the job. He was German by birth, a historian by training, an explorer by inclination, and a runologist by disposition.

Lowering the pitcher, Einstok caught Munro up to date by narrating an incredible series of adventures. Starting with the Rhinelander Korps. "The Rhinelander Korps was, or is, a secret association that began in the late nineteenth century, and one that comprised mostly American politicians, businessmen, and members of the military, most of whom were of German ancestry. German nationals made up the rest of the association. One of its earliest and most prominent American members was Theodore Roosevelt, who spent much of his youth out west, which included hunting in Utah. While there, he befriended an immigrant German, a Jacob Schnabel. Since TR spoke German, making friends was not an issue. After befriending Schnabel, he found out about the centuries-old diary Schnabel carried around. A diary started by one of Schnabel's ancestors."

Einstok paused his narration to let Zelda and Max light their cigars with Max's matches. Behind them, the coyotes stopped yelping.

"Now that the gravy is simmering, let us move onto the potatoes," Einstok said, continuing his narration.

That ancestor, a German Catholic, and mercenary, joined a company of Spanish conquistadors in 1520. Like young Theodore Roosevelt, that German ancestor was educated, literate, and equipped with an alert mind and stout backbone. He was also a devout Catholic. After five years in the Americas, the ancestor returned to the Rhineland well off and with a diary documenting his travels and observations. The diary included information Einstok recently used to redirect previous aerospace efforts. An effort centered around an Einstok Industries division called TETRA. The information swirled around a winged flying throne and an alien who landed in what were the dying days of the Mayan civilization. Knowing of their own impending collapse, Mayan leaders sent a Mayan messenger north to return a gold-like cylinder to another civilization, one that disappeared well before the end of the Mayan civilization. So the cylinder ended up in the possession of the Aztecs via the Toltecs.

While Zelda and Max knew what their employer spoke of, the fire in their eyes almost matched the ends of their newly lit cigars. That same narration also stoked a smoldering coalbed in the eyes of Einstok's special operations team leader.

Over time, Aztec priests created a repository outside a city they called Teotihuacán. A complex created before the rise of the Aztec Empire, but one they incorporated into their own cultural lore. Their mission was to understand the visit of a god they knew nothing about. But it did not take long after the arrival on Cortez in 1519 for the Aztecs to realize the Spanish thirst for gold and the wanton destruction of Mesoamerican literature. Therefore, the Aztecs sent a column of civilians and soldiers loaded down with gold and silver north to what is now Utah. Around the same time, a smaller select group traveled south taking the cylinder back to where the Mayan messenger came from, a site in Honduras known as Copán today. The alien cylinder contained information about a visitor, and his spacecraft hidden under a complex near the city itself.

Einstok sipped his lemonade, appreciating the fire in Munro's eyes. With Munro integral to his own future, Einstok continued.

"Being a literate man, that German mercenary documented what he could in the diary and kept what scraps of Mayan and Aztec bark cloth paper he found inside the diary. In the end, the mercenary threaded together a narrative about his observations in the context and understanding of his time. After his years in the Americas, he secured his wealth and returned to the Rhineland, where he accepted the Protestant Reformation. Knowing what the Catholics did with literature that challenged their beliefs and power, he kept his diary hidden from the Catholic Church and passed it down through the family until a descendant decided to ground truth his ancestor's documentation."

As Einstok detailed the reason they were at that table, Zelda and Max knocked the ash off their cigars into the ashtray. Cigars paired well with an excellent tale of the incredible.

"Jacob Schnabel arrived in the western hemisphere, and even added to where his ancestor left off. The additional text included a visit to Honduras, where he documented finding a site matching the descriptions his ancestor documented before visiting property in the American West near a town called Kanab in Utah. But before leaving Germany, he made an exact copy of the diary, including copies of the Mesoamerican scraps, and left it behind with his young son, a boy named Stassi. By the 1920s, that young boy had helped create the foundation for what would become a Nazi-sponsored rocket science and subsequent space program in the 1930s and 1940s."

Munro sat back in his chair as if a descending angel had placed its holy fingertip against his forehead.

"Excuse me," Munro said, taking a deep breath. "You have submerged to the deepest of oceans and climbed the highest of mountains in search of humankind's greatest achievements. Yet you have not found that spaceship? You seemed to have knowledge of its location, and I know that nothing has ever stood in your way. Or our way."

The skin at the corners of Einstok's eyes wrinkled from the proud smile consuming his face. He continued with his narration while answering Munro's question.

"According to what TR documented in his own biography, albeit in coded text, he found the German dead after falling off a cliff. Along with that original diary next to his body. TR continued the German's search for Aztec treasure. Using the diary as a compass, and his own intuition, he found the treasure buried in an underground vault outside of Kanab. Having come from a family with money and the fact that TR was a lover of nature, he purchased the property and kept it under the family's name. Leaving the gold where the Aztecs deposited it hundreds of years before. Hiding the original diary, Teddy wrote his bibliography and created a coded message within it. He also left a code key for his cousin, FDR, to access upon his death. TR, knowing his cousin FDR would also become a member of the Rhinelander Korps and have political potential, made sure FDR would receive the key on his death and make efforts to locate the treasure and the German's diary. And that he would use them wisely. That time came sooner than TR thought it would. World War I officially ended in 1919, the same year TR died, but it was the

Treaty of Versailles that destroyed Germany economically."

"There are, or were," Max interjected, "those who felt Great Britain was the actual culprit, and the countries behind the treaty blamed Germany for the war and unfairly punished them. Those pro-Germans, including members of the Rhinelander Korps, wanted to see Germany rise from the ashes and rechallenge Britain's power."

"Quite right," Einstok continued. "But assisting Germany's rebirth was something the American public had no taste for as half of the public supported Britain's power as global police, and the other half were isolationists who had no taste for foreign intrigue. Or another war. Therefore, any sort of funding helping Germany needed to remain off the books. As a member of the Rhinelander Korps, FDR decided to use that treasure as one means of secretly funneling clean money to Berlin. His goal: to see a challenger rise against the British empire and balance out the power."

"Much like the creation of the Protestant Reformation," Munro surmised quietly.

Einstok continued, "While FDR was not part of the federal government in the 1920s, he was active academically and internationally. Since he was the Secretary of the Navy during and just after World War I, he had access to naval vessels that could take him around the world. To search for treasure. Those travels included an island off the coast of Canada."

"Oak Island," Munro said slowly.

"Yes," Einstok replied. "Keeping the Schnabel diary handy, FDR even tried to find a fabled city buried in the Honduran jungle, but with no success. The local environs had changed since Schnabel visited the site, and the jungle reclaimed the site. Still, as membership in the Rhinelander Korps continued to grow in the mid-1920s, FDR had the Roosevelt family lease a tract of that land in Utah to the air mail service as an airfield. He also allowed Henry Ford and Harvey Firestone to create a testing ground for developing improved motor vehicle and aviation technology. But it was all a cover."

"How so?" Munro asked, absorbed in what Einstok was sharing.

"I had my time at the stove. It is now time for Max to oversee the completion of the entrée," Einstok stopped and wiped condensate off the side of his glass with the side of his index finger.

Max Steiner nodded as he lifted his glass of lemonade. After a sip, he started. "By the mid-1920s, Ford, with parts supplied by persons such as Firestone, used the privacy to develop more advanced airplanes, aircraft engines, and rockets along with heavy-duty trucks for the army. He, and military members of the Rhinelander Korps organized transcontinental convoy exercises. To evaluate newly constructed military trucks carrying supplies and towing wheeled artillery, and to continue the modernization of America's road system. The whole exercise was a ruse to get the gold out of Utah and to the East Coast, where a submarine, named the *Bremen*, received the gold, the original diary with the added text, and at least one German national by the name of Captain Erwin Rommel."

"Wait a minute," Munro said, "you're talking about General Rommel? The Desert Fox? Leader of the Afrika Korps?"

"Yes," Max answered. "Anyway, the *Bremen* was a commercial submarine. The company built that class of submarine to run the British blockade and conduct trade with the United States, since the US was not at war with Germany. At least until 1917. It disappeared in 1916, with authorities suspecting a tragedy at sea. Secretly, though, the company who owned the submarine arranged with the Rhinelander Korps to take it over in the mid-Atlantic. Built to transport cargo, the Rhinelander Korps used the submarine to smuggle gold, men, equipment, and weapons, and when Prohibition came into law, it smuggled alcohol. A German American merchant marine officer, Paul Danzig, commanded that submarine from 1916 to its demise in 1928. When not running missions for the Korps, Danzig housed the submarine at a private shipyard along the Amazon—one owned by a German ex-patriot."

Zelda said while exhaling cigar smoke. "Prohibition, and the resultant Volstead Act gave the government law enforcement capabilities and created a new arm with which the Rhinelander Korps could infiltrate. The author of that act, Andrew Volstead, was part of the Rhinelander Korps. It was a twofold success as Prohibition gave the Rhinelander Korps a new means of raising funds while at the same time getting the Rhinelander Korps further entrenched into the government."

"Correct Zelda," Einstok said. "Anyway, in 1926, after picking up the gold from a cove just north of the Maine border, along with that original diary, Danzig steamed from Canada to Central America, and onto Antarctica before turning north and arriving at a remote section along Germany's Baltic Sea coast. It was there, where Rommel disembarked, and Danzig offloaded the gold into the hands of German financiers. Danzig then took on a specialized cargo and expert passengers, including Stassi Schnabel. Like his father, Stassi was a scientist with a passion for rocket science. While academics and enthusiasts in Germany were publicly developing rocket science, Stassi Schnabel and his group, and the Korps, used the *Bremen* to lay the groundwork for a joint German and American secret rocket base in Antarctica. One that German financiers who received the gold would fund and supply through international banks."

"But what would be the purpose of their base in Antarctica?" Munro asked. "And did it amount to any significance?"

"Excellent questions," Max said. "Their initial goal was to develop a radio-guided rocket system to attack the British Royal Navy from afar while not having witnesses to the building of their base or the firing of the rockets. It started out as an exploratory operation with potential. We found out about it through recently uncovered secret communiqués between Henry Ford, Stassi Schnabel, and an up-and-coming rocket engineer by the name of Werner Von Braun."

"Sounds like you are about to tell me that things did not go as planned," Munro said.

"You are correct," said Max. "But I will address that piece of history momentarily. The setting up of the base went well between 1926 and 1928, but shifting ice crushed the submarine at the Antarctica base. So without a long-thought lost submarine, and the fact that money from the Aztec gold and rum running was not enough for all the cooperative efforts between Germany and the Rhinelander Korps, its members had to find new ways of funding their efforts and not risk the Korps' exposure; they needed a diversion—hence the Great Depression."

"Are you saying the Great Depression was created on purpose?" Munro asked.

"Yes," said Zelda, "and its authors included FDR and Henry Ford. They prepared themselves and the Rhinelander Korps for the financial collapse secretly, but on paper, the Depression hit members of the Rhinelander Korps just as hard as everybody else."

"But why?" Munro asked.

Einstok noted the disbelief in his team's leader's voice. He paused and looked at his glass of lemonade. "Politicians such as FDR were advocates for larger participation of the government in private lives, which requires public spending and taxation. However, most Americans would not accept such intrusions, so they manipulated the collapse of the American's financial foundation and banking system. From 1929 to 1933, the financial collapse threw Germany and the United States into turmoil. By 1932, America and Germany were at the depths of poverty, bankruptcy, and despair."

As Einstok, Zelda, and Max presented their knowledge to Einstok's special operations team leader, Munro's eyes glowed with wonderment.

"Creating a reason for two rising stars to emerge and save their populations," Einstok continued. "FDR and Adolf Hitler, who secretly met during their ascendancies. During the 1920s, when FDR used US Navy ships for his treasure-hunting excursions, and when German capitalists saw fit to smuggle Hitler out of Germany for such meetings. The Americans now welcomed FDR's massive spending spree, and German capitalists saw both a financial and cultural rescue in an Austrian corporal. However, soon after Hitler's accession, he tossed their well-laid plans into a trash heap. The right-wing businessmen thought they could control Hitler, but instead, Hitler took over all aspects of the German culture, politics, business, and military. By the late 1930s, they had to find a way to get rid of Hitler. However, they realized that doing so, through assassination or other means, would be even more disastrous. FDR knew that as well, and shelved plans to have Hitler assassinated. After reading the intelligence concerning Germany's efforts, and successes, in the years leading up to WWII, FDR knew he needed a reason to get involved in the future war. At the same time, FDR kept abreast of Japan's plans for the Pacific Ocean and Asia."

"Are you saying FDR let the Japanese bomb Pearl Harbor as well?" Munro asked. He narrowed his eyes.

"What a better way to excuse massive government spending," Zelda said. "While there have always been individual machinations, FDR sought to create a shadow government. The infamous *they* or the Deep State."

Zelda stopped to let Max take over.

"Once Hitler assumed power in Germany, he expanded the idea of the rocket efforts in Antarctica, as he liked the idea of the base in Antarctica. But, with Hitler always having the grandest of ideas, along with the knowledge of Schnabel's diary, if they could sink ships from hundreds, or even thousands, of miles away, why could they not send those rockets into space. To the moon or even Mars, especially if there was a time-warping spacecraft at the other end of the journey. Whoever found it first could build fleets of flying ships able to cross the Atlantic in minutes."

"So, while America was fighting Germany in WWII, they were collaborating with them?" Munro asked.

Einstok chimed in, taking over from Max. "I have come to appreciate the Nazi space program on which the current global space industry can base its success. And that the Nazi space program was able to capitalize on the fledgling rocket science program created by German engineers, scientists, and enthusiasts in the 1920s. Most were private individuals with vision. Just like me. Anyway, Antarctica was not in play in the beginning of the Nazi space effort in the mid-1930s, but, by the early 1940s, after World War Two began, the Nazis took a bigger interest in that continent. Secrecy was becoming increasingly important, and a massive Allied bombing campaign was causing concern in Nazi-controlled Europe. Using Trojan ships and long-range U-boats, along with key members of the US Navy leadership redirecting American naval ships from their routes, the Nazis did, indeed, establish not only a space base, but also a base to keep the Fascist movement going since the War turned against them in 1943."

"Hence the rumors of Antarctica buzzing with UFO activity," Munro said. "Or portals to an inner world."

"Exactly," Einstok replied.

"Part of that resource-relocation effort included vast wealth stolen from the banks and museums of Europe. A program cloaked under the code name Operation *Donar*. The Germanic god of lightning and thunder. Their base, Base 211, was in the Queen Maud Land area of Antarctica. An area they renamed *Neuschuabenland* or New Swabia. After the War, there continued to be rumors of die-hard Nazis holding out in a fortified underground bunker stuffed with treasure and secret weapons. One needed to create a fourth Reich. So to quell any rumors, the US government deployed an expedition under the command of Admiral Byrd, who, as it turned out, was also a member of the Rhinelander Korps. There were others of the staff who were members of the Rhinelander Korps as well. They named the expedition Operation High Jump and began the exploration in 1946. Right at the start of the Cold War with the Soviet Union."

"And the results?" Munro asked, sipping his iced lemonade.

"After a year, the American fleet expedition left Antarctica, announcing that there was no Nazi base in Antarctica, no evidence of a fortified hideout, or a cache of stolen treasure."

"Did you, or do you, believe those public statements?" Munro asked.

"All I know is they left, and by 1947, the Cold War became a reality. At the same time, we created a friendly West German government, while Great Britain, left economically devasted by the War, found themselves usurped by a new superpower, the US. If Byrd's expedition did find anything, whether stolen Nazi treasure or rockets capable of sending bombs to major cities thousands of miles away, or even into space, there was no way the American government could announce their findings even if it did find something. They removed any evidence of American-German collusion during the War. I had Max, and the Condor Division, look for any scraps that fell between the floorboards. They discovered that the American expedition did uncover a German presence starting with a couple of ships crushed in the ice along with the *Bremen*. There was also evidence of a landed facility. Max and his team followed up on their research, and they found that documented evidence along with a dozen dead Germans, which the Americans left behind. This information was withheld from the West German government until just recently. I used my outlets to inform the now unified German government of a German presence in the Antarctic along with dead Germans. A piece of news of which they were much appreciative. However, there was one finding that we did not inform the German government of. The effort has proved fortuitous in so many ways."

"And that is where you and your team come into play," Zelda added.

Munro turned to her with a smile before returning his gaze to Einstok.

"When Max, and his team arrived, he found a secret base within the secret base, and one item secured in that secret-secret base: the original diary started by Schnabel's mercenary ancestor and updated by Jacob and Teddy Roosevelt. I translated the diary Max gave me and compared it to the copy Stassi, Jacob's son, also brought to Antarctica, and both helped me understand that there was a spaceship buried in a stone facility in the Honduran jungle. But the reason I have not yet visited that site is that it is now being excavated by a team of archaeologists under the supervision of a Mesoamerican archaeologist, Geoff Manwaring. My involvement, or interest, would only draw unnecessary attention."

Munro sat back in his chair. He lifted his glass of vodka-lemonade.

Einstok, knowing of his team leader's habits and life, could see through the reflections in the Black man's eyes. Being an adopted child growing up in the Bahamas, Munro's backyard was rife with pirate lore and stories of legendary explorers. After watching Munro take a long sip of his drink, Einstok leaned forward. "Munro, you have been in my employ since the Legion, and I appreciate your service. Now I am asking if you are up for a new adventure."

"Sir." Munro turned his eyes to the mystery on the table in front of him. After tapping it with his finger, he looked up. "You know that I am always game."

Einstok accepted Munro's response with a smile. "I have referred to a division more than once today: TETRA. One I put together to address the adventure before us. One that includes an advanced weapon systems research and development group."

"I have heard rumors," Munro replied.

"Oh," Einstok said, with a slight smile. "Anything specific?"

"Only that your technicians have already given the research and development team a name. The Merlin Group." Munro answered with a steadiness in his eyes. "A group which will require a specialized cadre to evaluate their ideas. In the field. If you will excuse me sir, it all sounds a bit James Bondish. Q-branch and all."

"More like the US Navy's SEAL Team Six, which was created as a means to evaluate new special warfare operations methodologies and weapons," said Einstok. "Munro, while the US Navy have their SEALs, special operators who started their careers with BUDs or Basic Underwater Demolition training, I am proposing a similar capability within the United States Space Force: Special Orbital Combat Operators who must successfully complete Basic Orbital Special Combat training, or BOSC for short. Special operators who can operate at sea, on land, in the air, on any planet, and in space."

"I thought you said," Munro said with a mischievous smile on his face, "that according to developing treaties, any space initiatives are supposed to be free of any military aggression or intrigues?"

"On paper, yes," Einstok answered. "That said, do you think other countries haven't conceived ideas of standing up a corps of spaceborne operatives. Or even private individuals with such a vision?"

Munro nodded, letting Einstok continue.

"Even in the 1950s, the American government expended resources to develop orbiting spacecraft capable of housing specialized commando units that the government could drop from space in reaction to any communist aggression around the world. The originators called it Operation Overwatch. There was even a consideration of establishing a lunar-based commando reaction force. Those efforts were real enough, and so is my idea of BOSC. Like so many hundreds of volunteers who flock to the Navy base at Coronado and the drumbeat of glory twice a year and can pass the initial entry requirements, only a dozen or so individuals graduate as combatant swimmers six months later and move on to earn the right to wear the trident of US Navy SEALs. Well, the same will hold true for my vision. Although the vision is nothing more than an idea, I need you to bring that vision to reality and be among that first graduating class. A good swordsman is more important than a good sword."

Munro replied with a quote of his own, "The average man is hooked to his fellow men, while the warrior is hooked only to infinity."

Both men looked at each other while lifting their glasses. Einstok provided the toast. "Here's to The Merlin Group."

Everybody at the table paused to enjoy the moment. After a few seconds, Munro spoke. "Well, it seems like Max has Antarctica covered, but what is going on with the site in Honduras? And did the Nazis look for that site? In Honduras? And is it that spaceship still there?"

Zelda jumped in. "We know for sure that FDR did try to relocate the site Jacob Schnabel discovered, so we can assume the Nazis tried as well. However, we did not uncover any evidence that they found the site, or the flying—or winged—throne. Geoff Manwaring did manage to uncover the site outside of *Copán* and has been working on it the last four summers."

"You find any evidence that this man, Manwaring, knew of legends behind the site?" asked Munro.

"No," Zelda replied. "From what we know, Manwaring discovered the site just like he and other archaeologists do every day. Our source says his efforts seem innocent, with no knowledge of alien visitations. She says there is no indication that he is doing anything more than documenting a long-lost Mayan site, one of many consumed by the jungle. Our person on his team says that Manwaring's field project is nearing the end of the summer season, and he has uncovered the main building at the center of the site. They found the remains of fourteen people in the building who seemed to have been intentionally killed. Or committed suicide. The building itself resembles a working laboratory and there is a presence of radiation."

"Nothing else?" Munro asked.

"Nothing out of the ordinary in his communications with the university," Zelda continued. "Nor has he cached any information on his cell phone or personal laptop. Also, our contact says she has found nothing, nor has Manwaring officially announced any significant find other than that they discovered evidence of an Aztec presence at the bottom of a well at the site. However, she has noticed a change in Manwaring's demeanor, both in behavior and personality. A change that occurred overnight. She is certain he found something. Not a spaceship, but something small enough to hide."

"So, it is safe to assume," Einstok interrupted, "that while Manwaring has not announced a find of any significance, he is holding a discovery of consequence. We have crossed sharpened blades before, and I have come out the better while he claims victory in his own awkward manner. Regardless, my security division is keeping up with Manwaring's movements, communications, and any manner of transactions. If he did find something and is trying to keep it secret, he will slip up at some point in the future."

7

Shenandoah Valley, late July AD 2020

ater that evening, after Zelda left with Max to help start his travels back to Antarctica and to attend to her own duties in New York City, and Munro's team enjoyed showers, barbecue, and drinks, Einstok and Munro appreciated a soul-cleansing, five-mile hike while bearing moderately full rucksacks. During the hike they discussed future plans and Einstok's idea of BOSC. Afterward, they exchanged those packs for showers and a change of clothing before returning to the porch for coffee. On the table in front of them, along with their coffee, were the bound volumes and photos from earlier in the day and an electronic tablet. Under the soft white light from the ceiling fan, and the insects darting about the fixture, they rewatched a one-minute video.

"Quite impressive," Munro stated as he stirred sugar into his coffee with a spoon. "And to think it has remained undiscovered all these years. Now I can see why you secured that lunar plat for TETRA. By putting your property in place. How did you know?"

Einstok's eyes stayed focused on the slowly moving image. Taken by the same ROV that sent the photo with the metal label plate resting on gray soil, the camera panned across a small area sheltered by a rocky outcropping, revealing a scattered debris field. Shiny bits of plating, tubing, and foil poked out from the lunar soil and among rocks that had fallen from above over the years. Finally, Einstok answered.

"As you said before, I always have a need to know, and in this case, years of tracking down secret communications between Henry Ford, FDR, Stassi Schnabel, and others paid off. I gathered enough information to put a picture together and use my intuition as glue. What we are seeing are the remains of a WWII-era space plane. One developed by members of the Rhinelander Korps and German scientists and piloted by Captain Paul Danzig—a second-generation German American and former captain of the *Bremen*."

Einstok paused as the video ended with the image of a human's shoulders and head, enclosed in the remnants of a 1930s high-altitude pressure suit with a wide neck ring, and rounded helmet made of aluminum and transparent plastic. The desiccated face and shriveled eyes of a dead man visible through the helmet's face plate stared back at Einstok and Munro. The ROV also revealed a patch sewn onto the suit's upper right chest, embroidered with the name Danzig and a pair of wings under the name, along with the letters R and K at the ends of wings.

"Captain Danzig," Einstok said, "a skilled shipboard engineer, talented ship's captain, expert navigator, and adept pilot, volunteered to pilot a rocket-equipped space plane from Antarctica to the moon to explore the feasibility of establishing a moon base. He reached the moon, but crashed upon landing, but before the Rhinelander Korps could re-equip another lunar expedition, Hitler ordered the invasion of Poland, kicking off WWII. Before certain people could make plans. *They* felt it was time to go to wait for a better opportunity. That opportunity came with the start of the Cold War, when the ability to spend trillions of dollars unnoticed meant that they could develop and, or locate, technology without being noticed."

"Well," Munro chimed in, "it looks like you have the moon situation resolved, but what about Mars. You have already selected a plat there as well. Is there something at that spot that has revealed itself?"

Einstok leaned forward and picked up a sugar spoon, holding it in front of his face as if it were one of his newly recovered treasures. He smiled. "Yes, I do, and I have."

Lowering the spoon back into the sugar bowl, he looked out into the dark woods surrounding the house. "With you being an ex-legionnaire, and a qualified parachute jumper at that, I know that you, and others of your mindset, have that devil-may-care attitude, and are always willing to jump into the mix with no hesitation."

"Yes, sir."

"However, there are times when such bravado is such a waste of good men." He planted his eyes on Munro. "So, with you also being a voracious student of military history, I know you understand the concept, and use, of penal, or punishment, battalions."

Munro appreciated the forest while absorbing the information.

"Companies of incorrigibles, men unfit to be around disciplined soldiers, offenders convicted of heinous crimes and forced to clear mine fields with bayonets. Or their legs."

"While the real troops wait to rush in behind them to take the victory," Munro responded, keeping his eyes on the dark forest.

Einstok quipped, "Given the certainty of a hangman's noose, or sentenced to a penal battalion with a chance of survival, the choice is obvious."

Munro smiled, with a glean in his eyes.

Seeing his team leader's smile, Einstok continued, "Like you said, I always have a plan."

FIVE YEARS
LATER

8

Belize City, Belize, early August, AD 2025

"Hello, Geoff. I hope you don't mind me calling you by your first name."

"Just as long as you don't mind me calling you Angar," Manwaring, now wearing faded blue coveralls, a buzzed haircut, and a pair of handcuffs securing him to the wooden table he sat at, lifted one of his restrained hands and waved it at Zelda. "Zelda, I presume."

Dressed as if she were about to attend a corporate board meeting but standing next to a khaki-uniformed, dark-skinned, middle-aged prison guard in the room's open door, she offered a polite nod in return. Her face remained expressionless. The four of them occupied a drab room with a concrete floor and cinder-block walls. Though clean, the room needed a fresh coat of off-white paint. Other than a beat-up wooden table and a light fixture hanging from the ceiling, the room had a single door and one window with bars mounted to the outside of it. The horizontal slit panes cracked open at the window blessed the room with the flow of air.

Manwaring received the nod and continued his conversation with Einstok. "We have circled each other for years, and with drawn daggers. Yet we have never shared a bottle of fine merlot over good conversation." He stopped long enough to put tension on the chains attached to the handcuffs. "I know we have always traveled in different circles, but is there a reason behind us meeting now?"

Einstok sighed. "Geoff, you know that it was a duly appointed court here in Belize that found you guilty of murder three years ago. Strangling a prostitute to death, here in Belize. And every appeal since that decision has failed to overturn that court's decision."

The skepticism on Manwaring's face could have been seen by the man on the moon.

"Anyway, I hope you do not think less of me that I would appear here, in Belize, within hours of your execution, only to gloat over your execution."

Manwaring lowered his handcuffed hands to the scarred tabletop. He twerked his chin and twisted his neck slightly while doing so.

Dressed as if he were attending a garden cocktail party, Einstok tweaked at the cuff of his long-sleeved, white silk shirt poking out from the sleeve of a dark-blue blazer. "Of course, I am not here to gloat. And it is time to sheath those blades. At any other time, I would like to offer you a scotch and a seat next to me at the bar so that we might argue over our adventures. But, alas, we find ourselves here in Belize City. In prison. Waiting for the guards to wheel you down the hallway to a room where you will die by lethal injection while lying on a wheeled table. Abandoned by your university like a tramp with leprosy, and not a single protest from the British government, your execution will be carried out in"—Einstok lifted his wrist, exposing his Rolex —"in twenty-four hours and fifty-five minutes."

Manwaring tested his handcuffs again before answering. "I am sorry, but I'm having a tough time believing you'll sheath every blade in your kit. Even now. Instead, you are the single hair which keeps the Sword of Damocles, now hanging over my head, from plunging into the crown of my skull. Which is why I have the feeling you are willing to switch that single hair for a length of chain. Albeit momentarily."

Einstok paused in his answer long enough to look over his shoulder at Zelda.

Taking her cue, Zelda offered the hand at her side to the guard standing one foot from her.

In turn, the guard looked over his own shoulders, and into the hallway behind him. To the right and the left. Seeing the hallway empty, he accepted Zelda's hand, palming the folded, hundred-dollar notes in it. Once he slid the folded bills in his trouser pocket and took two steps backward, he pulled the door closed in front of him.

Now alone, Einstok pulled at the chair opposite his handcuffed competitor. He sat.

"If I may be direct, I have access to information, and you have access to information. Separately, that is all we have, just information. However, together, I believe, with my assets, we can recover the world's greatest archaeological treasure. Even if it is not of this world."

Manwaring leaned forward. His eyes searched his competitor's before responding.

"I remember times when we were at odds with each other. Including that time when I was trying to get vital information out of that gorge in Utah. It was my skill, and my team, which thwarted your team's efforts to stop me. I remember the article that young journalist wrote after my interview. The one where she compared us to Sherlock Holmes and Doctor Moriarty."

Einstok remembered that article too. He thought back to that raid on the ship when he blew up Swanson with a hand grenade. "The journalist was too gratuitous with her comparison between you and me. And, as always, you have a habit of assuming a grandeur about your actions, but there was no skill involved from your end—your escape was a matter of luck. My core team was employed elsewhere, and the team I put into place there in Utah did not have the time to iron out their methodologies. They were, in fact, still in their probationary period."

Einstok paused for a second. "Before you say anything, yes, I did think so little of you that I sent in an unproven operations team. I viewed it as a scrimmage match. My team of ex-military hires poised against your team of pub sweepings. A mere scrum where the players would walk away with black eyes and lessons learned. Especially concerning one's opponents."

Manwaring assessed his handcuffs again. "Somehow, you found a way to avoid repeating that issue. So, can I assume the game is afoot?"

Einstok sat back in his chair, adjusting the leg of his pressed khaki trousers as he did. Inspecting the crease in his pants, he said, "Like I said, you have information, and I have information. Together, we can discover one of humanity's greatest archaeological and historical finds."

Flicking a piece of lint away from his trouser leg, the Icelandic adventurer waited for a response. It came.

Manwaring spoke slowly and deliberately. "No, Mister Angar Einstok, what you have is a problem. I am not even going to try and guess how you know what you think I know. And have. But I will start with Bethany. She was on your payroll, correct."

Einstok nodded, but did not look up from his pant leg.

"I always thought she was a bit dodgy," Manwaring continued. "But she had nothing to offer you. I know that much. I also know that you have been quite busy these last few years, here on Earth and with your space efforts. I, on the other hand, am a disgraced archaeologist with no family willing to admit being related to me, and whose career ended up in the loo five years ago. I am also a first-degree murderer. Whatever remained of my life, and credibility, died soon after that conviction. Since I did not enjoy the luxury of being born a toff, I have nothing to live for. Which means I have no reason to give up what I know. I have never been a grasser, not even on myself, and especially if it benefits you. Simply put, you have a problem, and I am the solution. So, *Angar*, I have you by the bollocks."

Finally looking up from his trouser leg, Einstok answered. "Geoff, despite my present appearance, I was not born a toff either. I was born the son of a fisherman. But at the age of twelve, I knew there was more to life than gutting fish for a living."

Einstok raised his arms.

"And that included not wearing clothes soaked with fish guts. After realizing the world about me, I struck out on my own. So, yes, Geoff, the game is afoot. Shall we dance."

Minutes later, laying on his bunk, a metal frame half a century old and a mattress half its age, covered by a thread-bare sheet, Manwaring thought about Einstok's proposal. He also thought about his chances of survival. The numeric value he arrived at hovered one hair above zero. Though he enjoyed thinking about that number, no matter how small, he also thought about what he agreed to do to achieve that slim chance. His skin crawled.

9

Arizona,
early August, AD 2025

"Hi Tiburón. How's the Apache running?" the man asked as he walked toward the bar. "I heard you put a new motor into it."

Tiburón, enjoying a PBR Tall Boy, lifted his eyes from the open magazine on the bar next to the beer can and placed them on the mirror-covered wall in front of him. The door leading to the parking lot closed slowly, thankfully blocking out the harsh afternoon Arizona sun, but not before framing the outline of the man walking up behind him. From another corner of the bar, the smack of a cue ball interrupted a Johnny Cash song trying to escape the smoke-clogged speaker mounted in a corner of the bar. In front of Tiburón, behind the bar, an overly endowed, black-haired woman in her fifties pulled a lit cigarette from her lips. Hacking out a puff of smoke as she did.

The man stopped at the bar, and in front of the bartender. "I'll have a PBR, Gail, and put it on Tiburón's tab."

Gail smiled, revealing a missing upper front tooth. "Tiburón, you're either going to make TJ carry cash from now on, or you need to put him on your W-4."

Tiburón, removing the hand covering the top of his beer can and wiping the back of it on his jeans, scoffed. "Yeah, I did put a new motor in it, but I heard knocking on the way here. I'll look at it when we get back from our run. And Gail, I'll have another one as well."

Letting TJ sit next to him, Tiburón paused to finish his Tall Boy.

Tiburón wore jeans, square-toed cowboy boots, a short-sleeved fishing shirt, a shark tattoo on his neck, and a thick black mustache placed against his doeskin complexion. "Anyway, Gail, TJ will never carry anything but plastic, and that'll be his downfall. At this rate, the government will know, within five calories, how much TJ's consumed today. I've told you before, the IRS is an unconstitutional agency."

"Well," Gail replied, "just because you don't believe in the IRS doesn't mean you can't spend an occasional night with me. While the IRS keeps tabs of my tips, they don't keep track of what goes up my vagina."

"I wouldn't be too sure of that," Tiburón answered as TJ watched the well-endowed bartender bend over to pull PBR Tall Boys from the cooler under the bar. Tiburón had his eyes on the TV mounted in the corner. The anchorwoman's voice was muted, but Tiburón could read the caption under the anchorwoman's image: *Angar Einstok, CEO of Einstok Industries defends his lunar acquisitions before Congress.*

"That lying bastard," Tiburón cursed aloud.

"You sure do have a serious hard-on for that guy," TJ said. He sat back on his stool as Gail straightened up. "From what I've seen on TV, he's some sort of world class hero. Advancing space exploration and finding Nazi gold here on Earth. Are you jealous?"

"What?" Tiburón retorted, accepting the sixteen ounce can from Gail. "Jealous of that *Cabrón?* Hell, no. It's just that Einstok's slicker than snot, and twice as devious. I should know. I've been on him like a tick. So let me just say that you don't know what I know."

"Like what?"

"Like the fact that assholes like him, and governments, have been active in space for years. We landed on the moon well before the sixties. *They* just don't want the public to know about it. But, keeping it closer to home, you should think about getting an Apache yourself. If not an Apache. Any vehicle built before 1967. Or at least one made before 1982."

"Don't you ever take off your tinfoil hat?" TJ asked.

Just then, a man from the other end of the bar, a man wearing a cowboy hat, raised his empty glass.

Watching the backside of Gail's jeans as she walked away from the two men, TJ continued. "And are you still sleeping with a can of wasp spray under your pillowcase?"

"Shit, TJ. It's not a matter of wearing a tinfoil hat. There are governments right now who could conduct an EMP strike and knock out our electronics," Tiburón answered. He picked up his new beer and tilted it toward his companion. "And you never know when the sun will have another coronal mass ejection. As far as the wasp spray, the government may be able to track my over-the-counter purchases of ammunition, but they could not care less about my purchases of a few cans of wasp spray with a 27-foot range."

TJ surrendered by saluting with his beer. Tilting it toward his lips, he looked down at the open magazine on the bar in front of Tiburón. Cydonia: The Real Face of Mars; AND Its connection to Teotihuacán.

"Still reading about Martian pyramids and alien gas stations on Earth, I see. Anyway, with you and Fox News around, what could go wrong."

"Plenty could go wrong," Tiburón responded, "as the news stopped being real news when FDR became president."

"You've said that before," TJ said.

"And you've never argued against it."

"Maybe because I don't know as much as you do," TJ said as they placed their beer cans back on the bar. "Next, you're going to tell me Gail has microphones built into her nipples so the government can listen to our conversations. I mean, look at those things. They ain't normal."

"You never know," Tiburón answered. "Gail could be more than your average skanked-up bartender."

Pouring a draft for the trucker at the other end of the bar, Gail turned toward them. "What's that? Another round already?"

The gap in her front teeth was visible from their end of the bar.

"In a minute," Tiburón said as he reached into his pants pocket. As he withdrew his hand, a dull thump rung out from their feet.

"Still collecting those things?" TJ asked.

Tiburón slid off his bar stool to pick it up. "Laugh if you want, but a five-gallon bucket of beat-up lead tire weights will be worth its weight in gold when shit hits the fan. And when it does, I'll have enough lead to cast a thousand rounds for my black-powder rifles. *They* can put listening devices anywhere they want. Even in Gail's nipples. And without her even knowing. Next time you sleep with Gail, you could check."

The man jerked the beer from his lips. "I've never been that desperate."

Tiburón pulled a twenty-dollar bill from his pants pocket. "That's not what I hear, but anyway, we'll pull chocks after these beers. You put your cellphone in the lead case I gave you?"

TJ tapped the back pocket of his jeans. "What about the state police? The Border Patrol?"

"I've been monitoring their communications and know where every swinging dick is stationed between Nogales and Phoenix."

The men lifted and lowered their beers in silence. Tiburón spoke up. "After this load, I'm taking the next two weeks off. Shark Week is next week, and Sharknado Week follows that, so don't bother calling."

10

Amazon River Basin, early August, AD 2025

Eight persons in various stages of camouflage battle dress busied themselves along the shore of a muddied tributary feeding the Amazon River miles downstream. Einstok sat among them. On a rock with a gutted fish in his hand, and his pant legs rolled up to his knees. He used the water covering his feet to rinse off the fish. His canvas-leather boots, socks, and an open Swiss Army knife waited patiently on a rock next to him. He assessed the paperback in Munro's hand.

"I would think, in survival mode, a person would be more select about what they carried with them," Einstok stated. "Due to the weight of that book, or the space it takes up in your kit, I would think it would have better use as toilet paper."

Munro closed the book and placed it on the rock next to him. The title on the cover read *A New Voyage Around the World*. After letting go of the book, he reviewed their surroundings.

Einstok watched Munro for a second, noting the distant look in his eyes. It seemed as if the ex-legionnaire had placed himself in a faraway place. Einstok took in their familiar surroundings as well. Directly overhead, the equatorial sun baked away at the tropical forest on both sides of the narrow, mud-brown tributary. To their left, snarled in a clutch of tree roots, the remnants of a motorized fishing boat with an enclosed cabin and shattered windows lay canted over. Behind them, the rest of their team busied themselves with camp duties: assessing the dryness of clothing hanging from a line strung between two trees, tending to the cooking fire, boiling water in a salvaged tin can, and gutting a rainforest deer hanging from a tree.

Munro brought his eyes back to the present and turned to look at his team. His eyes landed on the only female in his team.

"All humans, all living beings, are creatures of habit. It provides security and comfort. Whether it be me carrying around a book about an English buccaneer-slash-explorer when I should be carrying an extra canteen of potable water instead. Or a small bottle of iodine to purify the water that goes into it. Or Lil' Sumptin' using a shard of windowpane from a wrecked fishing boat to gut and skin a deer we will never eat. While the weight of that book provided my heart and brain solace, the proper leafy vegetation here in the Amazon provided my ass that same comfort. Thus, balancing out the weight of a luxury in a survival situation."

Einstok nodded. Surrendering to wisdom, he withdrew the fish from the river, shaking it as he did.

"There are those in the world who think of persons such as Captain Cook and Charles Darwin as the first and most intrepid explorers to discover and document the world's mysteries. Those better read know that explorers such as Cook and Darwin used William Dampier's adventures to create their own success decades later."

Einstok paused to consider the bird over his head. A multicolored parrot clutching a tree branch and letting out a long, slow cry.

"Dampier sailed around the world three times, at a time when most Europeans were born, lived, and died within a mile of their own villages. He witnessed amazing adventures and mysteries. We have shared our own adventures, and we both know that you, I, and your team behind us are not simple villagers."

"Nor are we those who tend to waste such trailblazing efforts," Munro said. He reached for his book and leaned forward to stand. "But that path is on the other side of our final phase of Basic Orbital Combat Training, where we will become the first graduating class of Special Orbital Combat Operators for the United States Space Force."

Einstok also stood and finished his team leader's observation. "And ready for our first deployment as such."

11

A Million Miles from Mars, late January, AD 2026

Manwaring floated in front of the sealed module containing the mission's unconscious second officer.

"So, Doctor Elizabeth 'Lizzie' Borden-Montgomery," Manwaring said, "what did it feel like to watch him burn alive, trapped inside a car at the bottom of that ravine?"

He tilted his head as if expecting to hear an answer to a question he had asked a hundred times, but he knew none would come. His angled reflection in the module's plastic cover stared back at him. His hair, almost shaved off while in a Belize prison, started to grow back, allowing him to restart his ponytail. The reflection captured a partial image of another module behind his feet, making the interior of their spaceship's center—or habitation—stage feel that much smaller.

He, Elizabeth, and four others were crammed inside of what the six of them could only describe as the interior of a high-tech, self-sustaining, multimillion-dollar RV coach. But one without windows. From the outside, Manwaring thought it looked like a piece of hard candy in a gray-white wrapper, with the wrapper's twisted ends being the engine stage at one end, and an inverted control/lander capsule at the other end.

After TETRA had smuggled them off Earth, they boarded the vessel via an airlock built into the control/lander capsule while the ship orbited the moon. A vessel that, as far as the world's public knew, was nothing more than an unmanned supply vessel meant for a remotely controlled one-way trip to Mars.

He continued to look at Elizabth through the curved plastic cover. A woman he remembered as a teenage student who had attended two of his lectures over two decades ago. Now, he knew Elizabeth simply as Number Two, designated by the number stenciled on the top frame member of her module, embroidered into her issued clothing and spacesuit, and her position within the ship's crew. While being the assistant mission commander, she was also the mission's chief science and medical officer. Remembering her as a student, he appreciated her good looks. Then, and now. While she suffered from the same ravages as the rest of them, their four months of space travel failed to diminish her handsome Scandinavian features. Thinking back to those days when she'd attended his classes, he remembered her for reasons other than her looks. While every male in the class swooned all over her, she actually paid attention to his lectures. And asked relevant questions.

Speaking again, he lamented, "At least you had the luxury of watching your victims die in front of you. The nation of Belize saw fit to convict and execute me for a murder that, for the life of me, I cannot recall watching myself."

Thinking of his, and Elizabeth's, near future, the worn newspaper article taped to the inside frame of the module, and next to her head, caught his attention again. The occupant had rubbed away at the article's title over the months in space, but it was still legible: The Black Widow has been Executed in Texas.

Deep down, Manwaring knew that the government of Belize had not convicted him for strangling one prostitute in Belize City alone. Throughout his last few years in Central America, reported strangulations of prostitute always seemed to be cropping up when he worked in the area around the murders. Though he dreaded hearing talk of such murders when in town or seeing the reports in the local newspapers, he thought he had no connection with them. The doctors in England said they'd cured him.

As a fourteen-year-old growing up in a lower middle-class neighborhood in East London, he found himself embroiled in a murder case and the subject of a medical study. With no knowledge of his actions, the authorities brought the young lad to trial over the strangulation of a young girl in the neighborhood. Though only thirteen, she behaved in a fashion well beyond her young years. Through DNA evidence, the court proved he committed the murder, and medical professionals diagnosed young Manwaring with a psychosis they termed the Schlicken-Gruber Syndrome, a form of mental illness triggered by certain particulars where the victim conducts actions with no memory of doing so. Due to his age, the entire episode remained sealed in court records, and the diagnosis allowed him to receive treatment until he was twenty-one. By then, though, his family had disowned him, leaving him to his own means.

However, instead of falling into a life of crime, drugs, despondency, and loneliness and dying in a trash-filled alley in East London, he completed his college studies and moved into a university graduate program. Freeing himself of a childhood curse. Or at least he had thought.

Having read the article countless times, Manwaring knew the woman on the other side of that plexiglass suffered from no credible psychotic malady. Elizabeth was completely lucid during her murders.

"Why did you have to be such a memorable student in my class, Miss Elizabeth Borden-Montgomery," he said with a sigh. He reached over to the palm-sized keypad mounted under the medical monitor, both affixed to the latched side of the module, and punched in a series of numbers. After a minute or so, after her index finger jerked, he reached over and pulled himself to the module next to Number Two's.

Stopping in front of the module, stenciled Number Three, he contemplated the handsome man and his Red Sox ball cap, tucked under the Velcro strap going across his bare chest. What was once a fine, athletic frame topped with a strong, determined face when they first met had softened, and the man's once hard-core abdomen had become a little paunchy. Even the whitish-pinkish scars from two bullet wounds seemed more subdued. Looking at the mission's system specialist, Manwaring cautioned himself: *It wouldn't take much to rebuild those muscles on Mars.*

He turned to the palm-sized keypad mounted to Number Three's module. Manwaring recited a numbered code stored in his head, and his fingers hovered over those same numbers on the keypad. All it would take to kill the man was for Manwaring to punch that code, which would send a shot of nerve gas through the medical tubes and straight into the unconscious man's nostrils. He thought about the power he held in his fingertips while continuing to look at the handsome man behind the plexiglass, one he knew as Number Three, but who introduced himself as Finnegan. "How dependent you are that I do not simply type in the right numbers. It *would* be a quicker fate."

Number Three failed to respond.

"No. Now is not your time."

Other than Number Two, he first met his fellow astronauts less than six months ago. Brought, one by one, to a remote facility built inside lava tubes under the barren landscape of Iceland. However, the intense month of training under Iceland's landscape prevented any personal engagement. The truth, though, was he preferred it that way, even though he was the reason they were all there. To him, his five companions were mere tools in a field school: sifting screens, picnic tables, tote-boxes, and shovels. All needed to get him to that next artifact. And to satisfy his mortgage. One held by Einstok.

While talking to them in their comatose state allayed the loneliness of space, their unconsciousness assuaged Manwaring's guilt as their inability to speak reminded him they were inanimate objects, like G. I. Joes stacked on store shelves in their boxes, to be opened only when the time was right and disposed of after their owners had outgrown them or blew them up with firecrackers in childhood delight. Thinking about the death agreement he made with Angar Einstok, he wondered. *Was he just like them, a G. I. Joe in a box on the devil's shelf? Had he sentenced himself to that shelf?*

Answering his own question, he moved on.

Soon after Einstok had them smuggled from those lava tubes and into sub-lunar orbit, and then into deep space, they fell into the routine of keeping one person on watch for a three-day stint while the others went into torpor. The rotation of torpor helped them psychologically during their long confinement of space travel, along with reducing the consumption of supplies. But they all also knew it kept them from knowing each other as a group. However, since he was the mission commander and designated Number One, he got to know Number Two and Number Six better than the rest. When it was Number Two's turn to come on watch, he would initiate the recovery process and bring her out of hibernation. After hours of recuperating from two weeks of sleep, she would put him under for his two weeks. The rotation continued until Number Six completed his watch, where the cycle started all over again. The brief time during shift changes allowed for conversation, but not much. And thankfully so.

Leaving her, and Number Three alone, Manwaring glided around the habitation stage, inspecting the other astronauts—something he performed countless times in their journey to Mars. There was Number Four, or a man who went by Tiburón. A lithe Hispanic with the tattoo of a shark on his neck. His assigned position was that of the mission's botanist. Turning around, he looked at the remaining two modules. One inhabited by Number Five. A woman who called herself Spike. She wore TETRA-issued blue shorts, a T-shirt, short red hair, and a tattoo of a bulldog wearing a US Marine Corps drill sergeant hat on her upper right arm. She was the mission's equipment operator. She, and the machines now locked inside pre-staged lander modules on Mars, would finish constructing their base once on Mars.

Finishing his tour, he stopped in front of Number Six, a German who identified himself as Kroll strapped in his module with three blue Velcro straps holding him against the pleated gray padding lining the unit. The man weighed over five hundred pounds when they first met under Iceland. Weight brought on by quality food, fine wines, and human flesh. But now, after months in space, and wearing only gray shorts labeled with the black number six, the man's excess skin made him look like a partially inflated plastic animal in front of a barbecue joint. He was the mission's cook.

Like the others, Numbers Four, Five, and Six were pale and gaunt, a result of months in space and a minimal amount of physical exercise. The only signs of life came from the medical monitors fitted to the upper left corners of the modules' covers. Fixed at head level, the small lights of the medical monitors blinked red and white and black numbers and letters scrolled across the small monitor screen and tracked vital stats: blood pressure, body temperature, oxygen levels, and heart rhythm, along with the time and date based on Earth's time and date. Specifically, US Pacific time. Manwaring envisioned their craft hurtling itself at Mars at a speed of thousands of miles per hour. Yet, all he could hear from inside their vessel was the innocent hum of the air recycling machine hidden behind the vessel's bulkhead. Its job was to purify the air of particulates and to collect and recycle the smallest drop of moisture floating about. Enjoying the thought of one day less in space, and one day closer to his goal, he pushed himself away from Number Six's module to continue with his duties.

It was the job of the person on watch to ensure that the monitors and the medical systems remained hooked up correctly. The heating and cooling pads inside the modules and the orifice cooling tubes kept the bodies at a constant internal temperature of ninety-three degrees Fahrenheit. Medical leads, attached to the proper body parts with sticky pads, provided the medical data, while the intravenous feeding and waste-removal tubes remained clear of obstructions.

While Control on Earth did receive an automatic flow of data, including the medical status of each astronaut, it was Manwaring's task to provide regular data summaries concerning the entire voyage back to Earth. Ideally, TETRA would use that data to prepare future voyages after them. And to find out what went wrong if, indeed, forces beyond anybody's control destroyed them in space.

Turning from the six modules occupying the central section of their habitation stage, he opened the round hatchway at the forward end of the stage and pulled himself into the short tunnel leading to the command module. When the time came, or when forced to do so, they could detach the command/lander capsule from the spacecraft's center stage. Once on the surface of Mars, the command/lander capsule would also suffice as an emergency, short-term, living shelter, or storage place.

Closing the hatchway behind him, he turned to open the hatchway ahead of him and pulled himself through it. Once inside, he reviewed the cockpit. It resembled the cockpit of any modern airliner, but with seating for six. He pulled himself up from under the dashboard and into the left seat. Minus the control or steering yoke, the dashboard in front of him resembled that of a 747. Also, instead of a wraparound windshield, just as there would be on any airplane, there was only the slightly curved rectangular computer screen mounted just above the control dashboard. What they could see, when turned on, would be whatever the external camera recorded. While Manwaring could have turned the camera on to view the deep space in front of him, he opted not to. There would be time later.

Strapping himself in, he reached out to activate his communications and spent the next twenty minutes drafting the shipboard data and typing his own personal synopsis of the last rotation into a singular file. Buried within that file was the maintenance report from the ship's system specialist that Number Three left for him. In that report, Number Three indicated that, while out of torpor, he found an air-operated valve for the ship's engine was about to fail. He replaced it from the vessel's stores and noted the serial number of the air valve for Manwaring to include in his report. Although Number Three had sent off an immediate report of the parts replacement, and the reason for it, he made it part of the scheduled summarized report. After hitting the send button, Manwaring thought back to the other reports from Number Three while unstrapping himself.

An hour later, Manwaring and Elizabeth sat strapped at the small table in the habitation stage's kitchenette. Number Two took the time, before coming to the table, to brush her blond hair, tie it into a ponytail, and put on the uniform they were issued: blue, loose-fitting shirts and matching trousers, with large pockets closed off with Velcroed flaps. She also wore the issued white tennis shoes.

Elizabeth sipped hot coffee from a foil packet. Do you think we will have any more technical issues? Like the one Number Three found his last time out of torpor?"

"Hard to tell," Manwaring responded as he too sipped from a coffee packet. "But it seems Number Three has conducted a thorough inspection, and we should be sailing in calm waters for the remainder of our voyage. We still have seventy *sols* left to go, so you'd better get me into torpor. But let's finish our turnover."

✵

Mojave Desert, late January AD 2026

Zelda, wearing desert patterned battle-dress uniform, and a matching floppy hat, canvas-leather boots, and a holstered revolver on her right hip, sat in the driver's seat of a similarly patterned special operations-capable Land Rover. Her blond hair, combed back behind her ears, stuck out from under the brim of the floppy hat. She took a second to remove her sunglasses and wipe them with a bandana. Putting them back on, and lifting her face, thirty-one men, also dressed in desert BDUs, filed out of the canyon's entrance in front of her.

Each one of them hunched forward, easing the weight of the rucksacks on their backs while carrying black-painted automatic rifles at the ready. Completing her head count she reached over for the tablet sitting on the passenger seat. Flipping the cover under the tablet, she placed it on her lap and typed in the words. *Send med-air assistance to Spencer's Canyon. Six to recover. Medical status unknown.*

Twenty minutes later, twenty-nine of the men who slogged their way out of the canyon dropped their packs, and advanced technology rifles onto the dirt road behind the second SOC Land Rover parked behind Zelda's. They replaced those firearms with bottles of iced-down lager from coolers at the back of the vehicle. The driver, a Space Force medical tech, left his seat to assess the newly arrived persons.

Einstok and Max, who led them out of the canyon joined Zelda in her vehicle.

Einstok opened the rear of the vehicle, leaving the tailgate down. He slid the straps of the backpack off his shoulders and dumped the pack onto the tailgate along with his black-painted, Gauss SOC automatic rifle. Max did the same. Opening a cooler, Einstok grabbed a bottle of beer and handed it to Max. He grabbed three more before stepping around the tailgate and opening the passenger side front door. He passed a bottle over to Zelda while sliding onto the seat.

"Thank you, sir," Zelda said. "Welcome back to Earth."

Removing his floppy hat, Einstok threw it onto the dashboard before placing one bottle in the cup holder. Twisting the cap off the third bottle, he almost emptied the bottle in one swallow. Lowering the bottle, he wiped his forehead with the back of his other hand while turning toward Max, who quaffed the bottle of lager in his hand.

"Looks like you got over your disdain for American beer," said Einstok.

Max lowered his bottle and smacked his lips. "After two weeks on the moon's surface, and in sub-lunar orbit followed by thirty-six hours in that canyon surviving your tactical exercises, anything will do the trick, even American beer."

"Don't worry, Max, I got your brand back at headquarters," Zelda said as she also took a long slug of her beer. Pulling it away from her mouth, she said, "I've ordered a helicopter to pick up six men. Are they still alive?"

"They were when we left them," Einstok replied, after uncapping his second beer. "They either gave out because of the Mojave Desert or collapsed under snapped legbones. Two weeks in suborbital space and on the lunar surface for Phase Four training will do that to a man's bones. Sorry you could not join us."

"I understand, sir," she replied. "But you have kept me busy enough here on Earth. Even from the lunar surface."

"Speaking of which," Einstok said, "has my chief armorer finished modifications to my new model of space-capable Gauss rifles? I, we, need them ready by next Thursday."

Zelda sipped her beer. "I spent last week with The Merlin Group and oversaw the modifications based on your requests from the field. They will be ready."

"Very well," Einstok said. "Now, how about getting me up to speed. We have been in that canyon for thirty-six hours."

"Yes, sir," she said.

Einstok put his head against the seat headrest and waited as Zelda set aside her beer and tapped the tablet screen.

"For starters, we have received our regular update from Manwaring, and everything is on schedule for his arrival."

Einstok glanced over at Max, who had just turned to get more beer from the cooler. "And did Manwaring report any further problems."

"Manwaring reports that the system specialist did encounter another impending mechanical failure but resolved the problem before it came an issue."

"I remember the first two from his earlier reports," Einstok surmised. He accepted another bottle from Max while looking through the windshield. "So, it is possible our systems engineer is either overreacting, or we might have a supply-logistics issue. Or?"

"There is industrial sabotage afoot," Zelda said. "I have compared notes with the chief engineer for that project, and his analysis says that, left unfound, any of those problems would become catastrophic."

Einstok placed the empty beer bottle at his feet. "My competitors have been nipping at my heels for years. They have also been spying on my efforts to better themselves either financially or technically; however, sabotage at this level has not been in their modus operandi before."

"Do you think they were trying to stop the Mars mission all together," Max asked. "Or were they trying to slow down your effort?"

"I suspect," Einstok answered as he twisted the cap off another bottle and threw it on the dashboard, "somebody else may have at least some knowledge of our secret, and it would be in their best interest for Manwaring's team, or my team, to not be the first people on Mars. Have you made any further investigations?"

"Yes," Zelda answered. "After retracing our supply-chain organization with those parts, using their serial numbers, I have narrowed my suspicions down to three individuals. Americans connected with NASA, the Chinese National Space Administration, and the Iranian Space Agency. We have also started a re-inventory and the restocking of parts for our spacecraft from vendors closer to home. I also arranged to have those individuals dealt with."

Einstok smiled as he lifted his beer bottle. "Good detective work, Zelda. I must also congratulate you on another excellent choice, as it appears the Mars-bound assassin you found for that cleanup in the Bahamas has proven to be quite able. That said, it is a shame, and a waste, what will happen to the young man. He reminds me of me. On the other hand, Max and I have noted people just as capable behind us, but the next ten miles will be the final authority. Are the written exams ready back at base for those that make it back on their own two feet?"

"Yes, they are, sir," she replied. "I also have messages that require responses. Including one from the president."

Before Einstok could reply, Munro stepped up next to Max.

"Sir, they're enjoying their beer," Munro said, "and are anticipating their transportation."

Einstok's face broke into a wry smile. "Like in the Legion, just when you think you survived that one last evolution, and have beaten the odds, there is always one last, unsuspected, crucible. The transportation they are waiting for consists of whatever charge they can muster from their guts, and whatever petrol remains in their legs. Ruck up."

Turning toward Zelda, Einstok said, "The president can wait."

The following night, a full moon poured its haunting radiance against the naked, craggy peaks of the Currant Mountain Range. Miles to the south, a convex lens of a golden hue glowed in the darkness, trapping the city of Las Vegas like a lightning bug under a turned-over glass. The faraway moon competed with Las Vegas to illuminate the desert between them. Inside one of those roughhewn peaks, three people sat around one end of a stout and polished oaken table, which assumed the center of a richly decorated conference room. One of those three, Angar Einstok, assessed the room, and his successes.

Gold-trimmed lighting fixtures recessed into the reddish, mahogany-paneled ceiling that blanketed the ornate furnishings in the long room with a precious glow. At one end of the room was an enormous set of mahogany doors with ivory handles. At the other end of the room, an exquisitely stocked bar backed by a mirror ran the length of the wall. On the third wall of the rectangular room, a row of mounted, gold-framed photos highlighted the paneling. Though each photo projected a different image, they all had one item in common: Angar Einstok standing in front of or on top of his life's major achievements. Those photos displayed additional persons who had played a vital part in Einstok's endeavors over the years. Six of those people waited outside the conference room along with a bottle of Dalmore 62. The other two, Zelda and Max, sat in the room with him.

At the head of the table, Einstok wore blue jeans, a gray polo shirt with TETRA's logo on the left breast pocket, and a pleased smile on his face while holding a glass of scotch whiskey. He swirled the spirit slowly, appraising the mounted frames as if he had not a care in the world.

In the photo closest to the bar, Einstok was visible through the cockpit's windshield. Below and in front of him, the name *Dampier* was painted along the nose of the first generation X-Terra One. The first in a series of suborbital space planes capable of going anywhere on Earth, within hours, or into orbit. In the next photo, the second generation of that same space plane sat poised on a tarmac, surrounded by the flat Nevada Desert. Although twenty meters long, the craft's rotund body and stubby wings made it appear shorter. Capable of docking to any orbiting space station, it could also drop rocket-equipped pods full of adventure-seeking tourists or SOC operators. At the same time, it was capable of capturing those same pods rocketed back into lunar orbit. Einstok, wearing a green military flight suit, a TETRA ball cap, and sunglasses, stood under the space plane with his hand on its nose.

In the third photo, nine people, wearing tiger-striped camouflage BDUs and holding black M-4 carbines, kneeled around a Mayan statue made of gold. Einstok stood next to the idol holding his carbine across his chest. Sweat and grime stained the BDUs dark and matted their hair and beards—evidence of a long trek through the Yucatan jungle. In front of the kneeling people, the bodies of three men, dressed similarly to Einstok and his team, lay prone in the grass. Like prize elk dropped by proud Wyoming hunters. The dead men were, in fact, mercenaries working for a competitor.

Einstok's eyes continued down the row of framed photos, stopping at one photo of a white, self-propelled submersible floating in the blue ocean just behind the stern of Einstok's research vessel, *Neptune Explorer,* a vessel, equipped with the most advanced salvage equipment available, and one where Munro and his team helped crew. However, the piloted submersible looked more like an underwater airplane, but with the eyes, mouth, and claws of a crab. The eyes were a pair of forward-mounted lights remotely operated by the pilot inside the submersible. The mouth was the vessel's small and rounded window located under, and between, the projecting camera pods. On either side of the camera pods, mounted through the sides of the hull, was a jointed hydraulic arm. While both arms extended up like a referee signaling a touchdown, they were different in structure and purpose. The longer arm of the two held an object in its metal pincers: a mud-covered ship's bell the size of a beer keg. Just behind the celebrating mechanical arms, Einstok stood in an open hatchway wearing a blue flight suit. Surrounding the open hatch and sitting on the sloping sides of the craft were the same six people who waited outside the conference room. In the photo, they wore wetsuits. Now, those waiting people wore a different type of suit.

"Do you remember that adventure, Zelda?" Einstok asked as he lifted his glass to his lips.

Sitting at the table, intent on the computer screen and keyboard built into the table, and with a glass of the $58,000 scotch whiskey of her own, Zelda wore a business suit with a black skirt cut just above the knees and a snugly fitted gray jacket over a white silk blouse that clung to her athletic form. Her eyeglasses finished off her appearance.

"Of course," Zelda replied without looking up from her work. "You conducted the world's deepest manned salvage dive. The media labeled you as the master of the inner universe." She paused for a second. "We have received our regular situation report from Manwaring. There have been no more technical issues, so everything is on track for their scheduled arrival. *And* our scheduled departure."

"Very good," Einstok replied, looking at his executives. Zelda continued to look at the computer screen. Max, dressed similarly to Einstok, moved his focus from the photos to his whiskey.

"I am ready to speak with Munro and his team," Einstok said, "but is there any other business first?"

"Yes," she answered. "The crowned prince in Riyadh has agreed to your request to set up an Einstok Industries space base. I will fly to Washington tonight and meet with his ambassador to gather the proper signatures. The president also just sent a text and wishes to speak with you. He says it's important."

"Congratulate the prince on his decision, and tell the president I will respond momentarily," Einstok replied. "Go ahead and call in my team. The president can wait."

"Yes, sir," she said, typing a quick message.

A few seconds later, the double doors opened to reveal six smartly uniformed people, who marched in at sat at the long conference table. They placed their whiskey glasses and red berets, with silver crests designating them the elite Air Force-qualified combat controllers, on the polished table in front of them. Munro and his team looked around the underground room and marveled at its opulence. While familiar with Einstok's tastes, this visit to the room was their first. And it took them aback, including what they saw on the other side of one wall. The long wall opposite the wall with the framed photos. A glass wall.

"I must say you look resplendent in your Space Force dress uniforms," Einstok said. "And those special warfare insignia you wear means you have earned status within the United States Space Force. And *my organization*."

Einstok lifted the glass. The others followed suit.

After a long appreciation of the whiskey, and while Zelda continued with her flush-mounted computer, Einstok returned his gaze to the people waiting patiently. "Quite a change from yesterday morning, where you completed one last forced march and written exams, thus passing the final phase of Basic Orbital Special Combat training."

The six people, now clean-shaven and with regulation haircuts, nodded in acceptance. Proud smiles broadcast their satisfaction, and the smartness of their uniforms enhanced that satisfaction. Munro wore blue leadership tabs on his epaulets along with the single, gold bars, which designated him as a second lieutenant. The other five personnel wore triple blue chevrons on their sleeves, designating them as technical sergeants. They all wore silver parachute jump wings, qualifying them as Air Force pararescue-qualified parachute jumpers, above the left pocket of their uniform shirts. At the same time, though, they lacked the one item they all had slaved to pin on their uniforms.

"Nitro, along with a smart uniform and well-earned chevrons on your sleeves," Einstok continued. "I see the military forced you to give up your ridiculous man bun."

Nitro and Lil' Sumptin' reached up to touch their crew cuts.

Nitro nodded. "Aye, but I only wish my mates could see me now. The last time they saw me, the SAS drummed me out of my regiment, with no trooper stripes on my sleeves. Thanks for my redemption."

"Sir, he's right," said Lil' Sumptin' as she lowered her hand to flick an unseen speck of lint from her upper sleeve. "If it wasn't for you, we wouldn't be wearing the respectable uniforms of the United States Space Force."

"No thanks needed, Nitro," Einstok said. "I have a feeling your mates from your old regiment saw the graduation on television as well as millions of others around the world. Including space enthusiasts who see the graduation of this first class of Special Orbital Combat Operators as a next step in space exploration. On the other hand, Lil' Sumptin', there are military leaders from other nations who see a new step in space domination by a global military-industrial complex."

"Damned straight," Double Cannon threw out. "We ain't frigging keyboard warriors."

The rest of his team chuckled.

Einstok tilted his head forward in salute.

"Quite right, Double Cannon," Einstok said, lowering his glass. "By no means can you be considered desk jockeys. While it took two years to convince America's military leadership of my idea concerning a special operations-capable section for the Space Force, each of you posed a hurdle when it came to acceptance as recruits. That said, none of you lacked pluck when it came to the last two years, although I dare say that training was old hat. Starting out with spending just over a year completing all of the Air Force's special operations training—combat controllers, pararescuemen, special reconnaissance, and tactical air control parties—you completed all the training those special units go through. Once you completed that training, you spent the last eight months finishing training specific to BOSC. All wrapped up with your return to Earth and the crucible here in the Nevada Desert.

"Sorry to interrupt, sir," Double Cannon said, "but the last two years were nothing, so can we assume you have something more substantial waiting for us? One that will earn us our space tridents?"

"Yes, Double Cannon," Einstok said, "indeed. Just because you graduated BOSC, you do not have the right to wear your special warfare designator just yet. That merit will come after a rotation in the field. A deployment that you will all find quite fulfilling."

The recent Space Force special warfare graduates sat straighter in their chairs.

Einstok continued, "All of you had issues requiring attention: age, citizenship, and or legal issues. That said, with the pool of eligible recruits becoming smaller and smaller due to the American disease, namely obesity and illiteracy, leaving the United States Armed Forces in a crisis, your acceptance was not particularly difficult."

Einstok paused long enough to sip his whiskey.

"I must admit, Nitro, your process was the most difficult of all. You have been quite the rapscallion, so while the British Army and the SAS were unable to constrain your tendencies, I hope I have picked up where they failed."

Nitro smiled back at Einstok. "Well, those bloody IRA pigs had it coming, and what did I get for me troubles? Lost rank, and a discharge from the SAS with no pension. But at least I can go back to the UK whenever I feel like it and without fear of arrest, so thank you. Please feel free to take it out of my future pay."

Einstok chuckled dismissively. "No need. Just like your space tridents, *you will all* earn your pay, which is the reason you are here and not with your classmates celebrating your graduation." Einstok leaned forward in his chair at the head of the table. Sipping his scotch, he turned to look at the glass expanse making up the room's fourth wall, and the room on the other side. A room resembling NASA's flight control centers at Cape Canaveral and Houston. It was Einstok's personal control center for his space and lunar efforts. All of which operated under TETRA, Einstok's space-industrial complex.

Scientists and technicians sat at the computer kiosks lining the floor in front of a large, wall-mounted video screen or stepped intently to another person or computer kiosk while carrying files in their hands. They all wore polos and slacks, just as Einstok and Steiner did in the conference room above them. While nobody in the control room could see through the one-way window, they all knew Einstok was watching over them.

Just as the large one-way window assumed the length of the fourth wall in the conference room, so did the exceptionally large wall-mounted monitor in front of the computer kiosks in the control room. With smaller images to one side of the screen depicting activity on a lunar-based industrial complex, the center of the screen displayed the docking of a spaceship to Einstok's space station.

Einstok returned his gaze to the conference room and his staff.

"Of the over one hundred candidates who started Class 0001 of BOSC, only twenty-five were able to march through the gates of my desert training facility on their own two feet and pass the final examinations. Aside from you six, your class included veteran pilots, special operators from other armed forces, professional athletes, and law enforcement professionals. Of those nineteen, most will start out as BOSCs cadre of new instructors. The others will attend specialized schools. However, the secretary of the United States Space Force has issued orders detailing you to be part of TETRA's Orbital Special Research and Development Group a.k.a. The Merlin Group."

"At your request, of course," Sling Blade said.

"Of course," Einstok replied. "Your assignment with TETRA will be for an *indefinite* period. That said, you will have the weekend to bask in your limelight along with your classmates. However, by next Thursday your class will move onto their specific assignments. Which will provide us cover."

"Will that *cover* be old hat to us?" Slingblade asked, sipping his whiskey while looking over at Max.

Einstok replied, "While Max is not a member of the Space Force, he endured every forced march, flight hour, parachute jump, and bit of fish roe in the Amazon, just as we did. And with equal relish. He has also been the man behind the scenes, and the key player in our past successes in retrieving rare artifacts around the globe. Now, as part of the Space Force, you all will continue to serve my needs. You will all be my unofficial link to the military, which will prove useful to the further success of Einstok Industries and TETRA.

"All right sir, what's the op?" Solid Gold asked.

"Direct as always, Solid Gold," Einstok replied. "I have six expendables, misfits, smuggled aboard a spacecraft that, from what the majority of my organization knows and what the world's public has been told, is nothing more than a container ship with stores, robots, and drones to be remotely landed on Mars in preparation for the arrival of humans. It will be landing at a site already in the process of being remotely set up as a receiving station. They have been on their way throughout the last part of your training, and we have used every aspect of their training, and voyage, to prepare a similar supply space craft, and a subsequent voyage."

Einstok welcomed the gleams in the eyes of his team.

"What you are being asked to do is to follow those expendables in their footsteps and establish an official foothold on Mars."

"But while in doing so, we will recover something of value at the same time, right?" asked Double Cannon.

"Yes," Einstok said, sniffing the scotch in his glass. "And that depends on how you define the term valuable. Zelda has been behind the scenes during our training and has used her time to organize our mission, so she deserves a seat on that mission. Also, Max will be going to Mars with Zelda and myself."

Einstok set his eyes on Munro. "And so is your team leader. Munro will be the fourth crew member."

Lil' Sumptin' shot a look of confusion at Munro. "You already knew. You didn't tell me."

Einstok spoke before Munro could answer his lover. "Please, Lil' Sumptin', I ordered him not to say anything."

Lil' Sumptin' dropped her eyes and sighed heavily.

"We hope that you will not be averse to such a quest. I must also add to the intelligence gathered by the first spaceship, along with the fact that Earth and Mars are on the track of being much closer in proximity; our voyage will be appreciatively shorter."

Lil' Sumptin' spoke up with a cautious eye lifted in Munro's direction. "Sir, it sounds like a covert op, but with you being prominent in the public eye, your absence can't be missed. I would think the last thing you want to do is disappear from the world stage. People will notice."

"You are correct," Einstok said with a smirk. "So starting this evening, news will leak out that I have contracted a parasitic brain infection. One received during our survival training in the Amazon. My physicians feel my illness will force me to remain isolated at my villa for a period of treatment and recovery, with my much-noticed executive assistant, Zelda, by my side. Once this mission comes to a successful ending on Mars, I will reveal the truth to the world, which means the next time the public sees my face, it will be from Mars. The first human to complete interplanetary travel and set foot on Mars. However, there will be tertiary benefits that the public need not be aware of. One of those benefits being a deployment that will give you, and TETRA, opportunities to complete valuable combat testing of our new generations of spaceborne combat equipment and weapons."

"Do those misfits have any bench?" Double Cannon asked.

Einstok sipped his whiskey. "No. I have already arranged for the disposal of five of those misfits. All the sixth misfit must do is punch in the right codes at the right time. However, there is no such thing as a one-hundred-percent guarantee in life." He paused to look at the team. "Nothing wrong with a little spaceborne raid for practice."

"And another step in earning our space tridents," Slingblade offered.

"Yes," Einstok said as he leaned forward. "I realize that I am being forward having already started on plans that include you six; however, you still have a choice. I believe you have received enough information in the last few minutes to make up your mind. If you opt for this mission, our departure will be Thursday of next week, which means you will be back at this site Monday morning with kit in hand and the sleeves of your BDUs rolled up. Just in time for an officially announced departure of another remotely operated supply ship with stores and robotic machinery deployed to Mars. I will give everybody until 1600 hours tomorrow for a verbal response answer. If you choose not to go on this mission, Space Force Command will reassign you as an instructor for BOSC. You will not discuss anything you've heard in this room."

With that last statement, Einstok lifted his glass of whiskey, and the rest followed suit. Once they gulped down their drinks, the orbital space combat operators picked up their special operator's red berets. They stood in unison and filed toward the massive double doors. Munro reached the doors first and held the one on the left open. Being the last of them to leave the room, he pulled the door closed behind him.

Zelda put down her stylus, picked up her glass of whiskey, sat back in her chair, and took a slow sip. "So?"

"They have never turned down a mission request before."

Zelda looked at the computer screen. "Your wife is trying to get a hold of you. She is in London and wants to know when you'll be coming home. She is also asking if I will be accompanying you."

Einstok looked at Zelda and smiled. "I saw the video that you two made the last time you were together, and it looks like you seek adventures in numerous areas."

"Sorry to interrupt," Max said with a mischievous grin, "but I believe you put the president on hold."

"Oh. Him," Einstok sighed.

Zelda smiled as she looked back down at the screen. "The president got tired of being on hold. He said he had to attend a meeting and sent an email."

"What does he require?" Einstok asked.

"He wants to discuss your plans for the Trump-class of interplanetary cruisers."

"Give him a date. Sometime after next Thursday," Einstok replied. "We will not be around for it anyway. Anything else?"

Zelda picked up her glass and looked down at the screen again before speaking. "Do think you'll tell Nitro about one of those expendables?"

Einstok opened his mouth to answer, but a knock at the door stopped him. Einstok and the other two in the room looked to see the ivory door handle moving downward and the doors open. Munro and his team stood in the open doorway. All wore proud smiles.

"No," Einstok replied with a smile of his own. "I think not."

Three Sols from Mars, mid-April, AD 2026

Just as he had done so often in the last months, Manwaring reached out with his arms, stopping him in front of Number Two's torpor module. However, this *sol* was not the normal shift change between himself and Number Two. As soon as he completed punching the required codes into the keypad mounted to the frame of Number Two's module, he moved on to Number Three, repeating the process until he got to Number Six. Not since the first week of the voyage had everybody been awake at the same time. Pushing himself away from the module, his heart sank at the thought of the activity that would soon consume the spacecraft's habitation stage.

Turing away from his companions and his dread, he pulled himself through the short burrow leading to the command/lander stage. Once there, he strapped himself into the commander's seat and reached out to the console in front of him. Dismissing the thoughts of his companions, he mused: *it takes a minimum of six months to send a human to Mars but only twenty minutes to send an email back*. He rested his fingers on the console's keyboard and paused to think about the message he was about to send, why he "agreed" to this mission, and that night in Honduras. In his fieldhouse. In his room.

The night he started deciphering the languages on that metal container and into that spiral-bound notebook. With a chortle, he thought back, just as he had done so many times in the last few years, to how the writings of an over-indulged night clerk in Switzerland invalidated his life. Sighing, he leaned forward and typed in three words: *Dawn has arisen*.

"It's been hours since we woke up, and I still feel like shit. This sure isn't like it is in the movies." Tiburón stated. "Man, what I could do with a good coffee."

"How's that Tiburón?" Elizabeth asked. She sat opposite him, sipping water out of an aluminum foil pouch through the filling straw. She inspected the pallor of his skin as he leaned forward, holding the lower half of his face in his palms.

"Well, in the movies, the first person out of torpor was the space marine sergeant who plops his hat on his head and shoves a stale cigar into his mouth as soon as his module opens. He then hops out and yells at his space marines to hit the deck with their feet running. I just can't do anything but sit here."

"I've been reviewing everybody's data, including yours. Everything seems normal," Elizabeth said. Her eyes moved to others in the compartment. Comparing his skin color to everybody else's. "You don't look any worse than the rest of us."

"I did everything I was supposed to," Tiburón responded tiredly. "After recovery, I checked in with TETRA, answered emails, checked your tubes, refilled our water pouches, ate a pint-sized helping of rehydrated turd, spent an hour on the Nautilus, took *un cagar*, showered, shaved, and took a nap. And started the entire process over again. Until I had to wake up Spike."

Elizabeth turned her head toward Spike.

The twenty-five-year-old woman with short red hair, wide green eyes, and same build as Elizabeth, responded while strapped to the Versa bike in the aft corner of the habitation stage. "He looked okay to me."

Before Elizabeth could respond, the circular hatch penetrating the rear wall swung open. A man, holding a rag in one hand and wearing a Red Sox baseball cap and the company-issue shorts and tank top labeled Number Three, floated into the compartment.

"Everything all right back there, Finnegan?" Elizabeth asked.

"I had to kick the water recycling pump a couple of times, but it's back to making water out of everybody's piss and sweat," Finnegan replied, closing the hatch behind him. Tying the rag to the hatch's handle, he turned to face the others. "I don't know what eejit put that thing together, but I'm starting to question TETRA's advanced space technology and propulsion systems. I've scraped more knuckles on this tub than I did on my '57 Chevy. I'm starting to think Einstok procured his parts from Crazy Habib's Pneumatic Valve and Fireworks Emporium of Greater Karachi, Pakistan."

Since TETRA designated her as Number Two, and him Number Three, Elizabeth had the responsibility of bringing him out of torpor for his watch. Even still, he spoke little during their few hours awake together. When he did speak, though, he spoke well, but Elizabeth noticed an occasional slip of a Boston accent or slang.

"I'm having a time in believing in Einstok would be that cheap," Elizabeth answered. "From what you've said so far, the potential failures could have ended this mission, and our lives, without us knowing about it. Which made going into torpor a bit anxious. You sure you're not overreacting?"

"No," Finnegan replied. "I read TETRA's returned emails, and it seems like they're accepting Manwaring's weekly reports with credibility. And using our near-death experiences to help prepare for future missions, which includes sorting out their logistic supply-chain issues. It also means they're thinking the same thing I am, and that would be industrial sabotage. Based on what I already knew about Einstok, he's like any other entrepreneur billionaire-slash-corporate magnate. Meaning every competitor who wants to reach the finish line first has no problems with throwing a baseball bat at his feet."

"Well, whatever is going on," Elizabeth said, "I'm glad you're here."

"Just send the bill to Crazy Habib," Finnegan said. "What were you guys talking about?"

Watching Finnegan float past Spike, Elizabeth answered. "Tiburón feels like shit."

Reaching the others in the kitchenette corner, he pulled open a drawer under the microwave and grabbed for a packet of water held inside by a Velcro strap. Pushing himself around, he grabbed one of the chairs at the table and strapped himself down. "I'm no doctor, and I know we've all had hoses stuck in every orifice of our bodies, but my prognosis says you'll be fine."

Uncapping the straw to the refillable pouch, he continued. "But whatever it is Tiburón you're gonna have to shake it. Manwaring says we're getting close, so we need to get our heads in the game. Although TETRA will be controlling the landing, we need to be ready in case something goes wrong."

Elizabeth had already sucked the last of the water out of her pouch but pretended to suck water as she studied Finnegan. A hair over six feet, he presented a solid frame topped by strawberry-blond hair. His striking brown eyes and flowing mustache reminded her of a man from a Victorian-era photograph. All he needed was a bowler hat tilted at a rakish angle on his head while a dutiful woman in a flowing white dress stood behind him with her hand on his shoulder. Her eyes wandered over two pink rosebud scars: one on his upper right arm and one on his left shoulder. Although she detected a slight Boston accent, his speech and wording reflected an international, or even military background.

"*Ja*, I agree," Hermann Kroll said.

Like the others, Elizabeth turned to face the German. Remaining strapped upright in his open module, he occupied himself with an electric tablet. "How nice would it be to have a hot cup of strong black coffee. Even smelling it brewing would be such a treat."

"Agree about what?" Elizabeth asked. "And what kind of puzzle are you working on now?"

"Coffee. I was just agreeing with Tiburón about coffee. And I am working on a *New York Times* crossword." Kroll tapped the tablet's keypad with his index finger one last time. "Just like the smell of brewing coffee, even the simplest of puzzles activate the morning palette, thus wiping away the morning fog." He pushed the tablet under a piece of Velcro inside his module and reached for the Velcro strap holding him in place.

"Hey!" Elizabeth said as she pulled the straw from her mouth. "Remember what we said about putting on a shirt before coming to the table?"

Kroll nodded and reached for the blue shirt tucked under his head. He slipped it over his bald, bullet-shaped head as he floated to the table and the last open seat. He brought his hand up to rub his eyes after strapping himself in. "We need to make sure we do the landing correctly. I need to get out of this sardine tin and start cooking real food. I am nothing but bone and skin."

Elizabeth noted the sagging skin under his chin as he spoke. Having lost so much weight so quickly, she was concerned about any medical developments.

"I'd say a lot more skin than bone," Spike interjected.

Elizabeth turned in time to see Spike, the ex-marine float away from the stationary bicycle. Beads of sweat floated away from her skin, hair, and damp gym clothing, only to be sucked up by the air recycling unit in the ceiling—the only source of any mechanical noise inside the habitation stage.

Floating past her space mates, Spike reached out for the hatchway leading to the control/lander capsule. "I'm going up to see if I can get a clear picture of our new home."

"You do that, Spike," said Elizabeth. "But we've been up for three hours now, so I think it's time to get some nonmedically induced sleep. That should help you, Tiburón."

The Hispanic nodded in agreement, with his face still in his hands. The others retreated into their own thoughts.

Spike entered the other end of the tunnel headfirst, stopping at Manwaring's legs. Manwaring's stubby pigtail of gray hair floated behind his head, and his facial features, a hawkish nose, and a slightly protruding upper jaw were more pronounced by skin drawn tightly over them. And by the fact that she was looking at him from upside down. The muted blue and green glares from the dashboard computer screen reflected off the lenses of his glasses now positioned halfway down his nose and angled downward. Intent on the dashboard's console, or lost in thought, he failed to notice her entrance.

Spike reached out for a handhold bolted to the bottom of the dashboard console and pulled herself round to see the image of their new home on the center of the rectangular monitor screen above the instrument console. "So, Mr. Oxford, that's the God of War."

"Damn it, Spike!" Manwaring blurted out.

"Sorreee," she said smirking.

Manwaring twerked his chin to the side and returned his eyes to the console in front of him. "Is there something you require?"

"Not from you," she said. "I'm no doctor like you or Elizabeth, but I would recommend a rehydrated steak and a couple miles on the bicycle. It'll put color in your cheeks."

"I get plenty of exercise using my mind," he responded. "And leave any medical advice up to Elizabeth. She's the MD."

"How much longer?"

Keeping his eyes on the dashboard console in front of him, he answered, "Control has us a little less than sixty-eight hours out. Get some sleep. Once we enter orbit, we'll be busy."

Spike did not answer. Instead, she observed the Martian details on the center-mounted monitor. Backed by a deep blue-black, the pale red orb filled the center of the screen. Its surface, scarred by millions of years of erosion, meteor strikes, and geographical shifting, concealed the target of her inspection: a dry lakebed next to a low-running mountain range. Giving up, she pushed herself back into the tunnel, feet first, stopping only to show a small semi-spherical black glass lens mounted in the corner above Manwaring's head her middle finger.

✪

During her short absence, her shipmates had turned off the compartment's light and gone back to their modules for sleep, or to be alone with their thoughts. The only lighting in the compartment came from the individual medical monitors attached to the modules, including the one next to Elizabeth's head. Elizabeth, strapped into her module. With the clear, plastic cover closed, and with her arm across her chest, rubbed her index finger on the newspaper clipping taped to the curved inside of her module. Spike opened the hinged cover and latched it to the spacesuit locker built into the torpor module.

"Hi, Elizabeth," Spike whispered.

"What's going on up forward?" replied Elizabeth, while keeping her eyes on the article.

"Well, Mars is getting bigger, and Manwaring's an even bigger asshole."

"Don't get hung up on him." Elizabeth looked at Spike. "We'll be landing soon, and we'll be out of this tin can. And in our own quarters."

"I remember bitching about being locked up in the back of a Humvee with a bunch of sweaty marines who managed to bump into my tits every time we hit a pothole," Spike remarked. She paused long enough to narrow her eyes at Elizabeth. "Once I get to my own quarters, I'll never complain again. That's unless you don't come by to visit me now and then."

Listening to Spike, Elizabeth continued to stroke the title of a newspaper article duct-taped to the curved wall: *The Black Widow Has Been Executed in Texas.*

"Does your execution still bother you?" Spike asked.

"It's not being executed that bothers me. It's how. I just thought I would have more control over my own death," Elizabeth answered. "An execution tied to my tenth victim. A man connected to Texas oil, and I was put to death by lethal injection, strapped to a steel table in a Texas prison, and with only one person to witness: a woman I've never met before. One with a complete lack of soul. Now, all that remains of me is a short paragraph in a Napa Valley newspaper and a jar of ashes on my grandmother's fireplace mantle."

Elizabeth paused to think about the lie she had just offered. Although she never did meet the woman who entered the prison to offer her a secret pardon before, she remembered the woman from the cover of a magazine. The *Soldier of Fortune* magazine edition where the woman wore camouflage battle dress, carried an assault rifle, and stood next to Angar Einstok. Both of whom had stood with others on Peru's Altiplano.

"I know what you mean. They executed me the same way," Spike responded. "And had the same visitor: an Ivanka Trump look-alike who seemed like she completed two successful internships: one with the DMV and another with the IRS, which meant undergoing surgery to remove her soul and replace it with a complete lack of personality. Now, my ashes are sitting in my mom's garage, in the middle of Tennessee, under a pile of old denim. I would have liked to have gone out by sending M-203 grenades downrange at ISIS jerkwads with a Glock in my other hand." She paused for a moment before looking at Elizabeth inquisitively. "They convicted you for killing ten of your lovers. I hope that if I ever get you to switch teams, I won't be added to that tally."

Elizabeth smiled back at Spike. "Don't worry. There will never be any hope of that."

"What? Switching teams or pulling a Hillary Clinton?"

"Her name is Zelda."

Spike and Elizabeth turned their attention to the module five feet behind Spike. At Tiburón. He had left his module cover latched open but turned off the tiny lamp next to his head. Now, its glow hung about his head like a halo.

"Sorry to wake you," Spike said to Tiburón, before turning her attention back to Elizabeth.

"Wasn't sleeping. Just thinking. Anyway, her name is Zelda. Along with being Einstok's executive secretary, she can hold her own in the field. Just like Einstok's team of cutthroat mercenaries."

"His men have any bench?" Spike asked.

"Are you kidding? His team put the grrr in the term special operations-capable mercenary," Tiburón answered. "He doesn't go anywhere without them. Or her."

"You seem to know quite a bit about our *benefactor*," Elizabeth said. "More than one might read in a magazine article.

"I'm a hacker, and pretty good at it," Tiburón said. "Which explains why he had to go at great lengths to track me down and select me to join this little party. He was only able to track me last fall, which meant when it came the American judicial system, they chopped off my head, my ass, and served me up extra rare. Leaving my mother to spend an hour every day praying to *Santa Niño* and an urn filled with two pounds of ground-up plastic. Both surrounded by pictures of me in my *futbol* uniform."

"Didn't mean to bother you Tiburón," Spike apologized again.

"It's fine." Tiburón responded with a sigh. "I was just lying here thinking about how ironic it's been. For years, I smuggled drugs, guns, and humans across the border, and now I find myself smuggled off Earth. I remember lying on the table and looking at the doctor who had his hand on the switch that would send poison into my veins. Then, right before he flips the switch, he steps out of the room and Zelda saunters in. Standing there, lording over me with her tablet in her hand, and with that Zelda-from-the-Palace-of-Pain look, she asks if I prefer to die on this table or be willing to train for a secret mission, and die on Mars down the road?"

"And from that table," Spike added, "TETRA shuttled us about, in between our secret training phases on Earth, hidden in high-tech, life-support crates like crated-up IKEA wall-entertainment kits. The same crates that got us here."

"Well, however we feel about TETRA and the lady from the DMV," Elizabeth said, "they did their research and assembled one helluva group. For what, we don't know. But I do know I'd rather be here than in some urn on a fireplace mantle for real."

Elizabeth dropped her finger from the article. "Let's get some sleep."

"Aye, aye," Spike said, reaching out to unlatch the cover to Elizabeth's torpor module. Leaving Elizabeth to close her cover, Spike drifted past Finnegan sleeping in his module. She sighed. *If anybody could make her switch teams, albeit for just one night, it would be him.*

After watching Spike pause in front of Number Three's module before floating over to her own, Elizabeth turned out her module light, leaving her in darkness, to her own thoughts. Number Three was a good-looking man, and one with character. Elizabeth prided herself on her ability to read people, and she had already determined that he was a man she would have loved to have known on Earth. Her thoughts shifted to her grandmother. A woman who now shuffled about her house in Napa Valley. Alone. A woman who had lost both of her sons during her own life, and her only grandchild. A woman put to death for being a serial murderer. Thankfully, her grandmother never found out that one of her sons, Elizabeth's Uncle John, was Elizabeth's first victim.

Hours later, after a sound, nonmedically induced sleep, the astronauts found themselves back at the table.

Tiburón pulled apart the top of the plastic foil packet containing his breakfast of rehydrated ham and eggs. Steam from the heated bag curled up and around his doeskin complexion and thick black mustache, and the shark tattoo decorating his neck. "I don't mind rehydrated food, but I'm tired of having to use recycled piss and sweat to make it halfway edible. I can't wait to land so we can start making, or finding, real water."

"I agree," Elizabeth responded, "but I just want to be able to do something besides staring at gauges. And I've read all of the books and movies TETRA uploaded for us while on my watches. After we land, it will all be up to us to get Legoland up and running. I can't wait."

"This is shit," Tiburón said as he shoved a heaped spoonful of yellowish paste into his mouth. His black mustache snared a piece of it, and the tattoo of a mako shark outline pulsated on his neck muscles as he chewed the egg paste. "I wish there were cows on Mars. I could do with a freshly slaughtered *bistec*. Two inches thick and smothered with onions."

"Or at least the onions from your garden, Tiburón," Elizabeth said. Playing with the straw sticking out of her drink packet, she said pensively, "Something fresh."

The German, sitting in silence while holding a spoonful of egg paste in front of his face, caught Elizabeth's attention. It seemed to her that his mind had escaped their space-bound prison. "Are you okay?"

"*Ja*," Kroll answered with a sigh. "It is hard to appreciate decent food until you no longer have it. I remember making the best sausage and smoked meats. People came from as far away as Warsaw and Budapest to my bistro just to taste my sausages."

"And what was that sausage made from?" Spike asked warily.

"Ah," he said, turning his pudgy eyes toward the equipment lockers above his head and getting lost in his own thoughts. "The best Vestphalian, acorn- and truffle-fed, pork ground with just the right amount of freshly ground spices, and a Spaniard. Preferably an Andalusian. Or a Scandinavian."

He pushed that spoonful of egg paste into his mouth before continuing. "I must admit, though, I experimented. Associates kidnapped eastern Europeans, Polish mostly. They would gut them and sell the organs in the underground economy before selling me the flesh, which I fed to my swine on the farm I owned outside of Berlin. After living on that diet for a while, I would slaughter my stock and use their meat to make sausage without adding in human flesh. It made for an excellent breakfast. It also helped that I selected the best wood from the forest on my farm to smoke the meat and fuel my wood-fired stove. From trees I cut down myself. With my own axe. Like anything else in life, balance is necessary. To smoke the best meat, you need the proper wood. Oak, and wood from fruit trees: apple, pear, and cherry are the best. Wood properly cured."

With a smack of satisfaction on his lips, he dropped his eyes, turning them onto Elizabeth.

The appraising gaze in the German's eyes pushed her back into her chair. "Kroll, would it help if I told you my ancestors left Sweden in the 1880s and settled in northern Wisconsin."

"No worry," he said, wiping a finger across his upper lip. "You have good genes. I can tell."

"I have to ask," Spike interrupted. "Why just an Andalusian and a Swede? Why not a Frenchman? Don't they eat good, too?"

"*Nein*!" Kroll stated firmly, with a shake of his head. "The French would never do. Too many rich creams and desserts in their diet. They also smoke too much. Cigarettes taint the meat. However, much has been heralded about the Mediterranean diet, and the Swedish enjoy a good protein regime. And do not smoke as much."

"What about an American?" Spike asked. "What's wrong with a good old-fashioned, corn-fed American?"

Kroll recoiled, and his pudgy eyes closed as if struck by a severe spasm. "*Mien Gott*! Even cannibals have standards. Eating an American is like eating the cardboard cornflakes come in. All it would do is bind up my guts. I did have a colleague, though, who ate an American once. He had the runs for thirty-three days." Kroll looked back at Elizabeth. "I would, however, make an exception in your case."

"I'll take that as a compliment," she said. "That said, Spike, if I die before he does, do me a favor and kill him. I do not want to end up a coprolite for a future Martian colonist to find, or as part of his contribution to the compost in our mushroom bed."

"Sure, but what's a coprolite?" Spike asked.

"It's a fossilized turd," Finnegan responded crisply.

Everybody at the table turned to face him, including Elizabeth.

"I've been known to pick up an issue of *Archaeology Today* now and then," Finnegan stated.

Tiburón swallowed another spoonful of his breakfast and chimed in, interrupting Elizabeth's appraisal. "Count me in, too. The last thing I want is to be one of Kroll's bowel movements."

Spike looked at Kroll. "Why don't I just kill Kroll now? I can find something to use as a garrote or a shank."

Kroll looked at her blandly as he chewed.

Spike looked back at Kroll. "But I thought most Europeans were against the death penalty. Something about the Nazis gassing six million Jews. Anyway, so why'd the German government execute you?"

Kroll swallowed his mouthful of egg before answering. "I guess my crimes against humanity were too much for even the most progressive European."

Spike nodded. After pausing a second, she turned her eyes to everybody at the table.

"I know we've all thought about this before, but I'm still trying to figure out why our executions were faked and announced publicly while TETRA turns around and sneaks us to an undetectable training base under the lava fields of Iceland and trains us for a secret mission to Mars. We may be the first ones to set foot on the planet, but others are soon to follow. We'll have to explain our presence when they show up."

"I'm sure TETRA will have an excuse when the time arrives," Elizabeth interjected, "but I was to die by lethal injection for crimes against humanity. For real. I, for one, would rather die of old age with five strangers on Mars than a woman alone and in her forties on Earth."

Elizabeth turned her gaze to her module.

"I'm sure they will have some sort of excuse," Spike responded. Her eyes followed Elizabeth's and fell on her module. "But I'm also curious as to how TETRA was able to keep our training in Iceland, our transportation to a Mojave Desert spaceport then to a space station orbiting the moon, and our departure from there all a secret?"

"Are you kidding?" Tiburón scoffed. "TETRA, like other corporations and governments, has been overtly, and covertly, shipping all kinds of landers to Mars, mostly covertly. Prepping bases for the eventual arrival of humans."

"Some more of your computer hacking at work?" Elizabeth asked.

"Of course," he answered. "I've been keeping tabs on the military-industrial complex. The real government. The black or shadow government. You know, *they*."

"The same one President Eisenhower mentioned in one of his speeches back in the late fifties?" Elizabeth asked.

"The very same, but Eisenhower was at least twenty years too late," Tiburón stated.

"What do you mean twenty years too late?" Finnegan asked, mixing his breakfast with a plastic spoon. "You're talking about the FDR administration. During the thirties and WWII?"

Tiburón smiled as he answered Finnegan's question. "My friends have always accused me of being a conspiracy nutjob, but I've learned to pay attention, and not to what is being said on the BBC, CNN, or Fox News. You must learn to listen to what *they* are not saying. It takes focused intuition, targeted eavesdropping, and a shit-ton of research. While most Americans have heard about the military-industrial complex, most don't know of its real power. Or appreciate its depth behind American, and global society. Admirals and generals push for defense spending and research and development because they want a purpose, which includes playing soldier. Corporations and defense contractors have been pulling trillions of dollars, the dark money, out of the public cookie jar for decades, and once you get hooked on that kind of heroin, you just can't put the needle down. Lastly, politicians get to puff up their chests and inflate their egos by touting whatever *they* tell them to tout."

"Well, it sounds like your friends might've been on the right track," Spike chimed in with a smile. "But how does that include TETRA. And Einstok. Isn't he supposed to be a self-made billionaire?"

"From what the public is told, yes," Tiburón replied. "He started out as an underaged deck hand on his family's fishing boat and toughed out the North Atlantic's harshest weather. And that was before he reached puberty. By seventeen, he had earned his airplane pilot's license. He also qualified as a commercial hard-hat diver at eighteen, and finished his university studies, specializing in Viking archaeology, at nineteen. When he turned twenty, he filed his first patent."

"So, where did the billions come from?" asked Spike.

"Einstok created his billions from the other half of his life. A life kept hidden from the public," Tiburón said. "Making a living as a fishing boat captain is not a guaranteed income. Therefore, like skilled seafarers had done for hundreds of years, taking on side work was never an issue. He helped his father and grandfather smuggle cigarettes and alcohol past customs officials and into Iceland. And that was before he turned eight. By the time he became of legal age, he had graduated to narcotics, firearms, illegals, and survived a dozen shoot outs with navies and law enforcement agencies from Canada to northern Europe. When he turned twenty-one, he got involved with artifact smuggling. By then, though, he had learned the real-world side of business. Tutorials not lost on a simple mind."

"Now, I know you grew up under a cell phone tower," Spike added. "How do you know all this crap?"

"First of all, I learned to drive semi-trucks when I was twelve, and I've been making my living as a smuggler since I turned fourteen, and smugglers know smugglers. Second, this 'crap' has surrounded us for years. It's just a matter of filtering out the noise. Once you do that, then you will see the truth. If *they* can keep all that a secret, then getting us off Earth and onto the surface of Mars is simple. I also know who killed JFK, that the US Navy is covering up UFO encounters from twenty-nineteen, where all of Hillary's victims are buried, who D. B. Cooper really was, that the Egyptian and Mesoamerican pyramids, especially Teotihuacán just outside of Mexico City, served as power stations for alien spaceships, and the fact that Roosevelt knew exactly, to the hour, when the Japanese were going to bomb Pearl Harbor. To cover up illegal government spending and the start of the Deep State. While every president starting with FDR has passed down the Book of Secrets or started their own, so did I."

Listening to Tiburón, Elizabeth kept an eye on the hatch that sealed off the tunnel leading to the command module. Where Manwaring sequestered himself as often as possible.

"While those who lord over us millions of miles away may have their own Book of Secrets," Tiburón continued, "I've got a feeling Manwaring has his. Whether it's millions of miles away from here or mere feet from us and locked up in his head, it doesn't matter."

There was silence while everyone reflected on what they were about to do—the history they were making, the mere secrecy of the mission rolled a pall over any thoughts of historic achievements. After a few seconds, a distant smile broke out on Elizabeth's face.

"What are you smiling about?" Spike asked.

"Nothing really. I just thought about a school play I was in when I was a little girl. One based on that old Christmas show *The Island of Misfit Toys*."

"Yeah," Spike said. "I remember that one. It was about an island where all the screwed-up toys made in Santa's shop were dumped. Left alone and unloved."

"That's the one," Elizabeth responded.

"Well, for some reason," Spike said, "I'm thinking about the movie *The Dirty Dozen*."

"I know that movie," mused Tiburón. "Psychotic killers convicted of heinous crimes and offered a chance at survival in exchange for killing a bunch of German generals."

"Hey, I'm not psychotic," Elizabeth said with a wry smile. "I was, am, of sound mind and body, and knew exactly what I was doing. The State of Texas proved that which is why they executed me."

Tiburón sipped his coffee. "A gay German cannibal and a mass murderer. All of us convicted mass murderers."

"I am not a mass murderer," Spike said. "My commander gave me actionable information, which meant taking out an orphanage full of wanted terrorists. I went ahead and laid enough explosives to demolish that orphanage and everyone in it. However, my commander's info turned out to be sour. There were no terrorists. Just a few low-level scumbags holding Coptic Christians hostage. The world court of public opinion hauled Triple-Canopy International Security in before the bench, and they had to throw somebody under the bus. They even made up a fake file on me. Documenting my *uncontrollable urge to kill*." She paused for a second. "I should've stayed in the Corps. There, I was a qualified scout sniper, an experienced sapper, and capable of driving any military vehicle with a coat of camouflage paint on it. At least I knew who filled my rice bowl, and I knew who had my six."

"Well," Elizabeth chimed in, "I, for one, am guilty as sin, just as Kroll is guilty as sin. But you're saying you're here because of misguided political pressure, and the fact that you're a minority twice over."

"That's why I'm here," Tiburón jumped in.

"Because you're Mexican?" Spike asked.

Tiburón sighed. "They could've hung me on any number of crimes if they wanted to, but the one I was convicted of was letting one hundred and ten illegals die of suffocation and heatstroke in the back of my tractor-trailer in an Arizona canyon. Although I spent equal parts of my life on both sides of the border, I'm a Mexican citizen, and Mexico does not have the death penalty. Just like Germany, but just like Kroll, my government had no problem with executing me. It seemed as if they were obeying orders from the American government. Or somebody else."

"Did you do that?" Spike asked. "Leave those people in that trailer?"

Tiburón smiled sardonically. "I've been committing crimes my entire life, but I got convicted for one I didn't do. Another man, TJ, and I were smuggling a truckload of illegals into Las Vegas, but an Arizona State Police helicopter spooked us. We hid the semi in a ravine, and I told TJ to unlock the back doors as I was busy looking at our escape route. He said he did, and we lit out. Hours later, the state police on ATVs jumped us and ended up getting in a gun battle. TJ died in the shootout, and the state police found our cargo. All dead. My partner never let them out. He was white and dead, and I was Mexican and alive, so I got left holding the bag."

"So, that means of the six of us, you two are the only innocent ones here," Finnegan said, squishing his near-empty foil packet. "But we were all convicted for crimes against humanity and convicted by unknown pressures. What I'm saying is *they* did not just scoop us up like floor sweepings. We are here out of design."

"Which means we're The Dirty Half Dozen," Spike said with a half-smile.

"Well, I don't know about what fatal credentials each of us hold," Tiburón interjected, "but in my case, while I've always been a good operator, nimble with my mind, and handy with the steel, *they* knew I was getting a bit too wise, and too close, so I agree that we are not just your average floor sweepings."

Elizabeth watched as they fell silent and tended to their egg-and-ham-paste breakfast, foil-drink packets, and the thoughts in their heads. Their eyes had a distant stare including Elizabeth. While the State of Texas executed her for the murder she had committed in Texas, she knew they also executed her for the murders she had committed elsewhere. And rightfully so. After another spoonful of egg paste and a moment to reflect, Spike turned to Elizabeth. "Well, it looks like we're finally getting a chance to know each other, but what about His Royal Douchebag? He looks like your average dorky archaeologist, who could get lost at his own dig. I can't imagine him floating to the surface in the same cesspool as us. Didn't you know him from before?"

"I started on my first degree at sixteen, a BA in forensic anthropology, and declared a minor. In Mesoamerican studies. Back then, though, you couldn't take a single class about Mesoamerica without coming across Manwaring in one shape or form. He was quite the authority and top in his field, and because of my academic record, I was able to get a seat in two of his classes when he was a visiting professor for two semesters. But that was years ago. Since then, rumors of his sexual proclivities started to surface. At one point, about every police department from Mexico City to Bogotá wanted to talk to him. The final straw came when the police in Belize City questioned him about the body of a strangled prostitute. That incident went from questioning to execution in the blink of an eye."

"All I know," Spike continued, "is that he treats us like we have leprosy, and the only exposure we've had with him was right at the start of this mission while under the Icelandic lava fields, our time in the Mojave Desert, and our departure from lunar orbit. Since you are the mission co-commander, you're the only one with any sort of time spent with him. Why doesn't he want anything to do with us?"

"I don't know," Elizabeth responded, "but I do remember from his classes, and by reputation, that he did come off as a pretentious snob. And not because of his British accent. He had a terrible ego."

"Well, that was then," Spike answered, "but now is now, and he can get off his high horse. When we get to Mars, we'll all be buried up to our necks together in the same dung heap."

Elizabeth agreed with their assessment, but she wondered what fatal qualification secured her a seat on this mission to Mars. Although she knew she was blessed with looks and brains at birth, she never let those attributes go to her head. But somehow, after all those years and all those students, Manwaring seemed to remember her. How or why he remembered her, she could not fathom, but she thanked him for saving her life. And for what reason, she did not know, but she knew she would find out.

Day of landing, mid-April, AD2026

The astronauts spent the last *sol* in space conducting vital tasks starting with going over the landing procedures and practicing emergency drills. Although TETRA would control the landing, the crew needed to be proficient in the event of emergencies. During their one month of training under Iceland's lava fields on Earth Manwaring, and the others, did spend hours on a simulator practicing for this very day, but that was many millions of miles ago.

The six Martian astronauts sat enveloped in their assigned seats. TETRA built the seats with spacesuits and environmental backpacks in mind, but now, they wore only their company-issue clothing. Manwaring sat in the left seat, the mission commander's seat, and supervised the drills to the point of irritation. Elizabeth sat in the right seat: the assistant mission commander position. Directly behind her seat, the mission's systems specialist performed his duties. Finnegan monitored the life-support and landing systems on the control panel mounted to the command/lander capsule's bulkhead to his right. Spike, Tiburón, and Kroll followed along with the drills as backup to Manwaring, Elizabeth, and Finnegan, occupied the remaining three seats. They all flipped through loosely bound instruction binders with thick plastic pages.

Slogging through their drills, they glanced at the monitor above the spacecraft's console board and watched the image of Mars consume the black interior of the framed rectangle screen. When they finally flipped over the last plastic page in their binders, for the sixth time, Manwaring set his eyes on the screen in front of them. "Let's get our kits together. TETRA has started our countdown."

The others obeyed his orders, and all of them started in on the next task, which involved cramming the landing capsule full of supplies in case the habitation stage, landing separately, failed to reach the surface intact, or was destroyed upon landing.

Like submariners preparing for a war patrol, the astronauts stuffed their precious few personal items, cases of prepackaged food and water, spare parts, tools, and equipment into the landing capsule's lockers, cubbies, nooks, and crannies. They even crammed vacuum-sealed packets of compressed organic waste, including used coffee grounds, tea leaves, and recovered fecal matter into the space under their seats. What they could not take with them would remain aboard the habitation stage. Once abandoned by its passengers, TETRA controllers would control not only the landing of the command capsule but their living quarters as well. The modules in the habitation stage sustained their lives during their voyage to Mars, but once on Mars, those modules would become their caskets.

TETRA would send the engine stage past Mars. With it being the only real working stage of the ship, and out of fuel, it will have served its purpose. TETRA will have collected over six months of operational data from it, allowing them to build a second-generation version of that engine, with upgrades, and once past Mars, TETRA would detonate it remotely.

Once the astronauts had filled every available centimeter of usable space, each person floated to their modules to suit up for the landing. They carefully slipped on their fabric spacesuits one limb at a time. The white suits, designed by TETRA, were lightweight and flexible in design, but rugged in construction. Orangish pads were sewn onto the knee and elbow joints, and over their shoulders. While allowing the wearer to bend and squat, the suits could withstand almost any rigor placed on them.

TETRA had tailor made and numbered each suit for their wearers before leaving Earth, based on the assumption that they would lose weight during space travel and recover it on the Martian surface. The only exception was Kroll. He weighed over five hundred pounds, but after a month of training on Earth, and after months in space, he'd lost over three hundred of those and now the unfilled portions of the suit floated away from his body. He resembled one of those old-time hard-hat divers with their loose-fitting rubberized canvas and leather dive suits. While that suit would suffice for now, another suit, created in anticipation of him losing weight was stowed behind a locker door within the lander's bulkhead.

Once they'd sealed themselves into their spacesuits, they grabbed their helmets. Made entirely from clear acrylic and backed with a rounded piece of white plastic on the inside, allowing for padding, the spheres offered a great deal of peripheral vision. With their helmets in one hand, they floated from their home and through the tunnel. The last person out of the habitation stage was Elizabeth, who only stopped long enough to give their home for the last several months one final look before reaching for the hatch sealing them into the lander/control stage.

Since their landing procedure was all up to TETRA it would only take one signal from Manwaring to tell them they were sealed in the lander stage, and all was ready for their historic landing. As Elizabeth entered their lander capsule, she saw Manwaring's gloved hand type that same message onto the mission commander's keyboard.

"Right," said Manwaring. "Let's conduct our environmental and communications systems check."

As ordered, everybody donned their helmets and twisted them until they heard the seals in the neck click into place. Once sealed, they lifted the plastic dust covers protecting the rectangular-shaped keyboard and screen built into their spacesuit sleeves. Though they wore gloves, their covered fingers were nimble enough, and the buttons large enough so they could operate the minicomputer. They pushed the Open button, which allowed for group communication, and tapped the Select button, which allowed each astronaut to tap a number on their keypads and speak only with the person assigned that number.

As Elizabeth completed her comms checks, she could not help but notice her shipmate's voices. "Hey guys, we're about to make history, and you all sound like you're schlepping off to another shift at the coal mine."

"What do you expect," Tiburón answered. "We're making history, but do you think my mom will ever hear about it?"

"No. I guess not," Elizabeth replied. "I doubt any mother will hear about what we're about to do." Elizabeth thought for a moment about her disappointed grandmother, but her thoughts were interrupted by Finnegan's voice coming over her helmet's inside speaker.

"Shit!" Finnegan blurted out. The console next to his seat became active. Lights the size of pencil erasers started to blink, and codes and numbers flashed across the monitor screen. "What the fuck!"

"What's wrong?" Manwaring blurted out, turning to look behind him over his shoulder at Finnegan.

Repeatedly pushing a button on his console, Finnegan answered. "Shit! There's something wrong with the Number Two stabilizer rocket."

"Is that a bad thing?" Elizabeth asked, keeping her eyes on the console in front of her.

"If it doesn't fire when it's supposed to, it'll throw us out of our glidepath. We'll end up splinters on the Martian surface!"

"Can't TETRA fix it?" Manwaring shouted as he started to see readings on his console go awry.

Finnegan threw his hands up at his console and unbuckled his seatbelt. "Too much of a time delay! It'll only take a second to throw us out of whack."

Throwing himself out of his seat, he dove headfirst, past Spike and Kroll, who occupied the compartment's last two seats, and opened the compartment's rear hatch. He disappeared into the space behind them.

Tiburón, sitting opposite Finnegan and observing his drills, moved to occupy the vacant seat. Spike and Kroll remained in their seats as their eyes darted from the system specialist's console to the mission commander's console.

"Ain't sure what I'm supposed to do," Tiburón said as he buckled himself into Finnegan's seat. He reached for the drill booklet stuck in the back of Elizabeth's seat. "What page is this drill on?"

Before Manwaring could answer, Finnegan's helmeted head reappeared. "Fixed it."

Elizabeth focused on the instruments on her own console and glancing at the instruments in front of Manwaring, saw that things were indeed settling out. "That was quick."

"Now that we're on the surface of Mars, we have a moment to breathe," Elizabeth said to everyone through her intercom.

They found themselves standing in the center of an expansive, rust-colored depression roughened with reddish rocks and gravel of varying sizes. The slightly concaved surface reached out for a kilometer before rising to join the flat surface of the Martian plain. That plain, continuing eastward, reached a dull, orange-blue horizon kilometers away. Above that reddish line, a distant sun appeared strangely small and produced a subdued, yellowish glow. Opposite that horizon, behind Elizabeth and the others, the rise of a mountain range began immediately at the lip of the depressed surface.

Elizabeth looked over at Finnegan and saw the rising peaks of a red mountain range stretch across the horizon behind him. "Where the hell did you learn to become an expert on emergency spaceship repair? Crazy Habib's School of Rocket Repair and Dental Surgery of Greater Karachi, Pakistan?"

"Like most things in life," Finnegan replied, "technology is based on the fundamentals. So once you've solved one problem, any subsequent problem is easier to recognize and overcome. That's the boring part of fixing rocket ships that are about to blow us to smithereens when we're about to land on Mars. Also, there's nothing wrong with the proper, and timely, application of duct tape, and a plastic straw to save said multibillion-dollar spaceship."

Elizabeth, like the others, accepted Finnegan's dismissive reply with cheerful relief while inspecting their lander. With the broad base of the lander resting on the Martian surface, three collapsed orange-white parachutes dangling from the ship's nose by yards of parachute cord stretched away from the capsule's hull. The hull, conical-shaped and stained gray by the built-in side retro rockets, helped, along with the parachutes, to ease them into position for a soft landing.

"Well, thank God for the inventors of duct tape and plastic straws," Elizabeth said. She turned her head and panned her eyes across the flat surface around them.

"So, this is what a dry lakebed on Mars looks like," Spike said. "Is that why TETRA picked this spot?"

"Technically," Tiburón answered, "a geomorphologist would refer to it as a deflation basin, meaning that particulates, because of wind, water, gravity, minor tremors, or even full-blown Marsquakes, funneled down from the mountains, accelerated further deposition. Thus, creating a hard-packed surface. A form of desert pavement perfect for the landing of spacecraft, and an ideal setting for a base."

"So, it's an empty lakebed on Mars," Finnegan retorted.

"Hey, I'm only repeating what TETRA taught me. As the mission botanist, I needed to know something about geology," Tiburón responded. He paused to bend over and pick up a rock at his feet. Raising the reddish rock in the palm of his hand up and down to evaluate its weight, he turned west toward the row of mountains.

A narrow, sloping rise occupied the space between the lip of the lakebed and the base of the mountains, which they knew as the Coronae Montes. Rough-cut gullies and ravines, angling sideways, emptied into the broad ribbon of a dry riverbed, which sliced the rise in half. Pointing with the rock in his hand, Tiburón continued, "This rock came from there, back when water once flowed on Mars. When that was, who knows, but I do know there are caves up there, and I can't wait to get up there and set up our bomb shelter."

Turning back to the lakebed, he leaned to one side and launched the rock in his hand, as if he were skipping a stone across a pond.

"What do you mean bomb shelter?" Kroll asked. "Are we going to be attacked?"

"No," Tiburón answered as he bent forward. "It's just a phrase. You know, like having an Alamo, bat cave, or war room. Anyway, the greenhouses I'm going to build on the surface will be exposed to micrometeorites and radiation, which will destroy them at some point. Building a greenhouse in a cave or sheltered area in those mountains will provide an emergency source of food and a sheltered retreat. A place advantageous for its defenders."

"Who keeps the high ground wins, right?" Finnegan asked.

"Exactly," Tiburón responded still bent forward while looking for another stone. "Also, you always need a place to keep your information safe. Just in case something happens."

"You make it sound like we're about to be attacked by spaceborne CIA operatives gone rogue," Spike retorted.

"Don't laugh," Tiburón warned, finding another palm-sized stone. "Einstok brought us here for a reason."

"So, do you have a bomb shelter back on Earth?" Manwaring asked, surveying the nearby mountain range.

Elizabeth wasn't sure if the others heard it, but listening to Manwaring's voice through her helmet's earphone speaker, she sensed a hidden reasoning or purpose in his question.

"Three, in fact," Tiburón answered, hefting the stone in his gloved hand. "With two of them being red herrings. And all three booby trapped."

While Spike, Kroll, and Finnegan watched the Mexican finger the stone in his hand, Elizabeth's eyes followed Manwaring's. Accepting Tiburón's response, their mission commander set his eyes on the distant sun.

"The sky," Elizabeth said. "It reminds me of a winter afternoon in Northern

California: distant sun, short days, and vague sunlight. All so depressing. I remember my grandmother always made meals with mushrooms in it on days like that."

"Your grandmother knew what she was doing," Finnegan answered, turning his eyes toward the sky. "Short winter days equals the lack of vitamin D. That's what affects our brains and moods, as well as our bones. I grew up in New England, so I should know. Since we've vacuum sealed all our shit the last so many millions of miles, we'll have plenty of mushrooms when Tiburón gets our greenhouses operational."

"Well then," Tiburón said. "Let's get at it."

"Okay," said Elizabeth, "but remember to pace yourselves. Our bones are compromised, and it will be some time before we're fully acclimated."

Turning their attention to their immediate surroundings, Elizabeth and the others viewed TETRA's prestaging efforts. During their training, TETRA showed them maps and images of the base. Though TETRA assigned the base its own name, Spike called it Legoland. The name stuck. Now, on Mars, they found themselves among a collection of Lego pieces. Toys left behind by an invisible child's hand on the backyard sandbox. Some toys were more worse for wear than others.

Running in a rough line from north to south, four square-shaped habitation modules, spaced about ten meters apart from each other, rested on jointed support legs with hard-rubber wheels. The wheel and suspension system kept the modules about three feet, or one meter, off the reddish Martian soil. The remnants of parachutes and their attachment cords littered the area. Already briefed on the purpose of each module, the astronauts nicknamed each module during their training, starting with the module labeled Number One. The Kype or Keep. The subsequent living modules included The Hilton, The Office, and The Garage, each with a single-digit number stenciled on the sides. Starting tomorrow, it would be Spike's job to move the structures closer and join them with flexible, aboveground tunnel kits. Once fully activated, each module will display rotating beacons in its own color to provide reference to anybody on the surface at night.

To the west, other modules profiled themselves like disjointed railroad cars in a *Road Runner* cartoon, each one built for a specific purpose and stuffed with specific items. Four of them contained wheeled machines. Each meant for a certain job on Mars.

At the end of the profile, their living quarters squatted patiently on the Martian surface, along with its recently deployed parachute, waiting for its next task as their morgue, and their modules their caskets. Like all the other deposited containers, it too received a moniker.

"So, it's officially Boot Hill now," Tiburón stated. "I hope we don't need to put it to use too soon."

"Not if I can help it," Elizabeth responded. "But I can't put off the inevitable."

"Just remember to save the last stitch for the nose," Finnegan said.

Everybody turned toward Finnegan, but it was Elizabeth who answered the question on their faces.

"What he is referring to is a custom from the old sailing days. Back then, when sailors died of disease or combat, their shipmates wrapped their bodies in the hammocks they slept in. With the addition of a cannon ball to weigh the body, the last stitch, after sewing up the hammock, went through the bone between the nostrils. Just to make sure they were, in fact, dead."

Elizabeth gave Finnegan a wink as she finished. "Just as long as we don't end up like people in *Soylent Green*," Tiburón replied, still hefting the stone in his hand. "I don't care what happens to my body. They can study it all they want."

"Was that a movie?" Spike asked.

"Early seventies movie. About an overpopulated Earth, scarce resources, government deception, and turning dead humans into crackers to feed the living." Tiburón tilted his helmeted head toward Kroll. "Sorry."

"It was just a movie," Kroll responded.

"Yeah. Right," Tiburón said. He hefted the stone again and looked away from Boot Hill to survey the rest of the storage modules.

"Well," Manwaring said, taking his eyes from the dry riverbed running down from the mountain, "I'd say we bless our fortune to have survived a half a year in space and be the first humans landing on another planet. So, let's get busy."

Tiburón raised the stone still in his hand and pointed to the mountain range. "They remind me of the Superstition Mountains outside of Phoenix. Mountains I took advantage of more than once. I can't wait to get up in those mountains. And down to the other side of them."

"Why?" Spike asked. "What's on the other side?"

"Cydonia. Home to Martian pyramids, and the face of Mars."

Tiburón, lowering his hand and holding the rock, paused as he faced blank stares.

"I'm sure Tiburón will fill us in later on," Elizabeth chimed in. "Meanwhile, Manwaring, where are our neighbors?"

"Our nearest neighbor, The God's Fist of Thunderous Harmony, a.k.a., Little Beijing, is on the other side of those mountains about two hundred and fifty kilometers away. Base Europa is about one hundred kilometers further to the north, and the Iranian/North Korean base camp is even farther north. By another hundred kilometers. But I would not expect to have neighbors too soon. While TETRA has been staging this site these last few years, the Chinese have only just started, as they were more interested in setting up a station on the moon to compete with TETRA's efforts, and the Europeans and Iranians are just now catching up."

"I can't believe how quiet everything is," Kroll said.

"Currently, Mars has, and has had for a great deal of time, an insignificant atmosphere with only about two percent oxygen," Manwaring answered, "and with such a minimal atmosphere, there can be no wind or any storms despite what you see in the movies. Now, again, we're here, and we have a job to do."

"Finnegan," Manwaring said. "Climb back up the lander from habitations stages and deploy the solar panels and antennae. And detach the parachutes for future use. Tiburón, Kroll, and Spike pull out the ladder kit and assemble it for the lander stage. Elizabeth, follow me. We'll inspect the habitation modules."

Finnegan snorted as he turned to look at Manwaring. "Haven't you ever heard of the word 'please'? TETRA may have put you in charge of this expedition, but there is no point in treating us like peons."

Manwaring returned Finnegan's glare. "Elizabeth!"

Without waiting for a response, he turned from the rest of the astronauts, and the others turned in resignation to fulfill their duties. Spike raised a gloved middle finger at Manwaring's back. Tiburón shrugged his shoulders, then raised his hand to skip his stone. "What the hell?"

The others stopped and returned their attention to Tiburón. But it was Elizabeth who spoke. "What's that, Tiburón?"

Tiburón raised his hand to show everybody the rock in his hand. Another reddish-tinted rock about the size and shape of an avocado but cracked in half lengthwise. "Doesn't that look like a swastika?"

Stepping closer, everybody focused on the rock's flat surface. On its textured face, right where the seed of the avocado would be, they saw what looked like a partial swastika pressed into it.

Finnegan spoke up. "Yeah, it looks like a swastika to me. Along with a couple of letters on either side to boot. They could be R and K, but I ain't sure."

"And you should know," Elizabeth said. Finnegan gave her a sideways look. Embarrassed, she kept her eyes on the rock. "What I mean is that, since you are a military historian and all."

"It does look like a Nazi swastika," Manwaring threw in, as he snatched the rock from Tiburón's gloved palm. "But it is just an impression. One left behind as the rock exfoliated away from a bigger piece. Tiburón, as you work on your excavation to erect our greenhouses, I am sure you will find other such examples of nature at work. Now, let's get to work."

To end their conversation, Manwaring raised his hand and flung the stone toward the profiled line of pre-staged container modules. Drooping his arm, he stepped toward The Keep.

Shrugging their shoulders, they fell to their duties. Elizabeth fell in step behind Manwaring and turned in time to see Finnegan looking in the same direction Manwaring threw the rock. However, they were all so lost in their own thoughts that they all failed to see the shaking of Manwaring's gloved fingers. Even Elizabeth, who was walking behind Manwaring, did not notice the twitching fingers, but she did notice a sudden change in his voice over their helmets' speaker system. Though always terse in his demeanor toward the others, his voice seemed even harsher in tone. Keeping her step, she looked briefly back over her shoulder again at the mission's system specialist. Finnegan had turned to climb up the landing stage's handholds and footholds built into the side. He opened the round hatchway on the side, which led to an airlock inside and aft or now under of the capsule's cockpit. He entered the hatchway and shut it behind him as Spike, Kroll, and Tiburón stepped up to the base of the lander and opened a rectangular door flush with the side of the lander.

Just like the luggage compartment on a bus or RV, Tiburón pulled at the handle on the end of an aluminum box snugly secured inside the recess. As he pulled it, Spike reached out to support the box until the other end came out and she could grab the handle. Lowering it to the Martian surface, Tiburón bent to open the hinged lid. Pulling out two wrenches and a container of nuts and bolts, he handed them to Kroll before reaching for sections of the aluminum staircase that they were to assemble and bolt to the side of the command module.

Stopping to catch their breaths, covers high up on the capsule's fuselage popped open and rectangular-shaped solar panels and disk-shaped antenna unfolded themselves. While the crewmembers busied themselves, Elizabeth and Manwaring walked toward The Keep.

"Looks like our home made it just fine," Elizabeth interjected.

Manwaring did not answer. Instead, he approached the base of the square-shaped stage, just under the closed rectangular door. "Let's have a butchers."

He pushed against a panel, which popped open after removing his hand. Lifting the hinged cover, they saw a hand-sized monitor and a keypad next to it. He punched in a code, and the monitor screen started to fill with numbers. "Looks like the oxygen producing machine is in good nick: seventy-two degrees Fahrenheit or twenty-two degrees Celsius, a positive internal pressure, and it looks like the OPM was able to extract enough oxygen, argon, and nitrogen from the Martian atmosphere to create an internal atmosphere breathable for us. And the module's batteries have been keeping a good charge."

The built-in solar panel, visible higher up on their side of the module and partially sheltered by two open half doors, was covered with a little bit of dust.

"Then what are you waiting for?" Elizabeth said as she pulled up next to Manwaring. Now, being able to see his face, she noticed something different in Manwaring's eyes. They seemed wider and brighter.

"Hold on," Manwaring said, stepping to the side and pushing his gloved hand against a panel flush with its side. It popped open. Elizabeth, you start putting the staircase together. I'll assess the rest of the modules."

He stepped off without waiting for a reply.

Douchebag, she thought, as she obeyed the orders and moved to pull out the aluminum box. As she did, she thought about the change in his voice when he responded to the swastika question, and the look in his eyes just a minute ago. *Did something just happen in the last five minutes?*

An hour later, five astronauts crowded around the center table inside The Keep. Their helmets and spacesuit gloves occupied the room's only table, along with a complete coffee serving set and a bottle of open red wine. The sixth astronaut, Manwaring, sat with his back to others as he tapped away on a keyboard at a built-in computer desk. Around the astronauts was the overwhelming amount of equipment and locker space built into The Keep's interior. The habitation module of the spacecraft that brought them to Mars now seemed palatial compared to what could only be described as an overstuffed interior of a high-tech camping pod.

"Now this is more like it," Tiburón sighed as he sniffed at the aroma of freshly brewed coffee filling the module. He reclined in a chair with a flexible back and held a ceramic coffee cup in his hands. In front of him, and next to his helmet and gloves, a serving set complete with a tray, a matching sugar bowl and cream container, and silver spoons occupied the space. "I'm drinking real coffee, made from real water, and from a real ceramic cup."

A drop of black coffee fell from the end of his mustache, landing on the front of his spacesuit.

Elizabeth, enjoying a glass of wine, related to the relaxation in his dark eyes.

"It tastes like plastic," Spike responded as she spooned more sugar into her coffee.

"As long as I can drink from a real coffee cup, I won't complain," Tiburón responded with a soft sigh. "The secret is in the cup. How's the wine?"

While Tiburón and Spike decided to brew a pot of coffee and enjoy the coffee set, Finnegan, Elizabeth, and Kroll opted for a glass of merlot. Built in among the module's equipage was a single-door pantry stuffed with a variety of items, including two cases of red wine and a set of proper wine glasses.

"I can honestly state that this wine is the best I've had in months, and I am glad TETRA took the time to select proper glasses to pair with a rather decent merlot." Elizabeth replied. Savoring a sip of wine from a Riedel Ouverture red wine glass, she pulled the glass from her lips. "Thoughtful for TETRA to provide a sliver of civilization to assuage the rigors of living on Mars. That said, I cannot wait to get the greenhouses up and running. There is something about growing your own grapes and producing your own wine. I should know."

"I agree," Tiburón said, pointing at the palm-sized, cellophane-wrapped packet of marijuana next to his helmet. "But why couldn't TETRA have taken the time to score some decent weed. They spent billions on this place and even found the right kind of wine glasses, coffee cups, and stirring spoons, yet they gave me this ditch weed."

"Didn't you bring your own seeds?" Spike asked.

"I did, but I'll have to smoke what TETRA placed in the inventory until I can grow my own."

"Well, you're more than welcome to enjoy TETRA's bounty," Elizabeth said, "but until the time comes for you to reap your own harvests, you'll need to ration what TETRA provided."

While speaking, Elizabeth noticed that Manwaring had lost the bright look that possessed his eyes an hour ago and returned to his normal, haughty self. Now, he sat with his back to their merriment.

"And while I understand the restorative and medical benefits of marijuana, red wine, and coffee," Elizabeth continued, "especially since we've been in space for several months and exposed to solar radiation and will continue to be exposed while here on the surface, I need to monitor out daily intake. To build a medical algorithm."

"I'll smoke to that," Tiburón said, lifting his coffee mug and tapping the packet of weed with his index finger.

Manwaring made some final taps on the keyboard and turned to face his fellow astronauts. He pointed to the kitchenette just outside the reach of his left hand. Next to the pantry door was a short, waist-high countertop with a pair of cupboards above it and two doors beneath it. Aside from the built-in coffee pot was a faucet, sink, and microwave.

"Tiburón, we are not finished with recycled water. TETRA provided two water tanks per module that hold two hundred liters each, which is the reason it tastes like plastic. But that will eventually run out. All our waste—solid or liquid—will drain to the automatic recycling unit. Everything from piss to coffee grounds to fecal matter will be macerated and pumped into that storage tank, which is accessed from outside each module."

Manwaring looked at Tiburón. "Since you are our mission botanist, it will be your task to empty those tanks daily and turn their contents into potting soil. The liquids will be automatically distilled back into potable water."

Tiburón responded. "I'm the only Mexican on the planet, and I get stuck with shoveling shit."

Manwaring ignored Tiburón's remark. "Finnegan, after our aperitif, start on your task. According to TETRA, there should be a layer of embedded ice just meters under our feet. Now, let me finish the grand tour."

He stopped to lean in between Elizabeth and Finnegan and grabbed the open wine bottle and an empty glass. Pouring himself a portion, he nodded his head toward the side of the module opposite the pantry, kitchenette, and water closet, or toilet.

"Our oxygen producing machine is capable of extracting and compressing needed trace gases, including oxygen, from the Martian atmosphere. It keeps the module's oxygen tanks fully charged and our internal atmosphere breathable and pressurized like Earth's. Each module also has two charging stations for our environmental backpacks when we're not wearing them. It also keeps spare oxygen bottles charged and ready for use."

The others turned to inspect the two open, closet-like stations where they could hang their suits and helmets, and the hoses and connection fittings needed to recharge their environmental backpacks. To the left of the stations was a doorway with rounded corners, which would allow them to walk from one module to the next.

"Once Spike has tweaked the modules into position, she will assemble the tunnels to connect the habitation modules and wire up the intercom system so we can walk and communicate between modules. Now, all of us have used the airlock to get into The Keep, so you are aware of its operation. Just remember, since the exterior and inner doors are electrically connected, one door cannot be opened unless the other door is secure."

Elizabeth and the others turned to look at the inner airlock door and its orange-sized window at head level. They also inspected the built-in features on either side of it.

"All of us have specific duties. My duty, aside from being the mission commander, is to collect physical scientific data, which will require me to be away from this base for hours a day. And to check in with TETRA on a regular basis."

Manwaring stopped to point at the bunkbeds, with lockers under the bottom bunk, to the right of the airlock's inner door. "I'll sleep here."

The bunkbed system was not like the narrow beds one might have expected. The bunks were wider, another creature comfort afforded by TETRA. To the left side of the inner airlock door was a shelving system with suitcase-sized aluminum containers secured in their storage cubbies.

"Well, I am the mission botanist," Tiburón said, "which means I'll need to stretch my legs as well."

Manwaring sighed. "I doubt any of you want to spend the next few years stuck inside these modules, and there will be time for exploration. But we all have duties requiring your attention at this base for the next few weeks. Anything you need to fulfill your immediate priorities is in the modules around us. Leave it to me to prospect for useful materials. Exposed to the temperature extremes on the Martian surface and spaceborne micrometeorites, these modules will last only so long, so finding construction materials is my priority. Of course, one reason humans refer to Mars as the Red Planet is the overabundance of iron oxide on its surface, which we can use for later construction. I will also prospect for other metals such as aluminum, magnesium, and the like."

"Well," Tiburón said, "if you happen to run across any gold, silver, or platinum let me know. I'm not one to turn my nose up at precious metals."

Manwaring paused before answering. "The word 'precious' is relative here on Mars. When I am not in the field collecting samples, or here in The Keep, I will be in my laboratory module, The Westing House, experimenting with my collections. Again, all of us have specific tasks that TETRA expects us to complete and are vital to our survival. Spike, starting tomorrow, you will use The Beast to tweak our four habitation modules into position so you can start connecting them. Once you complete that task, you can start plowing trenches for the greenhouses."

Spike nodded in acknowledgment.

"Tiburón," Manwaring said. "You help Spike. Kroll, your chores are domestic, but since the greenhouses tie in with food production, you will assist Tiburón when needed."

Kroll answered, without looking up from the wine in his hands. "*Ja*."

"Finnegan, other than drilling for water sources, you'll be busy keeping all of our equipment in good nick."

Finnegan responded by jutting his chin slightly.

Manwaring turned to Elizabeth. "While our duties are important, yours may be more so. TETRA requires constant updates on how our space travel has affected our bodies and how our current environment is affecting us as well. With that information, TETRA can better prepare future astronauts for their missions here. It is your assignment to keep track of our diet and to monitor both our medical and psychological status and provide that information to me so I can send it to TETRA. In addition, you need to be on hand to assist with medical emergencies. For that reason, you will restrict your activities to the medical field so as not to risk injuries. You can also assist Kroll with his domestic duties."

She looked up at Manwaring. "You know, if we were back on Earth, there would be a whole line of women waiting to kick your ass for that comment."

"Well," he said, "I'm just trying to be pragmatic."

"I'm happy just being alive, being able to grow weed, and being able to enjoy a decent cup of coffee," said Tiburón. "And not sipping it through a straw."

Manwaring looked around the cramped room. "I want to remind everybody that we were dead the minute they wheeled our unconscious bodies out of our execution rooms. The mere fact that we survived months in space to get here has given TETRA so much information to work with. Our landing, and subsequent work on the planet, will be invaluable. That said, we have been exposed to zero gravity and solar radiation for months, and remember, we have not consumed fresh produce or water for months. Therefore, we can assume that at least one of us will suffer broken bones from reduced bone density. We might also develop gland or organ problems associated with cancer. Again, Elizabeth, your task is to monitor and track such developments."

"Well, I *was* enjoying this cup of coffee." Tiburón sighed as held the cup with reverence.

Manwaring ignored him. "The Martian *sol* is slightly longer than a day on Earth, so our meals will be at 0800, 1300, and 1800 hours. In between meals, we will need to be diligent at our tasks and use the hours after supper to relax, discuss problems, plan for the next day, and get a good night's sleep. A strict routine is good for the mind, soul, and body."

"Question," Tiburón said. "We know that TETRA has been setting up this base for years but isn't anybody besides TETRA who has access to satellite imagery going to start noticing that modules are being moved around. That should clue somebody into our presence here."

Manwaring raised his wine glass to his lips but stopped to answer. "TETRA owns all satellites orbiting this latitude of Mars and controls all imagery sent back to Earth. Also, all TETRA has to say, if anybody asks, is that TETRA is remotely controlling these modules from Earth or from the moon or moved about by remotely operated vehicles."

Manwaring paused. Then, looking at Kroll, he said, "I suggest you check us into The Hilton for our first night. I believe TETRA has included lasagna in the inventory. Pair it with an appropriate pudding. Ring me when dinner is ready."

Elizabeth reflected on their time inside The Keep, and the words spoken, mostly by Manwaring. While the magnitude of what had transpired over the last months could now be reflected upon with safety, Manwaring's last few words brought so much relief: check into The Hilton, lasagna, and dessert. Especially now that they can enjoy sleeping on a normal bed without having to strap themselves in first. Relishing such comfort Elizabeth still asked herself one question. *Why did he have to say it in such an asshole-like way?*

Twenty-One Sols from Mars, mid-April 2026

Einstok and Max, sitting in chairs, and held down by Velcro straps, enjoyed chilled apple juice from their refillable packets. Behind them, ten plexiglass-covered modules: five on each side of the habitation stage stretched the length of their spacecraft's main stage. Zelda, and Einstok's team of special space operators, all in torpor, occupied seven of them. The eighth one was stuffed full of food packets and spare parts. After a moment of silence, Einstok pulled the refilling straw from his lips. "I know I've said this before, but I am glad that you decided to join me on this expedition, Max."

Max removed the straw from his lips. "Again, did you have any doubt I would not join you on your greatest adventure? That is, to date." Pausing to give his juice packet a partial squeeze, he continued. "We are talking about a spaceplane capable of interplanetary travel in mere hours."

Einstok nodded. "Yes, we are."

Both men, who's chiseled Nordic looks could have graced a Nazi SS recruiting poster from days gone by or the cover of any modern men's adventure magazine, albeit slightly puffy after spending over three months in space, reflected on those past discoveries. Their intense and sparkling eyes now feasted on the reasons why they were weeks from landing on Mars, starting with the finding of a German mercenary's diary buried within the wastes of a secret German American space base in Antarctica. One which proffered hints to the visitation of aliens to Mesoamerica centuries ago. The second finding was the breaking of a code built into Theodore Roosevelt's autobiography. An intelligence revealing the secret of a massive Aztec treasure, which found its way into the hands of the Rhinelander Korps. The result: Einstok pursuing the greatest discovery of his lifetime and the greatest treason of humanity.

"Well," Einstok said as he inspected the clear, plastic straw in front of his face. "Here's to the Rhinelander Korps and its members."

Max lifted his juice packet in salute. They each took a sip, then lowered the packets and turned toward their fellow astronauts.

"Your team is quite impressive," Max said. "Not only have they followed you to the ends of the earth, but they are also literally following you to the ends of the solar system."

"Mars," Einstok said with a chuckle, "is not the end of the solar system, but it is a start. Also, I must admit that they are a rum lot, but I would not trade their *talents* for anything on Earth, heaven, or hell."

He turned his head.

"Look at them. G. I. Joes wrapped in nice, neat boxes, waiting on a shelf to fulfill a young boy's imagination."

Max smiled in response but remained silent.

Einstok heard the silence. "Question?"

"Not a question," Max replied. "I, we, always have a habit of assessing the situation at hand and, with me, it starts with your team up against your expendables. Although I doubt it will be much of a situation if the time comes."

"I agree," Einstok said as he reclined a bit further back in his chair. "Is that it?"

"No," Max answered. "I am also assessing the magnitude of what we may find or whether Manwaring will pull a fast one to cheat us of our history. It seems to me that your team leader, Munro, differs in temperament from the rest of his team."

"You are right to always have a critical eye. Starting with the expendables. All six of them, convicted mass murderers who received due process before being properly, and legally, executed for crimes against humanity. Yet, I don't think one of them has a mean bone in their body. As this entire saga came to fruition in my mind, I realized I needed nameless misfits; people nobody would miss, but not billiard hall drunkards. I needed people capable of helping Manwaring get to Mars. After months of research, a proper list started to float to the top from the pool of candidates at my disposal. So far, my intuition and my intervention in their convictions and executions has paid off."

"I know what you mean," Max said, "as I reviewed their files during my watches. Besides Manwaring, whose execution you ensured for murders he never committed, there is that physician who has been quite busy during her short forty-plus years on Earth. The system's specialist, who thwarted the attempts by your competitors to end your mission prematurely. Then there is that Mexican fellow."

"Ah, Tiburón, a.k.a. The Shark," Einstok surmised.

"While quite the deft criminal, his research was getting a bit close to home. So instead of him having a road accident back on Earth or being shot by a state trooper, I killed two birds with one stone. Anyway, TETRA said they have been on Mars for twenty *sols* now, and they used those days organizing their base camp. It also appears that while everybody has been busy around base camp, Manwaring keeps up with his daily excursions into the mountains, but his movements appear aimless and have reported no results."

Max flicked his straw again. "Do you think this expedition was a waste of time, as Manwaring was just trying to find a way to save himself from execution? Or that Manwaring has found that space plane and has other plans."

"No, Max." Einstok shook his head firmly. "By no means has this expedition been a waste of time. Even if Manwaring was just trying to save his own skin. Think about it. We are only twenty-one *sols* from Mars ourselves, even though we left Earth weeks after Manwaring's departure. His expedition has helped us with our own mission. Soon, I will be able to announce to the world that I, along with you and my team, are the first humans to have landed on Mars."

Max offered his employer a mischievous smile before continuing. "Is your story about being an impaired billionaire with a parasite-ridden brain sequestered behind the walls of one of your mansions still holding water?"

"As far as the public knows, I am facing the greatest physical challenge of my extraordinary life: drooling in my tapioca in my villa outside Rome."

Max thought purposefully for a minute. "Again, about Manwaring?"

Einstok answered immediately. "First, if Manwaring keeps up with his end of the bargain, TETRA will have acquired an extremely historic, and financially rewarding, asset, leaving my personnel to deal with Manwaring back on Earth. At the same time, we will make it to Mars and announce our achievement to the world while removing any evidence of the expendables' presence. Second, if he has not been successful at finding our acquisition upon our arrival, we will still take care of all of them and continue the search ourselves. In that case, we shall delay our announcement to the world."

"Of course, I have no concerns with your team," Max said, "as they have proven themselves to be ruthless, but like I said earlier, your man, Munro, differs in temperament."

"Yes," Einstok replied with a bit of contemplation, "but I would never consider Munro anybody's man, as he only honors his oath. On the other hand, I think it would be a waste to describe each member of my team individually, so let me just say that, while Manwaring and his team were executed, under my direction, for crimes against humanity, those persons here in this module most assuredly deserved to have been on those execution gurneys instead."

"Everybody except for Munro?" Steiner asked.

"Yes! While he is the consummate professional, he is more benevolent in nature. A trait he used to garner respect from those less benevolent. Still, he has quite an exercise keeping Nitro in line."

"Well, that man Nitro really does have something stuck up his ass."

"You are quite right, Max," Einstok responded, "but Munro can manage well enough. He has that type of personality. One forged by life's circumstances."

Although Max knew Munro's background, Einstok repeated it as an ode to his team leader's character.

"Munro was found as a five-year-old orphan floating alone on a Haitian refugee raft by a Bahamian fisherman who raised him as his own. At seventeen, he enlisted in the Commando Squadron of the Bahamian Defense Force and trained with visiting special forces units from other countries including US Navy SEALS and the Sayeret Matkal, Israel's special reconnaissance unit. After his enlistment, he attended university studies in England, earning degrees in literature and history. He had planned to return to the Bahamas, to teach, but the family that raised him died in a hurricane. With no ties to a place he could call home, he joined the French Foreign Legion and volunteered to join their parachute regiment."

Letting Einstok finish his narration, Max added, "Hence the romantic lore of the Legion. A band of restless men longing for a place to call home. Men seeking solace and romance while looking for adventure and death around every corner of the universe but bound by honor. Twice orphaned by fate, he sought a permanent home. *Legio Patria Nostra,* meaning the 'Legion is our Fatherland.'"

"Quite right," Einstok said. "While you cited the current motto of the Legion, please bear in mind the Legion used two others over their long history, with the previous motto being *Honneur et Fidelite,* or 'Honor and Fidelity.' Holding the convictions close, he did well and planned to make a career of it. However, his company was part of an international effort in Iraq, and they ended up in a firefight. That brief battle, historically known as the Massacre of Najib, resulted in the wrongful deaths of dozens of civilians. After the dust settled, someone had to take the fall, and it was his platoon that fell under the pull of the guillotine's lever. Since he was the platoon's senior sergeant, he was the first in line at the guillotine's step. He assumed all responsibility for the attack and opted to quite the Legion in disgrace."

Einstok paused to look over at his unconscious team leader. Munro, just like the others, wore TETRA-issued blue undergarments and medical tubes stuck into his body's orifices.

"I read the transcripts and knew the forces had wrongly accused him. As I formed my team, I knew some might have found the type of men I would need to perform duties a bit less desirable. Therefore, just as a good brandy deserves a fine cigar, and Sherlock Holmes cannot exist with Doctor Moriarty, I needed a formidable counterbalance to create an effective force. He has certainly proved effective in his duty. He also, as it turns out, is quite the writer."

"I've been busy with my own duties over the years, but I do enjoy a good read now and then," Max said. "Has he published anything I might have read?"

"He writes under the pen name Willem Dam Pierre, a version of William Dampier, a name with plenty of significant adjectives attached to its origins: protector, awareness, curiosity, glory, and faithfulness," Einstok replied as he reached out to touch the forward bulkhead of the habitation module. "And while those adjectives describe Munro, his thoughts match them as well. They are quite far-ranging. Like the trillions of miles of space on the other side of this aluminum-skinned hull. A hull no thicker than a Hersey bar."

Max flicked his straw.

Einstok paused to read his researcher's thoughts. "I must admit that I could have positioned the pieces on the board in front of us better, as there are variables out of my control. But with both of us being consummate chess players, I can guess that you have already supposed what moves Manwaring might make if, indeed, he has found what he claims he is looking for. I have made those same conjectures back on Earth, and they are in place. But we will deal with them when the time comes. Now, it is time to put me into torpor. When that period ends, we will use the last few days in space to review our equipment and operational procedures. So, to answer your previous question, no, I am not worried about anything."

Sol 21 on Mars, late April, AD 2026

"How about coffee and a strawberry pastry?"

Elizabeth, intent on adding data from the morning's blood work results, did not hear the door to The Office open, but she did hear the invitation to a late breakfast, and its smell. Sitting at the computer desk, wearing blue pants and a long-sleeved jersey, she turned in her chair. Finnegan stood in the open doorway. He held a tray with cups and a covered platter.

"Let me finish what I'm doing." Returning to her typing, she listened as Finnegan got comfortable behind her. Though he wore no cologne, she sniffed at the air in front of her while creating images of his movements. It was then she remembered her sketch pad sitting on the operating table. "Shit," she mumbled under her breath.

Finnegan pushed the door shut with his foot. Wearing the same TETRA-issued clothing as her, he placed the tray on the padded examination table taking up the center of the module. He opened the sketch pad. A nice pencil sketch of him, wearing his ball cap and a trimmed mustache stared back. Bumping his head on the jointed arm of the light extending over the table, he picked up one of the cups.

"It's amazing how a few lines from a mechanical pencil on a piece of paper can say so much. You think I need to trim my mustache?"

"No," she replied with her back to him, "and don't get ahead of yourself. I've got a sketch of everybody in that book."

He quietly accepted her answer and found a seat on the bottom bunk. He noticed daily while walking through the module to get to The Garage that she never made the bed. While they all took their meals as a group and spent time together after supper at The Hilton, Elizabeth and Finnegan slept at their workstations, just as Manwaring spent his nights in The Keep. Tiburón, Spike, and Kroll enjoyed the comforts of The Hilton.

Sipping his coffee, he appreciated the wrinkles pressed into the still warm sheet. They comforted Finnegan, as did the damp sports bra and cotton gym shorts hanging from a hanger above her pillow. As he sipped his coffee and listened to the tapping of the keyboard, he sniffed at the air and looked around. Though this module had the same basic components as the others, including two bunks and a bathroom, it looked just like any examination room found in any hospital or doctor's office back on Earth. Down to the eye chart on the wall. He looked at Elizabeth's back and noticed her wet hair, now cut a little shorter, combed back in 1950s greaser style. At the same time, he caressed the wrinkled sheet before reaching for the gym shorts.

Hitting the last key, Elizabeth turned. At the same second, Finnegan snatched his hand away from her sweaty shorts and pretended to smooth out his mustache.

Smiling, Elizabeth stood. "Kroll's getting good at turning out decent pastries. And now that you're producing fresh water, the coffee is just that much better."

"Help yourself."

Leaving her desk, she grabbed the second cup and a pastry before joining Finnegan on the bunk. She took a bite of the pastry and sipped her coffee, while looking from side to side. "Sorry for the mess. I never got into the habit of making my bed, as it seemed a waste of time to me. Something that drove my grandmother nuts."

"What happened to your parents?" Catching himself, Finnegan apologized. "Sorry."

"It's okay," she said and swallowed. "My father was a fighter pilot in the Air Force and continued to fly his own plane after his tour. He and my mother were in their Cherokee, flying to a business meeting and ran into a thunderstorm. They crashed in the middle of it. When I was eight. I was an only child, and my parents often left me with my grandparents before that day, so they became my legal guardians. My grandfather died when I turned twelve. From then on, it was just me and my grandmother."

"At least you had somebody to try and teach you manners, along with a bed to sleep in," Finnegan said. "I had to share a bedroom with two brothers, and they got the bed. All I had was a father who drank and slapped my stepmother around, a piece of hardwood floor, and a roll-up futon."

"Sorry," Elizabeth apologized. She paused but continued to look at Finnegan over the rim of her coffee cup. "You know, Finnegan, you walk through this module every day, and only stopped long enough to say hi. I'm glad you stopped by for a proper visit."

He sipped his coffee. "I'm glad you said that. I just thought you had more important things on your mind."

"I do, but I would never mind a visit from the best-looking Irishman on the planet."

"Thanks, but I'm Irish American. Sean Patrick Finnegan, of East Milton, Mass. One of about five thousand Sean Patrick Finnegans in East Milton. Or some combination thereof."

"Now, we're finally starting to find out more about you," Elizabeth said. "All of us have learned about each other, but you've always remained a bit more aloof than the others, except for Manwaring. But at least you aren't nasty about it like he is."

"Yeah," Finnegan said. He paused to inspect the coffee in his cup. "I guess it came with the job."

Elizabeth tilted her head slightly. "The same job that got you here?"

Finnegan nodded. "I was an international assassin."

"Intriguing," Elizabeth said coyly. "How did you get into that line of work?"

"Growing up in my neighborhood was rough, and I caught two felonies by the time I turned sixteen, which ruined any aspirations of becoming a military fighter pilot or eventually an astronaut."

A sly grin took over Finnegan's mouth while he raised his coffee and pastry.

"Go figure, eh. But, being a juvenile, I escaped serious jail time, and knew I caught a break. So, figuring I still had a shot of making something of myself and getting out of East Milton, albeit the hard way, I finished high school and started on a mechanical engineering degree at a local college. I always had a knack for the martial arts, so to pay for college, I used a combination of street fighting skills and karate to become a mixed martial arts cage fighter. That's where the IRA noticed me and asked me to join their American branch, which I did, as a street soldier."

"IRA? As in the Irish Republican Army? From Ireland?"

Finnegan tilted his head slightly. "An American branch of the IRA. One affiliated with Boston-area gangs."

"You got yourself back into the mix?" Elizabeth asked.

"The money was too good to turn down and, still being young and stupid, I thought I'd never be caught. Anyway, they must've seen something in me and asked me to conduct a hit for them. It turns out I had a knack for that line of work as well. But before you judge me, I only took out people who needed it."

Elizabeth paused to take a bite of the pastry. "So, you got caught up in the life and dropped out of college?"

"I carried out my first hit with a screwdriver, and trust me, he was a real piece of shit. While I didn't mind the work, I realized killing a man with a screwdriver wasn't challenging enough. I found out that after every hit, I wanted to top the previous one with a bit more ingenuity. I guess it's like someone who completes one crossword puzzle always looks for the next one to be a bit more difficult. So, I went from a screwdriver to a pistol to a sniper rifle to explosives, poison, and finally more extensive technology. Hell, I even used a five-hundred-year-old crossbow in one of my hits. However, it was my undoing, as I got a little too big for my britches. Each hit became a calling card, and the FBI, Scotland Yard, and Europol started to track my work, and my methodologies. Eventually, once they started to suspect me, they hacked my email and cell phone and found pictures I took of my contracts. In a way, I got myself convicted and executed, so I wasn't that smart."

"It's amazing how one can be one's worst enemy. That's pretty much how I got nabbed." She paused and looked deeply at Finnegan. "Why'd you lose the accent. And do you miss the job?"

Finnegan sighed and shrugged ahis shoulder. "I started to deal with higher-end clientele, and taking contracts overseas. I did not want to come across as East Milton trash. And no, I don't miss the job, but it does bother me that it took murder to make me realize the talents I had. Also, I don't want you to think I was just some mindless zombie or robot murderer who killed on command. I chose to accept or decline each contract as I saw fit. I only killed those who deserved it. Can I assume you fell into the same trap? You know, being a renowned physician with a pedigree a mile long? We've all read the clipping taped inside your module."

"We all have that one trigger that can send us down the wrong path. In your case, it was growing up in a rough neighborhood. For me, it was my uncle raping me at thirteen. I wanted to tell everybody that Uncle John raped me, but my parents were dead, and so was my grandfather. While the rest of my extended family tended to be a bit snobbish, I knew my grandmother wasn't. However, it was just her and I, and there was no way I could tell my grandmother her surviving son was a rapist and pedophile. It would break her heart. But when he died of a mysterious car accident, brake failure on his Lexus, my path was chosen for me. It was a way of solving my issue without breaking my grandmother's heart. So I guess I'm like you. I didn't just kill for killing sake. I only killed those married men who sought me out. But not just any cheating son of a bitch. I did my research and only hooked up with the ones that did more than cheat on their wives."

Ah," Finnegan said. "Pedophiles, tax cheats, and men who run over turtles in the road. On purpose."

"Especially those." Elizabeth leaned over and bumped his shoulder with hers. "I find it all ironic in that I share my name with a TV witch and an infamous axe murderer—ol' Lizzie Borden. Remember that old poem? Lizzie Borden gave her mother forty whacks, and when she had seen what she had done, she gave her father forty-one."

Finnegan took an extra-long sip of his coffee, speaking as he lowered. "You know, um... since you are the only heterosexual female on this planet, I was thinking about asking you out for a date one day, but after having read the newspaper article plastered to the side of your module, I had second thoughts. I don't want to end up like your uncle. Or married men who run over turtles."

Elizabeth let out a breath. "Well, I think this trip to Mars has cured me of any previous tendencies. I know where you're going, and I want to remind you that I have needs myself, especially since TETRA forced me to leave my vibrator behind. And it will be a while before Tiburón can grow decent cucumbers."

Taken aback for a moment, he recovered quickly. "You know it just seems so ironic that while we came from opposite ends of the socioeconomic scale, we ended up in the same mess."

"Well, Mars seems to be quite the equalizer. Even still, if we were back on Earth, my grandmother wouldn't have turned her nose up at you. And she is quite picky."

"Good," Finnegan replied, "but what about the other men on this planet? Won't they be knocking on your door with a breakfast tray themselves?"

"You're right, but let's look at them one at a time. For right now, Manwaring has his excursions in the Superstition Mountains, and when he comes back, he divides the rest of his day between The Keep and The Westing House. As for Kroll, he's as gay as you can get. Besides, he is happier than hell pampering us while listening to Neil Simon and Elton John music and working on his puzzles. That makes Tiburón the only real threat, but I've been watching him and Spike, and they have a budding relationship. Looks like Tiburón is man enough to take on an ex-marine scout sniper and get her interested in the other team."

Finnegan nodded before panning his eyes around the room. "So, we've spent months in space and been on this planet for three weeks now. What's the prognosis?"

"Actually, I'm pleased," Elizabeth said, pausing long enough to glance at the computer monitor screen mounted to her desk. "Everybody is getting their strength back and rebuilding muscle. The lab work is great for everybody, including Kroll, which surprises me. All those years of a rich diet, little exercise, and consuming humans hasn't seemed to affect him in the slightest. It must have been his habit of swinging his axe to collect his own wood. Anyway, the skin suit he is wearing is tightening up. He may soon be wearing the second suit TETRA made for him, for when he lost the weight. Everyone's X-rays show good bone density, so I don't think anybody's going to break a hip anytime soon. Lastly, the mere fact that everybody has a regular schedule, and activities has improved both the psychological and physical outlook for all concerned."

"Including Manwaring's personality?" Finnegan asked. "While he never had much of a personality to begin with, his disposition toward us seems to get worse. When we do see him at breakfast and supper, all he does is scarf down his food and throw his dirty crockery into the sink."

"Well, I would not get hung up on him," Elizabeth said. "I wouldn't want anything to ruin our first date. Speaking of which, do you have anything special in mind?"

"Do you know the difference between a screwdriver and a hammer?"

She sat up straighter and feigned a down-the-nose, how-dare-you look. "Weren't you listening? I was able to rig my uncle's Lexus and send him over a cliff. And that was on my fourteenth birthday."

"Didn't mean any offense," he said, "and I can see that your credentials are impeccable. Come to The Garage after lunch. Don't forget your spacesuit."

15

Sol 21 on Mars,
late April, AD 2026

Elizabeth closed the door leading into The Garage behind her. She wore her spacesuit and gripped her helmet by its neck ring. While The Garage contained all the basic hospitality components as the other modules, it lived up to its name. Wall-mounted spare-parts bins and a workbench, complete with under-the-counter pull-out tool drawers, a pegboard festooned with tools, and a bench-mounted vise competed for leftover space.

"So, this is the He-man Woman-hater's Clubhouse I've been hearing about," Elizabeth said. "All you need is a *Playboy* centerfold on the wall, biker magazines spread about, a twelve-gauge pump standing in the corner, and a half-fridge full of PBR tallboys."

Finnegan, wearing his own spacesuit and ball cap, sat on a shop stool at the workbench. His helmet sat next to the mounted vise. He turned to Elizabeth. "I could always have naked photos of you on the wall."

"Don't get ahead of yourself, Big Boy," she said with a smirk.

Finnegan turned to grab his helmet off the workbench. "We're going to start with the water extractor."

Lifting her helmet, she responded. "Lead on."

Finnegan stood and they both lifted their helmets over their heads. Lowering them they twisted their helmets on until they heard the neck locks click. Finnegan lifted his left arm and peeled the transparent plastic cover back from the keypad. He tapped the button labeled "closed" and hit the Number 2 button, "Comm check."

Elizabeth lifted her translucent plastic cover, tapped the "Closed" button, and the button labeled Number 3. "Got you loud and clear."

"Let's get started," Finnegan said. Leaning sideways, he reached for a wire basket hanging from a hook bolted to the side of the workbench. The basket held four aluminum containers, each the size of an old-fashioned coffee thermos. Carrying the basket by the handle, they entered the airlock, one at a time, and closed the interior door behind them. After checking their internal suit environmental control systems, Finnegan depressurized the airlock, and they stepped onto the aluminum staircase.

The light blue and cloudless sky, and the waning yellow sun slowly making its way toward a dull-red horizon, welcomed them. Elizabeth fixed her eyes on the work Spike had completed so far.

Spike's first task was to use The Beast, a four-wheeled, single-seat work vehicle, to tweak the four habitation modules into better alignment, assemble the tunnels to connect the modules, and clean up the detritus scattered about Legoland. Her second task was to gouge out knee-deep trenches for The Shit Shack and their greenhouses. Today, she was helping Tiburón set up growing racks inside The Shit Shack on the other side of the habitation modules.

In front of Finnegan and Elizabeth, four pods with a solar panel bolted to the side and a ramp extending from the closed doors of each one, pressed their flat bases into the Martian soil. Like the habitation modules, burn scars from the rockets, which helped cushion the landing, marred the grayish hulls. While each pod housed a specialized vehicle, the last one in line housed a four-wheeled water-extracting vehicle, one Finnegan referred to as The Oompa-Loompa.

The remaining containers profiled themselves against the rising lip of the lake behind the vehicle pods.

"Place looks like a junkyard behind NASA headquarters," Elizabeth said.

"Operated by Dr. Suess. Here, let me show you how to do my job."

He turned and stepped down the staircase onto the Martian surface.

Finnegan and Elizabeth retraced an exposed white hose back to The Oompa-Loompa, located about two hundred meters west of Legoland proper.

Approaching the vehicle, Elizabeth passed three knee-high mounds of churned-up dirt and gravel. Passing Finnegan's previous test drilling sites, something clicked in the back of her head. She did not know what made the hairs on the back of her neck stand up, but something did.

Reaching the vehicle, Elizabeth stopped next to The Oompa-Loompa. It resembled an oversized Smart car with an extended rear compartment, painted orange and white, with a flat solar panel on the roof and fixed with four balloon tires. What looked like an outboard motor attached to the front bumper, completed the vehicle's appearance. There was a front windshield, but there were no other windows. The hose they followed entered the vehicle's tailpipe.

Finnegan stepped up to the vehicle's rear hatch. "Mind you, most of the work I did is buried. To protect it from the elements. I left the hose going to our habitation modules exposed, though, to make it easier to find the wellhead if happens in the middle of the night."

Finnegan placed the basket of containers on the ground and pushed a button near the bottom of the hatchback. It opened slowly to reveal a well-stocked interior. On either side, shelves filled with drill bits, lengths of drill shafts, and sections of PVC piping ran lengthwise. A pull-out workbench occupied the available space between the shelving. An electronic tablet in a cloth pouch hung from one side of the workbench.

"I come out this time every day for a systems check," Finnegan said, pulling the tablet from its pouch and moving his finger about the screen. "Unfortunately, I could not detect a contiguous layer of ice under us. Life couldn't be that simple. Instead, The Oompa-Loompa did detect a pocket of frozen water five meters down. I had to hunt and peck for it, though, which is why you saw my test drilling. Anyway, the pump's maintaining a positive head pressure, the filters just did an automatic dump of particulate matter, and the purification levels are good. We're pumping out three liters an hour, but it looks like the charge to the vehicle's battery system is low."

Stepping out from under the lifted hatchback, he stood on booted tiptoes. Standing on her own booted toes next to him, Elizabeth raised her eye level with the mounted solar panels. Remembering what Tiburón had said about micrometeorite strikes on the day they arrived, she saw smaller panels joined as one. A spider web crack marred the surface of one of those panels. "Micrometeorite strike?"

Finnegan answered, "You'll find everything you'll need in the back."

Five minutes later, she tightened the last mounting nut under the solar panel, plugged in the wire connector, and held out the wrench. "Is it starting to charge properly now?"

"Too soon to tell, so let me show you how this system works in the meantime." Finnegan accepted the wrench and turned away from the open rear of The Oompa-Loompa. Elizabeth followed him to the front of the vehicle. "It's basic, really," Finnegan said, pointing to the battery-powered drilling unit with the wrench. "The unit works just like an outboard engine, which is why it looks like one. We have an electric motor attached to an angled coupling that drives the shaft and drill bit."

He pointed to a hole where the motor housing was attached to the front bumper.

Elizabeth reviewed the attaching drilling motor. "Does that thing swivel?"

"It can," Finnegan said. "Just in case I run into an underground obstacle. Like a buried boulder. Forty-five degrees to either side and thirty degrees to the front. Anyway, once I insert the first drill shaft section, I go underneath and attach a six-inch drill bit to the bottom end. When hooked up, I turn the machine on and let it do its work. Once it gets going, I connect extra sections of drill shaft from the top as it drills into the sediment. Since the entire machine is battery operated, it can only drill so fast. Fortunately, I only had to drill about five meters before contacting that pocket of ice. In the end, though, we can only extract so much water at any given time."

He turned and pointed to a round PVC cap two meters away, surrounded by a mound of dirt and gravel. "There's evidence that water once flowed on Mars, and the evidence is visible in the rounded pebbles mixed up in the soil."

Elizabeth appreciated the work Finnegan had accomplished so far. She started to turn away, but something told her to look back. What it was she did not know, but something in the mound hooked her subconscious. While looking at the mound, her mind went back to their first day on Mars, when Tiburón picked up the rock with lines that looked like a partial swastika pressed into its surface, along with what could be the letters R and K. She was about to step to the mound to see what attracted her attention, but Finnegan stopped her.

"Once I reached the frozen pocket," Finnegan continued, "I drilled for another meter before removing the drill shaft and bit and replacing it with an electrically wired well liner and heater core. Once in place, I capped it off and connected the wiring for the heater coil and the hose to the filter and pump built into The Oompa-Loompa. Once I turned on the heater inside the well, everything else became automatic."

A white hose and wiring led from the wellhead to a connection on the driver's side of the vehicle. "Looks simple enough," Elizabeth said.

"Good," Finnegan responded. "Now, I need to go on my milk run, so let me show you the routine. We'll come back to see how your solar panel repairs are working."

Finnegan returned to the rear of the machine to replace the wrench and close the hatchback. Retrieving his basket, they followed the hose back to The Garage, stopping on the other side. A distance away, they saw The Tank Farm, a pod partially buried in the Martian soil, mounded over by the dirt from Spike's excavations, and fitted with an airlock and a solar panel anchored to the dirt covering the structure. Closer to the habitation modules was another pod, dubbed The Shit Shack, also partially buried and mounded over with soil and fitted with an airlock and solar panel. Next to it was the pod that contained the components needed to construct connecting greenhouses. Components now stacked outside the pod and next to the foundation partially assembled in a one-meter-deep trench.

"This is how the milk run works," Finnegan said. Placing the basket on the ground, Finnegan opened a hinged flap at the base of The Garage. A container, like the ones in the handbasket, stuck out of it upside down and threaded into a coupling.

"Every day, I go to each module and remove containers connected to the waste recycling unit inside. Our waste produces methane gas, so there's a mini compressor that sucks it off and pressurizes these containers. Since TETRA does not want us to start polluting Mars by venting it off, we collect it. We may also have a use for it down the road. Nothing goes to waste on Mars."

He reached in to unscrew the container. "It has a self-sealing lid, so both the container and the recycling unit close themselves off once removed." He pulled the container away from the coupling, placed it on the ground, removed a fresh container from the basket, and screwed it into place. "That's it."

"Again, simple enough," Elizabeth said, "but since TETRA has spent billions of dollars getting us here and setting this place up, I would've thought our waste collection system would be a bit less hand's on."

"I agree," Finnegan said. He stooped to place the full container in the basket and pick it up. "But an installed piping system with automatic valves and pumps is in the future. Besides, I don't mind having something to do. In fact, this setup may have been the original idea. Something about idle hands being the devil's work."

"Don't mind if I do," Elizabeth said as she grabbed the basket from Finnegan's hand and stepped toward the next module in line, The Office. With Finnegan following. Elizabeth changed out the remaining containers in turn. Five minutes later, the two of them stood behind The Keep with a basket of four full containers.

"Now what?" Elizabeth asked.

"Next," Finnegan said, "I take them to The Tank Farm, but let's pop into The Shit Shack first."

Within a couple of minutes, Finnegan and Elizabeth stopped in front of the aluminum ramp leading down to the airlock built into The Shit Shack pod. Finnegan placed the basket on the ground and stepped down to the airlock. A weak light escaped through the small, round window of the airlock's door.

Once inside The Shit Shack, they removed their helmets. As soon as Elizabeth twisted hers, unsealing the neck ring, she was struck by a familiar odor. One that immediately brought back loving memories. After having breathed manufactured oxygen for months, the sudden smell of ammonia and compost shocked her senses. But, the sharp, acrid smell, along with the sight of a workbench and gardening tools hanging from the tool rack on the wall, was almost overwhelming. It was as if she were a child again and standing in her grandmother's garden shed.

The only difference, though, was an enclosed machine, painted light gray and with a keypad and monitor mounted on the front of it. It stood next to the workbench. Tiburón, wearing his spacesuit, and with his helmet sitting on the workbench, gave them a half wave while writing something in a notepad. Against the opposite wall were five-tiered metal shelves filled with opaque Tupperware totes with blue snap-on lids. One of them was almost full of something black, and the other had a white powdery substance lining the bottom.

Finishing her survey, she could still see herself in the garden shed, wearing cut-off jeans and a T-shirt, covering grape seeds with dirt and compost. The sound of her grandmother's caring voice and the touch of her hand helping her with the small pot took over her thoughts.

Now, Lizzie, don't press down too hard, or the seed won't grow.

Against the back wall, a closed door occupied space between the enclosed machine and tiered shelving.

"What do you think of my digs?" Tiburón asked.

Setting his pencil on the notepad, he stood in front of the enclosed machine mounted against the wall. A pipe led out of the top of the machine and went into a box-like item fixed to the wall.

"It reminds me of my grandmother's garden shed," Elizabeth said. "Except for that machine, of course."

"Well, Tiburón started, "I think your grandmother would recognize every step I make each day. I remove the waste collection tanks from each habitation module, bring them here, and put them into the machine where the waste is sucked out and macerated, dried, and mixed with Martian soil. The soil here isn't really soil. It's nothing more than pulverized rock with no organic value. And it's acidic. So the proper combination between our waste, the potting soil supplied by TETRA, and Martian *soil* makes it usable for horticulture."

He turned to Finnegan. "The machine makes a funny sound when the motor kicks in. The motors might be seizing up."

Sidestepping next to Tiburón, Finnegan tapped on a keypad mounted to the front of the gray-painted machine and scrolled through five screens on the small monitor before stopping. "Well, that's not good."

"What's wrong?" asked Elizabeth.

Just then, the door at the back of the module opened and Spike stood in the doorway. She wore her spacesuit and carried a wrench in one hand. "Hey, guys." She turned to Elizabeth. "What are you doing out here? Did Lord Douche give you a pardon?"

"Screw him," Elizabeth said.

"Yeah, screw him," Spike answered, looking over to Finnegan.

Finnegan looked past his shoulder at her. "I was just showing Elizabeth around." Turning back to the small screen in front of him, he reached up with his gloved hand and felt the box-like item that the pipe went through. After four or five seconds, he stuck his other hand out without turning his head. "Give me the wrench."

Spike placed it in his outreached hand, and Finnegan used it to tap the box-like item. He waited for another four or five seconds before speaking.

"You're right, Tiburón. The fan motor is seizing up."

"Is that bad?" Elizabeth asked.

Keeping his eyes on the vent piping, Finnegan answered. "The fan motor maintains a slight vacuum to prevent the buildup of methane gas and vents it off to The Tank Farm. Methane gas can be explosive if it builds up in quantity." He stopped to turn toward Elizabeth. "Haven't you ever seen anybody light a cabbage-beer-fart?"

Elizabeth balked. "I never traveled in those circles."

Nonplussed, Finnegan continued. "Anyway, we're going to have to replace it. Tiburón, look in the second drawer down under the bench. You'll see a package labeled Vent Fan Motor."

"Right," he said as he stepped around Finnegan.

Stepping to get out of Finnegan's way, Elizabeth asked, "I can guess what the black stuff is in the Tupperware tote, but what's the white stuff?"

"Powdered nitrate. From our pee and poop," Tiburón said as he bent over to open the drawer. "Even our solids have liquids, so what is siphoned off is converted back into water for our plants, and the extracted chemicals are saved for future use."

Elizabeth furrowed her eyebrows. "Could that also be explosive?"

"Almost anything can be made into an explosive," Spike replied. "I used to collect bat shit, you know, guano from caves back in Tennessee to make gunpowder. I used that powder to make practice bombs at my uncle's rock quarry. It's all a matter of quantity, the right conditions, and having the right detonator, but there isn't enough there to cause any concern. At least, not yet."

Elizabeth thought for a second. "You boys go ahead and fix the fart fan. Spike, mind showing me what's going on back there?"

"Sure," Spike said.

After hearing the door, Finnegan spoke to Tiburón. "So, how's it going with Spike?"

Tiburón, with the replacement part in his hand, turned toward Finnegan. "Great. I think I'm about to close the deal. What about you and Elizabeth?"

"So far, our first date is going great," Finnegan answered. "We're cool, right?"

"We are."

Both men smiled and turned to the task.

At the same time, Elizabeth entered the second half of The Shit Shack—a small room filled with more five-tiered racks and shallow pans, full of black potting soil TETRA provided, and illuminated by light fixtures.

Before Elizabeth had chance to speak, Spike said, "I've seen how you've been looking at Finnegan, and I know why you asked me to go to the powder room with you. But it's okay. I'm not interested in him."

Relieved, Elizabeth asked. "Are you sure?"

"Well, I haven't given up on trying to get into *your* panties, but I've been curious why I lost a previous girlfriend to a Latino. So I thought I'd give Tiburón a try, to see what all the fuss is about. Anyway, how's your first date going?"

"So far, I've fixed a solar panel and gathered four containers of methane gas. Not too shabby I don't mind saying."

After collecting his waste cylinders, the old vent fan, and the box the new one came in, Finnegan and Elizabeth walked toward The Tank Farm. As they walked, Elizabeth could hear Finnegan breathe slowly over the intercom. Enjoying the walk, she realized an emotion. One that made her stomach flutter, and her head swoon. During her years as a teenager and adult, she had never been able to walk with a man and not plot his death while smiling at him. Now, it was just like that time on the playground when she was eight years old, and little Tommy kissed her on the lips. An innocence returned.

They reached The Tank Farm's airlock and went inside to remove their helmets.

Elizabeth placed her helmet on a workbench and looked around. Aside from the workbench with a built-in compressor under the bench top, racks going from floor to ceiling held dozens of tanks lying on their sides. They looked like scuba tanks, only smaller. A black flexible hose led from the back of the workbench up the wall to the side of a retractable reel mounted to the ceiling in the center of the room. A hose from the reel was connected to the valve on one of the tanks.

"Reminds me of the back of a dive shop," Elizabeth said.

"You dive?" Finnegan asked as he placed the items in his hand on the workbench.

"I got certified in Cancun. During a high school trip. Dove along the coast and in cenotes. Since then, I've just dabbled. You?"

"It came with part of the job," Finnegan answered, reaching for one of the waste containers in the basket. "Mind me showing you what I do here?"

"Sure."

Finnegan smiled as he lifted one of them and bent over to thread the neck into a connection port on top of the compressor. "All I do is take a container and connect it to the compressor. The pipe from The Shit Shack is connected to the compressor, which is timed to kick on every few minutes and send it to whichever tank it's connected to."

The compressor started, and its motor gave off a soft hum.

Finnegan straightened and stepped to the tank connected to the hose. He read the gauge. "It's at 2,900 psi, almost 3,000 pounds of high-pressure methane. There should be enough room for the methane from today's milk run. Then we can shift to another tank."

With the milk run complete, Finnegan and Elizabeth walked from The Tank Farm back to The Oompa-Loompa in comfortable silence, which Finnegan ended just after they passed The Garage. "Looks like His Royal Highness is on his way back."

Elizabeth turned toward the dry riverbed snaking its way down from the sharp mountain rise. In the distance, The Minivan stirred up a slight cloud of dust behind it. Like the other vehicles, it was white and orange with oversized tires but, unlike the other vehicles, it had seating for six and enclosed with side and overhead windows. Even with the available seating,

Manwaring was its only operator and occupant.

Glancing over their shoulders a couple more times, Finnegan and Elizabeth continued toward The Oompa-Loompa. As the sun dropped closer to the Martian horizon, Elizabeth thought about her afternoon with Finnegan and how much she had relished the time with him. Then, she noticed the waning light glint off something in the mound of dirt surrounding the wellhead. As if the mound of dirt called out to Elizabeth, she obeyed the demand by veering away from Finnegan toward the mound, while he continued to the water-drilling vehicle. Now close to the mound, she saw what caught her subconscious earlier.

"No way," she blurted.

"What's up, Elizabeth?" Finnegan said into the microphone built into his neck ring as he approached the rear hatchback.

Waiting for an answer, Finnegan opened the rear door to The Oompa-Loompa and reached for his tablet. Elizabeth stepped up next to him.

"Looks like your repairs worked," he said. But it took only a second to realize he had yet to receive an answer. Taking his attention from the tablet's screen, he turned to face Elizabeth. She wore a huge grin and held out the open palm of her gloved hand. Centered on her palm was a length of dark green, almost black, glass in the shape of a one-bladed safety razor but twice its length.

"Okay, a sharp piece of shiny black rock."

"It's obsidian. An obsidian blade, and it's been worked by a human. It came from a *macuahuitl*."

"Whoa! Are you talking about an Aztec war club? The 'infamous' obsidian chainsaw?"

"Exactly! I've seen tons of pictures of these from my Mesoamerican classes. Even from Manwaring's textbooks. I've also knapped out some of these myself. In class and in Utah!"

"Okay, it's an obsidian blade," Finnegan said. He lowered his voice slightly while reaching out to pat Elizabeth's shanking hand. "From an Aztec weapon. Got it. Just slow down so we can figure out how it got here. Any ideas?"

"I have no idea," she said, closing her gloved fingers around the shard. "But it's mind-blowing. Just like the swastika imprint we found the first day here."

Finnegan reinserted the tablet into its cloth folder on the side of the vehicle's interior. "Well, if you show it to Lord Haw-Haw, he'll probably dismiss it just like he did with that swastika."

"So, do you think it was a swastika pressed into that rock? Not a fissure?"

"I do think you are right about that being an obsidian blade." Finnegan pointed his gloved finger at her closed fist. He looked up at the nearby mountain range and saw that Manwaring's vehicle had reached the dry river outlet. "And that impression did look like a swastika to me. And with one partial letter on either side of it."

Holy crap," Elizabeth blurted out.

"Now what?" Finnegan asked.

"I don't know why I didn't think of it earlier, but I remember seeing that impression before. Back in Utah."

"What? A swastika?"

"A swastika, along with the letters R and K.

"Well, shit," Finnegan said slowly. "Manwaring knows something we don't. And it looks like TETRA selected this spot for reasons other than as a source of water. The question is how they, Einstok, knew to pick this spot."

Elizabeth did not answer immediately. Instead, she turned to look at the edge of the lakebed where the river emptied into it. Manwaring's vehicle had just crested the lip and driven down the shallow slope, pointing his vehicle toward them. "My grandmother always said I loved a good mystery."

"Okay, Nancy Drew," Finnegan said, "show it to him. See how he reacts and let me know. In the meantime, let's see if we can find that rock. Hopefully, Manwaring didn't go back and get it. After that, let's get back inside and get cleaned up. If we're quick, we'll have time for an aperitif before dinner. I'll bring the wine, and you can break out your official Nancy Drew Detective Kit. Bring your Sherlock Holmes hat and magnifying glass."

Elizabeth dropped her still-closed hand and tilted the transparent plastic of her helmet. Giving Finnegan's helmet a slight bounce. "Ah, a little role play. Meet me in my quarters."

✹

Finnegan entered Elizabeth's quarters. He held a bottle of wine in one hand, the stopper cork barely stuck into the bottle's neck, and two glasses in the other, hanging upside down from his fingers. He wore his TETRA-issued uniform. Elizabeth, though, sitting at her desk and holding a magnifying glass, wore only a blue T-shirt and a pair of white panties. Her slicked back wet hair had stained her shirt a darker blue. The rock that Tiburón found on their first day sat next to the built-in keyboard along with two obsidian shards. One from the mound near The Oompa-Loompa, and another found in one of Finnegan's other test drills.

She turned to Finnegan as he placed the bottle and glasses on the operating table. Elizabeth held up the magnifying glass and placed it in front of her right eye.

"I thought you were joking about the role play, but if you're game..." Before he could continue, Manwaring's voice erupted from the module intercom loudspeaker mounted in the corner. "Elizabeth! I need your updates for my reports!"

Finnegan grabbed the bottle with one hand and pulled out the cork. Taking aim, he launched the cork like a dart at the speaker.

Thirty minutes later, the two of them reclined against the pillows, staring up at the bottom of the bunk above them. Naked, Finnegan cradled Elizabeth with his left arm.

"Don't take it the wrong way," said Elizabeth, "but you're the best lay I've had on Mars."

"Well, Doctor Elizabeth 'Lizzie' Mongomery-Borden, it must have been your bedside manner. Anyway, I've worked up quite an appetite. Kroll's making mac-and-cheese with Spam,"—Finnegan reached up with his hand and tweaked her nipple—"and I would not want to disappoint Kroll. Let's get dressed and give Manwaring our reports before dinner. I'll give you my jump drive."

✵

Elizabeth, now fully clothed in TETRA-issued clothing, entered The Keep. Manwaring, dressed just like her, sat at his computer desk.

"Where the bloody hell have you been?" Manwaring said, turning to face Elizabeth. "And what were you doing on the surface? Working with Finnegan? You knew my orders!"

Elizabeth stepped up to Manwaring's side and held out her hand. "Here are the reports."

Manwaring reached for the items in her palm. His eyes widened but only slightly. After a half-second, he looked up at Elizabeth's face. "Looks like you've been enjoying a hot shower or something."

"Yeah. Something."

Manwaring dropped his eyes and snatched two jump drives from her hand. He left the third item on her palm. Turning to face the monitor again, he said, "What do you have there?"

Still holding out her palm, Elizabeth answered. "While helping Finnegan, I found what I think is an obsidian blade, or bladelet."

Manwaring kept his focus on the computer portals while plugging in the drives. "What makes you think it's an obsidian blade?"

"My first minor was in Mesoamerican studies, and I used your textbooks for those classes. I took two of your classes, but I don't expect you to remember me." She observed Manwaring's hand plugging in the jump drives. It trembled ever so slightly. "I also took more than one flint-knapping session. It has a bulb of percussion. It reminds me of those images of the bladelets inserted into the edge of those Aztec wooden swords. You know, a *macuahuitl.*"

With a sigh, Manwaring took his attention from the computer and leaned to his side. He adjusted his glasses and inspected the item in her palm. "You must remember that I have had thousands of students, so no, I do not remember you specifically. Also, I can see where you might have assumed it to be a worked piece of obsidian, but I'm sorry to disappoint you. During my work up in the mountains, I've seen similar items—hundreds of them, in fact. Mars was once volcanically active and had a molten core. Since molten glass or silicon is lighter than molten stone, the subsurface volcanic activity forced liquid silicon through narrow fissures in the strata, creating long, thin blade-like items. You also must remember that Mars has little in terms of an atmosphere, and along with extremes in day and night temperatures, the conditions are conducive to creating such items."

"Are you sure," Elizabeth asked.

"Trust me," Manwaring said, with an impatient sigh. "All I can assume is that when water did flow, it washed that piece downriver. Along with more just like it."

After a second-long pause, she said, "All right."

Closing her fingers over the object, she turned to leave. Hiding the smile on her face, she reached for the door leading to The Hilton. She knew for certain what she held in her hand, and she knew that Manwaring also recognized it as such. *Hello Nancy Drew.*

He heard the door behind him close and pulled his fingers away from his keyboard, placing his palms over his glasses. He muttered, "It's too soon. I'm not ready yet."

Late April, AD 2026

"That was your best meal yet," Finnegan said, scraping his ceramic plate with a steel fork and bringing it to his mouth. "Even if it did include spam."

"*Vielen dank*," Kroll replied in German. With a pleased smile on his face, he patted his belly. "I am glad you did not mind the tinned meat on top of the pasta and cheese. I like the salty taste it adds to the meal."

"I agree," Elizabeth said as she pushed her empty plate forward. Reclining in her chair at the table, she patted her belly as well. "I just hope developing weight issues won't become a habit around here. Now, how about an after dinner coffee? Next round is on me."

The Hilton, though equipped with the same basic features as the other habitation modules, was much more pleasing to be in. Its soft, fake wood paneling veiled the obtrusive life-support and environmental systems supporting their lives. As an attempt to lessen the mental rigors of space travel and living on Mars in industrially built modules, TETRA had developed this module with all the creature comforts, including a well-equipped kitchenette and a circular dining room table with six padded wooden chairs taking up the center of the module, and a comfortable sofa. Five of the astronauts sat around the table, while Manwaring sat at the end of the sofa bolted against the wall opposite the kitchenette. A large-screen television monitor was bolted to the wall space above the computer desk between the sofa and kitchenette. The only item visible on the desk surface was Elizabeth's open sketch pad. A mechanical pencil sat on top of her latest sketch. A two-part rendering of the blade Elizabeth had shown Manwaring earlier. Complete with a hand-drawn scale.

"I see that the first greenhouse is coming together," Manwaring said. Standing with his empty plate in hand, he paused in front of Elizabeth's sketch pad before stopping at the kitchenette sink.

"Yes, it is, and I think we'll be enjoying nice salads in three weeks," Tiburón said, taking a sip of coffee.

Manwaring placed his plate in the sink and turned the tap on for a moment to let water fill the depression.

Everybody at the table stopped to notice the courtesy. Including Elizabeth.

Normally, Manwaring took his full plate back to The Keep, only occasionally eating his meals in The Hilton. Even then, he would only sit on the sofa, scarfing down his dinner in silence, unless he gave an order to somebody. Once finished, he would simply drop the dirty crockery and silverware into the sink while on his way back to The Keep. Tonight, though, he took the time to put water on his crockery. Taking stock of that gesture, Elizabeth sipped her coffee while thinking about his reaction to the obsidian blade in her hand. Acting as if she had accepted Manwaring's explanation with no further regard, she knew what she held in her hand. It was not a piece of molten rock forced through a volcanic fissure. She also knew that the partial impression of a swastika was not an act of nature either. Manwaring knew something they didn't, and she couldn't wait to meet with Finnegan after dinner.

After soaking his plate, Manwaring removed a cup from the dish rack next to the sink. While pouring his coffee, he looked down at the top of the computer desk again.

"Good," he said. He approached the table and reached out for the spoon in the sugar bowl. "I do miss my greens. What I wouldn't do for a cool cucumber sandwich and a crisp apple cider right now."

Everybody else sat at the table and sipped their coffee while taking in Manwaring's new demeanor.

Tiburón spoke, "I got the cucumbers handled, and we do have bread dough, mayo, and apple seeds. I had planned to grow greens in the first greenhouse and apple trees in the second. We're also going to grow marijuana and grapes there, too, and call that greenhouse Satan's Eden, but the weed and the grapes grow a lot faster than trees."

"We have apple juice concentrate, don't we?" Spike interjected.

Tiburón paused to look at Spike. "I knew some graduates from San Quentin Penitentiary, and they taught me how to brew good toilet wine. So I know about fermentation?"

"I grew up in Tennessee," Spike responded. "So I know moonshine."

"And don't forget me," Elizabeth chimed in. "I grew up in Napa Valley. Wine country."

"Good," Tiburón said. "After a good night's sleep, we can compare notes in the morning."

Everybody went silent to enjoy the moment. After the brief reflection, Elizabeth raised her coffee mug. "Here's to Satan's Eden."

Everybody answered the toast and settled in for a quiet and relaxing evening.

"What do you guys want to watch tonight?" Elizabeth asked. She moved to the computer. Sitting down, she closed her sketch pad and started to scroll through a list of titles.

"How about something uplifting," Kroll interjected. "*Silence of the Lambs?*"

"You find that movie uplifting?" Spike asked. "Or are you looking for cooking tips? How about *The Dirty Dozen* instead? Since we all started out with numbers and are convicted murderers sent on a suicide mission, I'm sort of in the mood."

"Okay," Elizabeth said as she turned to face the computer. "My grandmother watched it all the time. She had a thing for the actor playing Major Reisman, Lee Marvin."

"Your grandmother was spot on," Spike interjected. "Not only was Lee Marvin a man's man, but he was also a WWII combat veteran for real. A marine scout sniper who bagged a shitload of Japanese soldiers in the Pacific."

"Well, you lot go ahead and watch your movie," Manwaring said. Finished with stirring his coffee, he set the spoon back on the table. Onto a napkin. "Elizabeth, I see you're quite the artist."

"I find it relaxing," Elizabeth said.

He nodded. "And I do like the plans for Satan's Eden."

Everybody watched as he opened the door to the tunnel leading to The Keep and closed it behind him.

"He seemed almost human tonight," Finnegan said.

While agreeing with Finnegan, Elizabeth had to ask herself one question: *Why did he compliment me on my sketches?*

"So, he explained away that blade just like he did with the swastika," Finnegan said. He leaned against the workbench, flipping one of the obsidian pieces between his fingers like a card shark. "Which means he's up to something in 'dem dar hills.'"

Elizabeth, sitting next to him in front of the workbench, held a glass of wine. The magnifying glass and her sketch pad occupied space on the bench's surface in front of her. "Something is up there with bits and pieces of it ending up in the lakebed. Mars may not have much of an atmosphere, and no flowing water, but it did have flowing water one point, and it still has gravity. Now, we're collecting items that don't square with each other—a swastika and what looks like the letters R and K on either side of it pressed into a rock, and two Mesoamerican obsidian blades. I can't imagine what else we'll find out there. But I hope we can find enough to paint a real picture and do so before Spike or Tiburón find anything themselves."

Exchanging the obsidian blade with a glass of wine, Finnegan asked, "You want to keep those two out of the picture?

"For now," Elizabeth said, pausing to offer a tilt of her wine glass in salute. "I think that little show of humanity at dinner just might have shaken things up. So, once we get a better picture, we can have a better chance of reacting while keeping the upper hand."

"Well, I gotta agree," Finnegan said. "If we can keep Spike and Tiburón focused on the greenhouses, it will help. Since my duties allow me a bit more freedom, I'll get up early and scout the greenhouse excavations to see if they churned anything without realizing it. Once I clear that area, I'll keep an eye on the rest of Legoland."

"It just so happens I have Mesoamerican literature on my computer in The Office," Elizabeth said. "Brought it along as reading material. It can help you. Can't do much about Nazi swastikas, though. Herr Finnegan."

"No problem there," Finnegan said, reaching for the wine bottle on the bench. "But why did you assume the swastika was of Nazi origin?"

"Isn't the swastika a Nazi symbol?" Elizabeth said, holding out her glass for a refill.

"It is, but they weren't the original creators of that symbol. In fact, the swastika dates to at least 5,000 years ago. Maybe 7,500 years ago. And by cultures or societies across what is now China and India. Even in Mesoamerica."

"Are you saying ancient Hindus or Chinese may have visited Mars?" Elizabeth asked as she pulled her glass from Finnegan's now-upright bottle.

"Possibly, but doubtful," Finnegan said. "Or the swastika came from outer space, and what we found here on our first day was the result of an alien using Mars as a way stop on his way to Earth."

Elizabeth narrowed one eye at Finnegan.

"Or," Finnegan said, "I could stick with your original thought that the swastika is of Nazi origin, and the letters R and K prove it so."

"In what way?"

Finnegan paused for a second. "It has been a while since I had to put the letters R and K together, especially when they straddle a swastika, which is why I didn't think of it earlier. But what I am talking about is the Rhinelander Korps.

"Go ahead," Elizabeth said. As she lifted her wine glass, she thought back to her childhood back in Kanab, Utah, and the lunch boxes full of her desert treasures.

"The Rhinelander Korps is, *was*, a secret association of Americans and Germans. An association rumored to include Henry Ford and Adolf Hitler. Not much is known about the group, so I'll have to sleep on it. In any case, though, we're talking about a group of American military men and financiers who collaborated with the Germans during World Wars One *and* Two. Perhaps even before the First World War."

With the lip of the glass pressed against her lower lip, she narrowed one eye again. "Now you're starting to sound like Tiburón."

"Is that necessarily a bad thing?"

Elizabeth imagined the smell of brewing coffee and frying sausage as she stepped out of her module and through the tunnel leading to The Hilton. Stepping through the door, she saw Kroll at the kitchenette, and Spike and Tiburón reclining side by side on the sofa holding their coffee cups. They rested their heads against the sofa's back and appeared half asleep. Elizabeth's hair was wet and was sticking out from under Finnegan's ball cap. It had been a good night with Finnegan, and the next morning being just as satisfying. Now, she looked forward to a good breakfast and an active day. Last night, before sex, they'd brainstormed about what was going on with Manwaring, and their reason for being on Mars. They concluded that if they had already found worked Mesoamerican obsidian blades and the impression of a swastika on the Martian surface, the next find could be quite revealing.

Elizabeth accepted a mug of coffee from Kroll and pulled out a chair at the table. "Mind a little help with Satan's Eden? I need to work off Kroll's cooking."

"Sure thing," Spike replied sleepily.

"I ain't gonna complain either," Tiburón said. "I have plans, and Spike could use the help. Where's Finnegan? Sleeping in?"

"Said he wanted to recheck something out at The Tank Farm," Elizabeth answered. "He'll join us shortly." She paused for a second, noticing Tiburón giving Spike a nudge with his shoulder. "What do you mean by helping Spike. What do you have planned?"

Tiburón sipped his coffee. "We're going to start on the framing beams. Once we get started, I'm going to grab The Mule and do some rock hounding."

"What about Manwaring's orders to stay close to home?"

"Screw Mister Dill Hole," Tiburón responded. "The right kind of rocks help control water evaporation from the soil, and leach in good chemicals at the same time. Although I have some rocks that will work, most of the rocks in the lakebed are the wrong type, which means the rocks I'm looking for are probably locked up in seams. Up in the mountains."

Elizabeth shrugged. "Well, I would prefer you give us a more specific location as to where you want to go. Just in case we have to come looking for you."

"Don't know yet. I'll keep my comms open."

"Okay," Elizabeth responded, "but make sure you're back in time for lunch, just to be safe. Did Manwaring already leave?"

"He came in here, slammed a coffee, a link, and was off like a prom dress," Spike answered with a slight yawn.

The door from The Office opened, and Finnegan stepped through it. He joined Elizabeth at the table while accepting coffee from Kroll. Once he sat, next to Elizabeth, they ate and joked quietly, and as they were finishing their breakfast, Kroll offered his plans for lunch.

"I hope you don't mind a simple lunch today, a nosh. I would like to help outside myself. Are cheese sandwiches for lunch satisfactory?"

Elizabeth emptied her coffee. Before answering Kroll's request. "My grandmother made the best grilled cheese sandwiches. And with bacon. And with dill pickle spears."

Kroll smiled. "*Sehr gut*. Grilled cheese sandwiches with bacon and pickles it is."

Finnegan smiled and looked at Elizabeth. "Well, it looks like I need to earn my lunch. Elizabeth, do you mind helping me in The Garage before you mix it up with this mob?"

Thirty minutes later, Tiburón, Spike, and Elizabeth stood in front of the partially assembled greenhouse wearing their spacesuits. The distant morning sun climbed ever so slowly in the sky.

"I'll help you get started." Tiburón said as he reached down for a box of bolts and a wrench. He stood up and held the items out for Elizabeth. "But it's pretty straightforward."

Retrieving the box reminded Elizabeth about the time she helped her grandfather assemble an aluminum shed.

"You guys got this?" asked Tiburón.

"Go ahead, Tiburón," Spike said. "Just keep in touch and make it back by lunch."

"Yes, ma'am," Tiburón said while bending over again to pick up a plastic bucket with a rock hammer inside of it. Leaving the women to their work, he turned and walked around The Garage, intent on the module containing The Mule. Coming around the corner of the module he spotted Finnegan standing next to the lowered ramp.

"Coming with me?" Tiburón asked over his helmet's intercom as he pulled up to the ramp.

Finnegan, now inside the module, and on the vehicle's driver's side, unplugged the electric vehicle while answering. "Turns out Elizabeth was an immense help. Leaving me with time on my hands. You mind?"

Tiburón dropped the bucket and hammer into the bed before stepping into the passenger side of the module. "Fine with me."

Minutes later, as they pulled away from base camp, Finnegan could almost feel Elizabeth's eyes watching them drive toward up the lakebed's slight rise and the riverbed snaking down from the sharply inclined mountains. His mind still reeled at what he had found that morning. Quickly sharing his finds with Elizabeth, there was no way he could let Tiburón go up there by himself.

Notwithstanding the finds, or perhaps because of his finds, Finnegan genuinely enjoyed the drive into the red- and gray-mottled mountains. He could also see the smile on Tiburón's face through the helmet's transparent plastic. But they smiled for distinct reasons.

While Finnegan drove, Tiburón kept a wary eye on the riverbed in front and on the rising banks on either side of them. Occasionally, Tiburón told Finnegan to stop so he could inspect a rock outcropping further up the steepening riverbed. Each time they stopped, he would use his rock hammer to knock a sample loose, hold it up against the distant sun, twist it in his hand, then either drop it on the ground or toss it in the bed of The Mule before climbing back in the passenger seat. The morning continued as such, following the partial tire tracks in patches of loose dirt and gravel. Tracks from Manwaring's daily excursions. After three kilometers, they reached the first tributary emptying into the main riverbed.

Stopping at the intersection, Finnegan said, "Well?"

Tiburón didn't answer right away. Instead, his eyes traveled back and forth between the main riverbed and the tributary. While Finnegan waited for Tiburón to decide which direction to take, something on the ground pulled at his eyes. While not really understanding why, he leaned over and picked up two items.

"What do you got?" Tiburón asked.

"Oh, nothing," Finnegan answered. He straightened up and held up a pale gray rock with red streaks. "Just playing. Anyway, which direction?"

Tiburón took the rock from Finnegan's hand and looked up at the main riverbed. He tossed the rock aside. "Let's go straight ahead. That tributary ain't going nowhere."

"Straight ahead it is," Finnegan said as he pulled his hand from the spacesuit's pant pocket and placed it on the steering wheel along with the other hand. Taking his foot off the brake pedal, they continued further up the walled-in riverbed.

By around noon, they had passed four more narrow tributaries and collected about a hundred pounds of loose rocks in the bed of the vehicle. They stopped in front of another tributary. Tiburón looked at it from the passenger seat. "This place really does remind me of the Superstition Mountains outside of Phoenix, and that tributary reminds me of Copperhead Canyon."

Finnegan looked at the tributary Tiburón called Copperhead Canyon. It was narrow, with steep sides, but it looked wide enough for any of their vehicles to drive into. There was a partial tire track in the loose gravel, along with something else. He could imagine water funneling out of the tributary. "It reminds me of the cornfield mazes from Halloween."

"Except the Canyon wasn't a cornfield maze. Hence the name Copperhead Canyon," Tiburón replied as he threw his legs out of the vehicle to stand. "It was a great hideout. Sheltered, with a spring, hidden caves, and a back door, with one main entrance that we could block off and defend."

Tiburón stepped toward another rock outcropping poking out of the wall of the main riverbed. Finnegan got out as well and stepped around the front of the vehicle and toward the entrance of the tributary. Listening to Tiburón talk about his smuggling days and Copperhead Canyon, Finnegan stepped into the tributary, stopping about two meters in. Now that his eyes knew what to look for, he bent down to pick one up. Straightening up, he folded it over in his hand. Yes, it was just like the first item, but there was a difference. The item he found earlier was in the main riverbed, mixed in with millions of years of mottled rocky detritus, and at the junction of a tributary. This item was in the tributary, at its conjunction with the main riverbed. Clasping his fingers around the find, he peered into the canyon, at least as far as the first bend, and nodded his head. He repeated the name of the canyon to himself.

"You ready?" Tiburón asked through the helmet intercom.

Finnegan turned around. Tiburón stood at the canyon's entrance.

"Yeah, I could use a grilled cheese sandwich and a coffee."

The drive back seemed to take forever, especially with the lakebed, and Legoland, spread out in front of them below. Even though their battery-powered motor and wheels drove them forward, Legoland never seemed to get bigger in their eyes. Eventually, though, they stopped in front of The Shit Shack.

"Leave the rocks here," Tiburón said. "Spike and I can get at them later. Right now, I want a grilled cheese sandwich."

While Tiburón said he was looking forward to lunch and putting his rocks to use, Finnegan was looking forward to something else, but right now, his conversation with Elizabeth would have to wait. The two men walked around the side of The Keep and stepped toward The Hilton's airlock. They noticed that Manwaring's vehicle was not parked in front of the Westing House, the pod where Manwaring could plug The Minivan in to recharge whenever he came back for lunch, and where he could do his thing, whatever it was, inside the pod. Aside from being a spare-parts storage pod, the structure also served as Manwaring's field laboratory.

"I thought lunch would never end," Elizabeth said.

Finnegan, walking behind her, entered The Office, closing the door behind him. "Same here."

She turned to face him. "What did you find?"

Finnegan reached into his trouser pocket and pulled out his hand, palm side up. He opened his fingers. "I thought you would find them important."

Elizabeth's eyes widened as she zeroed in on the items he was holding. Elizabeth turned to look at the items on her desk. "It may not make sense, but it can also make all the sense in the world at the same time."

"I agree, but I wonder if Manwaring has found anything yet," Finnegan responded. "He did miss out on lunch."

"He's missed lunch before."

"I know," Finnegan said, stepping over to the computer desk to add the items in his hand to their collection, "and I think that's what's worrying me.

I saw partial tire tracks in the main riverbed and inside the canyon's entrance. These items were feet away from the tire tracks. I was able to pick them out of that rocky debris, and I'm not a trained archaeologist."

Elizabeth stepped over to her desk. It was as if she were a little girl again, back in her bedroom outside of Kanab, lining up the newest artifacts she'd found on the desert floor after camping with her grandparents. The same rusted and tarnished curios that still filled tin lunch boxes on one of her bookshelves back at her grandmother's house in Napa Valley. Now on Mars, her hand paused above the item third in line. The item that Finnegan had found that morning by The Shit Shack. With the realization that she'd seen something similar before, but not on Mars, she answered, "My grandmother always said I did love a good mystery."

Late April, AD 2026

With their heads spinning, Finnegan and Elizabeth speculated about the possibilities behind the artifacts lined up in front of them. It didn't take long for them to separate the artifacts into separate storylines, but the themes lacked a context to link them into a singular plot. First, there was the rock with the impression of a swastika and two partial letters, possibly R and K. Next to it were the two obsidian blades Elizabeth found. After that, a small-label plate. One like one any would see attached to a piece of machinery. A plate Finnegan found that morning on the lakebed. The next two items were palm-sized pieces of orangish gritty pottery. Ceramics Finnegan found in the riverbed, or at the nexus between the riverbed and the tributary. The one with the tire tracks leading into it.

Elizabeth sighed as she looked at the artifacts. "There are any number of possibilities, which is why I'm not saying Aztec, but let's just stay with Mesoamerican for now. Doing so will give us a starting point and a rough date range. A very rough date range."

"Sounds like a great starting point," Finnegan said. He tapped one of the pieces of pottery with his index finger. It, and the other one, the thicker of the two, fitted nicely in the palm of his hand. "So, you're saying that those two pieces are from two different terra-cotta containers?"

"By looking at the curvature, and thicknesses, I'd say one came from a drinking vessel, like a cup or bowl, and the other came from something bigger. A storage container. You said you found them both with the curved side up?"

"Yes, ma'am."

"Good," Elizabeth said, picking up her magnifying glass and the thinner of the two pieces. She bent over the computer desk to use the light from the lamp. Finnegan stood behind her, waiting.

"Ah ha," Elizabeth said. She straightened and turned to face Finnegan. "I found a fingerprint on the inside, which means it was human-made."

"Or just made by a being with fingerprints," Finnegan countered. "By the way, did I ever tell you playing Nancy Drew makes me horny."

"Me playing Nancy Drew? You staring at my ass while I'm bent over a desk?"

Finnegan smiled. "There's that, too."

Accepting his admission, she continued. "Whoever made these containers made them from wet clay and left their fingerprints on the inside while shaping the vessels. And not on a spinning wheel. *And* the fingerprints appear human."

"Okay, so we have found, here on Mars, four human-made, centuries-old Mesoamerican artifacts," Finnegan said. "We also have a rock with a partial imprint of a swastika and what could be the tops of the letters R and K, which links us to one other artifact. One that is human-made, and one not only made in the twentieth century, but made in 1939, in the good ol' USA, namely Dearborn, Michigan. Now, all we have to do is find something that can link those sets of artifacts together."

Elizabeth reached out to place the magnifying glass on the computer desk. She replaced the lens with the label plate Finnegan found this morning over by The Shit Shack.

Machined from aluminum and with a hole at each end, the label plate was the length and thickness of a stick of gum, but a bit wider and slightly curved. In between the holes were two lines of text in English. One ran lengthwise along the top of the plate, and the second ran along the bottom of the plate. In between those lines was the outline of an eagle with its head turned sideways, and in the label's center, the letters R and K straddled the eagle. The top line read Starboard jet primary arbiter. Under the central image, the second line read: Dearborn, Michigan, USA. 1939-A541-T3874.

Though stamped only on one side, Elizabeth flipped the label over in her fingers to give herself time to think.

"I was born in Fairchild, Wisconsin, but I grew up in Napa Valley, California, with my grandparents after my parents died, and spent my summers with them in Kanab, Utah. We camped out often, and I always found all kinds of junk—copper buttons from old denims, old coins from previous campers, and even brass or aluminum grommets from tents and tarps. And I would tell my grandma I found part of Coronado's treasure. My grandmother knew different, but she always played along. Anyway, one day, I found a piece of metal just like this one."

She stopped to hold it up for Finnegan to look at. "I remember the image of the eagle and the letters R and K. I also remember telling my grandmother it came off the shield of a Roman legionnaire when they invaded the southwest. She played along with my fantasies, like she always did. That said, there were also stories of Aztec treasure on the land, and a crazy German looking for it in the 1800s, so my mind had fuel to work with. Anyway, when I grew older, my grandmother told me about a US Army air mail service airfield and a testing ground where Firestone and Ford developed new types of army trucks and airplanes. She said Charles Lindberg flew out of that airfield when he flew for the air mail service. I'll bet that label I found as a kid came off one of those trucks or an airplane."

She stopped, as Finnegan seemed to have been suddenly time-warped to another dimension. But, just as suddenly, his eyes and mind returned to their dimension, and he snapped out a question. "You said the writing on the label you found wasn't in English?"

"I told my grandmother it was Latin, and she went along with me," Elizabeth answered. "Since I couldn't understand the writing, I focused on the image, and the letters R and K. Thinking back, though, it could've been in German."

She watched as Finnegan held up the label and pointed to the bottom line.

"The date, 1939, is important," Finnegan said. "The year World War Two started. Also, Lindbergh, though an isolationist, was also anti-Semitic and pro-German. He even visited German aircraft manufacturing plants and Luftwaffe bases both in Germany and Spain, where the German Condor Division fought in the Spanish Civil War. Because of his accomplishments, views, and status, Herman Goering awarded Lindbergh the Service Cross of the German Eagle. Goering was the head general of the Luftwaffe and their parachute divisions. The award was meant to recognize Lindbergh's contributions to world aviation. Congress dragged Lindbergh before them and forced him to publicly denounce Hitler and the Nazis. Still, he remained pro-German and an anti-Semite."

Elizabeth focused on the machined label in Finnegan's hand. "I've heard about Lindbergh's feelings, but it seems like you're about to tell me Ford's role in all of that."

"Ford was also pro-German, anti-Semitic, and a recipient of the Service Cross of the German Eagle. Along with other prominent American businessmen," Finnegan said. "He was also extraordinarily rich, knew how to run a business empire, and admired Hitler's ideas. In return, Hitler read Ford's biography often and studied his manufacturing practices. Stretching one's imagination, one could argue a coordinated effort between Ford, Lindbergh, other Americans, and the Germans, i.e., the Rhinelander Korps, to create a unified space effort. There must be a connection because we're holding the result of their efforts in our hands. I also think that Ford's proving ground near your grandparents' ranch in Utah put this piece of aluminum in our hands, and that includes real Aztec treasure. In other words, it's starting to come together. Aztec treasure used to fund an American and German alliance. On Earth, and in space."

"And my grandmother said *I* had an imagination," Elizabeth said with a smile. "But somehow, everything you've said makes perfect sense. Think about it. An American-German space effort in the middle of the Great Depression and WWII. And in Utah? But what do we do now? And do you think we're in danger? From Manwaring? Or somebody else? The Rhinelander Korps? Are they around? Is Einstok their leader?"

Finnegan handed the machined label plate back to Elizabeth and reached into his pants pocket. "I'm just piecing together what you've told me and what I already knew, and from what Tiburón said before. Turns out that Mexican isn't that crazy. Anyway, no one knows much about the Rhinelander Korps as it only exists in myths and rumors. There is no available historical evidence proving its existence. Still, what we do next is important, especially since I do think we're in danger. We were executed back on Earth and turned into ashes, and whoever is behind all of this can't have our presence here on Mars known to the world."

"All I know is," Elizabeth said, "at the rate were going, our next find will be a Roman coin in a Smucker's jelly jar."

A broad, beaming grin took control of Finnegan's face.

"Now what?" she asked.

Still grinning, he pulled his hand from his pocket and held out his palm.

"Holy shit!" Her shaking fingers picked up the two items.

"I would have showed them to you earlier, but I also know that no matter how good you are at playing Nancy Drew, we can manage only so much information at any given time."

Like a proud child holding two popsicles, one in each hand, Elizabeth focused her eyes on the item in her left hand. "This piece looks like it came from an aluminum beer can run over by a lawnmower. But one with five and a half characters embossed into the metal. They almost look like Nordic runes to me."

"Well, I don't speak, or read Klingon, but they look almost like the lettering you might see in a *Star Trek* movie. What I do know is that aircraft, especially military aircraft, are made from thousands of parts, and most of those parts have some sort of serial or manufacturing number. In case there is a crash or a mechanical failure. Even individual panels or pieces of the fuselage have serial numbers embossed on them."

Elizabeth, keeping her eyes on the scrap metal, finished Finnegan's concern. "Which means we're also dealing with an alien spacecraft."

"So, Nancy Drew, the plot thickens," Finnegan said. "Especially if you include that item in your right hand. It's a—"

"It's a nock," Elizabeth said firmly. "From a crossbow. And not a modern one. Am I correct?"

"Yes! Looks like it's from a Spanish crossbow. Fifteenth or sixteenth century, I'm guessing," Finnegan said. "How did you figure that out?"

"I did some target practice in Utah," Elizabeth said, still holding the items in front of her, "which includes pistols, rifles, bows and arrows, and crossbows. I also found one exactly like this one. It's in my *Treasure Island* lunch box in my bedroom."

The item in her right hand resembled a pen cap made from brass, with a notch at the non-open end. Made to fit on the end of a crossbow bolt, it was what the crossbow's drawstring fit into when made ready to fire.

Elizabeth lowered both hands. "I'll secure these items. And I still say we should keep this from Kroll, Tiburón, and Spike. For now. The only problem is that they might find artifacts themselves and change their behavior."

"Like speaking up," Elizabeth offered, "in front of Manwaring?"

"Chances are, Manwaring has already found whatever he was looking for, which means we're dead. The question then is, how will he, or somebody else, try to kill us?"

"I'll do my best to keep any remaining artifacts scattered about Legoland away from Spike and Tiburón," Finnegan said. "But, about Manwaring, I don't think he wants to kill us. Hell, I don't think he even has the stones to do so, but he'll need to, as we were only useful in helping him get here. But how will he do it? Somehow, I think poisoning our coffee or cheese sandwiches seems a bit inefficient, or even beneath him. And don't think strangling us one at a time will work, either."

"You're right," Elizabeth answered. "When he does try to kill us, he'll have to be as efficient, complete, and striking as possible."

Finnegan nodded. "He must have exact control, as even if one of us survives, he himself will be in danger. Shit, even you could take him if it came down to it. No offense."

"None taken," Elizabeth said. "And just like you said, it all suits me just fine."

The remainder of the afternoon passed quietly, and dinner passed with the normal talk of the day and the occasional banter. As they talked and ate, Finnegan and Elizabeth watched Manwaring. His thin, hawkish face, accentuated by his gray hair pulled back into a ponytail, failed to reveal the results of his daily prospecting.

"So, how's TETRA's marijuana working out for you?" Elizabeth asked. She sat back in her chair and sipped on her coffee. "I've been keeping track of the inventory, so it can't be that bad."

"Not as bad as I thought it would be," Tiburón replied, leaving the table to join Spike on the sofa. "That said, we should be done assembling the first greenhouse in another couple of *sols*, which means we can move our seedlings from The Shit Shack into it. Then, we can start on Satan's Eden."

"Here, here," Kroll said as he lifted a small glass of wine in salute. "By the way, I've been judging our schedule and inventorying our stores. I suspect we may have to scale back on our wine consumption. You know, until Satan's Eden is up and running."

"I agree," Manwaring said, "which means we need to focus our efforts on the greenhouses. So, Tiburón, no more prospecting for rocks. Give me samples of what you're looking for. Since I am up in the mountains every day, I can locate what you need."

Tiburón looked down at his coffee before answering. "Sure thing."

At the same time, Finnegan felt Elizabeth, sitting next to him, pinch his thigh under the table.

"Good," Manwaring responded as he stood from the table. "Let's get our crockery washed, and I'll see you at breakfast."

Two hours later, back at The Hilton, Kroll was sound asleep in his bunk, having completed a crossword while listening to ABBA. Being their cook, he always went to sleep early, as he was always the first one up in the morning. Secured in his bunk, and behind closed curtains, the German snored blissfully. Manwaring retreated to The Keep, and Elizabeth and Finnegan found their own security in The Office. Their departures to their own quarters left Tiburón and Spike alone to listen to Kroll's slumber.

"So," Spike said while exhaling marijuana smoke, "you're sure those two pieces you found this afternoon are from terra-cotta containers. And Mesoamerican?"

Spike and Tiburón and lay together in another bunk, behind closed curtains, in The Hilton. Tiburón lay flat on his back with his right shoulder supporting Spike's head as she lay on her side cuddled against him. His hand slowly rubbed the small of her back under their covers. Warmed by a weak bunk light above their heads, Tiburón accepted the half-smoked joint from Spike with his thumb and index finger. "I've smuggled enough drugs inside terra-cotta statues to know the pieces I found are real. And that little label plate I found is just as real." He took a hit of the joint. Holding the smoke in his lungs a few seconds, he exhaled and added to the fog of smoke gathered around the bunk light just above their heads.

"So," Spike said, "we have both Mesoamerican pottery pieces and a label from a machine sent here by a secret German American group. A group made up of both German and American business leaders and military men. And in the 1930s or 1940s."

"And in cooperation with the OSS," Tiburón added, while knocking off ash into the empty coffee cup resting on the blanket covering his stomach. "While I can't explain the terra-cotta by itself, I can explain the Rhinelander Korps, and its members, including those bastards Ford, Firestone, and Lindbergh, and that fucker FDR. They were all traitors, and they were conspiring with the Nazis. Even though formed in the late 1800s, the Rhinelander Korps became even more powerful during the Great Depression in the 1930s."

Accepting the joint from Tiburón, Spike took another hit while thinking about what Tiburón told her. While she did not know about any secret German American alliance, she did know something about the OSS, the forerunner of the CIA. The Office of Strategic Services, created in 1942 and under the FDR administration, served as an intelligence-gathering agency with operators working behind enemy lines, and its pilots conducting high-tech, high-resolution, and high-altitude aerial reconnaissance. A form of technological reconnaissance the future CIA would excel in. She also remembered the small-label plate Tiburón had found and shown her. Made from aluminum and about the size of a stick of gum, it had the image of an eagle with the letter R and K embossed on its center. The line above the eagle read: landing camera aperture: 1943-A132. The line underneath read Office of Strategic Services.

Spike exhaled and passed the joint back. "It all sounds a bit *Raiders of the Lost Ark*-like. Are you sure we can't tell Elizabeth and Finnegan? Maybe they've been finding stuff, too."

"First of all, it's more like *Indiana Jones and the Last Crusade*. The movie where the American businessman was in cahoots with, and who funded, the Nazis to find the Holy Grail, which is all the more reason why we can't tell them. At least not until we get a better grasp of what is going on here," Tiburón said. "I mean, if they did find anything like we've found, and they didn't tell us, that means they're up to something themselves. Remember that rock I found on our first day here? I couldn't find it, so either Manwaring threw it further than I thought, or maybe Finnegan went looking for it. If he did, then that means he knows something. And remember, we didn't know them until we started our training. They could be plants. They could be working for the reason we're here to begin with."

"Hey," Spike said as she exhaled. "You didn't know me before this mission, so why do you trust me?"

Taking the joint from her, he responded, "You, I've got you figured. And I've checked you out from head to toe and inside and out and didn't find any microphones in your nipples. And Kroll's a non-issue as well. It's Elizabeth and Finnegan that I haven't read yet. And there's always been something up with Manwaring that I never did like. It all surrounds his wanting us to stick around Legoland while he spends every day up in those mountains. There's something up there he doesn't want anybody else to see or find. He's part of the system. Remember: *Never trust the system.*"

Spike turned her head to look at Tiburón's chin three inches from hers. He did the same, and their noses touched. After a second, she said, "While we need to scale back on our wine, you need to slow down with the weed, too. That stuff is making you paranoid. Last night, you held my boob like a microphone and talked solid gibberish to my nipple."

"Hey, Chica, no weed has ever made me paranoid, and no weed has ever knocked my dick in the dirt. But I agree that TETRA, or the government, could've done something to the ditch weed they issued us. The DEA and CIA have been messing with weed for years." He smiled. "I'll just have to keep testing it to see if *they* did."

18

Late April, AD 2026

The next morning, Elizabeth stepped into The Hilton, wearing freshly pressed utilities and with her blond hair tucked behind her ears and sticking out of the bottom of Finnegan's ball cap. The smell of baked muffins and strong coffee enveloped her like a warm blanket on a wintry night.

Kroll stood near the sink pouring a cup of coffee.

"*Guten morgen*," Kroll said. He held out a cup of coffee.

"Thanks," she answered, reaching for the cup. "Breakfast smells good."

"*Danke*," he said, brushing the crumbs off a plate and into the drain. "By the way, I inventoried our stores for next week's menu, and I am missing rations. Do you know anything about that?"

Elizabeth's cup stopped halfway to her mouth, but before she could respond, the rustle of cloth and the scrape of plastic curtain rings seized their attention. Tiburón rolled out of his bunk, followed by Spike. Rubbing their eyes as they stood, they yawned simultaneously. Tiburón wore only TETRA-issued white boxer shorts, and Spike wore a short blue undershirt and matching panties.

"Hey, where's our coffee?" Tiburón asked, adjusting his scrotum under his boxers. Spike stepped up to Elizabeth and gave her a peck on her cheek, as she did every morning.

Elizabeth returned Spike's affection by patting her on her butt cheek. The second it took to do that gave Elizabeth an opportunity to absorb Kroll's question. "No, I don't. Might be a mistake in the loading. Or in the inventory. I can help you double-check. Anyway, where's Manwaring?"

While pouring coffee for Spike and Tiburón, Kroll answered, "He already ate. He said he wanted to get an early start on collecting more samples for himself and Tiburón. Where's Finnegan?"

Elizabeth tilted her head. "In The Garage tinkering with something. I'll take a cup of coffee to him and let him know about the muffins. After all, those muffins smell good." She turned to Tiburón and Spike just as they found their spot on the sofa. "You two seemed to be getting along nicely."

Both saluted with their coffee cups.

Elizabeth entered The Garage. Closing the door with one hand, she held out the coffee in her other. Finnegan stepped away from his workbench to accept the coffee, leaving his helmet lying sideways on the workbench. The padding secured against the back of the helmet's inside now lay next to it on the workbench. His spacesuit lay draped over the shop stool next to the workbench.

"Got something?"

He sipped his coffee before answering. "Remember when we agreed he had to kill us, and with sheer certainty. At the same time?"

Elizabeth nodded.

"I think I figured how he, or somebody, might carry it out. That is, when the time is right."

"Well, that time might be closer than we thought," Elizabeth responded. "Kroll said he's missing stores from his inventory."

"Shit," Finnegan said.

"Yeah, I know," Elizabeth said, grabbing her cup. "Let's get breakfast. You can explain what you found afterward."

After more coffee and a helping of blueberry muffins with Kroll, Tiburón, and Spike, Finnegan and Elizabeth were back in The Garage. A cylinder the size of a double AA battery with two coated wires sticking out of one end seized their focus.

"Like I said before," Finnegan said, "I never thought Manwaring had the stones or the strength to kill us by hand, which means he must do it remotely. When the time was right, or when told to do so. Anyway, since we all have to wear spacesuits and our wrist-mounted computers when on the planet's surface, all he has to do is get us together out on the surface. That way, he can type in a code without us being suspicious and explode these little cylinders. I found mine under the head padding right at the base of the neck ring. Probably filled with poison gas."

"But if one of us found it, we would just assume it being part of the spacesuit. A GPS locator," Elizabeth said. "You got yours out, and I can get mine out, but we still have Kroll, Tiburón, and Spike. While we shouldn't tell them yet, I'd feel better if we could disarm their suits at the same time. The problem is that we've already eaten our breakfast, so calling them in to draw blood now would be a dead giveaway."

"Especially since tomorrow is the normal lab day," Finnegan said. "We can wait until tomorrow, and I can do my thing while you have them in The Office drawing blood. In the meantime, I think it's time to figure out what Manwaring is up to. Especially since Kroll is missing rations from his inventory. Manwaring might be ready to pull chocks, but if he can't, or won't, kill us, then I'll bet there is somebody who can or will."

Elizabeth smiled. "Pulling chocks."

"Yeah, it's an aviation term," Finnegan replied. "What about it?"

"Oh nothing," Elizabeth said, with a nostalgic look in her eyes. "It's just that the last words I remember my father saying, after telling me he loved me, was telling my mother it was time to pull chocks. Something he said often. It was his *nice* way of telling my mother, it was time to move her ass."

By 8:00 a.m. the following morning, Elizabeth had Tiburón, Spike, and Kroll in The Office with their sleeves rolled up.

"Where's Finnegan?" Tiburón asked. "And Manwaring?"

Elizabeth stood in front of Tiburón, holding the syringe needle up.

"I already drew their blood. Finnegan's in The Garage tinkering with something again, and Manwaring said he wanted to get an early start on whatever he does up there. Why? You're not, all of a sudden scared of needles, are you?"

Tiburón shook his head. "No, just curious."

"Well," Elizabeth said as she turned the needle tip at his vein, "as much as you bring up government conspiracies, I'm not with the government, and I'm not going to inject a nano-transmitter into your system while drawing blood."

Minutes later, Kroll, Tiburón, and Spike were enjoying their breakfast in The Hilton, and Elizabeth found Finnegan in front of the bench in The Garage. At the sound of the door opening, he turned and greeted her with a big, cheesy grin.

"I told you," Tiburón said, turning to place his cup in the sink. "They're up to something. We're always together on lab day, but somehow, both Finnegan and Manwaring conveniently found excuses to have their blood drawn early. And now Kroll's bitching about missing stores."

Kroll, making his bunk inside The Hilton, turned to look at the two. "Excuse, but am I missing something?"

Tiburón and Spike paused to look at each other. After a second, Spike gave Tiburón the nod. Tiburón briefly explained what was going on.

"I'm starting to agree with you," Spike said, "but I can't believe Elizabeth's in on any plan to kill us."

"I don't either," Tiburón said, reaching for his spacesuit, "but I'm going back out on the surface to see what else I can find. Those pieces of terra-cotta I found are the start of one helluva mystery. I'd grab The Mule and get up in those mountains, but I don't want to tip our hand too soon. Care to join me?"

"You two do that," Kroll added. "I'll go through our stores to see exactly what's missing."

Thirty minutes later, Tiburón and Spike were on the surface finishing bolting a rafter beam in place in greenhouse Number One. Wearing spacesuits, Elizabeth and Finnegan drove The Mule around the corner of The Garage toward them. Finnegan sat in the driver's seat. Elizabeth, in the passenger seat, raised her hand toward them.

Tiburón waved back with a wrench in his hand. "Now, where the hell are they going?"

Watching them approach, Tiburón would soon have an answer to his question.

As Elizabeth and Finnegan approached the lip of the lakebed, Elizabeth pulled a pair of pliers and battery-sized gas bombs from the vehicle's glove compartment. She used the jaws of the pliers to crush the sealed tops and, as she did, wisps of escaping gas dissipated into the Martian atmosphere. Knowing they were now safe from that threat, Elizabeth placed the pliers and empty cylinders into the cargo pocket of her spacesuit.

As their deaths wafted away behind them, the explorers enjoyed bounding over the lip of the lakebed toward mountains, following the tracks left behind by Manwaring's daily trips. They drove, aiming for the dry riverbed leading out of the mountains. By noon, they were deep into the riverbed with its banks rising sharply on either side of them. They arrived at the junction where Finnegan found the second piece of pottery.

Finnegan had no problem seeing the tire tracks left by Manwaring and continued, in silence, to enter the offshoot. For Elizabeth, the ride through the winding Martian canyon was exhilarating. While appreciating the shear craggy walls towering above them, she said, "Reminds me of when I was a kid. When I explored Zion National Park with my grandparents."

Finnegan turned to face Elizabeth. "Are you trying to make me jealous of your childhood?"

"*And* it reminds me of what Tiburón said when we first got here. About having a defendable Alamo." Elizabeth nudged his shoulder with hers. "Let's go."

After a short distance, the tributary started to widen, although the rugged walls still towered over them. Evidence of a once-flowing tributary river and waterfalls cascading over the rocks above them was everywhere. She appreciated the alternating shades of red and gray layers of deposited soils in the canyon walls. Finnegan's voice erupted from the speakers inside Elizabeth's helmet. "What the hell!"

He brought their vehicle to a stop so quickly that Elizabeth was thrown forward. She threw her arms to the dashboard to stop herself. "What the hell?"

"Look," Finnegan said, pointing toward a waist-high boulder in front of them, and resting against the canyon wall.

Elizabeth's eyes followed Finnegan's extended finger, but she did not see anything except two vertical walls towering over them and the boulder ten feet in front of their vehicle. She was about to speak but stopped. The item that caught Finnegan's attention was finally realized in front of her. "Impossible," she blurted.

Impossible or not, both slowly absorbed the incredible in front of them. What poked out from behind that boulder was real enough. The withered remains of a human foot, enclosed in a tattered boot with a golden sole, stuck out of the dirt.

After moments of stunned silence, Finnegan pressed the accelerator pedal of The Mule and inched forward. Stopping next to the boulder where they could see the rest of the remains, Finnegan shifted the gear lever to park. "It looks human."

Elizabeth leaned forward to look around Finnegan.

The mummified remains of a human sitting up against the wall of the canyon wore a bulbous gold helmet inset with glass and a spacesuit of some sort, with the remains of a liner suit under it. The outer and inner suits were nothing, but rags stuck to desiccated flesh. Next to the body, partially buried under an accumulation of Martian dirt that covered the human's midsection, was a cylinder, like a scuba tank, also made of gold, with two hoses sticking out of one end. Elizabeth tried to peer into the opaque facemask of the helmet, but the abrasive micro-dust obscured the thick glass. Poking out of the dirt around the encased body were pieces of scattered pottery shards and the head of a metal-bladed axe. Also sticking out of the dirt was the top of the bone handle of a knife or dagger, and next to it, the top of a leather quiver containing five or six crossbow bolts. Most with nocks.

"Looks like one of those old-fashioned helmet divers," Finnegan observed as he bent over and pulled something from the loose soil piled against the left side of the body. Sitting up again, he held an obsidian-laced sword in his right hand. Five or six bladelets were missing. "Behold! The obsidian chainsaw."

Elizabeth provided a more scientific observation, but with a shaking voice. "Due to the lack of bacteria and oxygen, along with the extremes in temperature, and the fact that this area was sheltered, the body mummified naturally." Elizabeth paused as she heard the shock in her own voice. Never in her wildest dreams, even in her childhood, did her mind ever conjure up such an adventure. She took a deep breath. "He reminds me of *Ötzi*. That European mummy they found in the Alps back in the 1990s. A fully equipped hunter at least five thousand years old."

Finnegan, still looking down at the remains, sighed heavily.

"I remember reading about it, but the worst part is that I'm staring at a fortune in gold and can't do anything with it."

"So, I was right," Elizabeth exclaimed, her voice now shaking even more. "But now the question is: how did a Mesoamerican warrior end up on Mars?"

Finnegan looked up at the next turn in the canyon. "I'll bet that man walked out of this canyon. And it looks like Manwaring found his way deeper into it. Let's see what's going on, and maybe we'll run into whatever brought Montezuma here."

With her mind reeling at what they'd discovered, all she could say was, "Lead on."

"Yes sir!" Finnegan said as he put The Mule into gear. The machine lurched forward and made its way deeper into the winding canyon between the vertical walls. They drove slowly for another fifteen minutes, following the meandering canyon floor until they came to another bend. As Finnegan began the turn, Elizabeth looked down at the wrist computer to check the status of her air. Finnegan hit the brakes, throwing her forward again.

"Damn it!" she yelled into her helmet, before straightening herself.

Finnegan put the vehicle in reverse and backed up a meter. He turned, presenting her with a huge grin. "Do you remember that comment you made when we first got here. The one where you said Legoland looks like a junkyard behind NASA headquarters?"

A grin, one matching Finnegan's, pushed at the corners of her widening eyes. "Yes."

Late April, AD 2026

A lone figure floated in absolute bliss, hovering just feet above the spacecraft's hull. Though the vessel was hurling toward Mars at thousands of miles per hour, the man felt no sense of the fantastic speed. Like frozen in a still dream, he hoped it would never end.

As my eyes attempt to decern the other side of the universe, I imagine myself already there either with a sharpened quill in my hand or fine German

Sig-Sauer on my hip.

After penning that quote in his mind, Munro returned to the duties in front of him. Encased in his spacesuit, he floated above a solar panel while holding a wrench in his gloved hand. Satisfied with his repairs, he inserted the tool into a pocket before lifting the cover to his wrist mounted comms computer. He punched in the number to tell the others inside he was ready to reenter the spacecraft and took another second to enjoy the boundless space surrounding him. The Red Planet poised against the backdrop ahead of the ship's nose.

Receiving a reply in his headset, Munro reached down to turn on the electrically powered safety line winch secured to his waist, which pulled him to the airlock's outer hatch. Keeping his eyes on Mars ahead of him, he thought about their overall objective and the individuals he had never met before. Reflecting on a life of reading, and observations, he remembered the writings of William Dampier, who often lamented about the company of men he traveled with.

Reaching the hatch, he thought, *It is amazing how the limitless boundaries of space can force a man to focus on the finite core of his soul.*

Elizabeth lifted her legs from inside the vehicle and planted them on the canyon's floor. She walked up to the front of The Mule and leaned around the corner of the canyon wall. She gasped. After a second, she turned and looked disbelievingly at Finnegan before turning back to the wonderment spread before her eyes. He exited the vehicle and stepped up behind her.

A flat, circular area with a rock-strewn floor greeted them.

The enclosed area was the size of a football field surrounded by a rock wall that receded backward into blackness, creating an overhanging lip. It reminded Elizabeth of more than one cave, or exposed sinkhole, she'd visited while in Central America. All that was missing were the jungle vines and tree roots growing into the sinkhole from the surface above. However, it was not the natural setting that astounded her.

What stunned her the most was what looked like a jet-type aircraft sitting to the right side of the canyon as it emptied into the sinkhole. Its stubby port wing, touching the cliff wall and the fuselage, enjoyed the relative protection provided by the overhang; however, the starboard edge of the fuselage and the entire starboard wing were all but crushed from falling rocks. Despite being almost covered by rocks and dirt, she could still discern its dull-colored reddish-gray metal with thick, stumpy triangular-shaped wings and the remains of a bubbled canopy. A triangular landing gear system with square metal plates, instead of wheels, held the craft's remains off the ground. The craft's fuselage ended with an oval-shaped vertical tail assembly. The vision reminded her of a photo of her father sitting in the cockpit of his own fighter jet, taken on the tarmac right before takeoff.

The Minivan was parked behind the tail assembly.

She pulled her head back. "It looks like a MiG jet from the fifties."

"It reminds me more of a Harrier jet," Finnegan added. "Or space shuttle, but shorter and stubbier. It doesn't look much bigger than the Cessna I flew when I started on my private pilot's license."

"Either way," Elizabeth said, "we have a real spaceship—or spaceplane—sitting in front of us."

"Forget about that toy," Finnegan said. "Look beyond it. At the far wall. Under the overhang. In the shadows."

She turned and stepped forward to get a better view. In the center of the open, rock-strewn ground, light from the Martian sun entering the sinkhole revealed pieces of shredded metal, almost masked by the Martian dirt covering them. In the back of the open space, recessed in the dark shadow of an enclave carved into the rear wall of the canyon was an intact, larger spacecraft.

"It looks like the *Millennium Falcon*," she said as Finnegan pressed up behind her. His helmet bumped against hers. "Think Manwaring's inside that thing?"

"Yes," he said, laying a hand on her shoulder. "Which should give us time to inspect what remains of that spaceplane. Come on."

Finnegan stepped past Elizabeth and walked cautiously up to the stunted craft. Elizabeth followed.

The skin of the spaceplane was made from a sort of dull, reddish-grayish metal that almost matched the color of the Martian surface, but as they treaded closer, the extent of the damage from falling rocks became more apparent. While the portside wing remained intact, falling rocks had destroyed the entire surface of the craft's starboard side, exposing an internal frame system. Albeit mangled.

Stepping up next to the bubbled canopy, they picked at the skin of the craft with their gloved fingers.

"Well, it's clear this thing isn't taking us back to Earth. Or anywhere else for that matter," Elizabeth surmised. "That is, unless you can work your magic."

Finnegan appraised the scarred metal skin.

"I don't care how much duct tape I have or how many photocopied certificates I received from Crazy Habib's School of Spaceship Repair, I can't resurrect this thing. Whoever built this spacecraft built it for interplanetary space travel, which meant they had to use materials that could withstand the impact of micrometeors and space dust particles at high speeds." Finnegan turned to face the entrance to the sink hole. "But assuming our Mesoamerican friend used this thing to get him here, he got out, lived for a few hours before dying, leaving this craft exposed to the elements for, what, five or six hundred years? I don't care how robust anything is built; it can take only so much."

"How long do you think it took our friend to fly from Earth to Mars?" Elizabeth asked.

Finnegan pushed his gloved finger against the skin of the spaceplane's nose section. "Aren't you supposed to be Nancy Drew, or some kind of investigative archaeologist?"

"I've never been vain enough to *not* ask for a second opinion," Elizabeth retorted. "First lesson I learned at Crazy Habib's School of Private Investigatoring and Oral Surgery."

Finnegan smiled as he dropped his arm and studied the side of the craft. The severely damaged wing was about waist high and had a vent system running along the top of the trailing edge of the wing. A metal screen material covered the trailing edge. Two handles protruded from the fuselage just under the canopy. Curious, he reached up with both hands to pull himself up while lifting his left foot onto the frames of the wing. He peered through the remnants of the canopy, which appeared to be made from plastic or acrylic. Centuries of falling Martian dirt and rocks filled the cockpit, leaving only the top metal frame of the pilot seat exposed.

"I'd say no more than a few hours. There isn't enough room to support life for any longer than that. But you knew that." He stepped down and planted his feet on the ground. "Whoever built this thing was way ahead of us, and even though it has had the dog shit beat out of it, TETRA will be able to reverse engineer it."

"Which means anybody in control of a rebuilt model can have access to interplanetary space travel in less than a day," Elizabeth said slowly, remembering the images of Einstok, including the cover from an issue of *Soldier of Fortune,* where he stood with his band of mercenaries on the *Altiplano* in front of an advanced helicopter. the one where they had just survived a gunbattle with competing treasure hunters.

"Well," she said, "I'm going to assume that no matter which way you look at it, we're dead. Knowledge of this type is something that TETRA will want to keep to themselves. We need to find a way of destroying this thing or spreading every nut and bolt to the four corners of the globe. I mean, Mars."

Finnegan nodded as he surveyed the battered machine.

"Agreed. There is no way Einstok will share this technology with the rest of the world. And I'll bet there are others who might also be interested; that is, if they know about this thing. But from what you can see, and based on your anthropological knowledge, what kind of person or persons built and flew this thing? I mean, before our Mesoamerican friend."

Elizabeth's eyes returned to the craft.

"After watching you climb up the side, and by the shape of the cockpit, I'd say the pilot and builders walked upright, were bipedal, and had opposable thumbs for grasping. We also had the same approximate stature, and I'm guessing the same forward-facing eyes with stereoscopic vision."

"Yep," Finnegan said. "It still reminds me of a Harrier jet, though. Vertical lift capabilities, like a helicopter, but can fly forward, just like a jet."

"What kind of an engine did it have?" Elizabeth asked.

"Don't know. Let's have a look." Finnegan stooped to look at the underside of the wings. Elizabeth followed suit.

They inspected what resembled three upside-down flowerpots with bulbous sides attached to each wing, with each one covered by mesh material. They stood up and walked back to the tail. Its builders had constructed the empennage around an engine with the outlet, or exhaust, also covered with a mesh type of material. While the outlet was oval, the bottom was slightly tapered, and the edges running up and down were curved outward. At the more rounded top, and inside the engine outlet, they could see another rounded bulb or pot-like item.

Finnegan turned to drop one eye toward Elizabeth's crotch.

Snorting, she blurted, "Okay, so it looks like a vagina, but how does it work?"

He smiled before returning his attention to the engine. "Of course, we can rule out internal combustion engines or jet- or rocket-propulsion. Or any technology humans have created to date." He paused for a second. "I do remember an article in *Popular Science* that discussed theoretical or futuristic engine types. A type of engine that produces a negative field in front of it and a positive force behind it, which would allow for the speeds we're talking about. Also, the field may have provided a protective layer around the craft to prevent damage by objects while in flight. That said, just sitting here for a few centuries, without a protective force field or even being under cover of any sort, it's got the dog shit beat out of it."

"I guess that's one technological opinion." Elizabeth reached out to touch the machine with her gloved fingers. "But something Tiburón mentioned in one of his conspiracy rants is coming to mind. The rant about electromagnetic power."

Finnegan continued to survey the machine. "Well, after seeing those Mesoamerican weapons and listening to Tiburón going on about space ports in Mesoamerica, I'm reminded of a book I read once. *Rommel's Other Afrika Korps.*"

"Where the author wrote about the Germans seeking the power of the Pyramids?" Elizabeth asked.

"Yes. Put all that together with the bits and pieces we've found to date, I agree. But we can pick Tiburón's brain when we get back. In the meantime, though, I'm not comfortable with TETRA having access to this type of advanced technology, but we need to study it first. Just as Manwaring may have used his knowledge of previous visitations to Mesoamerica by aliens to save his skin, I think having this knowledge will save our skins in the future. I could start by putting together a homemade technical manual. You could create a sketchbook."

Elizabeth smiled before answering. "I knew I kept you around for more than great sex."

They turned to face the remains scattered in the center of the open cavern floor and the larger spacecraft secreted under the overhang.

"You know," Finnegan surmised, "still assuming it was this little spaceplane, our native friend flew back here in a day! Can you imagine what that thing inside the cavern is capable of? I'm talking about intergalactic travel!"

Finnegan and Elizabeth walked through the rock-strewn surface toward the scattered remains among the rocky debris. There were pieces of aluminum sheathing scattered about and coated with Martian soil. If the metal was painted at one time, then it was time, which removed the coating and camouflaged the remains. There were also lengths of wiring and pieces of machinery.

Finnegan stopped and bent over to pick up an item nestled between two hand-sized rocks. Straightening up, he held out a portion of a black box with a glass lens inserted into it. "Looks like what used to be a camera."

Watching dust fall from the item, Elizabeth leaned in to get a closer look at the label plate inside the camera's remains. While the writing was in German, she was able to discern the date: 1939, and its manufacturer: Zeiss

Glaswerke. The now familiar eagle and letters R and K, along with the swastika, accompanied the date, manufacturer's name, and subsequent serial number.

"So," Elizabeth said, "we have an alien spaceplane, flown here presumably by a Mesoamerican hundreds of years ago, a rocket ship equipped with a television camera, with parts made in Michigan and Germany and flown here presumably in 1939, or just afterward, and now that *Star Wars*-looking thing hidden in that cavern. I think it's time to let Spike and Tiburón in on what we've got here."

"I agree," Finnegan said as he walked toward the spaceship. "But let's get a closer look at that thing."

Disk-shaped and perched off the ground with four jointed legs fixed with metal plates, the spacecraft was about twenty meters in diameter and about four meters from top to bottom. The metal covering the ship's hull was also reddish-gray. At the front of the craft, toward its center, were two squared projections with a series of antennae-looking items sticking out of the top of each projection. In between was an open rectangular door and a ramp.

"It looks like the mouth of a crab," Elizabeth said.

"I'd say that our little plane was probably parked inside the spaceship," Finnegan said. "Just like people who house a motorcycle or ATV inside the back of an RV and lower the ramp and open the door for it."

"I agree, and one with two cockpits."

Both appraised the two rounded, tapered extensions off to the sides of the craft's hull—the eyes of the crab. Eyes faced with clear material. Suddenly, a dull bluish light moving about in the recesses of the craft became visible through the clear facing of the right-side projecting compartment.

"Looks like Manwaring's looking for the circuit breaker panel," Finnegan said with a smirk. "What do you think? Should we just walk in and surprise him? Or we could slink away and study these ships when Manwaring is not in either of them."

"Well, the latter may be quite difficult," Elizabeth answered, "so I think helping him find that blown fuse would be quite neighborly."

"Well," Finnegan said, straightening up his shoulders, "since we've disarmed his gas bombs, I doubt he'll have any other option except to accept our civility."

They walked to the base of the ramp and stood in front of the rectangular opening. A dancing bluish illumination, visible through a right-side interior door that was cracked open, helped to reveal the area inside. The bay was large enough to house the spaceplane, but not large enough for the spaceplane to rotate inside, which meant the pilot had to back the spaceplane in when landing. Or back it out on takeoff.

The only items visible to Eliabeth and Finnegan were two opposing doors in the rear corners. Both doors were ajar, and there was a flush-mounted panel next to each door and a flush-mounted fixture in the bay's ceiling. Taking the first step, Elizabeth placed her booted right foot on the lowered ramp. She stopped.

Manwaring exited the right-side door. He stopped at the sight of Elizabeth.

Finnegan lifted his left arm, opened the cover to the communication system, and punched the open key. "Need a hand finding that fuse panel?"

Manwaring's eyes widened. "No! You shouldn't be here. You can't be here. I'm not ready yet." He opened his arms as if he were trying to prevent a repo man from taking his prized car.

"You can't pretend anymore. We've pretty much figured out what's going on." Finnegan stepped forward, planting a foot on the ramp. "But my question is, what's going to happen to us once you pilot that thing back to Earth? We know you've made a deal with TETRA to save your ass, but were you supposed to kill us once you've figured out how to operate that thing? Or were you supposed to take it back and show TETRA how to operate it, and they will come back and kill us instead?"

Manwaring's eyes darted between Finnegan and Elizabeth. "Fools! They track our movements! Now they know you're here! With me! Now they know I've found it! And I'm not ready!" He sighed, lifted his left arm, and opened the cover to his communication system.

The sheer anguish on Manwaring's face hit Elizabeth in the gut.

All the pieces of the last few years, especially the last few months, came together. Elizabeth understood the torture on Manwaring's face. "I doubt that's going to work," Elizabeth said. She reached into her cargo pocket and pulled out a closed hand. Holding it out in front of her, she opened her gloved hand.

Manwaring dropped his arm. His eyes narrowed.

"Please, Geoff," Elizabeth said. "Please."

Manwaring clenched his fist and punched the wall panel next to him. The ramp jumped up and snapped shut in front of them.

"Shit!" Finnegan said.

Catching her breath, Elizabeth sighed. "Let him be. There's no use us trying to break in. And it looks like we've got plenty to do on our own."

Turning her head, she looked at the beat-up spaceplane and the pieces of the destroyed rocket. Finnegan's eyes followed.

"But," Elizabeth continued, "if he can figure out how to operate this craft before he runs out of food, air, and water, he's off to Earth, and we're dead."

Finnegan, still looking at the wrecked spaceplane, said. "Then I suggest we'd better get at it. And that includes asking Spike to find a way to blow that thing to smithereens."

Late April, AD 2026

"Hey, dill hole, wipe that shit-eating grin off your face," Spike ordered as she rolled her eyes at the overhead light fixture in The Hilton.

Finnegan rotated the twelve-inch crossbow bolt he held between his hands one more time. "Spike, let the man enjoy his fifteen minutes."

"Hey, if I have to spend one more minute listening to him say"—Spike deepened her voice and lowered her head into her shoulders—"'I told you so,' we won't have to wait for Einstok and his goons to show up. I'll sink that Aztec axe into his skull myself. And chop his body up with that war sword just to make sure he shuts up. Then, I'll use his balls for target practice. Does that crossbow still work?"

Everybody at the table, except Spike, chuckled.

Tiburón, still holding the bronze-bladed, three-foot long war axe in front of him, lowered his other hand to caress the obsidian-edged sword leaning against his thigh. Finnegan smiled at the sixteenth-century Iberian crossbow sitting on a white towel on the table in front of him. The Aztec's bone-handled obsidian dagger and the quiver for the crossbow's bolts, each the length of his forearm, accompanied the crossbow. All were covered with reddish Martian dirt, staining the white towel underneath them with what looked like sprinkled cinnamon. The last item of note was a set of steel chisels and tools, inserted into their own pockets sewn into an open leather case.

Finnegan answered Spike's concern. "Nothing that a stiff-bristle toothbrush, a bit of olive oil from Kroll's larder, and a little TLC can't fix."

"Good," Spike said. Stopping to turn her attention back to the items strewn about the tabletop, she asked. "He's still up there?'

"Yes," Finnegan answered, reaching out to finger the camera label plate from the rocket ship remains. "And while he stole food from our stores, he will run out of air and water at some point. That's unless he's figured out how to get that thing operational."

"We don't know when he found it. Right after our arrival, or only days ago, but either way. He's had time to figure something out," Elizabeth added. "He was able to find a way to power that ramp."

Finnegan nodded in surrender.

"All I can say is," Tiburón said, "whoever flew that thing, those things, must've had the same needs as us, whether we're talking Aztec or Klingon."

Elizabeth, flipping an Aztec bladelet over in her hand, listened to her tablemates. Her thoughts, though, were on other options that Manwaring might be envisioning.

"Should we discuss terms with Manwaring if he does arrive here?" Kroll asked. Stepping up to the table, he placed a plate of finger sandwiches on the table and sat down.

"I would rather kill him," Spike said. "Just like he tried to kill you two by exploding those gas bombs inside your helmets. And he would have done the same to us when the time came."

"He was desperate," Elizabeth mused. Although she heard the spew in Spike's voice, she remembered the torment on Manwaring's face when he opened the cover to his wrist-mounted computer back in that canyon.

"You're taking his side!" shouted Spike. She looked at Elizabeth, who promptly stopped flipping the bladelet.

"My grandmother taught me a lot of things. One of the things she taught me was never to name an animal you know you may have to kill someday. He didn't want to kill us. It was in his face. Instead, he made a deal with Einstok to use us, to get us here, so he could recover his artifact, or artifacts. But he knew, while he couldn't do it, Einstok and his mercenaries would. And will do. It explains why he was always so rude and kept his distance."

Elizabeth lifted her eyes from the obsidian bladelet.

"I suggest we understand his position, and the position we're in. We can use this opportunity to salvage all our lives, including Manwaring's. In a weird way, he saved our lives. And handed us a find of historic proportion at the same time."

She rested her eyes on Finnegan.

Taking his cue, Finnegan said, "Well, we've had our breakfast, so I suggest Elizabeth and I get back up to Copperhead Canyon. I need to start taking notes on the small spaceplane. And Elizabeth can start on her sketches. Spike, you need to find what you can in terms of improvised explosives around here. At the same time, we can see if he's going to respond to the note we left him."

"You're agreeing with Elizabeth?" Spike scoffed aloud.

Finnegan sighed as he turned to Elizabeth.

"Yes," Elizabeth said. "But we're looking at the bigger picture. Tiburón, you know quite a bit about the Rhinelander Korps, and more about Einstok. And let's not forget about your knowledge of pyramids. Hence that shit-eating grin on your mug."

"Oh, my friggin' God," Spike blurted out as she dropped her head back and stated at the ceiling.

Ignoring Spike, Elizabeth continued. "Do you think the Rhinelander Korps still exists and that Einstok is part of it? And how do the pyramids fit in here? Based on something you said before and material Finnegan and I have read in the past, something is starting to surface."

"Shit!" Spike buried her face in her arms on the tabletop. "Do you have to encourage him? Somebody, please curb stomp that son of a bitch now."

Elizabeth watched as Tiburón sat back in his chair. Self-satisfaction beamed broadly from his immense smile.

Spike lifted her head just above her folded arms and nudged Tiburón's arm with her elbow. "Hey, you sorry excuse for a skid mark. Get over yourself, and fill us in."

Tiburón, still grinning broadly, lowered the axe and looked around the table. He coughed slightly as if to clear his throat. "Well, the name Rhinelander Korps may have gone away, but the idea of the association still exists. Even updated. Multinational corporate leaders hell bent on controlling the world's economy and social order. Like Zuckerberg and Facebook, or the military-industrial complex Eisenhower warned us about when he left office in the late 1950s. Thus, replacing the idea of good old-fashioned nation-state governments."

"And with Einstok at the lead?" Finnegan countered.

"He's not part of that cabal. He is his own cabal, which is why he's trying to be the first one to get his dick skinners on those things in Copperhead Canyon." Tiburón saluted by picking up his coffee cup. "Still, he's nothing more than a self-aggrandizing treasure hunter. And good at it, which means we have to bust this thing wide open. Once people on Earth find out what's going on here, Einstok can't touch us. Nobody can."

"Oh God!" Spike groaned. "Will your head ever fit into your helmet again?"

"Agreed," Finnegan said. "I'm an avid reader and one book comes to mind: *Rommel's Other Afrika Korps*. It was about a group of archaeologists and engineers following Rommel's drive across North Africa. Like the Monuments Men who followed the Allied armies across Europe after D-Day. Or just like the plot in *Indiana Jones and Raiders of the Lost Ark*. You know, where Hitler and his deputies, like Himmler, had teams looking for lost treasures or archaeological evidence pointing to the supremacy of the Aryan race."

"Or just like the antiquarians and engineers who followed Napoleon's armies into Egypt," Elizabeth added, "in the discovery of the Rosetta Stone."

"Exactly," Finnegan said. "While Rommel's military goal was to seize the Suez Canal and shut off a vital shipping route, the author argued that the German specialists were intent upon seizing Egypt's pyramids."

Finnegan paused. Tilting his head to a slight angle, he looked at Tiburón. "Did the author's argument have credibility?"

Everybody's eyes followed Finnegan's and saw the satisfaction in Tiburón's eyes.

"Yes. Let me explain." Tiburón leaned forward as if he were about to tell a ghost story to cub scouts sitting around a campfire.

"Oh crap!' Spike blurted out with her face reburied in her arms.

"For believers, pyramids are markers for alien landing sites and served as portals to the heavens. Which is why priests, and specialists, buried Egyptian royalty in gold-lined tombs inside pyramids. So that the energy of their souls, and with the special properties that gold holds, could transport, or beam, the souls of the royalty to the stars. To stand with the gods. While their use as landing markers or as soul-transporting vehicles could be true, what *is* fact is that pyramids, whether they be Egyptian, Mesoamerican, or Asian, are located as close to the equator as possible on Earth. Just like the pyramids of Mars are here on this planet. Cydonia."

"Why is that important?" Kroll asked.

Elizabeth answered for Tiburón. "The Earth is widest at the equator, which is where the earth's electromagnetic energy is perceived to be the strongest."

Tiburón winked at Elizabeth before continuing his narration.

"Pyramids, built of stone, in specific ways, with access to special materials, and in certain locations, were meant to draw, or harness, the earth's electro-magnetic energy, and use that energy to power, or recharge, alien spacecraft."

"Like gas stations?" Spike asked. Her face remained buried in her arms on the table, muffling her voice.

"More like charging stations for electrically powered vehicles," Tiburón answered. He paused long enough to look at his tablemates, again, landing his eyes last on Elizabeth. "But some sites were more important or useful than others. Copán in Honduras and Teotihuacán in Mexico, for example."

With a captivated audience, Tiburón explained the significance of those sites, starting with Copán. His narration included those all-important murals depicting a Mesoamerican taking off while seated in a rocket ship. He also recalled when he first heard Manwaring's name, during his field school excavations near the site. Once he finished his narration about Copán, Tiburón started on Teotihuacán's significance, "Teotihuacán, located in the north of what once was Lake Texcoco, existed before the creation of the Aztec Empire. At least by a thousand years, and as the Aztecs expanded their empire in the 1300s, they came across the site and gave its current name: Teotihuacán. Although the Aztecs did not know who created the complex, they incorporated it within their own lore and honored it as a creation of the gods of the sky and the lords of thunder, and the home of the Feathered Serpent."

Listening to the Mexican's narration, Elizabeth recalled her youthful curiosity as an ambitious reader and how she often traveled to Latin America with her parents. She thought of a day-long visit she took to the ancient complex while visiting Mexico City. Then, her thoughts moved to the Nancy Drew mystery she conjured in her own eight-year-old mind while standing under the shadows of one of the ancient city's pyramids. A mystery she scrawled in a notebook when they returned to their hotel room in Mexico City that weekend. A mystery now among real Nancy Drew mysteries back in her bedroom at her grandmother's house.

Elizabeth eased back in her chair, absorbing the significance of Tiburón's words.

"The Teotihuacán complex consisted of structures centered around two main pyramids: the Pyramid of the Sun and the Pyramid of the Moon. Two massive structures separated by the Avenue of Death—a long, straight, and paved concourse that alien conspiracists claimed was a runway for spacecraft. There were those who argued that the creators of Teotihuacán intended the entire city to be a spaceport and used it as such. Believers coined the site the Cape Canaveral of Ancient Mesoamerica. They argued that the evidence supporting their claims existed within the pyramids. Namely, the lengths of squared conduits leading from enclosed vats were lined with a skin of mica—a material used to seal the vats and the conduits and function as a heat shield while they held and moved vast quantities of mercury."

Pausing to look around the table, Tiburón finished, "Their argument rested on the fact that, even today, mercury, used as a semi-super conductor, and mica, used as an insulator, are employed extensively in the aerospace industry."

After leaving their notebook, sketch pad, and measuring tape next to the mangled spaceplane, Elizabeth and Finnegan walked up to the closed ramp of the spacecraft. Two changes had occurred since their last visit. First, new landing pad prints in the dirt that covered the floor of the cavern. Second, a new item stood next to one of the spacecraft's articulated mechanical legs. Eyeing the item, Elizabeth asked, "Is that what I think it is?"

Finnegan replied, "I think Manwaring is willing to talk."

"Hurry up, Solid Gold," Double Cannon shouted. "It's my turn."

Sweat bubbled from Solid Gold's tanned skin as he finished his workout on the resistance band machine. Securing the handles with Velcro strips, he grabbed his face towel and wiped his armpits before loosening the waist strap. "So, you think they've found what they've been looking for?" he asked. Floating away from the seat, he rolled over and wiped off the machine.

"Dumb ass," Double Cannon cursed. "Wipe down the machine before your armpits."

"I will," Solid Gold retorted. "Just as soon as you stop farting. We're in a spaceship, for Christ's sake."

The other three members of Munro's team sat at the table. Munro and Max sipped apple juice from their pouches. All of them wore the same

TETRA-issued blue clothing as those on Mars. Max looked across the table at Munro. The ex-legionnaire, inserting a notebook and pen into his shirt pocket, returned the look.

Though the team has endured all manner of challenging deployments on Earth, the confines of the space capsule, and the time inside it, created rigors even the toughest mercenary would have a demanding time dealing with. Thinking back to his Foreign Legion days, Munro remembered a fellow legionnaire, an American whose first military enlistment was as a US Navy submariner. After that enlistment, the American joined the Legion and served under Munro. The American said more than once that it takes a special kind of mind to become a submariner and stick with it. While BOSC training did present a grueling series of eliminating events to its applicants, including spending time in suborbital lunar orbit and on the lunar surface, Munro knew it was time to get his team onto the Martian surface to focus on something besides themselves.

Double Cannon floated toward the table and both Munro and Max could see Double Cannon was about to mouth a response to Solid Gold's dig, but Einstok's arrival into the habitation module from the command/lander stage convinced him to remain silent.

"What's the latest?" Max asked quickly.

"As you know," Einstok said, "Manwaring spent his time wandering the mountains next to the lakebed since their arrival, but in the last few *sols*, he has stopped his wandering. That means he has found his, *our*, objective. Now, it appears that, by the movement of his companions, they too are aware of the reason for this mission. Manwaring included us in a message he sent to TETRA, stating that the spaceplane, and the Rhinelander Korps rocket, are both unusable."

"Wasn't he supposed to have killed them at this point?" Munro asked.

"Yes," Einstok answered.

Einstok stopped talking long enough to pull himself into an empty seat at the table. Strapping himself in and peeling a remote away from the Velcro attached to the table, he turned on the television monitor in the corner.

The brightening screen revealed an overview of the lakebed, and the rugged mountain range next to it.

"Now that he has found the correct location, we can focus our satellite imagery and have a better view of what is going on."

"I wouldn't mind a bit of bloody action myself," Nitro interjected. "I hope he lets them live."

Everybody at the table heard Nitro's comment, but it was Einstok who responded. "I, too, would not mind an interlude. In the meantime, shall we get updated?"

Adjusting the imagery of the satellite's camera, he narrowed the frames incrementally until the astronauts could focus on what looked like a volcano crater, or sinkhole, in the mountains. At first, they saw only that, but after listening to Einstok's direction, they saw what looked like the partial outline of a plane's wing extending from under the rim of the sinkhole. And among the stone rubble littering the sinkhole's floor.

"So, you're saying the rocket was just sacrificial?" Slingblade asked as he finished sipping his apple juice through a straw.

"Yes," Einstok answered. "Its operators sent the camera-equipped rocket from Antarctica as a one-way exploratory trip. Proving it feasible to send an unmanned rocket ship to Mars. In 1939. Their cameras were able to send seconds of rudimentary footage upon their descent into the sinkhole. Before losing their signal, which is the reason we are not attempting to land inside that geo-feature ourselves. Anyway, the Rhinelander Korps considered it a success and furthered plans for both a moon and Martian presence. However, Hitler's invasion of Poland kickstarted WWII, forcing their plans on to the back burner."

"Why did the Rhinelander Korps select that particular landing site for the rocket?" Nitro asked. He paused to pick something from the corner of his eye. "And why did TETRA select that dry lakebed for your future base?"

"The scientists from the Rhinelander Korps," Einstok said, "studied the diary created by the German mercenary I mentioned earlier, and the copy created by his descendant. The research helped them determine the specific area to send that rocket ship. But the Rhinelander Korps selected that cave, or sinkhole, simply out of sheer luck, as there are several other sheltered areas within that mountain range. As far as selecting the dry lakebed, it seemed a natural location with future operations in mind. I started on plans for that purpose, and while doing so, a clue fell into our laps."

Einstok paused to relish the moment.

"Years ago," he began again, "a YouTuber investigating basic satellite imagery said he found a spoon in one of those frames. In the lakebed where I planned to set up my base."

"Like a spoon-spoon?" Lil' Sumptin' asked.

"Yes. A wooden spoon. About eight inches long. Anyway, he posted his find on social media, but no one paid any attention to it. That said, I had my people investigate the matter. However, the discovery of that German mercenary's diary, and its copy in Antarctica, gave substance to the YouTuber's claim and galvanized the reason we are here right now. As far as sending Manwaring ahead of us, we could have gone ahead ourselves, but he found specific information that gave him the upper hand. At that time."

"So, there is no way Manwaring can fly that thing off Mars and back to Earth?" Lil' Sumptin' asked.

Max jumped in. "No. And since Manwaring hasn't secured his companions, you will dispose of them, leaving us to assume the completion of the project ourselves." He turned to Einstok, who wore a broad smile on his face.

Einstok turned to face his team leader. "Munro, you have less than three days to get your team ready."

Munro did not answer.

"Munro?"

Jerked from his distant thoughts, he answered, "Sorry. I guess I'm still trying to get out of torpor." He turned to his team. "All right, after everybody has thirty minutes on the exercise equipment, study the outlay of the base at the lakebed, and that canyon. I will make available the personnel files on Manwaring's crew. While Manwaring has the capability to kill them, it looks like it will be up to us. There is one person with military combat experience, an ex-marine who goes by Spike, but there is one other who could prove problematic. A hired killer. All of them, though, have had time to acclimate to the Martian surface while we've been in space for these number of months, so let's not take any chances."

"They may have been on the surface for a bit, but we're armed, and they're not. Also, aren't they just a bunch of toss-offs?" Nitro gestured as if he were masturbating.

Before Munro could answer, Einstok spoke up. "Munro's right. Manwaring's team seems not to be a threat as far as combat abilities, but I did not just collect sweepings from a local billiard hall. So, we should not leave anything to chance. Now, let us get about our tasks."

As everybody moved to follow Munro's orders, the ex-legionnaire remained seated. He sipped his juice through his straw and thought about those on Mars. Something he had done often in the last few days. In response to Nitro's last statement, he thought, *arrogance has killed more men than bullets.*

Finnegan and Elizabeth stood next to the spacecraft's hull, eyeing the item at the base of a jointed leg under the spacecraft. Manwaring lowered the ramp and joined them on the surface. They opened their conversation on friendly terms and after listening to Manwaring's side of the story, they asked for a tour of *his* spaceship. Manwaring readily agreed.

Not knowing what to expect, Elizabeth followed the two men up the ramp, through the rectangular spaceplane hold and into the airlock separating the spaceplane hold from the craft's starboard side flight control station, or cockpit. It was big enough to fit three of them. An aspect Elizabeth took note of.

Once inside the ship, they removed their helmets and stood in the cockpit. One of two cockpits, for redundancy. Since the spacecraft was disk-shaped, and about twelve feet high, the interior of the spacecraft provided ample head room despite the equipment and furnishing squeezed into its hull. While

Manwaring explained the flight control console to Finnegan, Elizabeth looked around the cockpit and the room on the other side of the open door. The ship did resemble the interior of the *Millennium Falcon*. "Did that alien fly and operate this ship all by himself?"

"Yes," Manwaring answered. "But I've found accommodations for more than one crew member. Let me show you."

Following the two men, Elizabeth found the ship divided into spacious, but equipment-filled compartments following the curvature of the hull with the craft's propulsion system taking up the center of the craft, inside its own compartment. Not really understanding how the ship's engine worked, Manwaring knew enough to explain that it provided both a downward force and outlets in the stern to push the craft forward.

Finishing their clockwise tour, the three of them stepped into the portside or second, cockpit. "So, it does fly like a Harrier jet," Finnegan said.

Finnegan placed his fingers on the slanted console top and stood next to the high-backed pilot's seat. Elizabeth felt uncomfortable. The far-reaching gaze in Finnegan's eyes reminded her of father when he left for a mission or deployment. Standing on the tarmac with her mother holding her hand, she could see the joy in his face before he climbed into the fighter jet's cockpit. At the same time, Elizabeth could feel her mother's heartbeat through the handhold.

"Know something about Harrier jets?" Manwaring asked. "I know that you are a licensed private pilot with single-engine, multi-engine, and seaplane ratings."

Dropping his hand and looking about wondrously, Finnegan answered, "Aside from what I've read, I've logged forty hours as a virtual pilot in a simulation platform."

"Meaning video games," Manwaring responded.

Shrugging his shoulders and turning for the door to the spaceplane hold's airlock, Finnegan flatly answered. "You could put it that way."

As they finished the tour and got ready to don their spacesuit helmets, Elizabeth faced Manwaring. "Thanks for the tour. I'm amazed at how much it reminds me of Han Solo's *Millenium Falcon.*"

Manwaring took on a broad smile. "Well, maybe George Lucas had access to information the rest of us didn't have. Now, please take my gift back to the others. I will be with you shortly."

✹

Back at The Hilton, Elizabeth asked Finnegan, "Do you think it's safe?" Finnegan took his attention from the bottle and placed it on the faces around him. Imploring faces searching for the right answer. "Why are you looking at me?"

Elizabeth smiled. "You're the only Irishman on Mars, so if anybody should know about liquor, it's gotta be you."

"And that didn't sound the least bit stereotypical?" Finnegan retorted. "Besides, I'm Irish American."

"Okay," Elizabeth said. "Just pretend you're at your local in East Milton, Mass, and somebody just gave you a double dog dare to drink the bartender's special out-of-the-corner hooker's shoe."

"Well, since you put that way," Finnegan said, reaching for the bottle. The bottle was clear and triangular, and held two liters of a thin, semi-brown liquid. While he could not read the lettering on the label, the image was apparent—a robust creature with a broad smile on a blue face and armed with futuristic ray guns. Wearing them in Mexican bandito or pirate fashion over a Robocop-like suit of armor. The alien, blue-faced creature held a tankard in his hand and propped a leg on the body of a boar-like animal.

"I can't believe that we have a bottle of alien whiskey," Spike said. "It reminds me of a Captain Morgan rum advertisement."

"The alien who flew those ships had the same stature and physiological makeup as us. And breathed air like us, so why shouldn't it have access to alcohol?" Elizabeth said. "Alcohol has been a cross-cultural staple, and currency, on Earth for thousands of years. Why, then, can't it be a universal staple? And be safe for humans."

With a determined sigh, Finnegan reached out, twisted off the screw cap, and poured some into his coffee cup. With all eyes still on him, Finnegan placed the bottle on the table, lifted the cup, and emptied the contents into his gaping mouth. Snapping his eyes shut, he took the cup from his lips. His face turned slightly red, and beads of sweat bubbled out of the skin on his forehead. After about ten seconds, he opened his eyes wide and exhaled forcibly. Catching his breath, he was about to speak, when the door from The Keep opened. Manwaring, wearing TETRA-issued clothing, stood at the open frame.

"We need to start locking the front door," Spike blurted out. She shot Manwaring a look of disdain.

Everybody remained silent as Manwaring stepped to the table and picked up the bottle.

"Although I've endured other kill devil in my time, this stuff is not too bad. That said"— Manwaring turned his attention from the bottle to Tiburón—"I'd refrain from lighting up a joint or being near open flames for a minimum of thirty minutes after consuming this liquor. And avoid spilling it onto your spacesuit."

Tiburón replied with a mixed expression. "Thanks for the advice. Now what do you have to tell us? And are you still trying to figure out that machine? They said you learned to levitate it."

Manwaring put the bottle back on the table. "I've made quite a bit of progress since I found those machines soon after our arrival. But, since I couldn't spend all day every day there, as I knew my movements were being tracked by satellite and the GPS hard-wired into The Minivan, I spent most of my time prospecting for mineral resources and other potentially usable sites, which was my original job. One I didn't mind fulfilling as I kept my eyes open to more evidence of alien, or human, visitations. That said, I often parked The Minivan at other locations and hiked to the sinkhole. I gathered enough information to get me started and to set up a timetable to complete my own training. But it was your visit to the site that threw my schedule down the loo. And giving away to Einstok that we'd found something."

He panned his eyes around the table. "We have quite a bit of work ahead of us, and not so much time to do so. Einstok and his team could be here any *sol* now, so please give me the opportunity to explain my plan. And myself."

"If you plan on flying that thing back to Earth," Spike jumped in, "you'll be dog meat the second you land. Also, our necks will still be in the noose here on Mars. Which means all we're doing is waiting for the hangman to pull the lever."

"She's right," Tiburón said. "*They* got us by the short and curlies."

Manwaring kept his eyes on Spike. "I know that."

Spike sat back in her chair. Pausing, she slowly lifted her hand and extended her index finger hand like the Grim Reaper summoning its next soul. "You're not going back to Earth."

Manwaring tilted his head to the side, appraising the Aztec weapons in Tiburón's possession and the weapons in front of Finnegan. "Here, let me get everybody a cup."

With coffee cups full of alien whiskey, they all sat at the table and listened to Manwaring's story.

According to Manwaring, the body Finnegan and Elizabeth encountered was an Aztec warrior named Achcauhatli—a Soldier of the Sun, or Eagle Warrior. A warrior accepted into that special fold because of skill and bravery. The Aztecs received a container, an alien container, from the Toltecs, who got it from the Maya, whose own civilization had collapsed centuries before. They held onto the container and studied its contents at a special location outside of Teotihuacán. When Cortez Spanish arrived in 1519 and started to destroy everything that resembled Aztec religion, architecture, and writing, the Aztec leadership made plans to save what they could. By 1521, a column of Aztecs loaded down with gold and examples of their writing escaped north into what is now Utah."

"Shit!" Elizabeth exclaimed. "I was right about Aztec treasure outside of Kanab, Utah."

"Yes," Manwaring answered. "I mounted an expedition to Utah to recover artifacts, proving that the Aztecs did, indeed, travel as far north as

The Great Basin. It was also where Einstok sent a team to steal my find. Not the first time I've crossed swords with Einstok. While I discovered Aztec items buried in a cave, I did not discover that specific treasure trove outside of Kanab. That treasure was found by a group of people..."

Thrusting the Aztec axe into the air as if he were Merlin about to shoot a bolt of magical power at an invading flying dragon, Tiburón shouted, "Fuck! A group of people known as the Rhinelander Korps. Knew it!"

"Oh, crap," Spike moaned. "Here we go again!"

"Correct again," Manwaring said, "and while that column of Aztecs headed north, Achcauhatli, armed with the weapons at this table—including a Spanish crossbow he captured from a previous encounter with the Spanish and a team of elite specialists—he escaped with the cylinder, a load of select metals including glass, and that set of Spanish steel tools there on the table. They made their way back to the site where the small spaceplane had landed hundreds of years before. It was just outside of Copán, Honduras, and, coincidentally, a site I worked for two seasons before I discovered the cylinder."

"God dammit!" Tiburón exploded. "I knew there was a connection between Copán and Teotihuacán! And Cydonia!"

"Fuck!" Spike turned and reached for the Aztec axe in Tiburón's hand. "Give me that thing. I'm gonna split your skull open right here and now, you son of a bitch!"

Tiburón pulled the axe out of her reach.

"Easy Spike," Elizabeth said. "Based on what Manwaring is saying, we'll need every asset we have, and every trick in the book. Go ahead, Geoff."

Listening to Manwaring's continued narration, Elizabeth assessed the weapons at the table. Remembering that *SOF* magazine article about Einstok and his team of mercenary operators fighting it out with treasure hunters on the Peruvian *Altiplano,* she reflected on her comment about a book of tricks. In doing so, Elizabeth appraised Spike. Though the ex-marine wore her red hair short and Elizabeth wore her blond hair longer, they were of the same build. She also looked at the number 5 embroidered into Spike's issued clothing. The same number was embroidered into her spacesuit.

"I'll explain the connection between those two sites in a minute." Manwaring sipped some alien whiskey and grimaced.

"The intellectuals studied the cylinder and its contents at the residence outside of Teotihuacán. So, when they arrived at the site of the spaceplane, they were able to instruct Achcauhatli about the basics of how to operate the computer systems for the spaceplane and how to use the environmental survival suit they made for him. Once educated, they sent him here, to Mars, and to the gods, to save a record of their civilization. They recorded their intentions on the container I found, just as the previous holders of that container did. The container, in effect, was a Rosetta Stone."

"Were the Aztecs that advanced in their knowledge of technology?" Finnegan asked. "It seems strange that they knew everything from making a spacesuit with a breathing apparatus to flying this craft all the way here."

"It really wasn't that difficult," Manwaring responded. "The Aztecs were not always great innovators of technology, science, and mathematics; however, they were experts at adopting technology from cultures they conquered or had interactions with. Anyway, after the Mayans burned the body of the alien pilot who landed in their midst, at his request, they stored his spacesuit, breathing equipment, and other items with the spaceplane. Take that bronze-bladed axe, for example."

"It's called a *tepoztli*," Elizabeth said.

"I know what it is called," Manwaring and Tiburón said simultaneously. Both men looked at each other before turning to face Elizabeth.

"What? Can't a female medical doctor know something about Mesoamerican weapons?"

Manwaring smiled. "Two- to three-foot handle made from tropical hardwood and with a curved poll at one end. With a slit cut into that poll to receive a curved blade of bronze. A tool appreciated by skilled wood workers, expertly wielded by warriors, and held aloft by the gods. And the fact they knew enough of metallurgy to alloy copper with other metals to fashion excellent bronze implements proves their ability to copy the alien's equipment."

"They, the Mayans, just didn't leave the ship out in the open, did they?" Finnegan asked.

"No, they didn't," Manwaring continued. "The Mayans recognized the significance of their guest and his equipment, and they secreted it with an enclosed complex. A complex I discovered centuries later. After arriving at the site, the specialists accompanying the warrior simply replicated the suit and breathing gear using materials they brought with them and found in the local jungle: deer hide for gaskets, bones for pistons, and tree gum as a sealant, for example. Since there was a significant difference in stature, they had to build a suit to fit our Aztec friend. They also realized that the alien who flew it to Earth had tracked his flight on a recorder. All they did was reverse the flight controls. So, theoretically, all the Aztec had to do was to suit up, climb in, and fly that spaceplane back to the gods and save a record of their culture. Something we can easily do right now."

"What's this *we* crap?" Spike asked.

"You seem to know quite a bit about this alien?" Finnegan said, trying to ignore Tiburón's huge grin. "Where was he from originally. And why did he land the bigger spaceship here on Mars but then fly the smaller one to Earth? And how does that connect Copán with Teotihuacán."

"And don't forget Cydonia," Tiburón threw in.

Giving Tiburón a side look, Manwaring reached for the whiskey bottle. "I'll give you the long answer, which will require a top off for everybody."

Everybody at the table held out their cups. While topping off everybody's cups, Manwaring resumed his narration. "The alien who landed at Copán was an ex-warrior-turned-adventure writer by the name of Nezhoda Roo. According to Manwaring, the first name meant something akin to Lone Wolf. The last name, Roo, turned out to be a designator of sorts. Like a military rank. The originators of Teotihuacán came from a galaxy called the *Centaurus* A/M83 Group. A galaxy twelve million light years away. Nezhoda Roo arrived on Earth in the year AD 650, which coincided with the collapse, or abandonment, of Teotihuacán, and the first stage of failure of the Mayan civilization further south. The final Mayan collapse came less than two hundred years later, in AD 822."

Spike had a stunned look on her face. "Why did Nezhoda Roo land on Mars first?"

"Like I stated before, Nezhoda Roo enjoyed a successful career as a warrior in his own galaxy, but after his celebrated service, he became a historian, or writer, with the goal of documenting the far-reaching adventures of his race. By AD 600 Earth time, his race no longer had a need for stations such as Teotihuacán or even planets in Earth's solar system. So, by the mid-600s AD, he came to record what his race had left behind, starting with a station they'd established but subsequently abandoned on Mars."

"Holy shit, I'm good!" Tiburón shouted. "I told you the pyramids of Mars were real. Long live the face of Mars!"

"Can't somebody curb stomp this sumbitch?" Spike yelled while reaching for the bottle of whiskey. "Please!"

Ignoring Spike's plea, Manwaring acknowledged that Tiburón was right and continued his narration. "Cydonia, and the area around it, served as a way station in support of their mining operation on Mars thousands of years before. However, because Mars lost its magnetic field, which was necessary for Mars to have an atmosphere and to recharge and power their spacecraft, Mars proved economically unfit. That abandonment coincided with a positive change in Earth's environment, which encouraged alien explorations of Earth centuries before establishing stations such as Teotihuacán on Earth. Such visitation gave credence to the stories, legends, and lore of skyborne craft, flown by gods, landing on Earth since before the birth of Jesus Christ.

"After finishing his recordings of the abandoned mining operation on Mars, he decided to leave the spacecraft in that cavern, and fly the spaceplane to Earth. Nezhoda Roo visited sites on Earth, such as Mesopotamia, Egypt, and Southeast Asia, before landing lastly at Teotihuacán. While there, he saw written evidence inscribed into the walls of certain structures of Teotihuacán. Evidence detailing a site further south. Having an intrepid spirit, he decided to visit the site, which turned out to be Copán. A city the Mayan established around 300 BC. Upon landing, a band of Mayan warriors, returning from a raid, witnessed his arrival from the sky and jumped him when he exited his craft, leaving him severely wounded in an ensuing fight. Although he killed a portion of their party, the hunters took him back to their city, where the city's elites presumed him a god from the stars. They nursed him back to health and befriended him."

"Kind of like a warrior's code." Elizabeth interrupted.

Manwaring nodded in agreement.

"After recovering, he voluntarily remained to document his adventure with the Maya, keeping his written observations on paper and contained in a cylinder. In return, he passed on information about himself, his craft, and his home planet. Unfortunately, while on a hunting trip with Mayan warriors, a jaguar severely mauled him. He lived long enough to pass on his burial instructions. The Maya honored his request, burned his body, and buried the ashes within a stone complex they built around the spaceplane and his equipment, including his breathing apparatus and spacesuit, so they could study it in secret. They also documented the alien's visitation with the murals now visible at Copán in Honduras. The drawings of a Mayan astronaut taking off in a spaceship. The intellects continued to study, and honor, the alien's presence, but by the early 800s AD, with the Mayan civilization in a total free fall, the intellects did not want to see the knowledge of the alien's visit fall victim to the jungle and time. They sent a messenger, with the cylinder, back to Teotihuacán, a city they knew of from their own lore, and from the alien himself.

"However, by the 800s AD, another population had occupied the site as their own. This population would become the Toltec civilization. The Toltecs revered the site and the cylinder as gifts from the gods. They, in turn, were overcome by the Aztecs who received the cylinder in the 1300s."

"So, we have come full circle," Manwaring said, lifting his coffee mug to drain it of the last of its whiskey.

"With the arrival of the Spanish in the 1520s," Manwaring continued, "the Aztec returned the cylinder to Copán. I worked on that site and found the cylinder secreted with a stela. Along with a building buried under a mound. It had been a lab or workshop and contained the bodies of more than a dozen Aztecs. We also found evidence that something containing or using radiation had once been there. As they were figuring out the spaceplane, they probably exposed themselves to radiation."

Finnegan looked up from his whiskey. "While exposure to radiation has always been a concern for us since we've spent months in space and are now on a planet with no ozone layer, so what about now. Do we have to worry about being around that wreck of a ship?"

Manwaring licked his lips and winced before answering.

"I used my equipment from The Keep and from the alien spacecraft to test the spaceplane for radiation. Fortunately, just like the machine surrounding the engine, the engine is quite neutered."

Everybody fell silent as they thought about what Manwaring had just told them.

After a long minute, Manwaring sighed heavily. "Do you realize what we have here? Two alien spacecraft, and the technology built within them."

"And don't forget about the rocket ship from the Rhinelander Korps, and those traitors FDR, Ford, Firestone, and Lindberg," added Tiburón. "We'll be able to rewrite history, and prove I was right! Do you think the American government, and corporations, waste billions of dollars out of ignorance? Who spends a half million dollars studying duck penises? It's a sideshow to keep the American populace confused. Smoke and mirrors, a shell game, and sleight of hand. This expedition, and TETRA, is the ultimate result of the military-industrial-congressional complex, the MICC. The Black Budget, the Committee to Save America, the Deep State. It all makes sense now."

They looked at Manwaring. Rereading the man as they did, including Elizabeth, who prided on herself on being able to read people. On Earth, he was a self-centered and arrogant man, a man convicted of strangling prostitutes and sentenced to death. Now, on Mars, he was a new man.

"Well," Elizabeth sighed. "Like Tiburón said, we've got enough to turn human history upside down. You think they're on their way here right now?"

"I agree, and yes, I do," Manwaring said. "Which is one reason I had not planned to take the larger spacecraft back to Earth. I told them only of the spaceplane before our departure from Earth, and I just reported to TETRA and Einstok that I found the spaceplane and the Rhinelander Korps rocket ship, but that both are in unflyable condition. I agreed that once I found the spaceplane, I would activate it, if still functional, and bring it back to the same spot Nezhoda Roo had landed centuries ago. TETRA would find an excuse to occupy the site outside of Copán to wait for my arrival. If it wasn't functional, I was supposed to report to TETRA that I found it and to wait for their arrival."

"And kill us," Spike interjected flatly.

"Yes," Manwaring responded with an equal flatness, "but that is behind us."

Elizabeth picked up her whiskey. "So, they know nothing about the intact spacecraft in that cavern?"

"The spacecraft was mentioned in the information inside the cylinder I found at my site," Manwaring said, "so I knew it was there. But as Einstok offered me his deal, I got the impression he knew only of the spaceplane. I deemed it best to not update him."

"Slick," Finnegan responded with a grin. "So, where's that cylinder now? And what do you have in mind?"

"First," Manwaring said, "I've been putting together a plan, as we may have only *sols* before we receive visitors. Second, I will inform one of you about the cylinder's location. And another person about the diary I created while translating the cylinder's inscriptions and its contents."

Spike asked. "Don't you trust the rest of us?"

Manwaring shook his head. "If all of us hold the same key, we are all dead. But, if each of us holds one secret key—a key not known to the others—then we all survive. I'm forming a plan. In the morning, I should have it solidified. Then, you can put it into action."

"Will we have time to complete my notes and Elizabeth's sketches on the space plane?" Finnegan asked.

"Yes," Manwaring responded. "In fact, Finnegan, finishing your home-spun tech manual will be your sole focus. Concentrate on the spaceplane's propulsion, navigation, flight control, and life-support systems. That will be your key. Elizabeth, even though you are an accomplished artist, you shall have another key. You have not spent much time with that craft, so you're good there. Hand your sketches over to Finnegan."

Elizabeth nodded.

"Spike though," Manwaring continued, "is an ex-marine scout sniper, which means being able to note and sketch details. Correct."

"Cameras and memory can't catch everything," Spike responded.

"And," Manwaring said, "being a qualified sapper, you have learned how structures are assembled and know how to best destroy those same structures with an economic application of explosives. Therefore, your secret shall be to detail the structural makeup of the spaceplane before you rig it for demolition." A pleased smile started to fill her face, but then fell. "But with what? All we have, besides the handheld weapons here on the table, are five or six scuba-tank-sized containers of pressurized methane gas and a tote full of nitrate powder."

Manwaring smiled. "While we may have created a limited number of explosive materials ourselves, there's more onboard the spacecraft than stores of spirits and wines."

Kroll gasped. "You said wines?"

Late April, AD 2026

The next morning, six Martian astronauts stood at the entrance to the sinkhole, near the wrecked spaceplane. They all set their eyes on the spacecraft nestled in the cavern opposite them. Even though three of them had stood in front of the craft before, they were all in awe, even Elizabeth, though she had more reason to be in awe. That morning, Manwaring revealed the location of Nezhoda Roo's cylinder to her. As he did, memories of being with her parents on that one trip to Mexico City and visit to Teotihuacán flooded back to her. As did the impromptu mystery she scrawled in her notebook that weekend. A mystery involving The Pyramid of the Sun. Thinking about what she scribbled in that notebook, Elizabeth thought about her grandmother. Alone, with practically no family and grieving for her only granddaughter. Elizabeth could imagine the proud look on her grandmother's face if the plans they are making go through.

Manwaring turned to face Kroll.

"We know you are bilingual. Even a polyglot. And we have seen your penchant for puzzles and endured your choice of music."

"*Si*," Kroll said with a cheery, Santa Claus-like smile. "I also speak Spanish and Polish, and I studied music at university."

"Good. Understanding music is key to understanding patterns," Manwaring said taking a step forward. "I'll provide you with the location of my diary back on Earth. Starting with the name of a young woman who worked as my assistant at Copán."

Kroll offered a thumb's up.

"Excellent," Manwaring responded, stepping forward and around the rocks littering the floor. "I also need you to finish stocking the spacecraft with my share of the rations and water. I inspected the alien's larder, which is still full of foodstuffs, as Nezhoda Roo prepared for an intergalactic exploratory voyage with no timetable to return to his galaxy. Although they are sealed in containers or dehydrated and nestled safely inside a spacecraft, itself secured inside a dry cavern, I can read some of the labels and see pictures of their contents. I'll hang onto them as lifeboat rations."

"*Ja*," said Kroll, "I will see to it, but if you do not mind, I would like to inspect your larder to see what might be of use in The Hilton."

"Whoa!" Spike shouted out. "We're not going to have to eat alien food, are we?"

Manwaring smiled. "You've enjoyed his whiskey, and you're still alive. Right, Elizabeth?"

Elizabeth answered. "He has a point."

"Shit," Spike mumbled.

"Don't worry," Elizabeth said. "I'll inspect the larder to see what would be useful in our diet. And I'll make sure Kroll doesn't slip it into our meals by calling it a Sunday surprise."

Elizabeth cautioned Kroll with a sideways look. Kroll smiled in return.

"Good," Manwaring said. "Finnegan, once you're done with recording the spaceplane's internals, could you start on the craft in front of us. While I've figured out how to operate it, I still don't know how the engine works."

Finnegan turned his eyes up to the dull blue sky outlining the rim of the sinkhole above. "There sure is a whole lot of space up there. Are you going to be able to manage all that space by yourself?"

Elizabeth, hearing the question, almost tripped over the rock in front of her.

Finnegan reached out to catch her. "You okay?"

"Yeah," she replied.

"Nezhoda Roo was able to operate that craft by himself," Manwaring answered.

"What! Now, all of sudden, you're Buzz Lightyear?" Spike blurted out behind him.

Manwaring half turned to look over his shoulder as he stepped over a rock. "Spike, while you and Finnegan will be busy with your recoding and sketching, I would not mind instruction in hand-to-hand combat."

"You know anything about fighting?" Spike asked.

Manwaring faced forward while lifting his gloved hands over his shoulders. "Word has it that I have a mean stranglehold."

"From what you told us last night," Finnegan replied, "we're all going to need a little limbering up."

"Quite right," Manwaring said. "In the meantime, aside from the various explosives, our alien friend has an armory complete with knives, and handheld and shoulder-fired firearms."

Spike turned her head to look back at the wrecked spaceplane and the entrance into the sinkhole behind them. "Limbering up will just be the start. We're going to need some CQB training."

"CQB?" Kroll asked.

"She means close quarters battle," Finnegan said, stepping around another rock. "Which means she's thinking marine."

"Good," Manwaring said. "As for you Tiburón, your key will have two codes. First, collect our Aztec friend and his kit from behind that boulder. Then, look for a spot to secure him. Afterward, collect every scrap of his presence, from this sinkhole down to Legoland."

"Everything except his weapons," Tiburón answered.

"For now," Manwaring said, moving one step closer to the spacecraft. "While having secret knowledge of an Aztecs warrior's presence on Mars will be profound enough, your second code, gathering up the remains of the rocket ship scattered about our feet, will prove Earth shattering."

"Got it," Tiburón responded.

Stepping closer toward Nezhoda Roo's spacecraft, Tiburón appreciated the wreckage of the Rhinelander Korps' rocket scattered about the floor of the sinkhole. Although WWI ended over a century ago, and WWII almost a century ago, the knowledge of collusion between the United States and Germany during those world wars, and in between, would be disastrous for families still in power today. Tiburón relished the power at his feet. Enjoying the exhilaration at the prospect, he turned to Elizabeth. "Sorry, Elizabeth, but you're going to have to give up your lunchbox treasures."

Elizabeth answered with a smile. "You're welcome to them." By now, they had crossed the open floor of the sinkhole and stood in front of the spacecraft.

"In the next few days," Manwaring said, "each of you will have enough to save your lives, just as that cylinder I discovered on Earth saved mine. And if I can fly the spacecraft off Mars before anybody from TETRA arrives, they will not dare kill you."

They went quiet, absorbing the tasks facing them.

After several seconds, Spike broke the silence. "Do you think you'll be able to breach TETRA's security system so we can announce our presence on Mars to Earth?"

"TETRA has the computer set up in The Keep so that we can only communicate with TETRA headquarters," Manwaring said, "but I'm going to find a way of hacking out of the system. Something that has been in the back of my head since all of this started. If I do figure it out, our communication is going to have to be quick and effective, as TETRA will shut down those communications within microseconds. All it will take is a well-written and well-timed sentence. Or two."

"Do you think you could do it?" Tiburón asked with a sideways look. "What do you know about hacking?"

Still looking at the spacecraft, Manwaring answered. "Sadly, not much. I spent my computer time drafting articles and compliance reports. Why? Do you know something about computers? Hacking?"

Tiburón scoffed. "If *they* could spy on us for all these years, then why couldn't I spy on them? Besides, isn't there some sort of communication system on that spacecraft? And don't forget about the communication system in our lander capsule."

"You guys can worry about that later," Spike said. "I haven't blown anything up since leaving Earth. Let's see what kind of demo Nezhoda Roo had."

After respectfully collecting the Aztec's body from behind the boulder, and everything associated with his visit, and securing him inside a body bag they brought from Boot Hill, Tiburón left the canyon in The Mule in search of a secure, resting place for the Aztec warrior.

At the same time, Spike fell to her duties with relish. Especially after what she found inside the spacecraft. Kroll took delight in inspecting the spacecraft's larder and wine stores. Elizabeth remained with Kroll to supervise his selections. Finnegan spent the day inspecting and documenting the space plane's particulars.

After a sip of alien whiskey, Finnegan placed his cup on the table next to his plate of half-eaten beef wellington. "I have to say, Manwaring, you have brass ones. Flying that thing back to Nezhoda Roo's home galaxy. All by yourself." Elizabeth winced at Finnegan's statement.

Not noticing Elizabeth's pain, Finnegan continued. "It's possible that the race of people that Mr. Roo was a part of has evolved into something too advanced for us to comprehend. They may have even transcended into a different dimension."

"They may have," Manwaring responded. "There have always been stories from people who've said they've been abducted by God-like or spiritual beings. What do you think a catfish senses when it bites on a hook and is snatched up from the bottom of a lake, or what a goldfish perceives when it looks out from its fishbowl at humans walking back and forth? Like ghostly forms passing just beyond its vision and understanding. It is possible to suggest aliens are all around us, with us being the goldfish or catfish. There is also the dark forest theory. One akin to aliens being stealthy hunters, and where the prey can only snatch brief glimpses of their stalkers."

"Is there an estimate as to how much life *is* in space?" Spike asked. "I mean, there must be more life out there. Besides Earth and the planet Nezhoda Roo came from."

"According to the Drake Equation," Manwaring answered, "there are any number of civilizations in Milky Way alone. And our galaxy is only one of millions. Therefore, the probability of more evolved civilizations capable of intergalactic travel is likely. These same civilizations kept evolving, which again supports the argument that they've transcended into a dimension that we humans cannot comprehend."

Pushing aside the thought that inner Elizabeth was pounding into her conscious, Elizabeth said, "On the other hand, what if they devolved instead?"

After a slight pause, Finnegan said, "I can understand one civilization, but all of them? Every single alien civilization went down the same toilet at the same time. Is that possible?"

"Anything is possible, which explains us being here." Manwaring raised the hand not holding his whiskey.

Elizabeth ran her finger around the rim of her coffee cup. "Who knows what's possible or impossible. Including an intergalactic blight. Or what if they outstripped available resources or fought wars that destroyed themselves? Or even created an artificial intelligence that wiped them out but then died off itself when there were no longer humans capable of taking care of it? Those are all threats humans are concerned about today."

"Like Easter Island," Finnegan said. "Where the population built those stone statues and destroyed the island's environment while doing so. After cutting all their trees down, they ended up imprisoning themselves to a point they could not escape their own self-made disaster."

Elizabeth seemed to accept Finnegan's proposal by looking at Manwaring. "What if you do make it to Alpha Centauri and run into planets full of people who went back to the Stone Age? Just like Nezhoda Roo did back on Earth. With the Maya?"

Manwaring's eyes panned across the others at the table one at a time. "Whether I become a goldfish in a bowl or another Nezhoda Roo, I do not know, but just in case... " His eyes stopped on Finnegan and Spike. "While each of you have your assigned tasks, instruction in combat—whether hand-to-hand or using Nezhoda Roo's weapons—will not only help us with soon-to-be-visitors, but it will also help me wherever it is I land that thing."

"Do you have anything we can start with?" Finnegan asked. "Aside from being an executed strangler."

"Well, as a trained archaeologist I know how to handle a sharpened six-inch Marshalltown trowel, a standard transfer shovel, and a bastard file," Manwaring answered. His fingers curled inward creating fists.

Finnegan raised his cup. "Good. Muscle memory."

"And do not forget me," Kroll said, eyeing the Aztec axe in Tiburón's hands. "I used to love chopping trees down for my smoke house."

After dinner and based on Manwaring's credible assertion that they would receive visitors from TETRA, the astronauts continued their tasks. They did not know whether the arrival would be in two days or two months, but they all agreed on two things. That the arrival would come sooner than later, headed by none other than Angar Einstok and his team of mercenary operators. There was no time to waste.

Manwaring packed his possessions into a TETRA-issued duffel and then spent time with Tiburón exploring the software in The Keep's computer. They were trying to find a way to announce their findings to the world before TETRA would shut them down. Kroll and Elizabeth gathered what rations they felt Manwaring needed to supplement the alien's rations. Spike and Finnegan dove into the most physically demanding tasks of them all.

Their first task was to detach the drilling motor from The Oompa-Loompa and attach it to the front bumper of The Minivan. If each vehicle had a GPS tracker installed, continuous trips by The Minivan to the sinkhole would not raise any new suspicions by TETRA or Einstok. They also took what they needed from the rear of The Oompa-Loompa, including a six-inch drill bit and a six-foot section of drill pipe. Their second task was to distribute the high-pressure methane gas from the six, fully pressurized cylinders inside The Tank Farm into four more tanks. Spike's idea was to leave room in those ten tanks to add compressed oxygen. Since Mars had a minimal atmosphere with only 2 percent oxygen, she said a proper ratio of methane and oxygen, pressurized to 3,000 psi, would add exponentially to the bombs' explosive potential. To detonate the cylinder bombs, Spike decided to use some of the breeching charges she'd spotted in Nezhoda Roo's armory.

As Finnegan had been standing next to Spike when they uncovered Nezhoda Roo's armory inside the spacecraft, he immediately recognized the various types of demolition charges available to them, including breeching charges. As big as a deck of cards, the blackish-green-colored boxes had a magnetic strip and an adhesive strip on one side, with a timer dial and switch on the other. Although he could not read the alien markings on the arming side of the demolitions, he knew immediately how to use them.

Now, back at Legoland, helping Spike, Finnegan thought that if he had no issue with figuring out those breeching charges, he would have no problem figuring out how to fly that ship nestled in the back of that sinkhole's cavern.

Once they loaded their explosive cylinders in the rear of The Minivan, Finnegan and Spike drove over to the Westing House to gather a spool of wire, a roll of electrical tape, portable power sources, and switches. As they walked out the door of the Westing House for the last time, Finnegan grabbed six roles of duct tape.

"We have enough electrical tape?" Spike asked. She sat in the driver's seat watching over her shoulder as Finnegan dumped his load on top of the gas cylinders. Why the duct tape?"

Finnegan turned to sit in the passenger seat. "Spacesuit repair kits."

"Got it," Spike answered.

Instead of returning to The Hilton, they drove from away Legoland, and into the dry riverbed.

Early May, AD 2026

"Well, our mission is upon us," Einstok said. Strapping himself into a seat in the habitation module's kitchenette, he appraised his team. Waking up, all at the same time, and not from torpor, they recovered color in their cheeks and alertness in their eyes. They were ready. Now that they had a real-world mission to focus on instead of only each other while cooped up inside the spaceship. Since waking up from torpor four days ago, they'd worked out on the exercise machines, eaten proper rations, hydrated themselves, and practiced with their main combat weapons outside their spaceship while tethered to its hull. Einstok had selected one himself: the GR-1 ANVIL Gauss rifle. The same rifle Einstok and his operators used during their BOSC training and sent to The Merlin Group for upgrades before their departure from lunar orbit. The rifles resembled black-painted, modern-day assault rifles but with a series of squared coils lined along the length of the barrel. They were built robustly enough to crack the hardest of space helmets if swung hard enough. Donning their spacesuits, they took turns in pairs to conduct extra vehicular activities outside the capsule. Part of the EVAs included operating their

Gauss rifles on an improvised range running the length of the spaceship's hull. Though they floated in zero gravity, and firing with any accuracy was out of the question, the fact that Einstok's team actively engaged themselves in something familiar meant more than anything.

When not physically engaged in preparing for their Martian objective, they spent time reviewing the images TETRA had been sending them the last few days. Images now pictured on the monitor in the habitation module, including one that provided a larger overview of their objective. A dark hole nestled among the craggy outcroppings of the mountain range towering over the lakebed. The other image showed a closeup of that sinkhole, and entrance into it.

Einstok waited for his team to gather at the kitchenette for their morning coffee and briefing.

"They have kept themselves busy inside that sinkhole, even during darkened hours. GPS locators have The Minivan making repeated trips between that sinkhole and their base at the lakebed. The question is, why such an effort on their part if all they have is a destroyed spacecraft and wrecked Rhinelander Korps rocket ship?"

The others at the table reflected on his question.

After a short pause, Max said. "We suspected that there is something besides the two destroyed machines, and we now have evidence."

"Which," Einstok said, "means we will be in for a fight. We have just over twenty-four hours before landing, so we need to be prepared."

Einstok could almost feel the anticipation shooting from the eyes of Munro's team. However, the look in Munro's eyes differed. A distant look Einstok had noticed more than once in the last few days.

"You know, Mr. Einstok," Nitro said, "if you had told me that I would be facing *that* Finnegan I would have done this mission for free. I don't know why I didn't put it all together before."

Pulled from his thoughts about his team leader, Einstok said. "I know that Nitro. Still, you will earn your pay. You always do."

"We've all read the same info," Double Cannon said, "and know who you are talking about; however, it'd be nice if the rest of us knew why you are talking about him."

Nitro turned to answer his teammate.

"Sean Patrick Finnegan. A contract hitman for the IRA. And one of his contracts involved Sergeant Major Thompson. Both he and I were part of a special ops team operating covertly in Dublin. Regimental Sergeant Major Thompson recruited me and brought me up in the SAS. Even though we were operating undercover, Finnegan, found us out and killed Thompson. With a kilo of plastique wired to a fucking toilet seat."

While Einstok listened to Nitro's explanation, he noticed that Nitro left out the part about the sergeant major being part of a previous team that beheaded the family members of an IRA soldier.

"I received information concerning Finnegan's location," Nitro continued. "I went after him. On my own. Turns out that the IRA planted the information. I ended up killing an innocent husband. The father of two. At my court-martial, the SAS found me guilty of manslaughter and drummed me out of the SAS: no stripes and no pension, all due to that IRA scum."

"Well," Einstok chimed in, "he is technically not an IRA member but more of a subcontractor. Or third-party employee."

Nitro gave his employer a sideways look.

Disregarding the silent rebuke, Einstok continued, "But he is still a target to be mindful of. Along with Spike. We need to eliminate Spike and Finnegan as soon as possible. Their spacesuits are labeled 5 and 3, respectively."

Einstok turned panned his gaze across his audience. "Agreed?"

Everybody, including Nitro, nodded.

"Good, and before we get to our duties," Einstok said, "about that proof we mentioned a second ago. Usually, our satellites fly directly overhead, but TETRA placed one at a more southerly latitude. Something done on occasion. Anyway, the change in latitude allowed its camera to send back photos taken at more oblique angles. One of them gave us a glimpse of something hidden under the lip of the sinkhole and recessed further back under that rim."

"So, it wasn't noticed before?" Solid Gold asked.

"The image we are talking about revealed a portion of a structure. We reviewed previous images taken from that latitude and did not see anything. Which means only one thing. Whatever we saw was portable. And was moved closer to the lips, if by only a few feet."

"Or flyable," Lil' Sumptin' interjected.

"Correct," Einstok said. "While we have no idea what is hidden in that cavern, Manwaring was selective in the information he offered while on Earth. I would have done the same if I were in his place. Touché, Mr. Manwaring, Touché."

"So, we're still landing at the dry lakebed, and not inside the sinkhole directly?" Solid Gold asked.

"Yes," Einstok responded. "Our chief concern remains with the loss of signal control while entering the sinkhole. That said, we have the equipment and training to achieve our mission."

Early May, AD 2026

"Good morning, Kroll," Manwaring said. Closing the door to The Keep behind him, the new vigor in his arm muscles reminded him of this morning's workout with Finnegan. "Breakfast smells good."

Kroll stood at the range, poking at a slice of meat frying in the skillet with a fork. In his other hand, he held a wine glass. "We're having steak and eggs."

"Beef steak or alien steak?" Manwaring asked.

"Both," Kroll answered.

"Okay, but make sure you keep them separate."

"*Ja Wohl*," Kroll raised his wine glass in salute. "Breakfast will be ready in five minutes. Coffee? Or an aperitif?"

"Coffee's fine," Manwaring said. "I'll pop into The Garage before breakfast."

"Very well," Kroll answered, while setting the fork down. "Looks like my cooking is putting you into fine form."

Waiting for his coffee, Manwaring could almost feel Kroll's eyes dismembering his body. "I appreciate the compliment, but would you please stop looking at me like that. You're making me nervous."

Kroll grinned. "Sorry. Bad habit."

Accepting his coffee, Manwaring turned toward the door leading to The Office. As he did, he cautioned Kroll. "And don't even think about turning my arse into ham."

Manwaring exited The Hilton and walked through the short tunnel connecting it to The Office. He walked past the empty bunkbed and its unmade linens, with damp wrinkles pressed into the bottom sheet, through the next tunnel, and entered The Garage. Both Finn and Elizabeth sat in front of the workbench drinking coffee. They turned toward Manwaring.

"Morning," Manwaring said. "Nice haircut."

"Morning," Elizabeth said, reaching up to touch what was now short, reddish-dyed hair sticking out from under Finnegan's Rex Sox ball cap on her head.

Finnegan saluted with his coffee mug. "How do you feel?"

"Splendid," Manwaring answered. Taking a second to rub his thigh, he stepped up to the workbench. "However, I did not realize doing squats while holding an Aztec war axe over your head could be so painful."

"Good, and just so you don't plateau, we have that Aztec war club ready for you," Finnegan said gesturing to the item on the table in front of them. "Tiburón found all but two of the missing teeth, and we glued them back into place. I copied the remaining two from my three-D printer. You should be able to incorporate this into your workout routine. Just as you said before, you were handy with a trowel and shovel, so you have muscle memory to start with."

Manwaring reached out and caressed the weapon with his index and middle finger. Shaped like a cricket bat with a row of sharp obsidian bladelets inserted lengthwise into the edge of the rich brown tropical dense wood, the weapon looked deadly. "I'm surprised at how well the wood has stood up to the Martian atmosphere."

"Can't beat mahogany for longevity," Elizabeth said.

"Or deadliness," Finnegan said. "No matter what planet we're on. But that's for later. For now, though, let's get at that alien steak and eggs. It's food we may have to get used to."

Reaching up to adjust the bill of her ball cap, Elizabeth's heart sank. It was the second time he'd said *we* when talking to Manwaring about the spaceship in Copperhead Canyon. In the few hours between last night and this morning, Elizabeth and Finnegan laid in her bunk in The Office discussing the impossible that had brought them to Mars. Finnegan went on about the adventures the alien, Nezhoda Roo, must have enjoyed. He mentioned his upbringing in East Milton, Massachusetts, and his family. His stepfather had died of liver disease, and his mother got hooked on painkillers and was now homeless. His two brothers were both doing life sentences in the state penitentiary. He had no family left on Earth. But Elizabeth did—a grandmother whom she longed to see one more time.

Finishing their breakfast, five astronauts, encased in their spacesuits, climbed into The Minivan, ready for another day of preparing for the unknown. Only Tiburón enjoyed the morning sleeping in, albeit for only an extra hour. After waking, his job was to show an active outside presence in Legoland. Assuming their movements were being tracked visually, and by a GPS locator built into The Minivan, TETRA would see what they have always seen: work being accomplished at Legoland while Manwaring continued his trips to the mountains. One of Tiburón's other tasks was to make sure The Oompa-Loompa remained visible, but also to make sure its front remained in the shadows or out of sight. Depending upon the quality of their satellite imagery, TETRA might notice the drilling motor's absence. A red flag for any alert special ops mercenary.

By sunset, four tired, but pleased astronauts returned to Legoland in The Minivan. They were greeted by Tiburón, who had just warmed up the supper Kroll prepared for them that morning. Only Manwaring remained with the spacecraft. Based on the circumstances, everybody agreed it was best for Manwaring to remain in the Alamo. Along with spending every minute possible getting to understand the spacecraft better, they agreed he might need to fly that craft out of the sinkhole at a moment's notice. Not really knowing what Einstok and TETRA had planned, they discussed the probability of their new arrivals landing straight into the sinkhole as it would be the most direct solution to their goal. Though they thought it more likely that Einstok and his mercenaries would land on the dry lakebed, where a safe landing was more assured and better controlled.

In either case, Manwaring and Elizabeth received instructions on how to detonate the explosives Spike and Finnegan rigged up inside the spaceplane and buried under strategic locations in the canyon walls. Though a trained sapper, Spike did not enter the Marine Corps without experience. Having grown up near her uncle's rock quarry in Tennessee, she bragged about learning how to spot fracture or stress points in geographical features and economically using the bombs she made from her bat-guano-based gunpowder to achieve the greatest result.

After the Martian astronauts ate their dinner and discussed the remaining tasks, they turned in for a good, but brief, sleep.

Elizabeth took a minute to clean up after Finnegan made love to her and slid back into her bunk. Finnegan, naked under the sheets, appeared half asleep. Sliding under the covers herself, she wanted to ask him one question, but she feared the answer. Remaining quiet and knowing she could only treasure what she held, she enjoyed listening to him breathe instead. However, after a lost amount of time, it was Finnegan who broke the silence.

"Are you sure you want to do it your way?"

Turning her head, bringing them nose to nose, she answered, "Yes."

"And just with the crossbow?" Finnegan asked.

"I've used crossbows before," she said. "Plus, we don't want to let them know we're packing serious firepower too soon."

"Well," Finnegan acquiesced, "just don't John Wayne it. Blow those charges at the right time, let them get a glimpse of you, or at least your spacesuit, land a well-placed shot, then pull chocks PDQ. Got it?"

Early May, AD 2026

Leaving Kroll behind this morning, the others set out from Legoland in The Minivan, each one lost in their thoughts with their helmets in their laps. Elizabeth, sitting in the rear bench seat next to Finnegan, looked over her shoulder and out the rear window. "What the hell is that?"

Everybody turned to look out the large rear window, including Spike. Legoland lay spread out behind them backed by the pale blue early morning sky, and a silvery glint shone like a piece of Christmas tinsel.

Without losing another second, Finnegan lifted his arm and punched the 'open' button on his wrist-mounted computer. "Manwaring, we got company! Kroll, get suited up and grab The Mule. Get to the Alamo! Now! You hear me?"

In a second, both Manwaring and Kroll's voices rang out from the inside of their helmets. As pre-arranged, Kroll kept his wrist-mounted computer nearby just in case. Now, knowing that the spaceship would be on the Martian surface within the next half hour, Elizabeth and the others envisioned a squad of armed astronauts piling out from that craft, bent on killing them. Though fully charged, a speed regulator governed The Minivan's engine, allowing it to go only so fast. As Spike continued to drive, the others kept looking behind them. In a few minutes, they saw Kroll, in The Mule, depart from Legoland. Behind Kroll, the spacecraft continued making its controlled descent toward the lakebed.

"Think we have a good enough head start?" Tiburón asked.

"I think so," Finnegan answered. "And don't forget they still have to land that thing and deploy whatever they have for vehicles. Assuming they have any. Either way, we should have time. All we can do now is keep driving."

By now, the spacecraft hung lower in the sky, and its white and orange parachutes suddenly ballooned over it.

They waited, and watched, as Spike drove The Minivan up the sloping dry riverbed. Kroll was still behind them. He had no problem keeping pace with The Minivan. This was important, not only for Kroll's survival, but also because the bed of The Mule was full of additional supplies. As they had no idea how long they might have to hold up in the Alamo, every bottle of oxygen, and packet of pear juice could prove to be lifesaving. Continuing to watch, they saw the white-silver spacecraft enveloped by a huge puff of red dust flaring up as retrorockets ignited to soften its landing in the lakebed.

With The Minivan now nearing the nexus of the riverbed and the entrance into Copperhead Canyon, Spike took her foot off the accelerator pedal. She turned, in time, to see a line of silvery-white dots racing across the surface of the dry lakebed, and toward the dry riverbed.

"Looks like they're riding motorcycles," Elizabeth said.

"Electrically powered dirt bikes more like it," Tiburón said. "They knew they would have access to our vehicles eventually, so why not bring dirt bikes. I would've. I count nine."

"Which makes those bastards more maneuverable, and faster, than we assumed," Spike said. "Get ready, Elizabeth."

"Got it," Elizabeth said. She reached for her helmet. The others did the same, as she would deplete the interior atmosphere inside while exiting the vehicle through the vehicle's side door.

✵

Elizabeth watched as The Minivan turned the first corner in the canyon, leaving her alone. Turning her focus back to the sloping riverbed, she could see Kroll was making progress and would soon be ready to pick her up. However, the nine recently landed astronauts were quickly catching up with him on their two-wheeled vehicles. After long minutes, Kroll finally stopped in front of her, giving Kroll a second to look behind him. Elizabeth, with her crossbow in hand, and quiver slung across her chest, dropped herself into the passenger seat. "Let's go. Stop at the next turn."

"*Ja, Wohl*!" Kroll answered. He turned to look in front of him while pressing down on the accelerator. "I hope Spike's booby traps work."

"They will," Elizabeth said assuredly.

The Mule lurched forward, throwing both against the backs of their seats.

At the next turn, Elizabeth told Kroll to stop. She climbed out and ran around the front of the machine and reached for a box switch buried behind a small pile of rocks. It was the size of her hand and had wires protruding from it. Picking up the device, she turned the yellow plastic knob from off to on. The walls at the entrance to the canyon, behind them, collapsed and threw up a cloud of Martian dust. Because Mars had no real atmosphere to carry any sound or shock wave, she only felt the result of the explosion through the soles of her space boots.

Dropping the switch box, Elizabeth turned toward their vehicle. "That'll take some wind out of their sails."

After two more turns, just where the canyon started to widen, and at the same spot where Finnegan and Elizabeth found the dead Aztec warrior, Kroll lurched to a stop again. Elizabeth stood from the seat and looked down the canyon. "Go ahead. I got this. I'll be there soon."

Kroll hit the accelerator pedal and rounded the next bend in the canyon. Elizabeth hid behind the same boulder that the Aztec sat down to die. She stood her crossbow up on the butt of its stock and reached for the small switch box secreted there as well. Picking up the switch box, with the wires protruding from it, she turned the switch and felt the result of the explosion again. The canyon walls crumbled, creating a pile of rubble as high as a human. As the rocks settled into place, a cloud of dust exploded and hung over the obstacle for a couple of minutes before settling.

Setting the switch box down, she reported blowing the second charge. After receiving a word of caution from Finnegan, she retrieved and shouldered the crossbow. Waiting for the new arrivals to climb over that rocky debris, she started asking herself questions. Although she already knew the answers.

The first one centered on the intentions of the new arrivals. *Were they really here to kill us?* However, the answer was readily available. If their arrival was a benevolent one, why did they not announce their arrival ahead of time? Adjusting the butt against her shoulder, she asked herself a second question: Why did she volunteer to pretend to be Spike, cutting and dying her hair, wearing Spike's spacesuit, and putting herself as the first one in the line of fire? Again, the answer to that question was also readily available.

The cadre coming at them, Einstok and his mercenaries, were trained operators and experienced killers, so they knew they needed to remove the greatest threat to their mission first. That threat being Spike, then Finnegan. With her pretending to be Spike, she could slow down their attack and debilitate them to a degree. At the same time, the real Spike, wearing Elizabeth's spacesuit, and newly dyed blond hair, would be controlling the fight when Einstok entered the sinkhole.

After some minutes, the top of a helmet popped over the top of the rocks. A second later, the rest of the mercenary's body followed, topping the pile of rocks only seven yards away. He wore a spacesuit and environmental backpack like they did, and Elizabeth recognized the black-painted, and robust-looking assault rifle. He also wore a fully stocked cartridge, or magazine, belt around his waist.

Shifting her position behind the boulder, she pressed the stock of her weapon against her shoulder, stood, and fired the weapon. Feeling a slight jerk against her shoulder, she could almost see the twelve-inch, iron-tipped bolt in flight. But a second later, the bolt drove itself into the man's chest. The victim dropped his weapon and clutched at his chest. He stumbled forward, down the sloping pile of rocks, to the ground. Falling to his knees, he clutched frantically at the end of the bolt protruding from his chest.

Elizabeth lowered her weapon and reported her contact. "One down. And they're armed. Coming your way."

She received an affirmation but with no names used.

She thought briefly about running forward and snatching up his weapons but realized it would be a useless, and dangerous, effort. Giving her crossbow a pat on the stock, she turned to race to her next position. The man she shot let go of the bolt and fell face-forward to the ground.

23

Early May, AD 2026

"They got Solid Gold!" Munro shouted as he peeked over the rocks blocking their route. At the same time, a figure holding a crossbow and crouching behind a boulder stood up and ran further into the canyon. Stooping back down behind the rocky dam, he looked at the others. "One person, a woman. It's Spike, and she's armed with a crossbow. She's fighting a delaying action."

While the environmental packs they wore on their backs supplied their air, the packs also recycled their exhaled breaths to remove carbon dioxide and moisture. Still, sweat started to run down his face, and he found himself breathing heavily. "And she knows what she's doing. She reported in with the others."

Knowing what frequency, the first arrivals would be using, Einstok and his team set their comms up so that they could listen while not being listened to.

"A fucking crossbow!" Slingblade blurted out. "And how the hell did they end up with explosives?"

Einstok caught his breath and furrowed his eyebrows. "How they got ahold of a crossbow, and explosives, is irrelevant for now. What's important is getting right at whatever they're trying to protect. And now! It'll take hours to backtrack and find another way to that sinkhole. But they also know they cannot keep us out forever."

Einstok inhaled deeply before running up the rocks and down the other side. Reaching the canyon's floor, he offered the man he had known for years a half-second condolence as he stepped past him, with his rifle shouldered and ready to fire. The others followed, with Max stopping long enough to unbuckle Solid Gold's cartridge belt and unsling the rifle from around the dead man's torso. Shouldering the extra firepower, he followed the others further into the canyon.

Einstok and his team moved quickly, following the canyon's floor as the canyon continued to widen and the walls towered over them. They approached another corner. Knowing that speed and firepower were key to the assault, they ran to the next corner. A sprint even Einstok found taxing. But just as they approached it, the corner exploded in front of them.

Stopping just long enough to let the rocks fall into place and to take deep breaths, the team charged into the hovering dust and over the new obstacle. Firing bursts of magnetically powered projectiles as they came down the other side. Exiting the other side of the cloud dust, Einstok heard another one of his team members scream. Unable to identify the voice, he looked over his left shoulder. Double Cannon, grabbing at his throat, stumbled and fell to his knees. Ignoring the man's garbled, blood-filled grunts, Einstok charged forward firing at the only cover available for Spike to use. Another boulder. But, as he jumped over the top of it, he saw nobody. Stopping to let the others catch up, he reviewed the satellite imagery in his head, noting what remained of the canyon before it emptied into the sinkhole.

"I got Double Cannon's weapons." Nitro said as he pulled up next to Einstok.

Now, hearing Nitro's ragged breath, he realized the threat to his plans. Einstok jumped off the boulder, landing heavily on the other side. "Everybody, change out with fresh magazines and power packs. Slingblade and Nitro, once we are at the sinkhole, take the left flank. Lil' Sumptin' and Munro take the right flank. Zelda and Max follow me up the center."

Acknowledging the attack plan, the group rearmed their technically advanced and modified Gauss rifles. Ready, they ran toward the canyon's outlet into the sinkhole, just around the next bend. Rounding that corner, they ran into the most incredible sight.

To their right was the spaceplane that had been their primary goal all these many millions of miles. It was wrecked from centuries of falling rocks. A pair of wires drooped from inside the craft's wrecked fuselage and led back to the cavern, which held the spacecraft they only recently suspected of being there.

Manwaring sat behind the transparent shield covering the right-side compartment that projected from its disk-shaped hull. A machine beyond their wildest dreams. Wearing his spacesuit, without his helmet, Manwaring looked smug. Under him and the spacecraft, a soft blue light warmed the soil.

Einstok smiled before speaking to himself. "So, Sherlock Holmes has bested Doctor Moriarty. At least for now." Einstok's eyes returned to the wires drooping, and stretching, from the wrecked spaceplane. Suddenly, it struck him.

"They're going to blow the spaceplane when that thing is out of here! Go! Go! Go!"

Launching their assault, Lil' Sumptin' and Munro veered toward the wrecked space plane. Intent on the drooping wires. Lil Sumptin' was in the lead, while Munro, running behind her, aimed his rifle at anybody who might be around the spaceplane. When female mercenary almost reached the space plane, a figure popped up from behind it. It was Spike with her crossbow.

Munro fired a three-round burst at the woman, at the same time she fired her crossbow. Chips of rock and dust flew away from the wall behind her helmet. Two of his rounds struck the wall. The third round ricochetted off the side of her helmet just as the bolt shot from the crossbow.

With Spike disappearing behind the spaceplane, the female mercenary launched herself forward, using her body to snap the wires from the wreckage. But just as she did, an invisible force struck her, causing her left shoulder and arm to explode from her body. Her body landed heavily on the sinkhole's floor, face down. She never uttered a sound.

"God dammit!" Munro cursed. With anguish ripping at his heart, he ran past Lil' Sumptin'. Now was not the time to grieve for his long-term friend and lover. Reaching the wires, he threw his body across them like a WWI Doughboy throwing his body over barbed wire to allow the soldiers behind him to use him as a bridge. The weight of his body and equipment yanked the wires from the space plane's tail.

Rolling to his right, he crawled forward and reached the empennage of the craft. Raising his rifle, he saw Spike run up the slope leading into the recessed wall in the back of the sinkhole. Turning to face him, Munro saw what looked like a strip of duct tape across the front of her helmet. "Shit," he said, while assessing the remaining members of his team.

Like him, the others were pinned down by fire coming from inside the cavern and from either side of the spaceship. While bolts of projectiles exploded against the rocks in front of the assault team, he could hear the curses and grunts from his teammates, and from Manwaring's group through his helmet's earpiece. This morning was not turning out like they had planned. Their opponents had the element of surprise, held the high ground, and were armed with potent firepower.

Cursing again, Munro sought an opportunity to charge forward without making himself a ready target. Suddenly, the spacecraft inside the cavern lifted off the floor by a couple of feet, then lurched forward. Like Aladdin's magic carpet, the disk-shaped spacecraft hovered over the center of the sinkhole, blocking out the faint Martian sun. What light was left turned an eerie blue. Yet, there was no noise or disturbance of the smallest grain of soil from the engines hovering above him. The firing stopped, giving him a chance to advance. The ex-legionnaire pushed himself up and bolted forward, running on the smooth ground, a path between the rocky debris. But after five wide steps, his leg fell through a fake covering hiding a hole under it. A wrenching pain shot up his leg and into his spine as he torqued his knee severely. Dropping his rifle and letting it hang from its body sling, he tried to pull his leg from the snare but realized that his booted foot was snared in a plate of metal that allowed his foot to hit the bottom of the hole but did not allow him to remove his leg.

"Fuck!"

From the middle of the sinkhole, and from behind a rock not much bigger than his helmet, Einstok assessed their situation. A carefully placed trap had snared his team leader, and Lil' Sumptin' lay dead, face down in the dirt of a Martian sinkhole. To his left, Slingblade and Nitro were hunkered behind rocks and having a firefight with somebody hidden in the corner of the cavern. It became apparent to him now that the rocky layout of the sinkhole's flooring had been modified to the benefit of Manwaring and his team. Thinking about what to do next, he cursed the man in the spaceship above him. The spacecraft hovered, with its engines producing soft blue light. Even though those engines could keep that craft hovering above them, he felt no pressure or down blast. Einstok took his eyes from the craft and placed them on the remaining Martian astronauts inside the cavern. He saw Spike, now with duct tape across her helmet's face piece, along with three others. All of them hid behind rocks in the back of the cavern's center, only exposing themselves enough to fire their weapons. Trying to get a better idea of what to do next, Einstok wondered if they were still going to blow up the space plane. He received his answer.

A person stood up from behind a boulder, with a tube-like weapon leveled over her shoulder. The number on the spacesuit read 2—the doctor named Elizabeth. His eyes, following the tube's line of sight, spotted the pinpoint of a red dot on the fuselage of the wrecked spaceplane. Manwaring took the spacecraft higher in the sky above them. Einstok realized two horrifying facts. First, those wires served only as a diversion. To distract and divide his assault force. Second, they were going to destroy that space plane but use the shoulder-fired weapon to set off the demolitions inside that craft.

He yelled into his helmet's microphone. "Munro! Get down! They're going to blow it!"

However, Einstok wasted his breath as Munro leaned backward and was able to stick his helmeted head between a pair of rocks about the size of bowling balls. Within a microsecond, a bolt of light impacted the space plane's perforated skin, setting off whatever explosives were rigged inside it.

Though nobody could hear the explosion, a voluminous dust storm consumed the cavity of the sinkhole, along with everybody inside it.

24

Early May, AD 2026

Einstok realized the sinking feeling in his gut and the irony of it all. He'd put together a crew to assist in the capture of one of his greatest achievements, and it was that crew who were able to snatch that triumph from him. Still enclosed in a cloud of red Martian dust, Einstok yelled into the helmet's microphone. "Report in!"

He received immediate responses accounting for everybody including Munro, who was closest to the detonation. Now knowing what remained of his force, he issued his next order. "Once we have visibility," he yelled, "get back to our vehicles, and back to base. We'll set up a perimeter and up-armor ourselves."

Everybody responded affirmatively, except for Nitro.

"Fuck that!" he yelled over the communications network. "I'm going in to get that bastard Finnegan!"

"No!" Einstok ordered as the dust started to clear above them. But as he protested Nitro's statement, two forms stood up in the thinning dust cloud and charged the corner of the cavern. "Dammit!" Einstok cursed. "Cover fire for Nitro and Slingblade!"

Max and Zelda, on either side of Einstok, fired their weapons into the cavern.

While Elizabeth, Spike, Kroll, and Tiburón fired from behind the rocks in the back of the cavern, Finnegan assumed a defiladed position in that corner of the cavern, which provided another angle of fire. Finnegan armed himself with two weapons, one being a shoulder-fired alien rifle. Finnegan noticed the firing stop from the two men in front of him. Knowing what they were doing, he turned to look around the rock and saw two forms emerge through the dust as they ran up the slope leading into the cavern. He pointed his weapon up, but a bullet from one of the attackers ricocheted off a rock next to his head distracting him. He quickly recovered and aimed the alien rifle at the two charging figures. He lined the sight with the man in front and pulled the trigger. His weapon fired, and he watched, in seemingly slow motion, as the explosive round tore through the man's abdomen. The unfortunate man let go of his weapon and clutched at his guts as they started to spill out at his feet.

Zelda and Max continued their fire, and Einstok, knowing he could still help Nitro, changed out magazines while yelling into his helmet microphone. "Max! Zelda! Go! Go! Go!"

Jumping up, the three attackers charged forward, up the slope leading into the cavern while emptying their fresh magazines. They saw Nitro charging at Finnegan, plowing into him and knocking him over by holding his rifle in front of him like a police baton controlling rioters. The astronauts firing at Einstok, Max, and Zelda suddenly ceased their fire. Einstok, and his team, could hear their opponent's voices and knew why. They had run out of ammunition.

The four people hiding behind the rocks stood to meet their charge. Astonishingly, one of them held an axe, while another held what Einstok recognized as a Mesoamerican war sword. The third person held an alien rifle by the end of its barrel, and the fourth held a hand-sized rock.

"I'm down to my last magazine," Spike shouted inside her helmet as she fired a round around the side of the rock she was hiding behind. "We should have taken more off the space craft."

"Too late now," Tiburón answered as he fired the last round from his weapon. Dropping his alien rifle, Tiburón grabbed the Aztec bronze-headed axe next to him and stood. "Now, it's time to get Medieval."

Spike dropped her weapon and reached for the obsidian-edged Aztec war club. Kroll turned his rifle over and grabbed it by the end of the barrel. Elizabeth armed herself with a hand-sized rock. Knowing that the best defense was a good offense, Spike and Tiburón leaped over the rocks they were hiding behind and charged into the three attackers now only feet in front of them. Kroll followed suit.

Still snared by the booby trap, and with his weapons out of reach, all Munro could do was watch the collision of fighters while trying to extricate himself. As he struggled, he watched what could only be described as a bar-room brawl involving pool cues and broken beer bottles.

In the corner of the cavern, Finnegan held his rifle in front of him like he was swinging a bat. The attacker held his rifle like a policeman holding back a line of protesters and bowled into the Irish American. Finnegan tried to swing at his attacker, but the man was too fast, and agile, and bowled straight into Finnegan's midsection. The force of the impact knocked the alien rifle from his hands. Now, pinned on the ground under the weight of the man who held his rifle across his throat, Finnegan's strained to throw the man off him, but he could not. Thankfully, the rigid construction of the spacesuit's collar and neck ring prevented the rifle from crushing his throat outright.

As Finnegan tried to fight off the attacker while trying to breathe, the attacker's face stared down at him from mere inches away. The attacker wore a mask of aggression and an intense hatred. His thin lips bared clench teeth and accentuated the hatred in his blue eyes. Sweat fell against the inside of the man's helmet. While using his weight and the rifle to attack Finnegan, the attacker let go of the rifle to reach to his side and brought a military-grade knife into view. He held the blade against Finnegan's helmet before pointing the tip at Finnegan's throat. Still straining to catch his breath, Finnegan forced one of his hands to reach down to his spacesuit leg. So intent was the man, with his modern, steel-bladed military assault knife, he failed to see the centuries-old obsidian-bladed knife. Once he realized its presence, it was too late because Finnegan had driven it into Nitro's side. Nitro's face, only inches away from Finnegan's, revealed his shock, but his wide eyes only remained open for a few seconds. Dark blood erupted from his mouth and dropped onto the clear face shield of his mask. It mixed with his pooled sweat. The man's eyes closed, and Finnegan felt the pressure release from his throat.

Pushing the body aside, Finnegan struggled to get to his feet. Catching his breath, the view in front of him could not have been created by even the most imaginative movie director. A scene encapsulating a fight between humans wearing spacesuits and clear bubble helmets while trying to kill each other with centuries-old Aztec weapons, modern human-made and alien-made arms, and sheer power. All captured by the slight blue tint being cast down by the spacecraft's engine still hovering over them.

25

Early May, AD 2026

In the center of the cavern, three Alamo defenders plowed into their attackers and, as they did, Spike recognized the lady behind the helmet face shield. "Hey lady from the DMV," Spike shouted.

Zelda met Spike's body just as she heard those words. Severely out of breath, and with shaking limbs, Zelda flew backward, as the weight of Spike's body plowed into her. Landing hard on the ground on her back, Zelda lost what breath she had. Spike, seeing Zelda's physical condition, and knowing that months in space was debilitating, rolled to her side and regained her footing. She swung the Aztec war sword at Zelda's lower legs. Holding the sword with both hands, the Aztec weapon ripped into Zelda's spacesuit and tore into the flesh and bone inside it.

At the same time, Kroll plowed into Max. Recognizing Kroll from his research, Max was amazed at the strength of the German cannibal as they clumsily grappled in their spacesuits and helmets. It was not much of a fight. Kroll pummeled Max severely about the chest while he lay on the ground. After five or six debilitating blows to the chest, which forced Max to cough up blood, Kroll smashed the rock into Max's right kneecap. Kroll sat up straight and dropped the rock just in time to see Tiburón cleave the blade of the Aztec axe straight into Einstok's chest.

From the side of the cavern, Finnegan rearmed himself and ran toward the melee. But, by the time he reached them, Kroll had subdued his opponent, who now lay on the cavern floor with Kroll standing over him. Max raised one knee and splayed it outward. Kroll looked up and waved at them. Near Kroll, Spike stood over her opponent and waved her free hand at Finnegan. She raised the Aztec war club in her other hand and pointed it like a baseball player telling spectators in the stands she was about to knock it out of the park. Everybody watched as Tiburón stepped away from his opponent.

Finnegan looked up at the sky above the sinkhole at the blue lights keeping the spacecraft and Manwaring skyborne. "I hope he enjoyed the show."

Tiburón, finally catching his breath, raised his axe over his head and shook it vigorously. "God dammit! I took down Angar 'Fuckin' Einstok! Holy shit."

Spike dropped the Aztec war club to her side and lowered her head. "Shit! There's no going to be living with him now."

Hovering over the sinkhole, Manwaring watched the fight develop as best he could through the blue-tinted dust cloud. While he controlled the ship using a flight control joystick center mounted on the switch- and light-strewn flight console, he kept an eye on a slanted screen about the size of a paperback book. Much like the backup camera installed on the dashboards of modern vehicles, Manwaring was able to view what could only be described as a low-budget, grainy video game, complete with flashes of exploding gunfire, highlighting the blue-tinted dust cloud filling the sinkhole under him.

Finally, both the flashes of alien gunfire ceased, and the blue-tinted dust cloud obscuring his camera's view started to settle. He received a call from Finnegan. Now, able to see the battle's aftermath under him, he gripped the spacecraft's flight control joystick tighter. Slowly descending back into the sinkhole, he saw five or six bodies wearing white spacesuits with orange chaffing patches lying about on the sinkhole's floor or under the ledge that had hidden the spacecraft for so many hundreds of years. Using his landing camera, he rotated the spacecraft and backed into the cavern, setting it down on its extended landing gear.

"Thanks for joining us," Tiburón said. "Have something more pressing?"

After securing the ship's engines, Manwaring donned his spacesuit helmet and joined his teammates now standing at the base of the extended ramp. Their victims lay spread about. Some were still moving, albeit slowly, as they lay on the sloping floor leading deeper into the sinkhole. Looking about, he immediately recognized Zelda and Einstok. Another person, lying near them seemed familiar, and after a second, he knew the man as Einstok's chief researcher. "Well," Manwaring said, "I do not mean to sound a bit haughty, but I am still quite a valuable piece of real estate."

"Lord," Spike said. "Can't you ever stop being a douchebag?"

"Douchebag or not, he's right," Elizabeth responded.

"Geoff."

Everybody standing heard the ragged voice and labored breath over their helmet speakers. They all turned to Angar Einstok, who struggled to sit up.

Manwaring turned toward Elizabeth. She returned the look and shook her head.

Sighing, Manwaring answered Einstok's beckoning.

Kneeling on one knee, he reviewed the faces of Einstok's two chief associates, Zelda and Max. Though clearly in pain, Zelda offered Manwaring a wink and a nod, but Max appeared to be almost unconscious. Both wore strips of bloodied duct tape across their abdomens and legs. Spacesuit First Aid at its best. Manwaring winked at Zelda before dropping his eyes to the man next to his knee. "Hello, Doctor Moriarty."

"Hello, Sherlock Holmes," Einstok coughed out with a ragged, and bloodied, spasm.

Like the other two, two strips of bloodied duct tape adorned Einstok's spacesuit, across his chest and abdomen. But unlike the other two, dark blood ran from the corner of Einstok's mouth.

"Did you come here to gloat at my demise," Einstok half joked. Drawing another ragged breath, he asked. "What are you going to do with that thing?"

So many memories flooded through Manwaring's mind, including their meeting the Belizean prison, and the escape out of that Utah canyon. Appreciating Einstok's handsome Scandinavian face, now drained of blood, Manwaring concentrated on the man's eyes as he tried to think of an answer. Einstok's eyes were still bright and clear.

"No, I am not here to gloat. In fact, I am quite saddened. Even Sherlock Holmes lamented at the demise of his nemesis. As one gives credit, balance to the other. I fear my existence will be much diminished with your absence."

Einstok reached out with a shaky, gloved hand, which he rested on Manwaring's knee. "I'll take that as a compliment. So, again, what are you going to do with that spacecraft?"

Not really knowing what else to say, Manwaring said, "I'm going to fly it back to its home galaxy."

Einstok smiled, before coughing up more blood, and a piece of pink flesh. Catching his breath, he forced out, "What! You're Buzz Lightyear all of a sudden."

26

Day of Commutation

Four people, wearing their spacesuits, but without their helmets, stood inside Boot Hill. The vertically mounted modules that kept Manwaring, Elizabeth, and the others alive during their voyage to Mars were now detached and rested horizontally on the floor. Elizabeth hooked tubes to the connectors sticking out of the transparent plastic body bag encasing the body. After doing so, she made sure the tubes leading from the cushioned liner under the body were straight and not tangled. Seeing everything was in order, Spike, Finnegan, and Munro took a half step forward to face the man who started it all.

"Anybody want to say anything before I close the lid?"

After a long, silent pause, Spike spoke. "Like the man or not, he did have some brass ones."

"Very good, Spike," Elizabeth said. "To be honest, I would have to agree. Anybody else?"

Receiving no response, Elizabeth reached up to grab the edge of the lid. Finnegan and Munro looked at Elizabeth and nodded. She nodded back and closed the lid. Securing the lock, she flipped up the lid covering the small keypad mounted to the side of her former module and punched in some numbers. Lights started to flash on the monitor next to the palm-sized keypad. "Well, Angar Einstok is now buried."

She turned toward the other locked and sealed, coffins. The little lights next to the keypads all blinked as well. They all scanned the short strips of duct tape covering the label plates with the names of the originally designated occupants. The duct tape strips, marked with felt marker, stated the names of the new occupants: Slingblade, Double Cannon, Lil' Sumptin', Solid Gold, and Nitro. Finnegan reached into the cargo pocket of his spacesuit trousers and pulled out a roll of duct tape and a marker. He turned to mark the grave of the most recently interned.

After marking the last grave, the four of them stepped over to the table in the module's kitchenette and retrieved their helmets, ready to exit Boot Hill. Elizabeth, holding her helmet in front of her with one hand, reached out to touch Einstok's team leader. "Stay behind, Munro. And take all the time you need."

Lowering the helmet, Munro glanced at the module marked Lil Sumptin'. "Annabelle Dee Ambrose, may you rest in peace."

He turned to face Elizabeth and raised his helmet. "Thank you."

Elizabeth sat at her desk, typing in the names, along with their mercenary code names, of the men they'd just buried. Typing in the last name, Angar Einstok, she heard the door open behind her. Hitting the Save key she turned to see Manwaring at the door. He held two glasses of red wine in one hand.

"Please come in."

Joining her at the desk and sitting in the patient seat, they would sit while Elizabeth drew blood and conducted physicals, he held out a glass of wine. "This wine is well deserved, Elizabeth."

Accepting it, she sighed slowly while appreciating the wine in her hand. After a moment, she spoke. "Geoff, why am I here? How did I end up on Mars?"

Manwaring sat back in the medical chair. "I lied about remembering you. As a student."

"I figured you did," she responded. "But you must have had thousands of students in the last twenty-plus years. Why do you remember me?"

"Your humility is the reason why you're here," Manwaring replied. He lifted his wine glass in salute at the same time. He appreciated the confused look on her face.

"The reason I remembered you was not only that are you one of the most beautiful young women that ever attended my classes and every male student constantly vied for your attention, but that you ignored all of that and focused on my lectures. You asked relevant questions. Instead of getting by on your looks, you used your intellect. It was your humbleness that brought you to Mars. Along with having a successful career as a medical doctor. When Einstok approached me in the prison cell hours before my execution and asked who I would recommend joining the voyage, your name was the first to come to mind. Knowing of your conviction and death sentence, and medical qualifications, you were the obvious first choice."

Finishing his wine, he stood. "Though the discovery of the spacecraft is more important than any of our lives, I never would have killed you."

"I know that, Geoff," Elizabeth said, "and I'm glad you didn't kill Finnegan."

"You like him, don't you?"

"Finnegan isn't going with you to Roo's galaxy, is he?" Elizabeth blurted out, her lips trembling.

The door from The Garage opened, and Manwaring and Elizabeth turned to see Finnegan standing in the open door.

"I'll see you in The Hilton," Manwaring said.

"I'm not interrupting anything, am I?"

Manwaring pointed at the chair he just stood from. "Here, take my seat."

Stepping in, Finnegan received a pat on the shoulder from Manwaring, who reached for the door latch.

"Are you okay, Elizabeth? Something wrong?"

"You're not going to pull chocks on me, are you?"

Finnegan sat down and drove his eyes deep into hers. He removed his ball cap and placed it on her head at a rakish angle.

Later that evening, Elizabeth and Finnegan joined the remaining Martian astronauts in The Hilton. The prefabricated structure that once offered solace to six convicted, and executed, astronauts now resembled an inner-city emergency room. Its confines offered relief to three additional guests. Without their spacesuits, they all relaxed as best they could in their TETRA-issued clothing. While some enjoyed an after dinner wine or alien whiskey, others enjoyed a coffee. They all enjoyed their survival, even though they sought to kill each other only that morning.

"How's the leg, lady from the DMV?" Spike asked as she refilled her coffee cup.

Zelda sitting at on one chair at the table, with her bandaged leg propped up on another, sipped her glass of alien whiskey. "I have had worse, and the name is Zelda. Not lady from the DMV."

"Okay, Zelda, not lady from DMV," Spike replied, "but be careful with that alien whiskey. Alcohol is a natural blood thinner, and that whiskey is strong stuff. You'll bleed right out. If you need a real pain killer, try Tiburón's weed."

"Hey," Tiburón interjected while sitting on the sofa. "What are you doing volunteering up my weed?"

"Don't worry," Elizabeth said. Sitting at the table opposite Zelda, she wore Finnegan's hat and held a glass of wine. "I've got plenty of meds in stock. For both her and Max."

"He's made of good Nordic stock," Kroll offered. Standing at the countertop next to the coffee pot, he busied himself with preparing a dinner tray for the German researcher, now asleep in Elizabeth's quarters. "He'll be fine, especially after my cooking."

"Hear, hear," Finnegan said. Sitting on the edge of Tiburón's bunk, he lifted his glass of wine and took a sip, then turned to the man sitting next to him. "So that's why the man called Nitro was so intent on me?"

Munro answered slowly. "You killed a mate of his and that was not something he took lightly."

"So, it's a small solar system after all," Tiburón half joked from the sofa.

Finnegan looked into Munro's eyes. "What about you? We killed your mates today. Including your lover."

Munro returned Finnegan's look. "They have been in my charge for years, and together, we *all* volunteered to follow Einstok. To the highest mountains peaks, across the greatest of deserts, and the darkest of jungles. But now that Einstok is dead, I am absolved of having to give an account for their deaths. And Lil' Sumptin' was her own woman. There is no need to worry. My team is dead, and Einstok has no hold over me."

Zelda tilted her head toward Munro. "Munro. The Boss never had a hold on you."

Zelda and Munro lifted their eyes and looked at each other. "I'll miss you," Zelda said, lowering her eyes.

Listening to them speak, Elizabeth knew that fate had just commuted everybody's sentences. "Well, Munro, are you really going to follow through with your plans? Manwaring's idea?"

"God or man does not bind me now. I am bound only by the infinite boundaries of the universe." Munro panned his eyes across the room. "Are you sure none of you want to join us?"

Everybody looked thoughtfully into their drinks. After a moment, Elizabeth spoke for the group. "We are all in agreement that our knowledge will better serve us if we stay on Mars. To wait for the next arrival. You, on the other hand, have no secrets binding you to us or this planet. What's that old saying: The world is your oyster, so now is the time to sharpen your knife."

Munro nodded in agreement. "I believe the phrase can now be stated as, the universe is my oyster, so now it is the time to sharpen my knife."

The door from The Keep opened. All heads turned toward the open door, and at the man who stepped through it. Nobody could miss the beaming smile on his face.

"Earth now knows what has happened here," Manwaring said. "Which absolves me of my mortgage with TETRA and commutes our sentences. Which frees me, us, up for our next adventure."

Manwaring stopped and focused his beaming smile on the ex-legionnaire. "Are you ready for your first spaceship flight lesson?"

Munro used his legs to push himself up from the bunk. Stretching, he took on a smile as broad as Manwaring's. He appraised the British archaeologist before speaking. "What? Now all of a sudden you're Buzz Lightyear."

ACKNOWLEDGMENTS

I would like to thank the staff at Indigo River Publishing, especially Deborah Froese, Jorge David Remy, and Jennie Seitz for their expert editing advice and assistance with this adventure.

www.ingramcontent.com/pod-product-compliance
Lightning Source LLC
Chambersburg PA
CBHW071841020726
47502CB00003B/566